About the authors

Flavia Ursino

is a mother, grandmother and gifted psychic with over thirty years' experience as a clairvoyant and public speaker. She has a passion for animal rights and for those without a voice, and a great empathy for all sentient beings. Flavia is married to Kevin Coleman.

Dr Kevin Coleman

MB.BS; DA, DCH, DTM&H, MPH, M GP Psychiatry, Dip. Clinical Hypnosis, Adv. Dip. Gestalt Therapy, FRACGP, is a father, grandfather and medical practitioner with over thirty-five years' experience in public health and family medicine. He has worked in rural and remote locations in Australia, Papua New Guinea and southern Africa, and travelled extensively in southern, east and central Africa. He maintains a deep affection for the African people.

Monkey Business

A Story of Soulmates and Primates

Flavia Ursino   **Kevin Coleman**

First published in Australia by USNCOL Pty Ltd ACN 603 977 966
colemanpublishing@outlook.com
monkeybusinessthebook.com

National Library of Australia Catalogue-in-Publication Entry:
Ursino, Flavia, author.
Coleman, Kevin. author
Monkey business: a story of soulmates and primates.
ISBN 9780994271600 (paperback)
Exploitation—Fiction
Social Psychology—Fiction
Suspense—Fiction
Love Stories.
A823.3

Cover design by Crystal Lyons and Toby Lyons
Book design by Vidal Creative and Australian eBook Publisher
Printed in Australia by Printed Matter. Redfern. 2015

Dedicated to The Voiceless
That they may be heard from the heart

"Not to hurt our humble brethren is our first duty to them, but to stop there is not enough. We have a higher mission — to be of service to them whenever they require it."

—Francis of Assisi.

Story inspired by documentaries:
Hidden Crimes by Supress and *The River... the origin of AIDS.*

Acknowledgments

A heartfelt thank you to our amazing children, Laura, Scott, Crystal, Toby, Lumka and Bryan, for their love and humour. To Damiana for lighting our path with her prayers and believing in us as only a mother can. To our friends Paul and Anne Marie, Diana Vegan-Field, Gail Beyer, Julie McNab, Steve and Barbara, Greg and Dawn Fitzgerald for their invaluable assistance. To Laura Tasker, David Chaikin, Zoe Fletcher and Tara King for their hours of reading and tactful advice. To kindred spirits Marilyn Newman and Sallie Newton for their spiritual guidance. Thank you to Sallie from whom Esther's character was inspired. To our manuscript analyst and editor Tom Flood for his ongoing patience with us and for not losing his hair in the process. To Lilyana Mullutin for travelling this journey with us, and what a journey it has been. To Bryan Latty who commenced us on this journey the night he handed Flavia the video Hidden Crimes. Whoever would have thought? And in loving memory of Mellow, may she Rest in Purrrfect Peace!

Poem Sits and Waits by Crystal Lyons
Front cover by Crystal Lyons and Tobias Lyons
Hugs and kisses for our earth angels for walking alongside us.

Our sincere thanks to Nick Prendergast, Gerard Gallagher and Australian eBook Publisher for their patient guidance in design and printing.

Are you and I simply little more than a random accident in a random time and place, randomly noticing how the world impacts upon us, whilst seldom contemplating on how it is we might impact upon the world...

OR

Are we an integral part of a dynamic web of creation, systematically aligned to an intelligent life force which drives us, as it awaits to help inform our choices, and if the significance of our existence does impact itself upon the world, what responsibility might we need to assume here?

Are we 'our brother's keeper'?

Chapter One

The African boy swung his legs over the windowsill, landing silently on the wooden floorboards. He approached the ornately carved escritoire, its panels inlaid with Congolese mahogany. A quiet, yet determined knock at the locked door signalled for his attention. Sliding open the top left-hand drawer, he withdrew a large iron key and unlocked the door from inside, allowing his nine-year-old co-conspirator entry.

"Verboten," he warned the girl as she made her way to the desk. It was her grandfather's treasure, its four curved wooden legs embellished with monkey heads, on top of which lay an exquisite slab of mahogany butterflied out, allowing front and back to mirror one another. A heart pattern decorated the shiny top, split down its mirrored centre. A brass microscope sat on the right-hand corner of the desk, next to a copy of Gazet van Antwerpen dated June 16th 1926.

The African boy, backed into a corner, sat on one of the three elephant footstools, one in each unoccupied angle of the room. The boy looked across anxiously to a menacing bust of King Leopold II, listening for the master's return. His younger European companion quickly opened one drawer after the next, rummaging for the hidden key. Finally she let out a quiet squeal of triumph. The key was smaller than the door key, but with an ornately carved head; a swastika crowned twin snakes of Asclepius, their coiled bodies entwined and opened mouths mirroring one another.

Though two years older, the boy was intimidated by all the unfamiliar paraphernalia; on one wall hung a mounting of an antelope head, and on the opposite wall, framed papyrus scrolls detailing images of Iris, Osiris and Horus. Atop a red cedar side table laid an ornate chess set inlaid with choice wood from the Ituri forest. The playing pieces were of ivory and obsidian. Nearby, upon an ivory pedestal, stood a monkey-paw ashtray inlaid with a copper crucible, its bluish discolouration partly blotted out by grey ash. Three skulls were sitting on a bookshelf, one of a mountain gorilla, another of homo sapiens-negroid, and another of a chimpanzee. A pair of callipers hung on the wall. On either side of the skulls

1

stood numerous books; the Bwana's forbidden books. The boy was oblivious to their scientific or esoteric meaning, but shuddered with his own knowing. His precociously erudite female companion would have read: Charles Darwin, On the Origin of Species; Friedrich Nietzsche's Beyond Good and Evil, and Lothrop Stoddard's The Revolt Against Civilisation: the Menace of the Underman, and the Book of Enoch.

The girl inserted the key into a central cabinet and swung open the door of the wooden tabernacle. Inside sat four formalin jars with their twined contents.

Estelle removed her father's journal from the bottom ledge of the wooden cabinet. She hesitated momentarily before laying the leather-bound journal on the desktop. Opening the title page, she deciphered: trans species grafting of primate testicular tissue. Turning over the first few pages, she paused to study the drawings made by her father.

The precise diagrams were of four primate male generative organs: testes and vas deferens. She noted the different sizes of the four primate testes: caucasoid-43 grams, negroid -52 grams, great ape-28 grams, and chimpanzee-110grams.

The distant sound of the returning flying boat alerted the young African, who stood in some agitation, hissing to his blond companion to hurry. They would have to leave now!

"Estelle!" cried her black nanny from the main house, a hint of anxiety in her voice. "Estelle!" she called again.

The girl slipped out of the museum with her African companion.

The all-too-soon arrival of her father had her black nanny even more agitated. "Estelle?" called her father, her nanny shuddering, holding up her hands helplessly. "Kaffir?" bellowed her father, glancing savagely in the nanny's direction, before snatching the chicote that hung on the veranda wall. He grasped the handle of the sun-dried hippopotamus whip in his powerful right hand. "Kaffir?" he bellowed.

The young black boy froze, wide-eyed, then took off, showing his companion the white soles of his feet. The blonde took off after him. Although he was two years older, she was the more mature biologically, and determined not to let him leave her behind to face her father's wrath.

The terrified African had made his exit to the rear of the house, disappearing into the engulfing evergreen along a well-worn track. His ragged khaki quickly blended into the jungle green. She, on the other hand, was less camouflaged in her simple off-white cotton dress. Her intense blue eyes riveted on his sinewy brown legs, her pre-adolescent chin betraying a grim determination to follow the older boy, no matter what.

"Wait!" she cried.

He pulled up, waiting for her to catch him, took her hand and ran deeper into the jungle. She followed him faithfully, her father's bellowing ever more distantly behind.

Her father had warned her off le Museum before, covetous of his curious inheritance. He had followed his own father's interest in the occult and alchemy, but was adamant his offspring keep her nose out of men's business.

Some half-hour into their escape, the two companions found themselves upriver, on the edge of the forest, the distant rush of the falls behind them. Suddenly chatter was heard toward a nearby clearing. The African signalled his companion to be silent as they crept forward. The two children lay huddled in the long grass, their hidey-hole concealed by overhanging foliage. Taking care not to expose their presence, they kept very still, spying on the intimate family gathering.

Mother, Father and toddler were unaware of their presence, enjoying what was left of lunch. Father and daughter were engaged in a friendly wrestle as Mum basked in the sun.

"Can they see us?" whispered the younger of the two secretively, her delicate face framed by golden ringlets.

"I don't think so," whispered the African boy.

The tranquil scene was disturbed by the cries of purple glossy starlings as they fled from overhanging branches. The father jumped to his feet, alert to the disturbance.

A loud crack shattered the afternoon peace. A bullet penetrated below the left eye of the father, exiting the back of his head. The mother panicked, reaching for the toddler before being felled with a machete, a single blow decapitating her. The toddler was petrified, pissing on the dusty ground. The kidnappers approached her, smiling, then grabbed the little girl, bundling her into a bag. Before departing, the assassins cut off the hands of her deceased parents, bagging them separately.

The older African boy pulled the younger girl closer, flinching and huddling as the young girl buried her tearful face into his chest.

"You've got to stop it. Promise me. You've got to stop it."

The older African boy put his arm protectively around her shoulders. Time stood still.

AN ALARM SCREAMED IN Estelle's brain, her flailing arm knocking her mobile to the floor as she shook off the rapidly fading remnants of the dream. The mobile flashed Monday 7th April 2003.

"Shit!" Wiping the stardust from her cheek, the groggy young woman wrenched herself out of bed and scrambled under a shower, her en-suite a jumble of half-used body lotions, shampoos and conditioners.

Bundling herself into a cab, she used the half hour ride to compose herself, finishing off her make-up as she crossed the bridge.

Estelle alighted in Miller Street, North Sydney. The attractive, leggy blond sighted her reflection in a dark, polished car parked near the kerb. Opening the door, a professional young man checked her out, just in time to notice her taking him in. Their eyes met. Estelle gave an all-too-knowing smile; fawning men were a dime a dozen.

Her focus this autumn day was on meeting with her boss, Alex Blumenthal, editor of New Woman, in just three minutes. Skipping up a few steps, Estelle marched into the foyer of the Unix building and took a lift to the eighth floor.

Alex swung around at Estelle's entry, her regal presence silhouetted against the spectacular vista of Sydney Harbour. Discreetly shuffling an envelope into a bottom drawer, she settled into the deep comfort of her burgundy leather chair.

"Just in time, Estelle! You're booked on South African Airways, flight 206 tomorrow. Here's tickets. Got yourself organised?" she asked, sizing up her young protégé with her penetrating brown eyes.

"Yeah. All good. I've been to South Africa before—in my gap year," Estelle reminded her mentor. She had graduated cum laude from Sydney Girls Grammar almost a decade earlier, before spending three months at the remote Holy Cross Hospital in Eastern Pondoland, a place she still felt nostalgia for.

"Of course." The older woman was pensive. At twenty-seven, Estelle still looked like a schoolie to the battle-worn journo. As a younger woman, Alex had cut her teeth covering the demise of the former Mozambican president, Samora Machele, in 1986. It was reported as an accident by the South African Broadcasting Commission, in an impeccable South African English accent; however, the South African Defence Forces were all too soon on the ground, smothering out any oxygen left in a suspicious story. Now here she was sending this wisp of a kid to cover the tragedy of AIDS in rural South Africa. Her novice looked the part in a smart blue business suit cut just above the knee. Pretty girl, her chin chiselled and determined, her eyes blue and intelligent, yet vulnerable—and naive!

"What on earth am I doing sending you out to South Africa?" grumbled the older woman, thinking out loud, her pursed lips accentuating the small creases on her upper lip.

"Because I'm right for the job," retorted Estelle with feigned confidence.

"Yes. Ripe for the job," mused the brittle South African.

"Have your ACTU connections made contact with COSATU?" chipped in Estelle assertively.

Snapping out of her reverie, the older journo replied, "Dave Barrow. He'll meet you at the Sandton Sun. He has the trade union connections."

The Australian Council of Trade Unions had mentored, or so it thought, the Council of South African Trade Unions during the Apartheid era.

"Scotch?" suggested the older woman, filling herself a second glass.

"Why not!" Estelle winked. "Sun's over the yard arm. Barrow? Hmm."

The two women chinked glasses and took in the stately views over Lavender Bay. The Sydney Harbour Bridge stood solid in the background. The harbour usually had a calming effect on Estelle, but as she gazed at the Ferris wheel slowly rotating anti-clockwise, her mind drifted back to the haunting myth of Moloch, whose leering face decorated the entrance to Luna Park. She shuddered, recollecting the god of Baal's biblical reputation as a deity to whom children were burnt alive as sacrificial offerings. It seemed the ancient god of Baal had woven his malevolence into the twentieth century. Estelle remembered the shadow cast over the amusement park by the Ghost Train disaster of 1979. Seven people, mostly school kids, were incinerated, as if burnt offerings to ghoulish technological entertainment.

"Estelle!" interrupted Alex. "When you arrive at Jan Smuts airport and you're feeling buggered, watch for your handbag and passport as you reach over to get your luggage off the carousel."

Estelle frowned.

"Watch your back!" quipped the older woman with an all-too-knowing look.

A fleeting shadow crimped her protégé's innocent enthusiasm. This was her first major assignment overseas. A lot was riding on the success of her report. Down with the Scotch!

Following Estelle's departure, Alex opened the bottom left-hand drawer of her mahogany desk, retrieving the envelope marked 'Private and confidential'. Leaning into the open palm of her left hand, Alex massaged the side of her head, combing her fingers through her bottled, jet-black hair.

RETURNING LATER THAT EVENING, Estelle made last minute preparations. It was eight pm, dark over the city, with flickering lights around the quay. Venus had risen in the east.

"Star light, star bright, the first star I see tonight,

I wish I may, I wish I might, have the wish I wish tonight."

The remembrance of a soft female voice floated through her consciousness. Switching back to present time, Estelle packed her last minute bits and pieces: MasterCard, cash, 2,000 rand, passport, tickets, laptop. Glancing at a World Vision AIDS doco on her laptop, she logged off.

Chapter Two

Flying into Johannesburg, Estelle was flooded with a wave of remembrance. Gold was discovered on the Rand by a random Aussie digger, George Harrison, in 1864. South Africa was one of the world's wealthiest countries in terms of natural resources.

Jo'burg evoked ambivalent feelings for Estelle. Yes, the mine dumps were the mine dumps, however gentrified. Soweto sprawled to the south-west and the northern suburbs had their own leafy, green beauty, with spectacular thunderstorms in late afternoon summer, not so different from her home town of Sydney.

Her mother's father, John Harris, was born in Johannesburg. Following World War Two he graduated from Wits University with a degree in Mining Engineering, and not long after, on a whirlwind visit to Sydney, met the madly passionate sixteen-year-old Esther. Estelle's mother, Judith, was born nine months later.

Pop was a jolly, clean-shaven old fella with sparkling navy blue eyes. She dimly recalled story time, when he'd read to her before bed, and the Freddo Frog chocolates he'd dispensed as a terminally-ill old man courageously struggling for breath. He'd undertaken some contract work at the Penge mine in the northern Transvaal earlier in his career and was subsequently felled by mesothelioma. Her mother died a year later, a subject far too difficult for her father to open up about. Was it breast cancer that had tipped her over the edge? What might have been if Pop Harris had never worked the Penge Mine? Crocidolite, or blue asbestos: so deadly once it takes hold. All it takes is a few fibres: and such an inexorable disease, just like AIDS.

"Get over it, Estelle!" she chided herself, snapping out of her trance.

Arriving in Jo'burg from the land down-under was electrifying. The sheer dynamism of the place hit her like a force field: really multicultural, black, happy, exuberantly youthful! The many armed guards were a reminder that violence was just beneath the surface. Estelle was taken by courtesy bus to the Sandton Sun. Her minibus was alive with chatter, mainly from the blacks, as her driver skilfully manoeuvred through the afternoon traffic. Time seemed compressed in the bustling metropolis, but as they approached the northern suburb of Sandon, time and space just seemed to open up.

Alighting at the Fifth Street entrance, Estelle tipped the driver and was immediately swept into the plush lobby of the Sandton Hotel by an enthusiastic young black porter eager to provide her with the utmost in South African hospitality.

"Dis way, danke, madam." Petrus beamed, his black face shining around a set of brilliant pearly whites.

Inside, the fine décor and rich earthy tones created an ambience of welcome. Estelle was surprised at the number of young black entrepreneurs in the lobby. Suave, elegantly dressed and multi-lingual, young black yuppies were finding a niche in the new South Africa. As a group they were usually more adept linguistically than their Afrikaans and English-speaking counterparts, and were being nurtured by the multinational corporations who now had a vested interest in accelerating the growth of a black middle-class.

"Hello, Estelle. Welcome back to South Africa."

Estelle swung around to look up at the speaker, the clipped Natalian accent immediately familiar. His distinctive accent was accompanied by a clean-cut military appearance as he stood a comfortable few feet away.

"Well, hello, Dave. Good to see you again," replied Estelle, quickly regaining her composure. "I thought I recognised the name. Small world, eh!"

"Six degrees of separation, is it? Perhaps you'd care to freshen up. You must be tired. What is it: a sixteen hour flight?" smoothed over Dave, searching her with piercing brown eyes, cautious but welcoming.

"I'm quite ready to be briefed: had a bit of a kip on the flight over."

"Shall we say seven in the brasserie then?" replied Dave, combing his fingers through his receding chestnut hair.

"Seven sounds just fine." Dave had always been chivalrous and precise.

Estelle turned to follow the obsequious Petrus trolleying her luggage. Escaping into the waiting lift, she felt her slight blush and remembered, with mild embarrassment, her teenage tryst with Dave almost a decade earlier. She sighed. Not the first or last of her passionate and jagged affairs. Still footloose and uncommitted, she mused. Whatever. Twenty-seven was still very young for her generation, and she had to get ahead in her career.

POWER-RESTED AND SHOWERED, ESTELLE unconsciously dabbed a little Prada on before skipping down to meet her ex-beau. Supper was a simple fare for a five-star hotel. Grilled langoustine and salad followed by a fruit and cheese platter. Estelle skipped the aqua minerale, and allowed the waiter to pour her a generous goblet of Nederburg chardonnay.

"Well! It all seems like a lifetime ago. I'm looking forward to seeing Holy Cross again," opened Estelle.

"Yes, they were lecker days," agreed Dave somewhat awkwardly. "A lot has happened in a decade: good, bad, ugly. Vaccination rates, primary school participation, electrification have all improved. We're still chasing our backside on housing, what with all the illegal immigrants from the rest of Africa. You'll have seen the squatter camps all over."

Just like a man, mused Estelle, hiding behind facts and figures. "And yourself?" she chimed.

"Married, divorced, moved sideways from clinical medicine into community health," Dave replied curtly. "Downtown Jo'burg has become a bit of a no-go zone and even Hillbrow has lost its charm."

Estelle savoured her cheese, allowing Dave to prattle on.

"Violence is everywhere now, and has spread to every suburb. Previously we'd managed to cocoon the white suburbs to an extent. Now, well, we've all been touched by the violence here, Estelle." Dave went quiet, pensive across the crisp white linen cloth. He settled back into his sisal wicker chair, gazing at the small candle flickering between them.

"Sounds like you've been touched, Dave."

"Yes, my older brother, Mike: a car jacking, two years ago," answered Dave, his square jaw taut, eyes riveted on the flame.

"I'm sorry, Dave." Her reply was almost a whisper.

"This is South Africa; we learn to live with it," replied her companion, deflecting further discussion.

"And Mbeki?" queried Estelle gently, following his lead.

Thabo Mbeki had been Mandela's CEO, and followed on as South Africa's second black president. A shy intellectual and shrewd tactician, his introspective, measured friendliness was a contrast to Mandela's charismatic presence. "He gets a lot of stick for being a HIV sceptic, if that's your query? Of course the Americans and

Europeans would love to get their antiretrovirals into the South African HIV market—until the gold runs out! But we have such a massive AIDS population load here. Thirty per cent now! This problem is just too big for a drug approach. The Blacks have to change their behaviour."

"And not just the Blacks, I suppose," teased Estelle.

"Yes, I guess that goes for us all." Dave glanced at the full breasted young Estelle across the table. "One theory has it that there will be two populations eventually; those that do practice safe sex, and those that don't."

"And those that do fuck are the Blacks?" jibed Estelle.

"Well, it's rife in Kwazulu—and you'll see the impact this has had at Bara tomorrow," retorted Dave a little defensively. This little blond Aussie was getting under his skin—again!

"Isn't this epidemic really more about class than race?" niggled Estelle.

"You Aussies can't afford to be too sanctimonious. Apartheid was a wonderful deflection from your own kuck. Your Abos aren't faring too well on the longevity stakes, I hear!"

"Hey! Nothing gives you Springboks more pleasure that screwing a Wallaby," teased Estelle, alluding to their rugby rivalry.

Now it was Dave's turn to blush. "OK! Truce! Truce!" he pleaded. "See you in the lobby at seven."

THE PHONE WAS RINGING as she opened the door to her room. "That man!" Estelle exclaimed. Answering, she blurted out, "Da-Dad," brightening as she realised it was her father on the line.

"How are you, sweetheart? You've arrived safe and sound?" His voice was warm and concerned.

"I'm fine: just had a meal with Dave Barrow, a thorough gentleman from Natal days. No, not an old boyfriend, Dad; you know you're the only man in my life," Estelle jested. "Stop worrying. I'm in safe hands. OK, Dad, OK, Dad. Goodnight! Love you too. Ring you from Holy Cross. 'Night."

Estelle slipped upstairs to the rooftop pool before retiring, grateful for some quiet space on her own, then descended to crash out for the night, and slept like the dead.

DAVE ARRIVED WITH MILITARY precision at seven hundred hours. "You've had breakfast?" A statement and question as her chauffer hurried her through the lobby.

"I've missed the guava. Delicious! Where to? What the—?" queried Estelle as Dave opened the left-side passenger door of a battered yellow bakkie, best described as a single-cabined, compressed version of an Aussie ute.

"No one will hijack this old lady," quipped Dave, pointing to the thick chain and lock at her feet.

It was a little chilly. The sky was bluer than blue, with a bright, almost alpine sun. At 1,800 metres, Jo'burg had a crispness in the air that was invigorating. Estelle slid herself into the passenger's side and locked her door. Strapping in, she lightly brushed against Dave's tight, muscular left arm. Several fine, long strands of wispy hair delicately caressed her right cheek whilst the faint smell of her perfume subtly suffused their compressed space. Overcome by warm, fuzzy feelings that flowed into her pelvis, she was just as instantly relieved by the intrusion of a random thought of her crazy grandmother. Smiling, she imagined her Nan with some politically incorrect, throwaway line like: "Any closer and you may require contraception, my dear!"

"We'll take the scenic route through Coronationville, and Bosmont," announced Dave perfunctorily.

"Coronation Hospital?" Estelle asked as they passed by a three-storied brick building.

"Yes, affectionately known as Cori. Served as the major maternal and child-health hospital for Indians and Coloureds in the old Apartheid era. In the old days, Black women in labour were forced to go the long way round to Bara; well, if they didn't pass the pencil test."

"The pencil test?" Estelle raised a curious eyebrow.

"Yea. If a pencil got caught up, so to speak, in a curly pepper-head, patients were deemed Black and turned away by the officials."

"That's shocking."

"Not everyone applied the rule. One Lebanese paediatrician snubbed his nose at the Provincial administration and fetched black babies from the sluice room, resuscitated them and stuck them on ventilators. Tell the truth, a lot of the staff had heart."

"I'm gobsmacked!"

"It's become a rehab hospital in the post-Apartheid era, with all races now able to access the J.G. Striedom Hospital, once a designated 'Whites only' hospital.

Passing through the former Coloured suburbs, Estelle was surprised to find the pot-holed, tarred roads lined with eucalypts. This almost felt like home. Imperceptibly, the outer southern suburbs of Jo'burg morphed into the backblocks of Soweto. The little yellow bakkie snaked its way around to Deipkloof, an older, respectable suburb of Soweto. A lot of the middle-class housing were low slung, mining-type, three bedroom homes, not so dissimilar to what Estelle remembered from the mining towns of Cobar and Broken Hill in western New South Wales. Although most houses had become electrified, the blacks stood around smoky forty-four gallon drums warming their hands at the dying coals of the night before. Dusty side roads shot off left and right. The streets were milling with school-aged children in black uniforms and white shirts, men and women in smart suits hailing down black taxis. Scrawny dogs and snotty nosed infants stared out at the world while the faint smell of paraffin, mixed with garbage, pervaded the neighbourhood. Soweto was a kaleidoscope of sensations impacting every sense organ.

The bakkie screeched to a halt behind a bus that had suddenly stopped without warning, its brake lights not working. Estelle felt her heart rate take off and her vision narrowed down on the rapidly approaching left rear.

"Damn!" muttered Dave. "Sorry, Estelle."

A lorry, packed to the rafters with mangy chooks, pulled off to the roadside opposite. The wretched fowl squatted mute, yet hyper-alert, in cramped cages.

"They're for the chop! The less well-to-do can have the Walkie-Talkies," quipped Dave.

"Walkie-Talkies?" parroted Estelle, eyeballing the scared chooks across the narrow road.

"Sowetans are very resourceful. Head and feet make a scrumptious stew for fifty cents!" Dave laughed.

Estelle's frowning face dissolved into a smile as she shifted her gaze to the laughing, boyish thirty-four-year old with rugged good looks and smooth olive skin. "Where are all the shops?" she deflected.

"Apart from the Shabeens and a few fast food outlets, there are very few shopping centres in Soweto. Most Blacks shop in white Jo'burg or at one of the surrounding Hyperamas. Black small business was constrained during the Apartheid era—except the black taxis. Well, the railways were run for blue collar Afrikaaners, probably as efficiently as your trains in Oz."

"The Shabeens? Bars, you mean?"

"Yes, the mining hostels have always had access to rail, informal pubs you'd call them, and brothels. What more does a lonely migrant miner want?"

Rounding a bend and descending into a slight gully, the enormous facade of the Chis Hani-Baragwanath Hospital loomed up on a ridge across the highway. Estelle noted the barbed wire-topped walls of the massive hospital. Bara was the main hospital servicing Soweto, and a showpiece of the Apartheid era, impressing overseas visitors with South Africa's commitment to the latest technological advances for its Black populace.

Darting across the main highway leading from Uncle Charley's servo to Zola, Dave cleared himself and Estelle with security, and they were both issued with visitor badges.

Behind the concrete walls, Bara was a beehive of activity: emergency cases being rushed from Casualty to the admitting Ward Twenty with bright orange 'Urgent' stickers stuck to their sweaty foreheads; squeaky trolleys, with intravenous fluids running, competed with the lollipop ladies, in red and white striped shirts, delivering tea along narrow concrete pathways sheltered by overhead sunroofs.

The Black staff shouting and laughing, greeting and singing; life, death, sadness and joy all compressed into a multi-coloured life space. By contrast, Estelle noted the harried look of some of the white-coated doctors.

"And them?" She motioned to a serious-looking White doctor.

"Over half of the medical cases are HIV/ TB cases. Bara was booming when gold was fetching three hundred an ounce in the early eighties, and the rand near parity with the dollar. The place is a little demoralised now," brooded Dave.

"I see." Estelle nodded.

"There're over forty-four wards here, Estelle, with St John of God's eye hospital next door and the Maternity wing this way," continued Dave, directing Estelle around to the left. Arriving at Maternity, Dave swung the doors open to the second stage ward harbouring fifty-odd women in various stages of labour.

They were immediately greeted by Daniel Molefe, a stocky, friendly Black doctor in his early thirties.

"Daniel, my brother!" Dave grinned. "Meet Estelle Goldstein, my colleague from Holy Cross days."

"Molo, Estelle. South African? Medical?" he interrogated with a warm and cheeky smile.

"Grandfather born here; I'm Australian born. Did a stint at Holy Cross for my gap year, and no, dropped the idea of medicine and pursued a career in science journalism."

"And this is Sister Pearl, our head midwife. Sister, this is Estelle Goldstein from Australia."

"A pleasure to meet you, Estelle. You are most welcome. I trust you'll respect the dignity of our mothers," the formidable black midwife greeted, eyeing the camera slung over Estelle's shoulder.

"Of course, but if I may just get some discreet shots?" replied Estelle, taking in the immense ward, some fifty metres in length, twin operating theatres at the far end.

Sister Pearl raised her eyebrow. "Doctor Molefe will direct you, I'm sure. Well, nice to meet you. Trust your article does justice to our situation," replied Sister Pearl, moving off to assist a junior colleague.

Any awkwardness was quickly dispelled by the entry of a tall, bespectacled man in his mid-sixties. Doctor Malcolm Stern was head of the department—and proud of his baby.

"Doctor Stern, may I introduce Estelle Goldstein from Sydney, who's doing a piece on HIV and its impact on rural health," introduced Daniel.

"Very good; you're very welcome, Miss Goldstein. You're from Sydney? My son's a cardiologist at the Children's Hospital," greeted the sombre-eyed, erudite doctor in a Jo'burg Jewish accent.

"Oh. That's nice, Doctor Stern. Please call me Estelle. Where's he stay?"

"I believe a beach called Tamarama?"

"It's a beautiful beach; just a stone's throw south of Bondi."

"Ahh. And how do you find Bara, Estelle?"

"Impressive!" exclaimed Estelle, snapping off some shots as Doctor Stern gestured to his ward.

"Baragwanath is the world's largest hospital. We have just under 3000 inpatient beds and a total staff of 6,760. This unit is one of the busiest maternity units in the world. We deliver about 22,000 babies here every year, and you'll note the two Caesar theatres at the end of this ward provide immediate access to an emergency surgical delivery, should our mothers require intervention."

"How many Caesarean sections do you do a day here?" enquired Estelle, clicking away.

"The record is 23 Caesars in 24 hours for one doctor," sighed Daniel, "and some women were given a sterilisation, free of charge."

"God! That's a record of Olympian proportions—and who holds that record?" asked Estelle in awe, though perturbed by his last comment.

"Joe van—"

"Of course, those were the bad old days," cut in the professor defensively. "We have a very safe record here, Miss Goldstein."

"And you mentioned that a lot of mothers deliver in the Soweto Clinics, Doctor Stern."

"Yes. Most of our Black patients deliver in the periphery and are transferred here if they are high risk, or have a delay in progress. You see, Miss Goldstein," the professor motioned to a labour graph, "this is a partogram, developed by my mentor, Doctor Hugh Philpott. He developed this chart in Rhodesia, and this simple technology has been exported all over the world. We expect all our mothers to dilate their cervix at a rate not less than one centimetre per hour, once they have established labour. The progress of labour is charted just like this," his finger ran along the steadily rising line, "and you can see that this mother has crossed the action line and is now being monitored very closely. She will have a safe delivery here and we can expedite surgical delivery for her if required."

As if on cue, one woman was wheeled out of the left hand Caesar theatre as another needy mother was rolled into a newly cleaned and sterilised theatre next door. All the while, a low-grade cacophony of groans and grunts pervaded the unit as scores of black women stoically laboured to crown and then deliver their precious offspring.

"Very impressive, Doctor Stern. And do Soweto women have a very high fertility rate?"

"Soweto has an official population of approximately three and a half million and a fertility rate of less than three children per woman. Of course our earlier successes in curtailing fertility were due to improvements in socio-economic conditions and better contraception. But now with AIDS—Agh!" Doctor Stern's voice drifted off.

"Is it true, then, that thirty percent of women in Soweto are HIV positive?" cut in Estelle.

"Sadly, thirty percent, give or take a percentage or two. Well, Miss Goldstein, I must leave you in the capable hands of Doctor Molefe. Thank you, Daniel." Doctor Stern nodded to his senior registrar. The erudite Doctor Stern then turned and left the ward abruptly.

"What of the children, Daniel?"

"We have a lot of HIV positive newborns, and children who subsequently become HIV positive with breast feeding."

"Surely antiretrovirals would make difference?"

"Ah, it's painful!" lamented Daniel. "The government is still playing poker with the multi-nationals over royalties. HIV has impacted our people in such a cruel way. There was a time when no Black South African child was an orphan. Now sometimes whole families are taken out. So who is going to support all these orphans?"

"I can see the dilemma."

"The horse had already bolted by the time Mandela got in, though he was slow off the mark. It was only when HIV was impacting on our GDP that the authorities and big business started to take the issue seriously. No doubt you'll get a fuller picture when you get to Eastern Pondoland. I'd better get going. Humba gahly, Estelle."

"He means go well, Estelle," added Dave, who had drifted into the background during Estelle's interview.

"Lala Gashly, bro." Dave grinned at Daniel.

"Stay well," explained Daniel to the confused Estelle, smiling at the two of them.

THE TRIP BACK TO Sandton circled via Nancefield cemetery, where dozens of funerals were in progress. Clusters of mourners gathered by open graves, farewelling loved ones, a chilling wind carrying mournful cries over the veldt as hearses and bakkies delivered their tragic cargo.

"AIDS?" Estelle frowned.

"Mostly: about two hundred burials here every weekend. Twenty years ago it was mainly diseases of poverty and malnutrition—kwashiorkor, marasmus, pellagra, beri-beri, scurvy—you name it. Now HIV dwarfs all those previous, and with it, TB has just exploded."

"Tragic."

"The African people have tremendous resilience," replied Dave despondently. "I love South Africa, Estelle." Dave paused pensively. "We just have to make a plan and get on with it."

"So what was it about the Caesar record the good professor was so anxious to avoid?" probed Estelle.

"I guess it's a young man's thing. A need for speed," replied Dave. "Young men will compete for anything. At Bara, in the old days, young doctors would compete to see who could do a Caesar, skin to skin, in the shortest time, and then who could do the most in a single day. I guess it got a bit over the top when some young Afrikaners who had moral scruples about performing sterilisations on young white women, were only too eager to perform the same procedure on black women with no real informed consent."

"I see." Estelle watched the steady procession of hearses trickle into the cemetery.

They continued the drive back to Sandton in silence, each lost in their thoughts. Arriving back at two in the afternoon, Estelle was overcome with soulful tiredness. The little bakkie pulled up conspicuously outside the five-star Sandton Sun.

"Thanks, Dave. I'm buggered."

"What the—? You Aussies!" Dave grimaced.

"Jet-lagged," Estelle laughed.

"You're off to Kokstadt in the morning then?"

"Yes, an early start: a Fokker to Kokstadt and…?"

"Stan Ntuli, a field worker and COSATU facilitator, will meet you. Will you get down to Mkambati?"

Mkambati Game Reserve was a secluded park some fifty miles east of Holy Cross Hospital and bordered by one of the most beautiful stretches of the Wild Coast. The remote outpost of Holy

Cross Hospital had hosted a leprosarium, where patients with TB and leprosy were held in isolation.

"I'm not sure I'll get to the coast this trip. Is the leprosarium still running?"

"I don't know. It may have closed down. Boet Stan will fill you in."

"Hey, what a beautiful place, but what were all those black-shirted guards all about?" remembered Estelle, casting Dave a quizzical glance.

"Probably waiting for you to skinny dip!" The South African chuckled, a glint in his eye and a hand on her thigh.

"You! I'm sure we were being spied on. They had binoculars on us the whole afternoon," Estelle deflected, ambivalently pulling back.

"Ah, you're paranoid. Too much Dakka," teased Dave.

"Go well," Estelle replied.

"Will I see you on your return?"

"We'll see." Estelle bit her bottom lip.

Estelle alighted from the battered yellow bakkie, grateful to be back in her hotel with its fine linen and creature comforts.

TAKING HER FLIGHT SOUTH-EAST from Jo'burg to Kokstadt, Estelle's spirits soared as the plane skirted the highest peak of the Drakensberg, South Africa's highest mountain range, aptly known to the Zulus as 'a barrier of spears'. The tiny Fokker prudently passed through a little corridor between Lesotho and KwaZulu, the bumpy flight shrouded with intermittent cloud.

Landing in Kokstad, Estelle disembarked, picked up her luggage and scanned the small crowd waiting. A short, robust man, mid-forties, in smart, casual attire held her gaze as he walked over to introduce himself.

"Molo, Miss Goldstein?"

"Molweni, Boet Stan Ntuli," Estelle replied, cautiously searching the Pondo's inscrutable face. His high cheekbones were almost Mongol in character. Vertical scarification betrayed his traditional Pondo roots, his nostrils broad, typical of the Bantu. "Dave sends greetings."

The older African smiled and nodded. "May I take your bags?" His voice was soft and enunciation precise as he sized up the young Australian journalist.

"Thank you." Estelle acquiesced to his offer. "Please call me Estelle." Stan nodded in assent.

Another bakkie, cheap and versatile, provided a dusty, somewhat bumpy ride to Holy Cross. Swinging onto the north-south highway, the bakkie took a turn off to Magusheni.

"The Place of Slaughtered Sheep," translated Stan.

From Flagstaff the tarred road swung south via Lusikisiki, and onto the popular tourist destination of Port St John. Instead Boet Stan drove through Flagstaff, past several small local shops, a post office and local inn, and struck out on the unsealed road to the east, seaward to Holy Cross Hospital.

"Have you been to the Bundus before, Estelle?"

"I spent three months of my gap year at Holy Cross, following my HSC."

"Gap year? I'm not familiar with the expression," he asked slowly and precisely.

"I took a year off after my Higher School Certificate, prior to starting a university degree. I came out as a sort of Rotary Exchange student with a former mission doctor from McCords?"

"McCords Hospital in Natal?"

"Yes. He organised for me to spend a few months at Holy Cross."

Boet Stan drove cautiously as he passed a noble Pondo man riding west on his stallion towards Flagstaff. Erect in his saddle, the grey-stubbled old man doffed his hat in recognition. Stan saluted as he slowed.

Further on they passed a little bent grandmother, widowed perhaps for many decades, wearing a black dress and headscarf. A little further along, a young black woman also dressed in black—mourning.

"TB used to be a disease of very young children, teenage girls and young people—and of course the gogwanas. Now with HIV, it's anyone's disease," Boet Stan explained, as if reading her questioning eyes.

"Gogwana?" Estelle frowned.

"Grandmother," Boet Stan interpreted.

They travelled on in silence, as the rolling green hills of eastern Pondoland stretched out in front of them. Off road, on what appeared to be goat tracks leading into myriad hills, were dotted clusters of whitewashed rondavels. Mud brick, round huts with thatched roofs, these traditional African dwellings were in most ways ideal for the climate. Estelle recalled how cow dung was compacted and polished into a shiny, green marblesque floor. Dave had described the floors as 'spit and polish' on their weekend at Mkambati.

"These little rondavels look so idyllic," murmured Estelle, entranced by the rolling green vista.

"I suppose they look romantic to the tourists," Boet Stan intoned, "but they can be lethal in a thunderstorm."

"Why so?"

"The most common cause of mass death in this idyllic part of the world is lightning strike. Opening a door or window during a storm can be very dangerous. Sometimes an entire family can die. Many huts still lack a lightning conductor," Boet Stan explained in a gentle, even voice.

"I thought that an old wives' tale."

"Hmm." The older Pondo man grimaced, shaking his head.

"Where are all the trees?" Estelle asked, breaking an awkward silence.

"Wood. All cut down for fuel. Energy costs," Stan replied tersely.

"Of course," Estelle murmured, remembering the extensive use of cow dung for fuel.

Ten miles on, they came to a prominent hill, south of the road, with a cluster of pine trees three-quarter of the way up the slope. Some housing was visible halfway down the path lying above the hospital.

Boet Stan swung the little bakkie hard to the right and accelerated past two ancient sentinel eucalypts on either side, then up a dusty, corrugated road to the entrance gate of Holy Cross Hospital. To the left stood the impressive red brick Holy Cross Church built by Anglican missionaries prior to the Apartheid government takeover of all mission hospitals. To the right a dusty soccer field, and snuggling up to what had been the Medical Superintendent's residence, a tennis court. Just outside the hospital gate was a small, low-slung Primary Health Care clinic designed to take the load off the Outpatients department inside. This primarily catered to those who required a doctor's consultation.

Boet Stan waved to the baton-carrying guard at the gate. He was old and dishevelled, and wore an official cap, his badge of authority.

The old man nodded to Stan in recognition and swung the creaky gates open.

"Dankie, Dadda." Stan nodded respectfully before driving in. He swung the bakkie around to the left into a small parking area next to a clump of pine trees.

Estelle alighted from the bakkie and stretched. The hospital was, like many ex-mission hospitals, old and dilapidated, but clean and organised, and while the staff wearied often, they were always cheery, especially to visitors.

They were greeted by Matron Ndlovu, a stout, imperial presence, the multi-coloured bars on her epaulettes testimony to her hard slog up through the nursing ranks and years of study through UNISA, the University of Southern Africa based in Pretoria.

"Molo, Boet Stan."

"Molweni, Matron Ndlovu," his greeting languid in the mild autumn sunshine, "meet Estelle Goldstein."

"Molo, Estelle. You are most welcome. I believe you've spent time at Holy Cross before. Oh, dears, you must be tired. Do come in for tea." She bustled them towards the tea room like a clucking mother hen. The guests were ushered into a cramped room, barely able to contain the four-seater table with matching pine servery. The cracked walls were coated with fading aquamarine paint. In the corner adjacent the entrance, a stainless steel wash basin rested on a stand. A cake of Sunlight soap and threadbare towel were provided for hand washing. A crucifix adorned the right wall.

"Yes, Matron, for three months over Easter in 1993," Estelle replied as she washed her hands and looked to wriggle into one of the plastic chairs.

"Ah, you were here when our son Chris Hani was assassinated, the leader of the unbanned South African Communist Party?"

"Yes, indeed. I believe his assassination was organised by Clive Darby-Lewis, whose wife Gaye was Australian born. Subsequently Mandela came to centre stage and the rest is history, as they say."

"Yes, it was a terrible time, but his assassination pushed us all beyond a fork in the road: a blood bath or a peaceful resolution. Thank the good Lord."

The conversation was interrupted as a portly serving girl, brought in hot morning tea. A set of fine English china on a faded silver tray accompanied a dozen hot, fat cakes, their rich cinnamon aroma permeating the cramped tearoom. Estelle swallowed in anticipation of the delicious local donuts.

"Thank you, Olga." Matron nodded as the serving girl bowed out of the room.

"I didn't realise Chris Hani was a Pondo," Estelle continued.

"Xhosa, my dear; he was from my clan. I'm of the Tembu. These Pondo are rough, poorly educated people—and rebellious!"

Boet Stan joined the collective laughter. "Yes we are, Matron!"

The Pondo were a notorious lot and had run more than one doctor out of town in an earlier time, if they considered him unsuitable. To teach them a lesson, the Pretorian government left the hospital doctor-less for a year. It was in that time that Stan, as a lowly orderly, had taken over the circumcisions at Holy Cross. The midwives took on a lot more responsibility, but if a Caesar was needed, they had to ship the labouring mother out to St Elizabeth's Hospital, only twenty miles away but several hours south by road to Lusikisiki. That delay could be lethal.

"This Pondo boy will escort you around then." Matron Ndlovu laughed.

"Doctor Ngubani will be happy to orient you when he's finished the autopsies with Doctor Mabunda."

"Thank you, Matron," Estelle replied.

"You're most welcome, my dear." The matron smiled with delight.

"Autopsy session?" Estelle quizzed.

Estelle gasped at the many emaciated men of all ages languishing in the ward. Although ventilated with overhead fans, the sickly smell of body fluids and soiled linen seemed to permeate every pore of Estelle's body.

"This is a mixed medical and surgical ward, Estelle. As you can see, with HIV and TB, the wards are overrun." He motioned to a ward packed to the rafters, with a floor mattress between every second bed. "We are overcrowded but no patient in need is turned away."

"Hopefully my article will stir enough interest to get more funding to flow your way."

Stan smiled in acknowledgement of Estelle's good intentions, shrugging his shoulders.

Doctor Wilson Ngubane joined them in Calloway ward, the children's ward.

"Molo, Wilson. Meet Estelle Goldstein, an Australian journalist associated with the Australian Council of Trade Unions." Turning to Estelle: "Wilson is doing some work with the South African Congress of Trade Unions."

"Pleased to meet you, Doctor Ngubane," Estelle bubbled.

"You're welcome, Miss Goldstein." The dapper young black doctor, courteous and open, motioned Estelle deeper into the ward. Estelle noted the somewhat sweeter odour of the children's ward. They paused at a cot where an emaciated four-year-old with big soulful eyes languished. An inter-costal clear plastic tubing drained blood and serous fluid from the left side of her thorax.

"Innocence has a TB effusion and she is HIV positive. Both parents succumbed to HIV, and her grandfather is in the male ward with TB pericarditis. The Transkei has the highest incidence of TB pericarditis in the world." Doctor Ngubane rattled off the young girl's history in a matter-of-fact manner, though Estelle could sense the compassion in his eyes.

A wave of sadness arose in Estelle's chest: not just a mother, but both parents. "And the grandmother?"

"I'm not sure? I believe she's a sangoma."

Estelle cast her mind on Esther, her clairvoyant grandmother, who'd on occasion mentioned the sangomas, the traditional healers that practice by way of herbal remedies, divination and counselling, and who'd outnumbered Western-trained doctors in South Africa, and indeed were more popular with the black population than orthodox Western medicine, especially in the rural areas.

"May I take a photo?" Estelle requested, distracting herself from her own grief over maternal loss. Somehow, writing and photographing this tragedy in a remote rural community gave her an illusion of control. She could look at it and analyse it, and make pictures of it which resonated, and yet it was beyond herself.

Farewelling Wilson Ngubane, they moved off to other wards, and later to the Nutritional Rehabilitation Unit. After the worst of their acute illness, the children were discharged with their mothers from Calloway ward to the nearby women's kraal to skill up in gardening and nutrition. A dollop of peanut butter in a plate of mealy porridge went a long way, and the deep trench gardens, while not meeting caloric needs, could provide dense nutrition with greens and beans.

"Shite!" Estelle swore as her attempts with a spade bounced off the hard, dry earth.

Sister Beauty smothered a giggle at Estelle's clumsy efforts. Two solid women had arrived carrying twenty-litre containers on their heads, smiling as they gracefully off loaded the precious water. Estelle handed the spade back to Sister Beauty and stretched up to take some more shots.

Communal vegetable gardens surrounded the Holy Cross precinct and were tended on terraced plots carved into the hills. The gardens abutted the Women's Kraal, a circular cluster of several rondavels, and were an earlier effort to impact on malnutrition in this remote rural community. With every able-bodied man from fifteen to sixty-five recruited to the mines in Johannesburg for up to eleven months of the year, the burden of keeping the family alive on a day to-day basis rested on rural African women.

Beauty, the community health sister, was very informative, explaining how the program was inspired by two Jewish doctors, Sidney and Emily Kark, community health innovators in the thirties, who'd gone on to establish a School of Community Health at Hadassah University in Jerusalem. They had helped Holy Cross's founding Superintendent, Doctor Drew, with an early successful pilot. However in 1983, during savage droughts in the southern hemisphere, the under-five mortality rate in Eastern Pondoland was three hundred per thousand.

"But surely the government—the international community—just couldn't stand by and do nothing?" demanded Estelle.

"The international milk companies donated several tons of powdered milk as emergency relief. Alas, children weaned early off the breast face a death sentence. Gastroenteritis goes hand-in-glove with bottle feeds." Beauty explained how gastroenteritis stripped the child of her borderline nutrition and ushered in marasmus and kwashiorkor. "Shame! The poor condition of the elephants in Kruger National Park and the generous donations of the multinationals made the headlines." Beauty shrugged in resignation.

SWEATING IN THE OVER-WARM mid-morning, Doctor Solomon Mabunda rolled another corpse onto the autopsy table, stabilising the head on a block and double-checking the tag on his left toe. His young protégé had excused himself. A visiting foreign journalist from Sydney, Australia by the name of Goldstein had arrived. "Goldstein," Solomon quietly mused as he attended to the last emaciated former miner, still cool from the mortuary fridge. A bucket of sweet formalin waited at the side for its guest.

Although in his sixties, the deceased Pondo male had the body of a twenty-five-year old. Vertical scarification on his cheeks marked his ethnicity. The elderly doctor made a vertical incision with a size fifteen blade from the supra-sternal notch to the base of his sternum. He drilled through the sternum with a rotary saw, then wedged open the chest with a rib spreader. A lifeless heart and still lungs lay resting in the thorax. The stench of death embraced his nostrils.

Cutting through trachea, oesophagus and carotid vessels, Doctor Mabunda dissected the pleura away from the thorax, snipping off the remaining tenacious fibrous strands holding the heart and lungs captive. He briefly surveyed the lungs, noting their black discolouration, as much from urban smog as from tobacco. The tell-tale white, cheesy matter occupying the apex of the lungs signified tuberculosis, but the real prize lay deep in the spongy lung matter. The old doctor respectfully lifted the organs out of their tabernacle into a clear plastic bag of formalin, and then placed the lot into a waiting white bucket. From here the heart and lungs would be transported to the South African Institute of Medical Research in Johannesburg for pathological analysis. The histology would confirm silicosis, and in due course the family of the deceased would be sent a cheque for 4,000 rand. Had he been a White miner, the cheque would have been for 20,000 rand. Although racially biased and bureaucratic, the South African Mining Compensation Act had been more progressive than others: cold comfort for poor Black rural families.

Thus far, Mabunda's forensic endeavours had brought in over 600,000 rand to this remote part of South Africa, and still there was no atonement. Sighing with heavy heart, Mabunda completed a perfunctory stitch-up of the thorax and returned the majestic deceased male to the fridge. Now he had time for a nip.

RETURNING FROM THE WOMEN'S Kraal, Estelle was weary from the morning's tour and amused by Boet Stan's irreverent branding of the matrons' quarters as 'Menopause Mansions'. As they walked past the unkempt tennis courts and across the soccer field, the beauty of Holy Cross Church stood as a sentinel to the east of the hospital gates.

At the far end of the soccer field, retired Matron Winifred broke from Xhosa into fluent Shakespearean English as she energetically stabbed the air with her finger in front of an emaciated woman's face. "You left the church. You've sinned. Now look where you are now—dying!"

"Sister of no mercy," Estelle whispered under her breath.

"The Lord is coming. Repent or be damned! Good people, repent or be damned!" the matron ranted with even greater vigour, casting a condemning glance at Estelle in her safari shorts.

"The South African Catholic Bishops' Council spoke out against the use of condoms." Boet Stan's tone was controlled and even.

"Fucking Christians," Estelle muttered under her breath.

Boet Stan raised his eyebrows, pulling back in surprise.

Estelle, missing his reaction, noted a dwindling line of young women in school uniform snaking into and out of the Primary Care Clinic. The young women all had their left upper buttock exposed through a hiatus in their black dresses. As they queued through, each was injected with a half ml syringe of the depo-contraception.

Boet Stan greeted a harassed sister-in-charge walking out of the clinic.

"Molo, Sister," Estelle greeted as the African nurse reached out to take the young Australian's hands in hers. "You've had a busy morning, Sister."

"Yes, today is family planning clinic and we've just about finished the depo line. These young women come from miles away every three months," Sister Agnes explained.

"What about AIDS?"

"All our clients are given education on sexually transmitted infections," Sister Agnes replied defensively.

"Do the men here wear condoms?"

"My dear, most of our young people still prefer flesh to flesh and our young men are against condoms. And besides, would you want your man wearing one of these?" Sister Agnes bent over to pick out one of scores of unwrapped condoms sitting in a large box of talcum powder.

"What the f...!" Estelle gasped.

"The overseas companies provide factory rejects for free," Boet Stan explained, unable to hide his cynicism.

Estelle clicked away.

Turning to leave, Estelle spied a box of Nestlé bottle formula in the corner of the clinic.

Sister Agnes opened her arms in helpless resignation. "We try to encourage breast feeding." She looked down. "But the mothers prefer the powdered milk. What can we do? We all have to make a living—our families," apologised the little black woman, shuffling in shoes that had been re-soled too often.

Estelle struggled to find compassion for the sister, her judgement interrupted by three tolls of the bell resonating from the tower beside the church.

The sun was clouded out as if in silent respect for the deceased. Dust swirled up from a cool wind that blew in from the east. A tall, frail, elderly black man in a white coat, unsteady on his feet, lurched towards them, his pousa lips red, de-pigmented from years of alcohol abuse. Solomon Mabunda was going home for the day, his duty completed. For a moment he stood stock still, a shocked look on his face, as if mesmerised by Estelle.

"This is our blood debt to the chimpanzeeees!" the staggering old man muttered, half turning to point towards the church.

His face protruded grotesquely as his lower lip dribbled saliva from the side of his mouth. He stank of formalin, scotch and vomit. His wide-eyed face came right up to Estelle's. "Project Coast: do you know? Anthrax! Anthrax in Rhodesia! The depo!" Mabunda staggered back, wagging his finger at Sister Agnes. "We are killing our young people. Cancer. AIDS."

"Dada," Boet Stan gently implored.

"What do you know? What do yooou know? I know. Hamilton knew. Tell her!" The old doctor pushed Boet Stan away.

"Ah! The scotch is talking," Sister Agnes chided.

Doctor Mabunda fumbled in his ink-stained white coat for some documents. "It's in the river. They try to hide it."

The matron, with the loudspeaker, arrived to rescue the old doctor, leading him off, resisting, to Menopause Mansions. Mabunda staggered off with the stern matron gripping his elbow, preventing him the indignity of falling into the dust.

"Agh! Shame." Sister Agnes shook her head as the pathetic figure staggered off.

"You have a plane to catch, Estelle," Boet Stan gently interrupted. "I'll get our vehicle."

Estelle stood in silent contemplation as Boet Stan retrieved the bakkie from inside the hospital compound. Mabunda had disappeared into the matrons' quarters and Estelle had cut off from listening to Agnes's apologies for the old doctor's behaviour, and her farewell.

THE BAKKIE RATTLED BACK slowly towards Flagstaff, slowing as they passed the old men on horseback. Estelle, lost in her ruminations, briefly recalled Agnes' farewell: "God-speed." How quaint, she thought. Her mind flitted from this to that as her chauffeur concentrated on avoiding potholes and rocks.

"What's the answer? Surely these people need access to water."

"More than water, they need organisation," Boet Stan replied.

"You sound like a Marxist."

"Is that so, comrade?" chuckled the older African man, bemused. "Comrade, how many of the so-called People's Co-ops, say in the north-eastern Transvaal, are independent of their overseas funders after a decade?"

"No idea," Estelle replied, irritated, looking ahead to the dusty, corrugated road. "How many?"

"None!" he replied emphatically.

They hit the tar road with a bump on the outskirts of Flagstaff. Although grateful for a smoother ride, Estelle's mind was still spinning and her ears ringing as she scribbled into a small notebook.

"The poor will never forgive us for our charity." His tone was flat.

Estelle cast a puzzled look across to Boet Stan.

"George Bernard Shaw," the older man added enigmatically.

"Simple problem, complex solution to the uneven distribution of wealth," Estelle challenged.

"Please continue." Boet Stan shrugged, glancing briefly across to his young companion.

"In the poorer nations, death is all too frequently the result of scarcity and lack: lack of clean running water, lack of nutrition, lack of health care, and so on. While in the wealthier nations, death is often the result of over-indulgence and excess: excess calories, excess fat, excess sugar, excess salt, and so on," Estelle preached.

"Complex indeed." Boet Stan shrugged as they continued their travels in silence to Kokstadt. Estelle sank into the mute comfort afforded by the tar road. As they arrived in Kokstadt, Estelle perked up.

"What of Doctor Mabunda?"

"A broken man of much intelligence and compassion; he was one of our most brilliant medical scientists, a virologist. Did some work on Ebola at Wits at one time: studied in Belgium and the United States. Unfortunately he had a nervous breakdown: has come to Holy Cross in retirement. He harvested my father's organs."

Estelle looked at Stan as if for the first time. The tightness constricted her chest. "My Pop died of mesothelioma. Penge Mine."

The African looked across with a spark of camaraderie.

DURING HER FLIGHT BACK to Jo'burg, Estelle scribbled into her notebook, recapping on the diversity of information she'd gleaned during her brief visit: so many loose threads to tie up.

Back at the Sandton Sun, she found the opulent extravagance a jarring contrast to the poverty and neglect of the rural homelands. South Africa really was a world in one.

Dave had left a note excusing himself for being unable to meet her before her return to Oz. Though somewhat relieved, she was also torn by a mild pang of loss. "Better to have loved and lost, than never to have loved at all." She sighed with a tinge of nostalgia; her heart ached with yearning for a bygone era. "Don't kid yourself, girl, you neither loved, nor lost."

Chapter Three

 $\mathcal{J}$ he trip home from Jo'burg was long and arduous. To boot, South African Airways had screwed up Estelle's booking, plonking her behind a group of South Africans packing for Perth. Two irritating sprogs sat immediately in front: a cheeky pepperhead aged about nine and his cute Afrikaans companion of about seven. The two antagonists skylarked and teased each other, the younger dishing out as good as she got.

Intermittently flipping through her pencilled notes, Estelle shuffled between movies before settling for the Nature Channel: elephants in East-Central Africa. Oh yeah—she was aware that China's rapidly expanding investment in development in East and Central Africa had seen a parallel ramping up of demand for ivory and rhino horn. Blah, blah blah. Exhausted, she closed her eyes.

THE TWO CHILDREN LAY huddled in the long grass, their hidey-hole concealed by overhanging foliage. Taking care to not expose their presence, they kept very still, spying on the intimate family gathering. Mother, father and the toddler were unaware of their presence, enjoying what was left of lunch. Father and daughter were engaged in a friendly wrestle as mum basked in the sun.

"Can they see us?" whispered the younger of the two secretively, her delicate face framed by golden ringlets.

"I don't think so," whispered the older black African boy.

A loud crack shattered the late afternoon peace.

A FLASH OF LIGHTNING rocked the plane violently. "You've got to stop it! Please stop it! Stop it!" cried the little girl tearfully.

Under the stern gaze of his father, her playmate sank back uneasily into his seat.

Finally! What took them so bloody long, a yawning Estelle thought, rubbing her eyes as she stretched, shaking off a half-forgotten dream. She was relieved the children had disembarked in Perth. A good case for contraception, she mused.

Over the long, trans-national flight from Perth to Sydney, Estelle worked on a draft document, mentally compiling a story that would rival any of her peers. Yes! This was it! This was going to be the news story that would make all the international ground-breaking difference needed for South Africa and its long suffering people. Bravo, Estelle, go to the top of the class!

She indulgently imagined how her compelling first-hand report and heart-wrenching images would soon hit front page newsstands throughout Australia, and from there, who knows, maybe a job with The New York Times.

She vividly recalled her Nan's prediction that she would one day inspire a rise in consciousness bringing about a revolutionary change to the world. Well, perhaps Nan got it right this time? As an international icon, with her passion and tenacity, she pictured herself a crusader fighting for justice every step of the way.

A bumpy touchdown on a Sydney runway fraught with strong crosswinds bounced the young crusader out of her delusions of grandeur. Her lap belt reminded her of a full bladder, and she had to be mindful of her hand luggage, even at Sydney Airport.

Making her way through customs, she looked up to see the brightest and the most colourful of them all. After all, how could she miss her? It was Esther, her iridescently dressed bohemian grandmother, exploding through the crowd with a smile as wide as her arms. The two rushed towards each other, cutting their way through the cluttered airport crowd.

"OK, sweet pea: give me the lowdown. Fill me in on all the details? How was it? What was the hospitality like? Were you made feel welcome?"

"So much to tell you, I barely know where to start," Estelle gasped, struggling to keep pace with the older woman's longer legs. Her overwhelming helpfulness in assisting Estelle with her luggage gave no hint of her almost seven decades.

The two women made their way to Esther's old HR Holden. Esther jingled and jangled all the way in her multi-coloured gypsy skirt with little bells attached by hand beading right the way around. "Bet you're excited! When will we get to read your scoop? Think they'll all be impressed with your efforts? I can just feel it in my bones! You've got the world at your feet, sweet pea!"

There was that sweet pea tag; a term of endearment given to Estelle by Nan as a child: now anything but endearing, but too precious to throw away.

"Tell me, sweet pea, did you take good care of yourself? Did you get adequate sleep and good nourishment? What was the weather like?" the old lady continued without pause, fumbling with an oversized cluster of keys at the boot of her hot pink car.

"Still traumatising impressionable young minds, I see." Estelle smirked, sighting the curious attention of passing children to the graphics on rear and side windows. The ghoulish stickers depicted everything from defenceless, featherless caged hens to heat-stricken, leg bound, blood-drenched lambs with their throats slit as they lay conscious, dying in pools of their own blood.

"I'm sure we're slowly getting the message across," Esther boasted.

"What? That your Animal Liberation group has quite a flair for inferior decorating?"

"Don't be silly. Besides, never did you any harm, sweet pea," the old lady retorted defiantly.

"You're kidding? Do you recall my childhood introduction to your cruelty-free cause?"

"No. But I'm sure that you are about to remind me."

"As a pre-schooler, I once asked what McDonalds was as we drove past the golden arches."

"I imagine I gave you a clear and concise answer," Esther responded with an expectant smile.

"Oh, that you certainly did! It's like Old McDonald had a farm, except all their animals are dead, sweet pea. Quote, unquote."

"Honesty is the best policy!"

"Hardly cruelty-free at such a tender age." Estelle laughed.

"Meat is murder, sweet pea. Now where were we up to?" Esther continued as she jingled and jangled from one side of the car to the other, opening both doors. "We're all here for a higher purpose. That is if we allow ourselves. Of course, there are many who'd rather waste their energies on addiction to cheap day-to-day drama. You do feel on track, do you not?" She looked quizzically at her grand-daughter.

"You know, Nan," Estelle bit her bottom lip as she swivelled into her seat, "I swear you could make any hardcore investigative journalist appear shamefully incompetent. You somehow manage to fire more questions in just half a minute than I'm paid to ask in a year."

"Now, now, dear; strap in so we can get you home safely."

Raising her eyebrows, Estelle gave a cheeky smile.

"Of course, at twenty-seven your vibration comes to a nine: very hard to pocket love at a personal level under the influence of a nine. The cosmic intent of this vibration is mainly to give of oneself to the world." The old lady rattled on, driving off in a car that rattled every bit as much.

Within moments, the true nature of cosmic intent had indeed begun to unravel. It appeared that the universe was conspiring against her. Fastening her seatbelt with one hand while fishing for sunglasses with the other, Estelle's handbag tilted out passport and mango condom. The bright wrapping was enough to make Esther's shoulder-length, fire-red hair seem dull and insipid by comparison. Bingo! Own Goal! Although the offending package managed to land between foot and bag, Estelle suspected it was all too late. Instantly she shrunk back into that old familiar feeling, dating back to childhood, where she'd spent a great deal of time escaping the gaze of Nan's third eye. Or was it nothing more than finely tuned peripheral vision? She was snookered and she knew it! Just knowing that Nan knew that Estelle knew that Nan knew.

She held her breath, almost rivalling her Nan's ability to go on for hours without taking one. Who could go without breath for longer? This moment could have become part of a scientific study, based around the theory that the brain needs oxygen to survive. Sure, but how long before there would be irreparable damage, or at the very least nerve damage as Estelle sat perched on the edge of eternity.

"Now did you remember my advice about no hanky-panky on your trip? Far too dangerous over there! Better to take it out on some nice boy back home." Esther looked at Estelle smiling, but didn't stop to allow her to answer. "I say never sleep with anyone that you don't want to become more like."

Yes, snookered.

"Talk about danger. I've had Frank and Maria on the phone non-stop, reciting the gospel according to themselves. The trouble with those two; they were hoping he'd meet and marry the Virgin Mary.

Instead he met and married Mary. As far as I'm concerned, I kept my vows. Till death do us part; the marriage died and I did part. Went through the list thoroughly: for better, for worse, for richer, for poorer, in sickness and in health. I'm sure I ticked all the right boxes." Esther looked at her grand-daughter as if with x-ray vision. "Hmm." She slowly nodded. "The men we align ourselves with can alter the course of our destiny."

"I hear you, Nan." Estelle smiled, the sermon a strangely welcome relief from the intensity of the previous few days.

Suddenly the car in front provided a merciful distraction.

"Slow down, Nan!"

The Holden's bumper halted close enough to kiss the other car's arse. Esther honked her horn impatiently.

"Granny Rage!" Estelle smirked. It appeared the universe had just shown some mercy.

"Look at him!" The old lady raised both hands to the heavens in exclamation as the poor old fellow in front struggled with the Auto Pay at the airport boom gate. "Any slower he'd be driving backwards!"

"You tell 'em, Nan." Estelle chuckled.

Esther weaved her way through traffic, more like an impatient motorcyclist than a placid senior.

They took the back route to the city via Redfern, finding themselves in the midst of a roadside action group looking more like a forest of protesters. Several people dressed in various shades of green held up signs: Save the planet – go Veg!

Reflexively, Esther wound down her squeaky window to give them the thumbs up. With any greater show of support, she'd have fallen out entirely. It seemed as if she had just defied the laws of gravity: move over, Isaac Newton.

"Bit extreme?" Estelle raised her youthful eyebrow at one young, muscular activist, his manhood camouflaged by a bush of dill.

"Animals carry our karma, dear: must be nice to them!" The old lady nodded her head approvingly, her blue eyes brimming with amusement.

"With any luck the protest will be over before his dill starts to wilt." Estelle grinned.

"The carnivores will have to change their ways, my dear. They are eating our planet out of existence!"

"I wonder who'll eat the last of the dill?"

"You know the livestock sector alone generates more greenhouse emissions than the world's entire transport system. An immediate stop to all animal products consumed and sold would stop up to eighty percent of global warming it's impact would be instantly experienced!" Esther stopped long enough to sigh, nodding pensively as she drew breath. "I am deeply concerned for our beautiful planet."

"And so am I!"

Taken by surprise, Esther looked across at her grand-daughter. "You are?"

"Yes: your consumption of the world's oxygen supply!"

"Now don't be cheeky." Esther laughed. "And you know what else I think?"

"No, but I'm sure that you're about to tell me."

"Claiming to be an animal lover or an environmentalist and eating animals is a contradiction. The poor dears raised as food are given no legal protection whatsoever! Their lives are nothing more than a perpetual cycle of violence. Dear! Dear! Dear!" Esther shook her head. "I'll chew my way through anything with a face only after it has given me written consent."

"That's what they're bred for," Estelle retorted, looking out onto the dreary back streets of Redfern.

"Well, stop breeding them! If the public were to witness a dog mistreated in the same way as a pig in a piggery, there'd be a public outcry for prosecution. When is an animal not an animal?" Esther sighed deeply. "If I can be happy and healthy without harming another, why wouldn't I? Our culture is being held together by animal sacrifice!"

"God, Nan. Animal sacrifice went out with the Old Testament."

"Our human culture needs a periodic scapegoat, my dear. We feel better, and our men bond better when they have a common enemy. It's all projection, of course. Thank God for Saddam Hussein, poor fellow. His an absolutely terrible demise."

"Deservedly so." Estelle shrugged, her attention drawn to the dilapidated Aboriginal public housing as they passed by what was notoriously known as 'The Block'.

"Perhaps. But I'm sure his mother loved him. It's the animals I feel for, poor things. They have no free will in this at all," mused the old lady, softening.

"It's the natural cycle of life and death. Eating meat is how we've evolved; besides, a lion eats flesh."

"We look nothing like early man, who had a life expectancy of 33 years. Thank God we have evolved towards other choices! As a species our addiction to flesh is scandalous. We'll go to war over water. Mark my word."

"Not oil?" Estelle gazed upwards to low-slung overhead power cables, the city skyline dazzling ahead, not ten minutes away.

"It takes up to100,000 litres of water to put a kilo of rump on a plate, and only 900 litres for a kilo of wheat. A vegan lifestyle is equivalent to not showering for a year. You don't need to be an Einstein to work it out."

"Vegetarian at home is my limit," Estelle replied as she continued to follow the knock-down dwellings, dreary industrial yards and cheap corner take-away outlets, their advertising signs faded and peeling.

"Easier to talk about the problems of the world over a steak and red wine than make a change in lifestyle. Have I taught you nothing, sweet pea?" The old crone raised her eyes to the heavens. "Jung predicted our second Odinic experience would be of global proportions."

"Odinic?"

"Odin! The god of war! Testosterone-driven power! And power is the midwife to war, dear child."

"Now would you like a hand down from your soap box?" Estelle laughed.

"I'm sure meat does something to the human psyche," Esther rattled on, honking her horn as she muscled her way through the dense city traffic. "Mining and abattoir towns have a raw feel about them. Slaughtering animals or hacking the earth must impact on our souls. Lots of pain in those towns, my dear."

"You sound soo judgemental, Nan!"

"Not at all, my dear. The miners are very decent people and pay their bills, cash up front. Heaven knows I've always found the smaller communities hospitable and generous, but human pain is human pain—and there's lots of pain—and a thick coat of religion does not heal the soul or conceal pain. If it did, we would not be running off to war, creating another generation of scapegoats."

"All helps the economy."

"Fear-mongering politicians brainwashing the populace to distract 'em from the real issues. An interdependent synergy is what's needed for the planet to survive! My stance on the economy: no eco, no me!"

Nan was so passionate. A caring woman who had little time for institutionalised religious humbug or political rhetoric. When she became pregnant to John Harris at such a young age, he being Church of England and she nominally Catholic, they eschewed the judgement of both institutions and married at the Wayside Chapel in Kings Cross. This initial sleight notwithstanding, Esther educated her daughter Judith at a Catholic convent.

Looking straight ahead, Esther impatiently tapped her fingers on the steering wheel, beeping her horn at the car in front, slow off the mark at a set of lights just turned green. "What is it, love? Can't find a colour you like?"

Estelle smiled and rolled her eyes.

"Oh! That reminds me. Need to drop by The Sanctuary."

Making her way through the congested traffic, Esther made her usual claim for a parking place. "Hail Mary, full of grace, thank you for my perfect parking space."

Sure enough, there it was! An older, distinguished-looking gentleman appeared from nowhere, acknowledging Esther with an apologetic smile for his delay. Then as if given his marching orders from heaven, he made his way to his car with military precision. Driving off in a timely fashion, he left the gap open for Esther to ease her way into her divinely appointed space.

Estelle wondered if perhaps Esther was making the most of the 'ask and you shall receive' principle around parking spaces—and how she loved her parking space trick! But was she a one-trick Nan? For all her affirmations, how did she account for still driving around some old clanger held together by rust and about to fall off its muffler? And in no greater hurry to retire than she was! Well, she did often make reference to her broomstick. Parking trick no longer required. Perhaps she needed to review her psychic priorities?

"Don't you worry, dear, there's still plenty of go in the old girl! We won't be stuffed away in some dusty old closet, like the poor old farts who think getting a home next to a chemist or hospital is real living—hmm—from chemist to ambulance to hearse in three easy steps."

"Sure," Estelle agreed sheepishly.

"I'll take that as an apology, shall I?" Nan looked across sharply.

Maybe she did hear that thought, Estelle worried. Nah. Just coincidence?

The two women headed towards the grand entrance of a large public building. The foyer was claimed by an impressive antique clock, the caption declaring in old, bold lettering: Time conquers all. Once out of the elevator, they made their way through to the doors of The Sanctuary. Within seconds Esther was leaning over the reception desk to check her answering machine.

"Leave your name and number..."

"No. I won't leave my name or number. If you're psychic like you say you are, you'll know both and return my call."

Like a raging torrent, Esther lunged from the reception desk and past the waiting lounges to stand resolutely in front of the annual moon calendar. "Where's the bloody moon today?" she growled. With her index finger she traced her way across the chart tacked to the wall. "Moon in Sagittarius. Typical! Bloody pranksters," she grumbled.

"Like I really get it." Estelle rolled her eyes.

With a huff Esther put her hands on her hips. "'Bout time you get your head around this, sweet pea." She led a reluctant Estelle toward the Moon chart. "Look." She retraced. "Sun sign is what many call their star sign: has an annual rotation. The lunar cycle has a monthly rotation, visiting each sign of the zodiac for about two and a half days each twenty-seven day cycle. Comprendez?"

"And your point is?"

"The moon profoundly affects our emotions. When in Aries it brings out our impulsiveness, in Virgo our nit-pickiness, in Sag, our playfulness. Your moon was in Scorpio at the time of your birth: explains your curious nature, sweet pea. In any case, some people are so totally off the planet. I just know today is going to be a lunatic, fringe-element day."

Esther resumed her huffing and puffing as she and Estelle picked up astrological mugs and spiritual magazines left on the coffee table by clients and staff.

"Seems your brilliant, hip-shaking, tree-hugging clairvoyants can see the future, but not the mess they leave behind," moaned Estelle as she helped tidy a bookcase full of crystals, tarot, etc., each holding a promise of enlightenment, healing, or perhaps even Nirvana.

"My brilliant clairvoyants see and offer an aerial view of their clients' lives: in some cases a view of their hereafter." Esther stopped, turning sharply to face Estelle. "How are you feeling, dear?" A look of concern swept across her face as she stood taking that optional breath.

"I'm fine. What's with looking at me that way, Nan?"

"Your aura's a little off-colour. Are you OK, sweet pea?" she insisted, reaching to feel Estelle's forehead.

"Just need a good night's sleep, else I feel fine. You need to stop worrying about me. I can take care of myself," Estelle assured, throwing her arms around Esther, with a peck on the cheek as they made their way to the staff room.

Estelle sat at the end of a cluttered table. The staff room was adorned with all manner of spiritual paraphernalia. Unlike other businesses where one might expect to find copies of 'Reader's Digest' or the 'Australian Financial Review', Esther's kitchen was jumbled with copies of 'Nexus' and assorted astrological magazines. The tea cups were claimed by the psychic readers' astrological sun signs. The walls were papered with Florence Scovel Shinn affirmations, and other gurus with their eternal wisdom. The place mats signified the planets, and even the plants were given Reiki on a daily basis. This was hands-on spiritual healing, or were the plants giving the psychic readers daily blessings, Estelle mused. Whatever, Nan had a PhD in quirkiness upon which she traded successfully, and no one could argue with success. Well, with the exception of her old clunker, that was. Nan might be a mover and shaker, she confirmed, but shake, rattle and rust?

"My Spirit Guides have told me I need to get my hands on the books before that grandfather of yours, Frank-enstein, makes them disappear on Monday," Esther raved as she rummaged through cupboards and drawers.

"Esther the psychic divorcing Frank the lawyer! Poor grandpa doesn't stand a chance."

"Your grandfather might know the law intimately enough to bend it without breaking it, but I know his and his legal team's moves well in advance of their deciding. All is fair in divorce and war!"

Esther snorted gleefully. "Frank may have his legal team, but I have my psychic army."

Esther stumbled across a tatty shoebox full of old photos sitting in the same dusty cupboard as some old business records. She skimmed through them briefly before handing them to Estelle.

"Frank and his mother have often accused me of being too preoccupied cooking the books to cook him a decent Italian evening meal. I told him from the very beginning my objections to performing any such unnatural acts for any man!" the old lady fumed.

"So is that why he often resorted to having dinner at his mother's spaghetti mansion?" Estelle replied absent-mindedly, flicking through the photos.

"To be expected, my dear. After all, she always did have him by the meatballs!"

Esther took a few moments to ponder upon a cream-coloured farewell card with gold lettering. 'If I don't get to see you before I go, I know that we will stay in touch. Love J. C.' The handwriting had a vulnerable quality about it. Esther smiled wistfully then distracted herself by referring back to the shoebox. "All treasures and secrets, long forgotten, are coming back with us and are going to be brought back to life."

Estelle had been curiously studying a photo taken in the hospital ward within days of her own birth. In the background was a mixed couple proudly holding their newborn.

Esther glanced over Estelle's shoulder and snorted. "Serves her right!"

"Serves who right?"

"That woman!" Esther replied, pointing to a middle-eastern woman in the background.

"What? For having a baby?" Estelle frowned as she gently ran her fingers across the picture.

"She had a bloody hide jumping the queue!" Esther squawked with increasing outrage.

"What queue? When? Na-an?"

"It meant that she had her Caesarean two hours before your mother's. Your poor mother laboured away for another two hours. Incompetent anaesthetist stuffed up the epidural. Cretin! All he had to do was stick the needle in the right space."

"OK?" Estelle replied, her question lingering on the air.

"Two hours before your delivery. Hmmm. That would have made this little guy a triple Scorpio."

"A triple Scorpio?" Estelle crinkled her nose.

"Scorpio sun, Scorpio moon, Scorpio rising. You do the calculation, sweet pea."

"What's rising?" Estelle shook her head, frowning.

"Running on a twenty-four hour cycle, whatever zodiac sign is on the eastern horizon at the moment of your birth imprints its energy upon your psyche. This impacts the impression we make on others at first encounter."

"Wouldn't expect anything less." Estelle grinned.

"Scorpio, as you well know, represents life, death, birth, sexuality, the spirit world, and the need to uncover the truth at any cost. No stopping this fella."

"I'm sure you're right." Estelle laughed.

"I simply shudder to imagine life with this little man. Nothing personal, dear: a triple Scorpio—grounds for adoption. Start life anew, have a new baby: whatever it takes. Lord only knows we all make mistakes. Or perhaps he might have given them reason not to have any more children."

"But Nan, aren't you an Aqueerious? You're anything but normal."

"Why be normal when I can be myself? Now, thanks, dear; just take these boxes and let's skedaddle."

ACCELERATING THROUGH AN ORANGE to red light on New South Head Road, Samuel Goldstein swung his silver Mercedes hard left, then gunned up the incline at the start of Worsley Road. The number plates on his car read 'STELLA'. On a good day his exclusive Point Piper address was just thirty minutes from his work in Ryde, a short drive over the Sydney Harbour Bridge. Reaching for his remote, he opened the imposing wrought iron gates that served to create a protective distance from the hubbub of the outside world. Proceeding beyond the vine-covered sandstone façade, he swept up a red gravel driveway, a border of rose bushes and oleanders serving as his guard of honour. Leaving behind the life-draining demands of his executive position, Sam breathed in the smell of oleander, relieved at being home. He slowed before his two-car garage and slid into melancholia as he became aware of a deeply treasured song playing on his radio:

"…And honey, I miss you, And I'm bein' good…"

The paunchy sixty-three year old absent-mindedly fished for his wedding ring, hanging on an eighteen-carat gold chain under his shirt. He took the ring between thumb and index finger, feeling for the emptiness inside the circle.

"…One day while I was not at home, the angels came…" The sad love song's closing stanzas synchronised with dusk closing in.

Sam entered the cloistered world of his elegant mansion, once representing a promise of tomorrow as spectacular as its surrounding panoramic view. While not harbour-side, his secluded green haven had enough altitude to gather the sea breezes from both the Rose Bay and the Harbour Bridge side of Port Jackson. To the west, Clarke Island stood solitaire. This was no Van Diemen's Land, though it sure felt like it to Sam sometimes.

Sam remained a condemned man, a prisoner hostage to a melancholic heart. Guilt stood vigilant as his relentless prison guard, a constant reminder of his crime: his failure to recognise her anguish, his failure to act. He lived in a void of unfulfilled promises, with just one exception: his posthumous promise to his beloved. He had vowed to discover the key that might have saved her life, releasing her from a cruel world of internal torment.

Sam rubbed his thumb along the texture of the ring. "Till death do us part," he murmured. He had always felt her death was premature, and surely they weren't meant to part. As for Yahweh and an after-life; a merciful god would have spared her life.

From the kitchen window, Esther spotted Sam. "Now here comes a laugh a minute."

Sam made his way up the stairs of his tri-level home and entered the open living space adjoining the kitchen. He could hear Esther's chatter with his daughter, who sat perched on a stool at the end of the black granite kitchen bench. She busied herself painting an assortment of crazily decorated Easter eggs, while Esther's voice competed with the kitchen orchestra. Amongst the major players: a surge of on again, off again, state-of-the-art appliances, the occasional piercing noise of the blender, the pinging of the microwave, all against the background humming of the dishwasher.

"...of course, you are now about to enter your Saturn return where life-changing events will bring about learning and personal growth for you. During Saturn return we grow from innocence to wisdom."

"Now listen to your grandmother; she knows everything without any real qualifications. It amazes me that she has the ability to run a successful business given she barely completed school."

The clicking speed of Esther's knife on the cutting board increased apace. "What has always amazed me is how you ever managed to get through university without any clairvoyant ability."

"I've never had the need to proclaim abilities to talk to the spirit world. I suspect that half your problem is rooted in having been deprived of imaginary childhood friends."

"Careful or you may soon join them. Besides, most of the ones I get to talk to are the ones that your company has managed to bury," Esther hissed playfully.

It was game on. Sam's entrance all too often heralded his first off-the-cuff serve in his mother in-law's direction. Esther always gave as good as she got. She was the mother-in-law he loved to hate, or perhaps he simply hated to admit he loved, and after all these years a love match had never quite been declared.

"Oh, you two; don't you ever tire of this?" Estelle teased.

"Aahh!" breathed Sam, running his fingers through his thinning grey hair, his day's exhaustion clearly advertised from beneath his five o'clock shadow.

Estelle rose from her stool and into her dad's open arms.

"Tell me, Stella, how was it?" Sam released himself from his grey suit jacket and tie. "What did you find out that isn't in the UN and WHO reports?" He carefully placed both tie and jacket on a soft cream leather lounge.

"Not how I imagined it. Despite all my research before leaving, on the ground it's not quite so straight forward. I guess when all that suffering is so in your face, it's hard to stay statistical about it all."

"I understand." Her father smiled tenderly, dropping into a moment of silence.

"What are you thinking, Dad?"

"My little girl has grown into a mature young lady. Your mother would be proud."

She's my world, Sam would often be heard saying in a moment quiet enough that only the truth could be spoken. In Sam's game, making the world a better place often meant tweaking the truth just enough to make the medicine he was endorsing more palatable to the market. For Sam, the purpose of his words was often to conceal the truth. For Estelle, the purpose of her words was to reveal the truth. For Esther, she simply loved to play with words. Whether or not they revealed or concealed any real meaning, Esther simply claimed the higher truth.

Sitting around a solid oak table, the three broke bread.

Sam was distracted by the ABC News announcing another car-bombing in Kabul. "Barbaric. We really need regime change there." He cast his gaze toward the large television screen in the adjoining lounge room.

"Well, the British failed, the Russians failed. God only knows, the only legacy of this adventure will be an assembly line of body bags. Our young men deserve better!" Esther sniped as she served three bowls of steaming minestrone.

"We have a moral responsibility to take out the Taliban. The sooner the world is rid of those terrorists, the safer we'll all be. For God's sake, look at how they oppress their women on religious grounds."

"It's evil how those male chauvinists genitally mutilate Muslim girls for male control and domination," Estelle snapped.

"Agreed!" Sam nodded to his daughter.

"Well, don't think it's so different here." Esther eyeballed her son-in-law over a glass of wine. "In our culture, females are cosmetically mutilated for sexual exploitation."

"Give us a break." Sam crunched into his bread roll slathered with butter.

"I get the lovesick young girls coming in, encouraged by their plastic surgeons to take out a loan they can ill afford for a boob job or genital cosmetics they don't need. So what's the bloody difference?"

"The difference is they have a choice!" Sam riposted.

"Let's just take off our blinkers, shall we? When we point a finger at them, three more point right back! Females are sacrificed, mutilated and sexually exploited in all manner of ways around the globe by gutless men who seek control and domination!" Esther fumed, crunching on a stick of celery.

"Just gutless men of church and state terrified of feminine power. Perhaps, if there is a God, she's female." Self-righteous anger burnt in Estelle's chest, giving rise to a trace of perspiration.

The conversation was abruptly interrupted by Esther's mobile: on the other end, one of her confidantes. During the brief exchange they shared psychic insight with one another: Sally regarding her financial concerns, Esther her divorce.

"Your grandmother is obviously under the illusion that if she can't talk, she can't breathe," Sam jested.

"Can't you just leave Nan alone for once?" Estelle smirked.

"And miss out on all the fun? Her friends are just as bad, totally incapable of thinking for themselves. It's nothing more than a case of the blind leading the blind, looking for their third eye." He laughed. "It would help if they could find one another's left brain—or is it their right brain?"

"Da-ad." Estelle frowned playfully, warning him to back off.

"As for that place she runs; all those lost souls pathetically dependent on moment-to-moment advice for the most mundane events in their lives."

"So? Nan specialises in selling hope."

"Some need more than hope, Stella. They need psychic rehab!"

"Maybe, but at least Nan provides her so-called psychics with jobs."

"I was actually referring to the psychics themselves." Sam smirked boyishly.

"Agreed. Psychics Anonymous: bring it on," Estelle whispered teasingly.

Releasing herself from her call, Nan glared at father and daughter. "You'll get your comeuppance, the pair of you. Just expect it when you least expect it," she chortled.

Darkness shrouded Point Piper as the hum of traffic dwindled. Clarke Island stood solitaire on a harbour dimly lit by a new moon. Announcing her retirement for the day, Esther swung around in time to witness her son-in-law washing down his blood pressure and cholesterol medication with a generous glass of whisky.

"Work-related stress, uh? Maybe you should consider leaving your high-flying mob."

"My high-flying mob provides a real service to the community: all doing the best we can to support our families."

"Hmm, with matching high-flying blood pressure!"

"At least we're not all on high-flying broomsticks!"

"I'm sure the greasy pole you are all climbing will see you lot reach greater heights than my high-flying broomstick. Just make sure you're not just high flying over a cliff edge," riposted Esther, her voice escalating several decibels.

"I'm simply focusing on getting ahead, Nan!" retorted Sam defensively.

"Dismiss my concerns if you will, but do make sure getting ahead is not just getting a bigger headstone!" Esther turned to her grand-daughter. "Remind me to make allowances for your father, dear. He has some kind of rare verbal disability. I'm sure he doesn't mean half of what he says."

"By the way, Dad," Estelle interrupted, "have you ever heard of a South African virologist by the name of Mabunda; strange old guy going on about blood debts to chimps, anthrax and cancer?"

Sam blinked a couple of times. "Not sure I recall the name. You must have met quite a few characters over there. Where else did you manage to get to?" He redirected his attention to Esther. "Off home then?"

Esther kissed her grand-daughter goodnight and playfully punched her son-in-law on the arm. "My family await me," the zany old lady chirped, ready to head off to her semi in Paddington, fifteen minutes away. Close enough to care, but far enough to maintain a respectful distance between her bloodline and a very different lifestyle.

Estelle slipped out the veranda doors, retreating to the pool house for the night, where she lay lightly perspiring. Sam ascended the spiral staircase to his master bedroom where he paced the polished floorboards before turning off the lights.

Six kilometres away, Esther was bowled over at her door by her dogs, Romeo and Juliet, and cats, Napoleon and Josephine, as she scrambled her way in.

She quickly fussed about fetching her family their nightcaps before sitting in their company. She remembered with affection, and slight sadness, explaining to Estelle why her cat, Sophia, could not have any more kittens.

"She's been spayed," Esther had gently explained to the curious four-year-old.

"Have you been spayed, Nan?" The little girl's brilliant blue eyes shone with innocence.

"No, darling, your mother is enough for me." Her only child was gone within a year. Still, she thanked God for the daughter she'd cherished for twenty-seven years, and now her beloved grand-daughter, Estelle, the spitting image of her mother.

She and John Harris had been destined. There was brief talk of an abortion, she being so young and their impulsive passion burning so fiercely. That idea was abruptly vanquished by both, and her youthful trauma aside, life with John had been a joy. Her second pregnancy had ended in a spontaneous abortion at thirteen weeks, messy and complicated by infection. A curative uterine curettage cured Esther of more than an incomplete miscarriage. An over-enthusiastic womb-scrape rendered her infertile with Ashermann's Syndrome, the walls of her uterus adhering together, eliminating menstruation and preventing any further pregnancies. Infertile at eighteen, she'd suffered a deep depression that ushered in a deepening spirituality. She would have liked a brother for Judith. Whatever, she mused. The Lord giveth, the Lord taketh away.

WITH HER USUAL COFFEE from the railway café across the road, Estelle fast became restless waiting for the elevator. She moved her weight from one foot to the other, her chest tight with anticipation of a challenging day ahead. Her article was due just after the upcoming Easter weekend. With a sudden change of heart, she headed for the stairs.

At the top of the first flight, Estelle found herself unusually short of breath. She stopped, caught her breath, and headed for the elevator. No exercise for just a couple of weeks; Estelle made a mental note to renew her gym contract.

At her desk, Estelle's morning started with her regular routine: another coffee and a quick scan of the news on the net. Headline:

'Teacher extradited from Thailand'. She read through the article briefly. 'Male teacher in regional Queensland accused of molesting a thirteen-year-old female student in a local pool.'

"Bloody pervert, hope he gets the book thrown at him," she mumbled.

By mid-morning Estelle was head down, engrossed in crafting her story. Her desk was awash with a tattered travel notebook, a dozen or so articles downloaded from the net, and her screen slowly turning over scores of digital images she'd uploaded onto her desktop. She had gone to South Africa with a lot of preconceptions about the tenor and thrust of her story, but she knew there was more to this epidemic in South Africa than just a male chauvinist tribal culture. Black South African culture was chauvinist, to be sure, but so was white. The clicking noise matched her fast appearing text on the computer screen:

'South Africa is an exhilarating, spectacular and complex country. With its post-Apartheid identity still in the process of evolution, there is undoubtedly an abundance of energy and a sense of progress—'

Momentarily confronted with writer's block, she further scanned the net for advancements in AIDS research. Her focus quickly turned to an article on a new HIV antiretroviral being trialled. Reading on, Estelle became increasingly excited and couldn't wait to interview one of the recipients. All going well, it appeared this drug would soon be hailed as a leading medical breakthrough for the twenty-first century. What a coup for her dad's company, she thought excitedly.

Estelle hesitated as she further marshalled her thoughts. Reminiscing, she flicked back to past images. So many: the box of defective condoms in talc; the clinic; the conga line of schoolgirls awaiting their three-monthly depo-contraception. Protection from pregnancy perhaps—and then?

The cursor pulsed next to and partly behind an open Word document: a coloured image of an emaciated black toddler.

Estelle felt her article deserved more than the usual pat, feminist, patronising backdrop. Depleted and blocked, she had so much to write, so little inspiration. On impulse, she phoned her father.

"Dad, I need some info on antiretrovirals for HIV and some inside info on your company's HIV vaccine trial. OK? OK. Sorry for the disturbance. Thanks heaps, Dad."

A faint film of perspiration settled on Estelle's brow. She suddenly felt weary and desperate for a cold glass of chardonnay.

AFTER THE QUICK FEW words with his daughter, Sam returned to his sales figures at a quarterly meeting chaired by Doctor Wolfgang Schaffell. Wolf, as he was respectfully called, was in an expansive mood and a little annoyed at the unnecessary interruption.

"Our aim is for compulsory immunisation before mums leave the hospital with their newborns. Our figures are way down. A captive audience is what we need. And, as a free bonus, our funded post-natal nurses will follow through with telephone screening for postnatal depression at three and six weeks. Right, Sam?" Wolf punched out his message with large, hirsute hands, more like a karate assassin than the eloquent European he liked to portray.

"We're working on that one. Still a few issues with privacy legislation, but our allies in the Divisions of General Practice are putting this out as a discussion paper. The GPs are overwhelmed and this strategy, along with our web-based options, offers a real opportunity to pick up the vulnerable mums," Sam expanded.

"Yes, quite so," cut in Wolf, leaning his ample frame forward astride a plush leather executive chair. "And our market share? You are mindful of lagging sales."

"The Fluffy Friday campaign is on track to kick off with Your Doctor week in August. This approach augments our reputation as a model corporate citizen and provides a platform for holistic intervention," Sam replied assertively.

"I like this idea of linking the immunisation schedule with a mental health check. The demographics and mortgage stress may just work in our favour," Wolf said, stroking his chin.

Sam uncrossed his legs and leaned forward, elbows on his knees. "Soft, cuddly, pink, blue and yellow teddies: ones that children can't resist. Guilt-ridden working mothers will buy for leaving their kids in long daycare centres, and grannies, because they just can't bear the thought that their grandchildren could end up as a statistic."

Wolf watched as Sam glanced at the ever-present portrait of Judith that adorned his desk. Wolf caressed a large ruby ring that graced his finger. "You're doing great work, son," the older man beamed, Sam basking in his appreciation.

AT THE CLOSE OF day, Estelle and Alex dropped into their favourite haunt, a popular, semi-crowded wine bar a block away from work. Alex leaned her breasts into the bar as she ordered a Cab Sav for herself and a Chardonnay for her young protégé.

"Hmmm. Don't know that's a good idea. Think I'd rather a mineral water. I've had this niggling headache all day. There when I woke: seems to have gotten worse," Estelle fretted.

"A glass of bubbly will help you relax. It's probably stress. You haven't been yourself all day. Maybe you need to do some speed dating? Besides, I'm here to celebrate."

"Celebrate?"

"John Curtis: a delicious morsel."

"John Curtis from marketing; haven't they just had a new baby? Didn't you recently attend his wedding?" Estelle smirked incredulously. "I thought you two were just friends?"

"Pull yourself together, child. Minor detail; we're not friends, just intimate acquaintances!" The older woman winked. "I'm busy looking into a hard body of evidence." She chuckled wickedly. "We all have free will. I'm just giving his wifey a well-earned rest. She's got what she wanted. It's a win-win."

Alex raised her glass in mock salute. Estelle put her glass to her forehead, massaging her fevered brow against the cool frost enveloping her glass.

"Come on—cheers. Here's to the stats and facts." Alex poured another generous glass of red.

"The facts and stats?" The tired young rookie sighed. "This trip to Holy Cross has opened a can of worms." Estelle began flipping over the pages of her tattered notebook. "Fact: Lancet, 1997, p350. Mostad et al. Women using depo-progestin 2.9 times more likely to have HIV-1 cells in cervical & vaginal secretions. Fact: Nature Medicine, 1996, p2. Preston Marx. Progesterone increases risk of getting AIDS in monkeys. It causes thinning of the vaginal mucosa, reducing the barrier to viruses and bacteria. Fact: Journal of the American Medical Association, 1995. Skegg & Noonan. Pooled analysis of WHO and New Zealand Studies. Women taking depo-progestins for two to three years before the age of twenty-five have a 310 percent increased risk of getting invasive breast cancer. Fact: WHO trial. The Lancet, 1991. p. 338. Thomas et—"

"OK. OK. Let's stop here," the older woman cut Estelle off.

"What do I do with this?" Estelle protested. "Depo-progestins are the main strategy for birth control in South Africa: have been since the mid-sixties—and Black South African women are far more likely to have used these contraceptives than their white counterparts."

"You're going beyond your brief, Estelle. What is your focus? This is scattered."

"But—"

"But nothing. OK, you've touched on the political economy and African male chauvinism. OK. Good. Now leave the crap on the pharmaceutical industry alone. That's what the medical establishment and the W.H.O. are there for."

"But...I thought—"

"Our market—your market is the twenty-five to thirty-five year old, liberated, responsible, twenty-first century women. They don't need scare tactics or Bible bashing. Get off your soap-box! We have a magazine to sell. Hey, these professional women are way too busy to settle into middle-class domesticity. Some would love to sponsor a little African orphan."

An hour or so, and a bottle of red later, Alex began to give her understudy uncensored counsel. "Estelle, we live in the free world and we can print what we like, but if you go beyond the pale, you're going to find yourself on the outer: self-censorship by osmosis. Get it?"

"I just want to get to the truth," Estelle protested.

"It's really not about the world out there, is it?" The older woman's argument was hardening. "It's all about you making a name for yourself. That's what it's all about for you young do-gooders. You've really got to get real with yourself."

Estelle felt a little affronted by Alex's haranguing, but still felt she had to take a stand. She was determined to defend her position on this—but tonight she was buggered.

"Hey, I have an implant, and oral sex is great! Get yourself some flavoured condoms, kid. We've gotta support our sponsors. Always look on the bright side of life, da-da, da-da, da-da," the veteran journo joked, skipping out of the bar, much to Estelle's amusement.

Estelle returned home, south over the harbour bridge. She looked forward to regaining her licence after her stint in the sin bin for mid-range driving under the influence. While bristling at her loss of independence, she was grateful to her Dad and Nan, who'd both been more than generous with their rides.

After a brief chat with her Dad, she crashed out for the night. Tossing and turning, she woke in a sweat, fire in her chest. She wasn't beat yet!

THE WEEK DRAGGED ON and Estelle struggled to focus as she waded through a deluge of research. Alex was on her case to produce the goods and Estelle was relieved when Good Friday arrived, enabling a respite from this opus.

Easter Sunday found the Goldstein–Harris clan gathering for a traditional Easter lunch. Sam, with his Jewish heritage, had long forgotten the ambiguity of this ritual. Judith had always loved Christmas and Easter, and following her death, Esther had continued the tradition, more for Estelle's sake. This year was diminished by the absence of Frank and his mother. Sam had enjoyed Frank's company, especially as they'd teamed up to tease Esther.

The three of them sat out on the patio, shaded from the bright Easter sunlight. Esther and Estelle wore silly Easter hats. Sam had his hat on the dining table beside him.

"I hope you ladies are well prepared for flu season. Have you had your shots?" Sam fired.

"Which flu are we in for this season: bandicoot, horse, cow, duck, rhinoceros, rooster, or should I just make my way through the entire Chinese astrology, in case we miss one? I'll consider serious action when they announce pear flu or apple fever," Esther shot back.

"Well, enter winter without proper preparation at your own peril! I can do nothing about your intransigent bias against vaccination, but at least consider Tamiflu!"

"I'm quite happy with homeo-immunisation."

Sam rolled his eyes.

"Well, I thank God for my childhood mumps, which has given me life-saving immunity against ovarian cancer, denied to a generation forced to vaccinate. And you talk of freedom?"

"Well, it's only a marginal protection," conceded Sam.

"I'll take the margin, thank you very much," Esther retorted.

"Well, consider the marginal benefits of flu vaccination then."

"Dear God! Someone, quick, fetch me the Sydney papers. I'm going to scan the death and funeral notices for a head count of any surviving friends. The obituaries, I imagine, are overrun with poor, innocent victims of the last animal flu. Have all the zoos been put on notice?"

"At least keep in mind herd immunity, if it's not too much trouble for you, dear. I trust you'll consider you responsibility to the rest of us."

"Firstly, I'm not a cow. Secondly, if you are so worried, just go ahead and get yourself shot so as to protect yourself from me!"

"One might beg to differ on both counts," grunted Sam.

"Please, darling, fix me a Valium and Prozac sandwich and hand me a glass of wine to wash it down, given I've gotta listen to the crap that flows out of your father's mouth. I'm sure he half believes his own propaganda."

"I'm warning you. We're headed for a crisis with the latest flu. Don't say I didn't try."

"There is absolutely no scientific evidence that the flu shot works for anyone past the age of sixty-five. Am I not correct, Sam?" Eyeing her son in law off, she patiently awaited his reply as she sipped on her vino.

"Time will tell. Mark my words!"

"Dear, dear, I'm sure time will tell. Besides, the only crisis that I'm aware of is your inability to make contact with reality. You are labouring under the delusion that your prognostications are listened to by an informed public."

Sam refused to make eye contact with Esther. "Perhaps a little research wouldn't go too far astray. Try reading, or at least have one of your literate friends read to you. If you have any, that is."

"What crap. You Flat-Earthers simply refuse to ask the right questions. I am reading one of Doctor Deepak Chopra's books. I'll happily flick it to you once I'm through with it. I take it you know who Deepak is."

"No, not personally, dear, but I do believe I know his drunken brother Six-pack." Exasperation was clearly written on Sam's reddened face.

Another half hour of ongoing sparring between Sam and Esther, each attempting to outshine, outwit and outdrink the other, and Estelle felt herself slowly sliding out of the here and now. She could feel the fullness in her gut, her sloth-like limbs, and a wave of nausea rising in her throat.

"Excuse me," Estelle barely whispered, rising with death-like pallor to find the bathroom. A loud crack, as if from a bull-whip, startled the jostling in-laws. As one they arose and raced in to find Estelle lathered in sweat, struggling to a crouch, with soft, grunting respiration. Bright red flowed from a gash over her right eyebrow.

"Heart!" Esther took two deep, controlled breaths. "Calm!" she commanded herself. "Ring for an ambulance, Sam. I'll clean her up."

Sam turned to make arrangements, noting somewhere that his daughter had wet herself, and was grateful Esther had taken charge.

Estelle felt the crack reverberate in her head. A high-pitched tone pierced her consciousness as she grunted to get breath. The blue tiled bathroom floor was so, so cool against her right cheek. A hazy redness on the tip of her nose sharpened to the chequered blue tiles, white channels slowly filling with a thin red line as her vision refocused.

Chapter Four

The emergency siren of the high-tech vehicle contrasted with the languid afternoon. Bright flashing red and blue lights weaved through the lazy Sunday traffic and on to St Vincent's Hospital. The experienced paramedics remained calm and in control, reassuring Estelle as she lay inert, wired to a monitor and harnessed with an OxyMask. An intravenous catheter appeared on her left wrist and Estelle suddenly felt claustrophobic under the misting mask.

Arriving at Accident and Emergency, Estelle was efficiently processed by a registered nurse, prior to a young Indian intern attending to the gash on her brow. As she was laid flat to enable the intern to suture the gash, Estelle felt like a ton of bricks had been placed on her chest. With the green drape smothering out any fresh air, Estelle panicked. Her pulse rate took off. She felt entombed.

"She's gone into V.T." The voice of her attendant nurse pitched high as she desperately hit the red emergency button. Estelle faded out as the team went into a well-rehearsed drill.

"I.V. Amiodarone, Doctor?"

"Thank you, Sister."

The young nurse regained her composure as a staff specialist burst through the curtains to assist with the resuscitation.

Out in the waiting room, Esther and Sam sat quietly, side by side.

"What do you think?" asked Sam anxiously.

"Critical, but—she'll come through OK." Esther tilted her head to one side and gently rolled her right thumb, index, and middle fingers together. "Thank you, God, for a safe passage through troubled waters," she affirmed as she breathed out, relaxing faithfully into the moment.

In the resuscitation bay, Estelle was all but oblivious to a blood pressure cuff, pulse oximeter and cardiac monitor constantly taking measurements as hands, fingers, and a stethoscope probed her body for diagnostic evidence. She continued to gently grunt, her heart rate returning to a lower, more respectable level while her oxygen saturation rose to ninety-five per cent on an oxygen mask.

"Might be a tamponade; let's get her to coronary care. They have a bed. See if Jacob can do an ECHO there. Stay with her;

keep her sitting up at forty-five degrees. Better get family; we may need consent." The staff specialist dispatched Estelle to make way for another urgent case.

Estelle had become an inanimate appendage to a trolley connected to green tubing, monitor leads, red dots and intravenous catheters. Seven tiny neat sutures had closed the gash on her eyebrow. She continued to hide behind a misting oxygen mask.

Arriving in coronary care, Estelle was distantly aware of familiar faces beginning to merge with faintly recognisable voices reaching her, it seemed, through a long-distance tunnel. In her feeble state, she attempted to mentally construct the images before her. A white-coated male with a deep, compassionate voice was conversing with Sam and Esther.

"...recently come back from an assignment in South Africa. Hasn't really seemed all that well since her return," Esther replied, anxious to assist the older doctor before both she and Sam were again ushered to a waiting room.

Estelle was painfully aroused from her stupor by a hard, gel-coated probe digging up under her rib cage.

"Sorry. This will feel a little cold and uncomfortable," explained the young sonographer.

Estelle felt a soft, grating murmur continuously see-sawing in her chest.

"Big effusion, Doctor Schneider: a litre, maybe one and a half of fluid."

"Let's have a closer look at that pericardium." The old cardiologist took over. "Five millimetres; that's thick. Get a diagnostic aspirate, Chandran: Mantoux, HIV, etc. Probably viral, but we'll do a formal drainage: biopsy in the morning. Book her for theatre."

Jacob Schneider entered the visitors' room to meet with the anxious family.

"How is she, Doctor?" Sam was immediately on his feet, scrutinising the older cardiologist's demeanour for a prognosis.

"I'm Jacob Schneider," the old cardiologist greeted, extending his hand to both Sam and Esther. "I'll be looking after Estelle during her stay. We've managed to stabilise her." He motioned Esther and Sam to take a seat.

"Estelle has pericarditis, an inflammation of the usually gossamer-thin membrane around the heart. She's accumulated a lot of fluid around her heart, and this has compromised her heart's ability to pump: hence her collapse. We call this a tamponade," Doctor Schneider gently explained to the nod of heads. "We've taken off a couple of hundred mls of inflamed fluid, but little clots hampered this procedure. So in order to get a proper diagnosis, we'll need to make a little cut just beneath her breast bone." He motioned to just under his rib cage. "The biopsy is important to rule out tuberculosis."

"How long? Will she be OK?" interrogated Sam.

"She had a little arrhythmia while downstairs, but that's settled down now. I should think here for some weeks. But let's get the biopsy first."

Sam and Esther nodded.

"You both look exhausted. I suggest you both go home and rest."

Sam and his mother-in-law departed, an odd couple united in loving concern. Soft rain started to drizzle as they exited the parking station.

"Not again." Sam gripped the leather-textured steering wheel.

Esther sat quietly on the passenger side of the Merc, mesmerised as the windscreen wipers synchronised with a soft grating. She gently rolled thumb and two fingers together. "Should have seen this coming: too close to see," she muttered.

Violent shaking started just after midnight, the soft grating sound blasted out of her consciousness as Estelle's teeth chattered like a high-pitched jackhammer. She felt frozen, as if in a remote igloo, peeking out over layers of white cotton blankets. Nausea rose in her throat. Estelle sat up abruptly, heaving bright, bilious vomit into a green plastic bowl. She fell back, whimpering, onto a firm, uncomforting pillow, pleading for the nausea to pass. A young intern placed a tourniquet around her right arm, struggling to get more blood for a culture from an arm which shook in defiance. Shutdown veins hid beneath Estelle's pallid skin. The overwhelming nausea gradually subsided. Estelle attempted to lift her head, but slumped back into the starched pillow. Her eyelids dropped like bags of cement. Her heart raced, jumbled thoughts spinning out of control.

A shadowy figure beckoned her. Trustingly she moved towards him. He handed her a sharp, shiny object protruding from a rolled newspaper. His eyes immediately changed. She had to get away. Walking fast, then faster and faster, she escaped into a long, dark tunnel. Loud, heavy footsteps followed, and breathing, becoming louder and louder. She ran. The tunnel led to a dark pool of water. A figure lay drowning, face down, as blood foamed out into a river. A voice called her name. She couldn't respond. Her body was paralysed. She trembled, engulfed by violent shaking.

She awoke, disoriented, sweat dripping from every pore. Her heart pounded violently, the drilling sensation in her head excruciating. Sobbing with exhaustion, she fought to stay awake.

"Make it stop," Estelle pleaded, grunting, depleted by the viciousness of the rigor. "Shit!" she cried, realising she'd soiled herself. "Oh, fuck! Fuck! Please, God."

Surrender came as gentle nursing hands stripped Estelle of her privacy, yet somehow preserved her dignity.

"The noise in my chest?" cried Estelle, feeling the vibration deep in her chest cavity.

"'Tis only a murmur, sweetheart." Her Irish tones were reassuring as cool hands rubbed Estelle's tense back.

"Am I going to die?" whimpered Estelle.

"Not just yet, darlin'. 'Tis the Lord pruning ye," soothed the Irish sister. "Now take my hand." The nurse's sparkling blue eyes pierced Estelle's soul. "I'll be with ye all the way."

Estelle nodded in gratitude. Tears welled, cracking the dam of her fear, flowing softly, a healing balm to her jagged emotions. Kind hands rubbed and soothed, warmth replacing cool as taut muscles let go. Estelle's chest softened, allowing her to succumb to a deep sleep.

GLORIOUS MORNING SUNLIGHT STREAMED in through the seventh floor window of Estelle's hospital room. She lay quietly, aware of slight pain in her upper abdomen and chest. Slowly her fingers felt out a three-centimetre vertical dressing below the notch protruding beneath her rib cage.

Crisp, white curtains were parted by a nurse in her mid-forties. "Ye decided to join us then," the nurse greeted in a familiar Irish accent. Dust particles appeared to dance around her head like a halo as she stood with her back to the risen sun. The nurse's eyes locked onto Estelle's with tenderness.

"Where am I? What's happened?"

"Ye've been promoted, darlin', from the fourth floor to the seventh." The older woman smiled mischievously. "Ye've been on a Cook's Tour."

Estelle nodded. "I met you last night?"

"Yes, I'm Sister Angelica. I've been assigned to ye care."

"Where are you from?"

"Oohh, meself, from Ireland; me mother, she was Irish, and me father, German. They both had a love of music and a nip of whiskey."

Estelle smiled. Apart from the beeping heart monitor, there was a peaceful silence in the air. The colourful floral displays set against neutral cream walls warmed an otherwise sterile room, giving a touch of serenity.

Two doctors entered. After a brief greeting, Estelle was requested to lie on her left side as the older of the two placed a stethoscope under her left breast.

"Dressing down," commanded the older doctor. "Lumbar puncture OK? Serum Rhubarbs?"

"Sodium still a tad low; transaminases a little out, L.P; slightly elevated protein," replied the taller, gangly younger doctor.

"Goodo." Turning to Estelle, as if finally seeing her, he confided, "You've had a bit of a torrid time, Miss Goldstein, but on the mend now, I should think. Your pericardial biopsy site will feel a bit tight. You can stretch that up over a few weeks. The clever docs will have you on Rifampicin for four to six months, I imagine; or till they've decided whether you've had a spot of TB. You'll have to put up with the bright orange urine, I'm afraid. You're not long back from South Africa?"

Estelle nodded blankly.

"Your pericardial thickening looks like it's been there for longer." The kindly older man looked down, his intelligent eyes searching Estelle's face. "Look after your heart, Miss Goldstein." With that, the dynamic duo turned and left.

Estelle sank back into her bed, gazing out onto a sea of little red-tiled rooftops tiering up from Paddington to Edgecliff. Random spouts of green shot up here and there, the occasional majestic tree having survived the suburban invasion. Spicer Lane, where Nan lived, was not so far away. She felt exhausted and overwhelmed by information overload.

"They hardly acknowledged you." She frowned, looking at Sister Angelica.

"Big boys with their toys, darlin'!" Angelica chortled as she went about checking Estelle's chart. "We let 'em think they're important, but I can tell ye, we really run the place!"

Estelle caught her impulse to laugh, nursing the small wound in her upper abdomen.

Esther, a little weary, re-entered at that moment. "You never know what the night will bring. I prayed last night my grand-daughter would be in good hands. Thank you." A knowing look transpired between the two women. A ripple of relief and gratitude washed over Esther's face.

"So how are we this morning, sweet pea?" Nan asked, tenderly caressing her grand-daughter's wasted hand. The skin on Estelle's palms was waterlogged and crinkled from hours of sweat. Her soft, motherly tones, soothing to the blond waif, were the same soft, motherly tones she'd once reserved for Estelle as a four year old.

"Feels like I've been to hell and back."

"Ooh, heaven or hell is what we choose to see and how we choose to be; 'tis an inside job, if I dare say so," added Angelica.

"As will be your healing," Esther softly comforted as she continued to stroke Estelle's hand.

"Some places I've worked, the conditions are hell on earth. Need to do something…" Estelle's voice trailed off.

"Yes, and you will! But now is your time to rest." Esther kissed her grandchild on the cheek. "You're in good hands," she again reassured. "Rest is what we all need. Not so?" Esther asked, casting a glance towards Angelica.

Exhausted, Estelle complied with her grandmother's injunction and drifted off. Her illness would claim up to twenty hours sleep a day.

"Not so different to a cat's slumber schedule," Esther chuckled.

SITTING AT HIS DESK eating a ham, cheese and tomato sandwich, Sam carefully perused a robust set of figures. The Fluffy Friday Campaign was fast making a killing: a great marketing success. A media blitz and ad campaign, along with celebrity endorsements, had whipped up a frenzy of public awareness. The net was cast far and wide. Calls were sent out urgently and loudly for research dollars towards depression and mental illness. Everywhere one looked, the hype was impossible to escape. There were telethons and marathons, research literature and diagnostic manuals, statistical data on suicide juxtaposed pharmaceutical claims of successful interventions, doctors appealing to stay-at-home mothers on popular morning shows and morning news, experts appealing to working mothers on popular evening shows and evening news. Schools issued reminder notes to parents for lamington drives, kind-hearted folk everywhere coming together to fundraise.

A fearful public was nudged out of complacency. Would be victims were only too happy to dig deep. Money was donated beyond the grave, the most vulnerable donating funeral legacies to the cause, the bereaved requesting donations to the charity instead of flowers, all vowing to end the scourge of post-natal depression. At the other end of the spectrum, the enlisted pester power was hard at work, cute pink, blue and yellow teddies fast flying off supermarket shelves and chemist counters.

AS EVENING FELL, SAM found himself doing what had now become his after work routine: visiting hour lift-shuffle. A handful of visitors marched in from the immaculately manicured hospital grounds. Ping. They shuffle into the ground floor lift. Ping. One or two shuffle out. Ping and ping again saw Sam scurry out of the lift and head for Estelle's room: number nine.

Upon entering, Sam found Esther sitting by Estelle's bed, softly stroking her hand and talking to her in reassuring tones.

"I've been sending you healing, sweet pea, and I can see that it's working."

Sam passed Angelica, who stood at the foot of the bed, clipboard in hand. Sitting opposite Esther, Sam immediately claimed Estelle's other hand. "Of course: nothing to do with the marvels of modern medicine!" He smiled, patting her hand. "You'll soon be on your feet."

"How are ye feelin' this evenin', darlin'?" inquired Angelica.

"I've been having some weird dreams," responded Estelle listlessly.

"Just side-effects of the medication; you'll be right soon," Sam responded authoritatively.

"We'll have you on a healthier lifestyle just as soon as we can get you home," added Esther tenderly.

"Premature to talk about exercising, I should think." Sam raised his eyebrows.

"I'm sure your father could do with some exorcising. My healing carries no side-effects. Besides, you're simply opening into other dimensions," countered Esther.

Sam threw up his hands dismissively. "About the only dimensions your grandmother manages to open up are LSD throwbacks from the sixties."

Estelle grabbed her rib cage to stifle an irrepressible laugh. "Stop. Pain!"

"Don't worry too much about your father, dear. His personality bypass removed most of his manners. Unfortunately the more aggressive ones were left behind in his system!"

"If your grandmother ever gets dementia, it's most likely she'll go undiagnosed for years, given there'd be no detectable changes in her personality!"

"My stitches are breaking," squealed Estelle with a pained smile, holding her abdomen. For all its dysfunction, this was family.

Sam's mobile rang. He fumbled for the phone on his hip, glanced at the screen, then hesitated for a second before slowly making his way to the door. Preoccupied, he motioned over his shoulder. "Back in just a moment."

Outside, Sam began to nervously pace up and down the corridor as he talked on the phone. His free hand began twirling the ring on his chain. "No, I don't think anything specific was said."

Further down the corridor, a young Afro-Aussie in his late twenties, dressed in earthy shades, stopped to ask for directions. Sam observed a large duffle bag with airport tags at the man's feet.

"Well, no, because she didn't know." Sam bit his lip. "OK, I'll try. In any case, the implications—"

Listening intently, Sam continued to observe the young man at the nurse's station. The ward clerk pointed down the corridor towards the lifts, gesticulating to the young man, who mirrored her gestures back to her, then walked past Sam. Telephone conversation terminated, Sam took a deep breath, pensively paced a few moments and turned back towards Estelle's room.

The young man had stopped at Estelle's doorway. Their eyes locked for a moment, losing themselves in each other's gaze. He gave a sheepish smile. Pulling himself out of the trance, he looked to each side of the door for the room number. "Sorry for barging in, Miss," he apologised, a New York accent detectable. "I'm all sixes and sevens today."

Still in a trance of her own, Estelle's heart monitors beeped faster. She made no attempt to avert her gaze. He stood there, the moment prolonged, before hesitantly turning to walk away.

Esther smiled at Estelle. "Now he's cute."

Sam re-entered the room. "You're obviously referring to me. Thank you. Of course there are very few handsome, outstanding gentlemen of refined character, such as myself, left in the world," he announced, raising his eyebrows and clearing his throat with a theatrical sway of his head.

"Ah, men; they're all the same everywhere, I tell ye," Angelica wise-cracked from the side.

"Maybe your father should have been left out standing!" taunted Esther.

The comic relief was interrupted by the entry of a dark-haired nurse in her early thirties. Angelica smiled warmly, acknowledging her presence.

"How are we tonight, Miss Goldstein?" enquired the dutiful nurse before administering Estelle her evening anti-TB medication.

"Makin' remarkable progress, to be sure," Angelica replied.

"She'll be home before we know it! Isn't that right, Stella?" encouraged Sam.

"I'm sure she will," agreed the young nurse.

"She's in wonderful hands." Angelica smiled at her colleague with pride.

"OH DEAR," MUTTERED THE old lady, gently stooping to examine a bloodied possum dumped on her doorstep. The critter's eyes glazed, her breathing shallow, her limbs partially severed. Carefully turning the dying female over to her back, Esther reached into her moist pouch: luckily no baby this time. Mindfully wrapping the limp body in a towel, she took it inside. There she nursed it during its dying moments. As with so many, she knew this little girl had sat in terror, deep within a tree hollow, seeking protection from man's chainsaws.

After a word with God, Esther turned in for the night.

WITH ALL LIGHTS OUT, Estelle fell into another fitful night's sleep. It was as if she had been sucked into a demonic black hole. She was running, running, footsteps in pursuit getting louder and louder. The shadowy figure re-emerged, blood dripping from his hands. They were being spied upon. He vaporised into thin air. Running for her life, she began to pant harder and harder. In the distance a building! From within, the chilling, high-pitched whimpering of tortured animals, their excruciating screams getting louder and louder. Angry cats traversed the road, fighting viciously. Fur started to fly, condensing into a blinding, suffocating wall of dust. She couldn't breathe. She couldn't see. Paralysed, she was fighting for her life!

During brief intervals she awoke, drenched and disorientated, lying like a rag doll. She felt too helpless to fight away the horrors and too exhausted to call for help.

She again found herself sobbing into an unyielding pillow. "God help me! God help me!"

ESTELLE AWOKE TO SUNSHINE filtering through her window, her eyelids imperceptibly opening and closing in the brilliance illuminating her face, her hair glistening with a golden glow. Esther was quietly sitting by her bed. She had not long arrived, having rushed to organise her animals for the day, and en route to the Sanctuary. Angelica was preoccupied, checking the monitors and IV bag.

"Everythin' OK then?" inquired Angelica, turning towards the frail waif.

"Last night I felt like I was dying."

"Oh, heavens! We can't have you dying now." Esther gently wiped her granddaughter's forehead.

"Strange. This morning I feel like I'm making a comeback."

"Now that's what we like to hear!" replied Esther energetically.

"'Tis nice to be given a chance to make a comeback," added Angelica warmly. "Bein' blessed by the radiant mornin' sun brings its own healin'."

"Are you always so cheery?" asked Estelle.

"Oh, I'm always in good spirits for those to whom I've been appointed."

"That's nice." Estelle smiled.

"'Tis the sheer wonder of life. Indeed the world is such a magical place."

Estelle sighed with gratitude for the upliftment of two spirited women. Both were so nurturing, each offering similar, yet different perspectives. Estelle, Nan and Angelica had created a tight women's club, conferring and consulting on a number of issues, mainly girly subjects: sales and bargains, clothes and shoes, make-up and hairstyles, and the truth about men. Esther, always quick off the mark, gave her finest tips for auditioning members of the opposite sex.

Beyond all the extraordinary high tech and competent staff efficiently tending to her every need, it was mostly the loving connections and affirming conversations that accelerated the pace of Estelle's recovery.

Increasingly Estelle began to notice how she felt in the presence of each individual visiting her room. Some people left her feeling energised, while others left her depleted. There were the givers and the takers. Estelle tried to avoid engaging with the vampires as they really did suck her dry. Thankfully her Nan was always so full of enthusiasm.

"Are you up for a game?" Nan pulled out a surprise parcel.

"Scrabble—my favourite!" Estelle's eyes lit up.

"Ah, the magical power of words," enthused Nan.

Esther had introduced Scrabble as an early childhood learning device. Over the years the game had brought the family together on countless joyful occasions. It had helped teach Estelle not only to spell, but perhaps had become a springboard to her career.

Board laid out. All tiles face down. No cheating! Six letters each on letter holders facing away from opponents. Both choose a face-down tile. Closest to the letter A wins the right to go first. Esther wins, squealing with as much ELATION as that very word; a bonus fifty points for using her first seven letters straight off the bat. Estelle fired up with a REV to precede Esther's ELATION. Nan's letters announced EXPECT to which Estelle added ANCY. Nan moved in with VOYAGE. Estelle utilised Nan's G with the space available for GUIDE. Nan decided upon RETURN, Estelle adding ING. Nan chose WARN to which Estelle again came back with an ING. As the board spaces closed in, leaving few available options, Estelle went on to play her sleepy, final hand with the last of her user-friendly letters, and with that added her F to Nan's ATE.

As she continued to make gradual progress, her mornings were better, but afternoons challenging. She was often irritated by the noise of jack-hammers, a torture in the long, sweaty afternoons. Sometimes she noted the handsome young man she'd laid eyes on weeks before. When he'd see her in bed as he passed her room, they'd exchange a friendly smile, perhaps a little shy, perhaps not quite appropriate. Whatever the case, he never made any greater attempt to strike up a conversation with her.

From her window she spied him, his athletic form dancing through the rain as he approached the back entrance to the hospital. She wasn't about to let this chance slip by her feminine charms. Without hesitation she ran her fingers through her hair and headed straight for the water cooler. With the sound of the lift doors opening, her heart skipped a beat. Her mind instantly blank, Estelle felt suddenly unable to breathe. Determined to keep her cool, she remained focused on the cooler before turning in his direction as if quite by chance. Though looking directly at her, he headed past without so much as the blink of an eye and kept walking right on down the corridor. Estelle felt totally ridiculous and briefly wondered if anyone else had witnessed how she'd made a fool of herself. Deflated, she shuffled back to her bed, gazing absently at her empty cup, its whiteness matching her waterlogged palms.

"Felt like stretchin' your legs, eh?" Angelica's voice startled her.

"Aaaah—just needed some water."

Angelica, unable to help herself, tilted her head towards the water jug on Estelle's bedside table. "Mmm-hmmm?"

Estelle hesitated before answering, "Cold water," then became lost in her thoughts. "Like he just looked straight through me," her voice echoed softly.

"'Tis always so refreshin' to find a real, down-to-earth man who can give us a run for our money. I still remember how it felt."

As she slid her feet under the sheets, Estelle redirected her attention back to Angelica. "Felt? Sounds like you're still missing someone."

"Ah, we were accidently torn apart almost a year ago. I'm afraid we have such different views on life these days."

"So sad; can't you get him to see your side?"

A trace of vulnerability filled the space between the two women, Angelica pausing to reflect. "It takes all the love I have to let him live his life."

"You've given up on him?"

"Sometimes it takes a far greater love to let someone go than it does to hold on." Again Angelica paused. "To live and let live, as they say." A wistful shadow flitted across her eyes.

"Do you believe in soul mates, Angelica?"

Angelica pondered for a second. "Ah, love eternal. Let me tell ye, me girl, I know there are soul mates."

"And yours may just be around the corner, sweet pea!" Esther declared with infectious zaniness, having just entered the room.

"Sometimes I'm just not so sure." Estelle shrugged, her smile almost deflated.

Esther caressed her grand-daughter's hair, gently removing strands from her face. "Destiny has its own date, angel," she replied, casting a smile in Angelica's direction.

Nodding, Angelica left the room.

"Did you have an instant knowing when you met Grandpa John?"

"An instant soul recognition!" Nan smiled tenderly. "But I wasn't about to let on." The older woman's eyes were soft.

"Oh? Why not?"

"I was going to allow that wonderful man to chase me until I finally caught him." She beamed.

"You were pregnant within a fortnight of meeting him?"

"The longest fortnight of my life, sweet pea, the longest fortnight of my life—and I didn't make it easy for him either!"

"Of course." Estelle grinned.

"You know what they say; you can hook a mate or you can attract a mate. Attraction is a sacred phenomenon; it works on spiritual principles. If you hook a man, at some level he will be aware of it and he will never be truly yours. Sooner or later he will become resentful and leave, emotionally or physically. I've seen it time and time again!"

"You attracted Grand-dad?"

"It was an unbreakable karmic bond—and we both knew it."

"And the difference?"

"Desperation, sweet pea! So many young girls these days have it all wrong. They sit glued to the phone, the screen. They chase. They hound. They hunt. They get pregnant. Of course both father and child are then issued with an instant job description that neither asked for."

"But Nan, you got pregnant."

"Oh, there is a difference, and if you're totally honest with yourself, you will always know it in your heart."

"And the difference?"

"Intention, sweet pea; your motives and intentions for anything in life will always show up—be it sooner, be it later—by way of results. Spiritual laws are no different to the laws of physics; they cannot be manipulated by any man, man-made religion, or institution. Ignorance spares no one from their effects."

Weaving her way through late afternoon gridlock, Alex muscled her way towards the hospital. Outside, near the car park, she could hear a number of birds noisily calling to their flocks as they organised themselves in their protective groups in the fading light.

"Up for a visit?" announced Alex, ambling towards Estelle's bed.

Estelle smiled as Alex welcomed herself in.

"Released from his tour of duty," sniped Alex, distracted by an incoming mobile message as she pulled up a chair.

"Released?" invited Estelle as Alex flipped shut her phone.

"Released from work; his dumb bitch has her claws into him. Dumb and dumber: left his phone lying around, so the wifey decided on a bit of a snoop. Obviously doesn't trust him."

"Maybe guilt got the better of him."

"I only ever say respectable things about the wives so that my boys can let go of guilt and have a good time with me."

"Maybe a turning point for them as a couple."

"Doubt it; she wants him back home on his knees, just not the right way. In any case, I'm not a home wrecker: happy to return him to that parasite. Anyway, so how are you going, kiddo."

"Wanting out of this place."

"Escape from Alcatraz. Hmm, don't blame you. I'd want out of this hell hole too."

"Be great to get back to work: keep having frantic dreams of missing my deadline. It's like I'm back in South Africa watching familiar faces die in front of me from disease and starvation. I call and call and no one is there to assist."

"Now stop fretting, kiddo." Alex scrutinised her wasted protégé. "Your AIDS article will be a first-class success."

"But I still need to sharpen it up. Hopefully I'll be out of here in no time."

"Not so fast there. I gather your doctors think you'll need a while to fully recover." Alex noted Estelle's sallow complexion. "TB or Viral?"

"The old doc wasn't sure, though I have been treated for TB. Whatever the case, seems as though I might have had it before leaving for South Africa," answered Estelle thoughtfully. "Not work-related."

"Not to worry," Alex's look of relief almost imperceptible, "you can start back on part-time hours. Maybe some research from home as soon as your health permits."

WEEKS PASSED, DAYS SHORTENED. Estelle's night terrors had eased. On the whole there was an increased sense of calmness, with the exception of the mid-afternoon trolleys as they made their clanging and banging rounds through the wards. Estelle's room, being a single, was a one-stop shop for the tea lady, who served with cordial efficiency before moving on to the next room.

This time spent in hospital was the quietest Estelle had ever known Nan to be—well, for Nan that was. To anyone else, Esther's quiet was still akin to the hyper-manic verbosity of a real-estate auctioneer.

It appeared to Estelle that her quiet moments were somehow orchestrated by the universe; a way of slowing her down in order to create a fertile void for self-awareness and growth. She felt somehow inspired—in spirit, as Nan would say. It was as if an inner voice had taken her over, leaving a subtle and tantalising trace of as yet unanswered questions.

Till this moment she'd unconsciously striven for her dad's approval: atonement for her mother's death, perhaps. Her mum's suicide had gutted Sam. In her efforts to compensate, she'd modelled herself on him by aspiring to the top of the corporate ladder, but what of her own self-approval; what did that mean to her? Was it possible for her to truly find herself in the external world without discovering her own internal world?

"May I?" A gentle Irish accent broke the silence.

"Sure, be my guest." Estelle wriggled aside, giving Angelica space on her bed. The two had become intimate friends. Estelle wasn't sure why Angelica had entered her life the way she had, nor did she really care. All she cared about was that she had.

"A penny for ye thoughts, young lady?" Angelica nudged softly.

"Not sure. Funny: thinking 'bout how Dad's approval has always meant so much to me."

"The world, to be sure, is filled with people starvin' for approval. Most humans only love themselves via others."

"Why, do you think?"

"Ooh, I believe most never outgrow the need for their mummy and daddy's approval. 'Tis what I think." Angelica's answer floated through the air.

"How sad," reflected Estelle, inhaling and exhaling slowly.

"There is, however, a sure way to know if ye have already been fully approved of."

"How so?" Estelle looked across with childlike innocence.

"Are ye here?"

"Here? Here, where?"

"Ye know. Here: in the here and now. Alive! A part of God's wondrous creation."

"I guess." The young woman frowned.

"Well then, it means ye have already been approved of. And that, me girl, is the only approval ye will ever need." Angelica smiled warmly, stroking Estelle's upper arm.

A silence briefly filled the air.

"How wise."

"Life's simple. We make it complicated. We are born with our intelligence, but we earn our wisdom, to be sure." Angelica shrugged. "How's we stretch our legs then? Up for a walk?" invited Angelica, stretching her hand towards Estelle.

The two quietly strolled past several rooms and down a lift, jack-hammers rattling away. Exiting at ground level, they ventured out into an open space. A subtle scent of blossom floated through the air. One could almost taste the freshness of the protected green oasis. The atmosphere was alive, buzzing with bees and the chirping of birds as they fluttered in and out of trees.

"I haven't been to this section before: so beautiful. It's like—"

"I know. Ye've come to appreciate the true beauty of simplicity."

"I have." Varying rose colours glistened with rain droplets in the magical late afternoon sun. Breathing their perfume, Estelle was delighted with her newfound sense of smell.

"When ye've been where I've been and witnessed the things that I have, ye just get to see things a whole lot differently. Ye just know. Besides, what do ye think of me secret garden?"

"Out of this world!"

"'Tis, to be sure." Angelica grinned. "'Tis where I retreat to when I need to rest. Mind ye, these days I'm far too busy takin' care of the likes of ye to get too much rest. Oh, and I really don't at all mind. Not at all." She squeezed Estelle's hand.

They strolled for a while before retreating to a park bench. In the background were a couple of multi-coloured butterflies doing a sweet courtship dance over a memorial plaque.

"I've been noticin' ye doin' quite a lot of thinkin' lately, ah? Anythin' botherin' ye?"

"Lot of time to think—stuck here so long."

"I hope ye don't feel stuck with me." Angelica nudged playfully with her elbow. "It seems like ye've only arrived yesterday."

"It's not so bad," conceded Estelle.

"Do ye ever question?"

"Question what?"

"Like," tilting her head towards Estelle, "like the truly mysterious questions of life. Ye know. Who are ye? How did ye get here? Where did ye come from? Where are ye goin'? Where is ye home?"

"Stop! Stop!" Estelle laughed. "You're making my head pound."

"Oh, I could go on." Angelica laughed. "Is there intelligence beyond ye own? Are the events of ye life a random series of happenin's? Are ye in control?"

"Boy, you really know how to fire them when you get going. I swear you've been having tea with my Nan. She reads palms."

"And so do I!"

"Oh no, don't tell me. No! Go ahead, tell me." She tentatively placed her open palm inside Angelica's hand.

"Did ye know that only about ten per cent of ye choices are made from an awakened state of consciousness? So what of the other ninety per cent? How does this affect ye relationships? It is said that in the cosmos we are all made of the same matter, so why do ye matter? Some say there are no accidents in the universe, and that everythin' happens for a special reason. Ye are that special reason." She softly nudged.

"You're not reading my palm, just sharing your philosophy." Estelle laughed.

"What! Now ye don't like me philosophy?" Jesting, she went on. "Like the man coming back in for that very special reason."

"What man? What reason? I've met a lot of men for no real reason."

"No. This one is the one. Ye are bound together by a sacred promise."

"I don't remember any man promising me anything. They're all bastards! I certainly didn't promise any man anything!"

"Ye've been heartbroken on more than one occasion. Ye know all pain and regret happens when our hearts are closed."

"Ok then! How will I recognise this promised man? Next you are going to tell me that he is some paragon of virtue," she sniped.

"Like any soul mate, he is not perfect, but perfect for ye, and he is the doorway to ye destiny."

Estelle smiled nervously. Deep in thought, she walked alongside her friend back to her room.

Chapter Five

The lift doors opened, Sam and Estelle moved across, making room for others. Filling quickly, all stood staring at the panel indicating the level of descent. Estelle felt remarkably confident re-entering her new life. She had no clear recollection of the day she'd been rushed into emergency in a semi-conscious state. Now here she was, feeling far more conscious, far more alert, far more of a free spirit and far more in control than she'd ever experienced. She felt she was leaving behind part of herself, an old paradigm, a worn-out benchmark for success. She could feel some kind of soul calling. Not one that she entirely understood, nor one that she could entirely ignore either. It was as if her internal spirit was being led by some external force.

With tenderness, Estelle studied her father's battle-weary face. "Dad, I'd like to arrange for an interview with your boss, Doctor Schaffell, so that I can follow up on my AIDS article."

Softly smiling, Sam nodded.

CAUTIOUS OF ANY LIABILITY for the company relating to Estelle's illness, Alex had agreed to allot her protégé a little work, mainly from home, with limited office hours.

With a late morning start, Estelle dropped in to the Sanctuary. She was entranced by an instant inner peace. Floating through the air, light, relaxing music complemented the sweet scent of incense. Next to reception, clients were buzzing around the psychic display board, carefully choosing whom they wished to consult. The board showcased the readers' photos with a brief synopsis of their specialties. Some first-timers stood mesmerised by the psychic menu. Some nominated who they wished to see based on word of mouth. Some had seen their clairvoyant of choice on previous occasions. All the while the atmosphere was alive with chatter as clients exchanged stories of how their regular clairvoyant had never missed a beat.

And then there was the usual satire. Waiting at reception was a client agitated by a disruption of her schedule caused by her psychic, Lena, who was running late.

"I know. I know, dear. If she leaves you waiting any longer she may be required to give you a discount on your reading, given that some of your future will have already passed." Esther turned to check the wall clock. "Of course from a spiritual perspective all time is now. I see you're up and about, darling. How are we this morning?" Esther chuckled.

"Thought I'd drop in for a while before heading into work," replied Estelle cheerfully.

"Great to see you!" The warmth in Nan's eyes was an instant welcome.

Without warning, a sudden, angry outburst stormed through the double doors, taking everyone by surprise. "You wouldn't believe what happened to me this morning!" Lena bounced in, a buxom blond in her late teens with a plunging, braless neckline. "Some pervert on the bus refused to keep his eyes on his newspaper."

"Well, my dear, you will insist on keeping the goods out on display. Perhaps if you'd place a ticket on each, we'd at least know how much for the pair," replied Esther dryly.

Barely fazed by the incident, the Sanctuary's loyal following understood Esther, the readers, and all the quirkiness to be a package deal.

While Esther went about serving customers, Estelle immersed herself in some of the books on sale. *Cancer. Another Way?* by Ainslie Meares, *You Can Conquer Cancer* by Ian Gawler, *Eat to Live* by Joel Fuhrman, *Green for Life* by Victoria Boutenko, *Skinny Bitch* by Rory Freedman and Kim Barnouin, and a number of books by Doctor David Suzuki. Nan had such an eclectic collection, though she claimed to access most of her knowledge via the spirit world.

"Time to feed little Marvin," announced Esther eagerly, having attended to the last of the line-up. She peered into a darkened box beneath the desk. The previous forty-eight hours had seen Esther on a round-the-clock feeding schedule for a juvenile galah that'd fallen out of his tree. With the little bird too heavy for his mother to lift back into his nest and vulnerable on the ground to predators, Esther took it upon herself to mother the featherless orphan till such time as he could reclaim the wild as his home.

Estelle moved towards the box. "I'll keep an eye on this little guy while you get his dinner," she offered, peeping in curiously.

Esther headed for the kitchen to mix and heat the little critter's formula. Sitting at reception, the squawking orphan quickly began devouring the formula with great gusto. His little beak jerked greedily at the improvised spoon in the shape of his mother's mouth. Both Nan and Estelle cackled as the ravenous chick shook his head, splattering the formula all over Nan's hair and outfit.

"Hardly fair not to have a mother," Estelle reflected.

"Life's not about fairness, certainly not for you, beautiful." Nan smiled in amusement as the noisy juvenile began vigorously pecking at her floral blouse.

"Something I remember you teaching me as a little girl." A soft smile lit Estelle's face.

"And what's that?" invited Nan as she went on enjoying her little mate.

"You taught me that prey animals have eyes to the side of their heads for greater protection from predators, while predators have eyes to the front."

"Come on now," coaxed Esther, firmly holding the spoon to the bird's mouth, encouraging him to continue eating.

Estelle sat watching as the chick continued to feed. She thought of prey animals, birds in particular, and how they would seldom display injury or sickness so as not to attract the attention of predators. She reflected on how, by the time weakness was detected, it was often too late to save their lives.

"Done now, are we?" Esther asked the downy bird as she lowered him back into his darkened box.

"Now let me give you some spiritual healing, sweet pea," offered Nan, focussing her concentration on Estelle.

"My God! The time!" exclaimed Estelle, leaping to her feet. "Where did the time go?"

"Relax, sweet pea."

"No! Sorry! Got to go! You may well be right about your concept of time, and the nature of reality and illusion, however explaining it to the likes of Alex might be an entirely different matter."

The way Esther explained time was her Olympic pool analogy. Though we may swim the length of the pool linearly, the body of water itself is not linear. With that, Estelle took a number of linear steps across to Esther, pecked her on the cheek and darted across to work.

ACKNOWLEDGING HER HEADS-DOWN COLLEAGUES, Estelle made her way to her cubicle. After rummaging around, frustrated by misplaced items, reshuffled in her absence, Estelle settled down to research.

The morning ran smoothly. Estelle ticked off her to-do list. Dovetailing with the success of her South African AIDS article, that had been polished and submitted by Alex during Estelle's hospital stay, she was pleased to have secured an interview for a follow-up article with Julian Clarke, a recipient of the new antiretroviral. Putting her computer on sleep, with time and date flashing, she pulled together notebook and pen and headed out for her day's meetings.

ESTELLE FOLLOWED JULIAN'S HOUSEKEEPER, Mary, a middle-aged woman wearing a nondescript tight, grey bun, nondescript blue dress covered by a nondescript white apron and nondescript flat, black shoes. Estelle trailing behind, they made their way through a long hallway filled with photos and memorabilia and an eclectic collection of books: science, history, travel and archaeology.

"Obviously a bookworm," remarked Estelle as Mary opened the lounge room door where Julian had been sitting quietly, his knees covered by a warm crocheted blanket.

"Come in," invited Julian, motioning as he lifted his eyes from his book.

"Thanks for agreeing to see me," greeted Estelle warmly, extending her hand to the short, balding man with a sad face and kind, dimly lit grey eyes.

"Can I get you anything?" offered Mary.

"Maybe a glass of water," requested Estelle, centring herself in a seat opposite Julian.

"Something for this bloody cough," requested Julian impatiently. Estelle observed the extensive bruising on his hand as he lifted it to cover his mouth.

"Bit of a bad day with it. Might be the dry air?" reassured the older woman, wiping her hands on her cotton apron before setting about to readjust the air con.

"Doesn't sound too good. How long have you had it?" empathised Estelle.

"It's been going on for far too damn long." Julian stopped to catch his breath, allowing the return of a little colour to his jaundiced face. "Got too much to do to get bogged down like this."

Mary exited the room, then re-entered with a tray. Julian reached for a lozenge and a sip of water, dabbing the excess from his parched, reddened lips.

"You're about to commence trials with the antiretrovirals. What outcome are you hoping for?" opened Estelle.

"The sooner we get underway with the new drugs, the sooner I can get back to a normal life," spluttered the middle-aged man. "Not that I'll be back to work any time soon." Julian's voice trailed off, as did the light from his eyes.

"Though you sound hopeful of a good outcome," replied Estelle.

"I've done my homework this time around!" he asserted, pointing to an amassed stack of research articles on AIDS vaccines and antiretrovirals on the coffee table between them. "Perhaps this time I get to benefit from medical research." He shrugged, resuming his more upright posture.

"You're a good man, Julian—much loved." Mary gently patted his right shoulder.

"Have you received adequate support since agreeing to this antiretroviral trial?" asked Estelle softly.

"I'm a blessed man." Julian's deeply sunken eyes softened, allowing light to re-enter the empty void. "I have all the love one could ever ask for." He smiled warmly, Estelle returning his smile with equal warmth.

"Now just call out if you need anything." Mary headed back out of the room.

The time with Julian passed quickly. Estelle felt privileged to sit in the presence of a truly courageous individual, who'd been previously let down by the failed AIDS vaccine. She penned him in for a follow-up meeting to monitor his progress and long-term response to the new wonder drug, before flitting across town for her next port of call with her dad's boss, Wolfgang Schaffell.

PONDERING HER EARLIER DISCUSSION and the testimony of love in Julian's eyes, Estelle made her way through the lunch hour crowds.

She was mindful of the city streets awash with thousands of people. In a collective dash, the multitude rushed about, glancing at elegant watches, all the while deftly negotiating eyes and bodies around each other. What were they most afraid of and so determined to avoid? Was it contact, or having precious moments stolen from their private inner worlds? She couldn't help but see differently the crowded city of strangers with far-away looks in their eyes, the life force drained from their faces as they rushed back to their offices. Estelle suspected that for many, joy and happiness had been deferred till the elusive finish of business.

Estelle negotiated her way around a jack-hammering building site. She flashed back to conversations she'd had previously with Alex. Now there was one example of someone who desperately craved intimacy, though couldn't bear to admit it. What Alex had so proficiently mastered, in lieu of intimacy, was the game of seducer-betrayer. She was a typical corporate high-flyer with little time to spare. After all, time equals money. Perhaps this was why there was such a growing market for speed dating and fast sex. Sex sells, but at what price? Well, sex at least, but how could anyone market love, chemistry and intimacy? Pseudo-intimacy: sex as a commodity with negotiable time. Though what was intimacy: in- to- me-see, perhaps? Estelle frowned. We all want to be seen, to be loved, she thought, but what if to look into one another's eyes deeply is to reveal nothing more than a shameful, secret reflection of one's own painful longing? Paradise lost? Is there a soul mate awaiting somewhere in the ether for me, she wondered wistfully.

She knew she was a product of an instant and disposable era: instant disposable sex and instant disposable relationships. What did this say about her era? What did this say about her? What does it mean when we lock eyes with a passing stranger? The instant our breath is taken away, our heart beats a little faster and our temperature starts to rise.

Estelle was fast coming to suspect that living, in the real sense of the word, was all about loving. She could now almost make sense of why Nan loved to talk with the dead, and why she joked about her séance group joining hands and contacting the living. Perhaps they really were more alive than the so-called living, some of who were waiting for some kind of delayed gratification in an afterlife, like the countless faithful who flocked to hard, wooden church pews on Sundays, dutifully paying off their insurance policy for some utopian hereafter. For Estelle, the gift of almost dying was that she would no longer postpone living life more fully. Live in the present with an attitude of gratitude, Nan would say. She smiled. She had come to understand that a life devoid of joy was little more than a desperate clinging for survival.

Estelle headed towards the head office of her father's company. Exiting the lift, she was quite surprised to find no one at reception. Knowing she was expected, she adjusted her dusk pink suit, and with head held high, marched on down the corridor towards the office. As she approached, she became aware of an agitated, angry voice. Though she had only met him on less than a handful of occasions, she was able to identify the voice as that of Doctor Wolfgang Schaffell, the very man she was about to see.

"…he's been sponsored, groomed, nurtured, and well paid to keep his fuckin' mouth shut! Ungrateful bastard! Perhaps it's time to send someone around for a little reminder."

Estelle hesitated, and with three deep breaths proceeded further down the corridor.

"No need to go overboard. He's a forgotten has-been on his last legs." It was her dad's voice, unusually tense. "We have a vast stable of eminent champions to counter any slur. Our Foundation has achieved three recipients of the Order of Australia in the last decade. Our American colleagues have achieved even greater recognition. The evidence-based defence of our position is seamless," soothed Sam.

Wolf rebutted with venom. "Yes, well, through our petrochemical cousins, at arms' fuckin' length. We do enormous good in society. Fucking lawyers! Bunch of hyenas sniffing for blood at emergency departments. They even advertise in hospital lifts, for Christ's sake. We don't need another fucking class action. I'm telling you that poofter won't be standing on his last legs much longer. I'll deal with him. I'm warning you, Sam. It's in everyone's best interest that nothing else is leaked or investigated. Now, do we understand each other?"

"The evidence, if there is any, is buried in dusty archives. We can just let sleeping dogs lie."

Estelle stood frozen, and then quickly retraced her steps back to reception, letting the door slam behind her. The loud slam was enough warning to modulate the masculine tones a few decibels. Allowing enough cooling-off period, she made her way back down the corridor.

Entering the room, she greeted both men with eye contact. "Hello, Dad, hello, Doctor Schaffell." With masking confidence, she extended her hand.

Sliding herself into a black leather chair, Estelle rested her open notebook on her knee. Pausing for a moment, she calibrated her approach. "I believe we have a common interest in seeing the expansion of your antiretroviral products into South African and other regions affected by HIV. For starters I am most interested in hearing about any plans that your company has to get the new antiretrovirals into South Africa."

"The New York conference will provide a strategic forum to facilitate political action and get our products into the South African market."

"I see!" She nodded encouragingly.

"All the major pharmaceutical players are going to be in the one place at the one time. Though we are still waiting approval from the Medicine Control Council, the South African national regulatory agency, I am confident that we will soon be given the green light to go ahead." Wolf rose from behind his mahogany desk and moved across his office, pouring himself a glass of water. "We just need to ensure there are no hiccups," he continued, squaring off to Sam.

"Of course," agreed Sam, turning to leave. "I think we can come up with a strategy to massage this through."

Rubbing his ruby ring, Wolfgang retraced his steps to his high-backed, black leather chair.

Estelle continued as Sam left the room. "I'm aware of the difficulties your company has come up against. There seems to be an influential group of naysayers who have held sway so far. Are their concerns bio-ethical or budgetary? I note that some eminent scientists, Omar Bagasra, for instance, have raised concerns about rogue recombinants emerging in the process of developing an AIDS vaccine, giving rise to even deadlier strains of HIV." Estelle noted her name-dropping got a rise out of Doctor Schaffell.

Over the next twenty minutes, Schaffell went on to defend the company's products and to explain petty politics and budgetary implications, more especially in a post-Apartheid Rainbow nation.

Satisfied with her interview efforts and hopeful for a brighter future for the people of South Africa, Estelle made her way with her dad to his car. The day had stretched to the point of exhaustion.

The drive home was, for the most part, blanketed in silence with both father and daughter in their own agitated preoccupations. Their thoughts, though worlds apart, seemed set on a collision course. Recalling the overheard conversation, Estelle became increasingly disturbed. Her stomach churned with anxiety. Drained by a sequence of jumbled thoughts, she fell asleep.

Sam observed his sleeping daughter with heart-felt compassion. She mumbled something about the meeting, and a need for more answers. With her tiny body having taken such a king hit, it would be some time before she'd be her vibrant, effervescent self, and perhaps even longer before being well enough to handle the onerous demands of her career.

THE HIRSUTE HAND HELD the earpiece close to his ear. "No, I don't think this will come to anything. How about our little friend?" He paused, listening intently. "So, no electronic footprint. OK. Keep me in the loop." Leaning back into his black leather chair, the corpulent executive clasped both hands behind his head and smiled with anticipatory satisfaction.

THAT NIGHT, ESTELLE TOSSED and turned into the early hours. Her heart pounded loudly. She felt barely able to breathe. Her palms poured with sweat. Her gut churned with an ominous knowing. It appeared the one man she had looked up to her entire life could be involved in some kind of cover-up. She questioned whether she really knew her father or was just bound to him by blind loyalty.

She had to find this mysterious 'forgotten has-been' who was in some kind of danger. And what of the archived data? Perhaps she'd start by making her way to the main laboratory. Her attention turned to Angelica. She'd become aware of how much she was missing her. She hoped to see her the following day before her check-up.

THE PREVIOUS NIGHT'S QUESTIONING somewhat faded, Estelle began second-guessing herself. Perhaps she had taken things out of context. Her father was a decent and ethical man who had worked hard his entire life providing for her and giving her a solid education. Where would she be without him? At the very least she owed him the benefit of the doubt.

Strolling through the well-manicured hospital gardens, Estelle realised it was too early for her check-up, so she made her way towards the cafeteria.

"Hey there!" came a familiar voice from behind her as Estelle stood at the counter. Instantly her heart melted.

"Hi." With a soft, feminine smile, she turned to face him, barely able to maintain her composure.

"Breakfast?" invited the young Afro-Aussie.

"Ah, yeah, breakfast." she echoed awkwardly. It was as if some helpless, flaky female had taken over her entire being.

"Can I interest you in joining me? I take it this place is a favourite haunt. I've seen you here before." He grinned cheekily.

"Oh, ah, sorry, ah, must rush: medical check-up." She scurried out like a shy, love-struck schoolgirl and was relieved to run into Angelica. "Damn! I just blew it," she muttered.

"What? Cat got ye tongue?" chortled the Sister.

"Perfect opportunity staring me in the face: just let it slip away."

"'Tis never too late, me girl." Angelica motioned her back with a warm smile and open palm.

Estelle turned just in time to see him make his way straight out the door, and perhaps straight out of her life. "Bugger!" she moaned.

Despondency gave way to good cheer as Angelica put her arm around Estelle's waist. She had something special to show her. There had been a poem left behind by someone deceased at the hospital:

> Travelling through time and space
> He knew that girl before.
> Ever haunted by her face
> Searching tomorrow for a time before.
>
> Beckoned by the longing of his heart
> Entranced by the call of his soul

A lonely voyager standing well apart
For in finding her, he would again be whole.

Her gentle voice echoing so tender
She awaits his return by day and by night
Tracing back memories he could barely remember
She watched and guided with her bright burning light

Soon to return to a time of yesteryear
Faint recollections dancing upon his mind.
Each enchanting encounter held preciously dear
Relentlessly seeking, determined to find.

Making his way back to her mysterious essence
Never distant nor forgotten, his heart felt desire
Longing for just one more moment, her graceful presence
Her memory: His twin flame and eternal fire.

Estelle stood quietly taking it in. "He must have truly loved her."

"I'm sure he still does, to be sure. Love never dies," replied Angelica wistfully.

Waiting for her check-up, Estelle was only too happy to spend some cherished moments with her dear friend, talking, sharing, laughing, and just seeing an entirely different side of life.

Finally Estelle stood patiently before the cardiology registrar who poked, probed and quizzed her.

"How am I doing?"

"I'm pleased to say your pericardial effusion, at least, is ninety per cent resolved and we're generally pleased with your progress. It seems the morning's suit you best," reassured the young Indian registrar.

LATER THAT DAY, ESTELLE winged back to the Sanctuary. Spending more time there had fast become her norm, and besides, the comic relief encouraged her to lighten up. Perhaps the more enlightened had indeed learnt to take life a little more lightly. Nan had a cherished piece of art in a decorative gold frame. It was an angel with the caption 'The reason angels can fly is because they take themselves lightly.' And sure enough, Estelle had again stepped into comedy hour.

"Yes, yes, I know dear. Sorry, dear, I didn't quite hear what you said. There seems to be quite a lot of noise at your end of the line. It sounds like rosary beads rattling. What did you say, dear? Oh, I need to be burnt at the stake for making your poor boy 'washed-brain'. Oh, I see. Yes. Yes, dear. You go on praying. I'm sure that sooner or later you will make God an offer he can't refuse." Rolling her eyes, Esther wrote on a piece of paper for Estelle to read: 'Cold-blooded murder is the order of the day.' "Oh, I see, he couldn't think properly after he married me. Well, dear, I suggest that your son has a prosthetic brain and you forgot to put it back in for him. What? A prosthetic brain! You no understand? Well, perhaps if it's not being used, he can lend it to you. After all, he doesn't use it all that often. Now I must go, dear. Do take care of yourself and don't strain too hard."

Putting the phone down, Esther looked up. "Back to see me, darling? How are we feeling today?" she asked with gentle concern.

"Feeling brighter," assured Estelle, stepping aside in order to allow Nan to continue with her business.

Esther took a deep breath before calmly proceeding to attend to one of her die-hard devotees who had been patiently waiting for her to finish her telephone conversation.

"Don't tell me. Let me see. Let me see," butted in the tall, flamboyant male client in his early fifties. Teasingly, he put his index finger to his head as if tuning in. "Mother-in-law—again?"

"Well, Jim, you know Frank—half man, half mother: needs some Viagra eye-drops so he can take a long hard look at himself."

"That bad?" he teased.

"Lord, grant me patience, but hurry. And if you can't hurry," sighed Esther, "grant me a wish: that Frank and his mother resemble nothing more than a blank space in a room next court session. Better still, Lord, have both just stay the hell away from me."

"I can't imagine why any of us would want to stay away from you!" responded her gangly client mischievously.

"Nor can I," interjected Estelle, laughing.

"You see. We all just want a piece of you," quipped her client with exaggerated body movements.

"Nice to see you're still at least able to laugh," smiled Esther, reaching for Jim's hand.

"Laugh and the world laughs at you," he replied, warmly returning her hand squeeze.

"Well, what piece of me would you like today? Is it my enlightened mind, my spiritual genius, or my body that nowadays has a mind of its own?" replied Esther rambunctiously.

"Pleezze! I wish to be enlightened by your spiritual genius."

"Well, I'm sure I have that on today's menu, fresh with a side serve of divine patience and universal understanding!"

"Don't forget the generous garnish of insanity that also comes with each serving!" Estelle quipped.

"Though you know what they say; there's a fine line between genius and insanity." Esther laughed.

As if on cue, a reader sauntered in for his afternoon shift. It was Michael. Last time Estelle had seen him, he'd walked in sporting a patch over one of his eyes in order to strengthen the opposite hemisphere of his brain!

"Just wait till I set up my cubicle," Michael announced excitedly. "I've got to fill you in on last night's love-making!"

"Oh, do tell," encouraged the client, leaning in Michael's direction.

"There was an incredible twist at the peak of our connection. It was so intense that I dematerialised," he announced, barely stopping to take a breath.

"Where's the bloody moon today?" bellowed Esther, lifting her eyes to the heavens.

"Straightforward enough! A genius might at least want to stick around for the action." Estelle suspected that even for Nan, Michael was a little more on the fringe than even she could cope with at times. Still she proclaimed Michael to be a superb reader with a following that would often travel across state just to take in an hour of his insightful, spiritual counsel.

"A hard act to follow, I'd imagine," replied Esther dryly.

"Insanely twisted," muttered Estelle.

"More twists than a corkscrew," mumbled Esther as she gathered the late afternoon mail.

"Heard that," retorted Michael.

Within twenty minutes, the afternoon readers had converged in the kitchen to contemplate life and extrapolate spiritual cures for the planet and all its occupants as they sipped on their hot beverages.

Esther sat sifting through mail, noting a bill she'd overlooked. "Final notice! Thank God! I won't be hearing from them again. By the way, please, dear, go a little easier on your clients today. Remember a little tact goes a long way. And besides, I may be too busy to pick them up off the floor and fluff them up before they leave the premises after your consultation," instructed Esther without lifting her eyes.

"Honesty is the best policy. Besides, tact is a luxury that neither I, nor many of my clients can afford," riposted Amanda. A psychic in her late sixties, Amanda had seen so much of the world that she had become somewhat jaded and couldn't be bothered with wishy-washy, wimpy approaches.

"Check this out!" demanded Roberta, the iridologist, flicking through a news rag. She began reading aloud: "News poll reveals extent of concerns over mandatory reporting. Medical defence organisations have previously warned that reporting laws could see innocent practitioners on the receiving end of vexatious claims."

"Yes, interesting. That'll keep all the good little boys and girls under control. Wonder where this will go?" replied Esther curtly.

"Surely the public need to be protected from shonky doctors," interjected Estelle.

"Mandatory anything is all about control," responded Esther. "Medicine has drifted from being a healing profession to providing a policing function for their corporate clients." She cast a sharp look in Roberta's direction. The mood took a sudden shift as a loud, angry silence darkened the room.

"What is it, Nan?" Estelle frowned.

"It's a legal letter from Frank's sue-and-screw team, hot on the scorched-earth policy." muttered Esther.

"And angling to have you bankrupt? He's so busy trying to push you over the edge that he isn't seeing just how close he is to it himself," volunteered Amanda, tuning in.

"Divorce is easy. Settlement is hard!" groaned Esther. "Prat! Needs to hang a mirror at the end of his bed so he can wake up to himself. Bastard thinks that with all those letters after his name, he's a law unto himself." Raising her octave, Esther continued her ranting, then reached for her tarot cards. "Calabrese with a gun! Thinks he's the one calling the shots! Frank and his friggin' legal team. Law without justice, I tell you!"

Silence fell as Esther studied the cards.

"You OK, Nan?"

"Right! Off we go!" The old lady was livid.

At the foot of the building, Nan flew out in a cyclonic dash, collecting crowds of pedestrians while sweeping small children off their feet.

"Where we off to?" Estelle had barely caught her breath.

"I'll fix the bastard."

In no time at all, they were both standing in line at Nan's bank, Esther's ever-increasing irritability and impatience almost audible.

"Finally!" Esther marched stridently towards the teller, Estelle in tow.

"How can I help you, madam?"

"About time! I've been waiting in that far queue way too bloody long. I want this account frozen—now!" she sternly instructed the teller as she handed over her account details.

"For what purpose do you require this account frozen, madam?" inquired the teller politely.

"My ex-husband is about to embezzle over sixty thousand in funds," declared Esther dramatically.

The bank teller's expression said it all. Nutter! The reply on Nan's face also said it all. I hope you die a slow and insidious death if you don't immediately do what I ask.

"So far your funds are well in order, madam." Almost immediately, the teller double-blinked and pulled back from the screen.

"You look like you've just seen a ghost, dear." Esther frowned in morbid anticipation.

The teller signalled for the attention of her colleague. Whispering, the two stood mesmerised by the screen for what seemed an eternity.

"I'll just see if our manager, Mr Perish, is available," replied the first teller, unable to shift her focus from the screen.

Mr Perish was aptly named, according to Esther, given the regular rise in interest rates.

"Welcome." Mr Perish ushered them in obsequiously. "There seems to have been a remarkable coincidence this afternoon! Funds were removed from your account just as you stood at the counter requesting to have them frozen."

Leaning forward with calm and deliberation reserved only for bank managers, solicitors and real estate agents, Esther spoke. "I strongly suggest you follow the money trail."

What followed was a series of questions and answers from Perish to Esther, and Esther to Perish, as they worked to help resolve the matter.

Outside, Nan roared with laughter. "What's the point of it all if we forget to laugh?"

"I guess EQ is every bit as important as IQ?" Estelle joined in the laughter.

THE BLOOD RED S-CLASS Mercedes with tinted windows pulled up in a cloud of red dust, the engine kept running. Getting out of his equally dusty bakkie, the elderly African in a crumpled suit walked over to be ushered into the back seat of the humming Mercedes.

"Molo, comrade," greeted the high-cheekboned patrician elder, grasping the old man's hand, "my apologies for the informality of this meeting."

The quiet hum of the engine muffled out the confidential conversation, lasting two, possibly three minutes.

Having got out of the car, the old man stood awaiting the departure of the dusty Mercedes. His patrician elder raised his right fist.

"Aluta continua," replied the old African, his posture now remarkably erect.

The Mercedes moved off gently, mitigating the red dust cloud in its wake.

ESTELLE SCANNED HER SCREEN for information relating to the international network of laboratories owned by her father's company. Anticipating her licence being reinstated, Estelle tucked into bed with a plan to drive out and investigate the main laboratory.

The following day investigations came to an abrupt dead end. The intensely guarded research facility with it's pristine façade was not only off-limits to the prying eyes of the general public, but totally impervious to investigative journalists. Though she wasn't about to lay claim to any of her grandmother's abilities, Estelle felt an ominous vibe about the place.

Propelled by a nagging sense of ambiguity, Estelle retraced her steps later that night. Her inconspicuously parked car was hidden from the facility's view by a perfectly maintained hedge. The crisp midnight air, along with the rush of adrenalin, kept her hyper-vigilant to any potential dangers. Several towering, ghost-like trees provided shadow from the full moon overhead as menacing storm clouds threatened to obliterate the lunar brilliance. The ancient, silvery face asserted its right to spy upon the night. Pitiful howls of dogs crying for mercy filled the darkness.

The howls subsided, leaving the sanitised landscape to the silent illumination of man's oldest witness. Estelle held her breath, listening to the wind whispering through the trees. A bright spotlight shone on the company's proud shield: 'To Defend Humanity'.

A shadowy form in balaclava and gloves emerged from the building's exit. Estelle struggled to identify the solitary figure as it disappeared to the rear of the facility. Impulsively she set off in pursuit of a departing vehicle, undaunted as she followed the fleeing taillights through a maze of streets, lanes and alleyways.

Finally the car came to a halt outside an old brownstone apartment block. Without thought, Estelle ventured into the building, darting through a door left slightly ajar. Suddenly she found herself inside a dimly lit ground floor apartment. Her heart pounded like an African voodoo drum. She feared he might hear her breathe. She slipped into a dark, well-concealed corner of the room. Holding her breath, she hid motionless next to a bookcase. The shadowy figure made his way into the next room. Estelle stood frozen, regretting her impulsiveness. Scheming to make her way out, she was startled by the sound of his mobile. Re-entering the room and speaking with his back to her, she recognised a vague familiarity in his voice. Paralysed, she tried harder to control her breathing.

"All set to go. Got metal cutters? Right. Spoke to the others. Problems with security all seen to." A silent pause followed as he moved towards a window, allowing more visibility courtesy of a streetlight. "Two a.m. sharp. Staff all left."

Estelle took in what looked like degrees framed on a wall. She noticed a carved wooden box beneath a windowsill where he'd placed his black gloves and balaclava.

"Enter from back lane. Park vans closest to the left side entrance: will send a signal on approach." The faceless male ended the call and exited the room. Estelle lunged out the door, knocking several books off the shelf. Loud, heavy footsteps followed as she lengthened her stride towards her car. Leaping in, she sped off into the fog.

Who was he? Estelle racked her brains to identify the voice. What was he doing around the research facility? Was he one of the scientists? Did her dad know him? Was he connected to Wolf's threats?

Desperate to stop obsessive thoughts burning her circuits, she turned on late night radio to some random monologue: "Are you one of the millions of modern-day sleepwalkers treading through life, moving through a fog of other people's thoughts? What seductive messages are being drip-fed into modern-day consciousness? By whom, and why? Who is buying your silent obedience? Are you ready to awaken from this drip-fed state of consciousness?"

STARTLED, ESTELLE AWOKE TO find an open smile and warm brown eyes gazing down upon her: in the background, the sound of a television.

"What a beautiful day to be released back out into the world."

Taking in her bearings, Estelle realised she was in an all-too-familiar room being smiled at by an all-too-familiar nurse in an all-too-familiar uniform.

A little dazed, and struggling to get her bearings, Estelle dressed to reunite with the world. She gingerly made her way to the Nurses' Station where she was given discharge papers to sign.

"Is Sister Angelica here today?"

"Angelica? Sorry, Miss Goldstein, we don't have a Sister Angelica here at present."

Bemused by the response, Estelle pressed on with her request. "You know, the wise, blue-eyed Irish nurse who was in charge of looking after me."

"I'm sorry, Miss Goldstein, surely you must be thinking of someone else. There is no Sister Angelica on this ward."

"But I spent a great deal of time with her."

"Are you sure?" requested the young ward clerk.

"Of course I'm sure. How can I not be, after all this time with her looking after me?"

As she approached from the far end of the ward, a nursing sister greeted Estelle, smiling warmly. "Hello, Miss Goldstein: everything OK? It's a wonderful day for going home: a fresh start."

"Miss Goldstein was just enquiring about a nursing sister," piped up the young ward clerk.

"I'd like to get in touch with Sister Angelica."

"Sister Angelica?" parroted the nursing sister.

"You know: caring Irish sister about mid-forties with lots of great advice—umm, wiser than the world. She was appointed to my care and loves her rose garden on the other side of the nurses' quarters," explained Estelle intently.

"Are you sure?" questioned the sister with raised eyebrows.

"Not you too; of course I'm sure!" insisted Estelle.

The perturbed nursing sister folded her arms across her chest, her right hand gripping the clipboard. "Sister Angelica?"

Sighting the desk calendar, the young clerk announced, "It's so hard to believe. It's a year to the day."

"A year to what day?" Estelle frowned.

Led to the familiar hospital garden where Angelica claimed to rest, Estelle stood silently by the sister's side as she read the details inscribed on the memorial plaque:

Angelica Lucius

21.6.1959-9.06.2002.

Angel in disguise.

Uncontrollable tears streamed down Estelle's bewildered face. Slowly she was led back to the Nurses' Station.

PRATTLING ON, WITHOUT SO much as taking a breath, Esther assisted Estelle to load her bag into the boot. Hesitantly Estelle climbed into the passenger's side. As Esther put her key in the ignition, Estelle glanced back over her shoulder.

"Wait! This is crazy," she cried, leaping out.

"Unfinished business, sweet pea?" uttered Esther in a gentle and understanding voice.

Making her way back to the Nurse's Station, Estelle excitedly began to interrogate the nurses, requesting information on the dark-skinned young man that kept visiting someone in the ward. Perplexed by her intrusive behaviour, the ward clerk and nursing sister tried to calm her by asking for further information. Neither knowing his name, nor that of the patient he was visiting, they were unable to assist her.

Deciding to take matters into her own hands, Estelle discreetly began criss-crossing from one room to the next, checking for a potential dark-skinned relative. Each time she exited with an awkward apology. Frustrated in her attempts, she stepped into the doorway of a room with curtains drawn around a bed to find a doctor doing an abdominal examination.

"Sorry, just needed to see something for myself."

Backing out, she bumped into a small child larking about in the hallway. Squatting down to eyeball the child, Estelle cajoled her as she pointed towards a room opposite.

"Hey, kid, come here. Can you tell me if there are any dark people in that room?"

Distressed, the small child rushed back into the room, flying directly into her father's protective arms, just about collecting the tea lady on the way in. Pointing towards the corridor, she said, "Daddy, there's a scary lady out there. She wants me to find dark people."

Having noticed the confusion, Estelle was offered further assistance by a passing nurse.

"Just looking for someone. You know, large hospital and all: a little confusing at the best of times. Seems people here just vanish into thin air."

She was encouraged to follow the nurse back to the Nurse's Station for further assistance. Enlisting her powers of persuasion, Estelle stood in front of a nurse at her computer. With pleading eyes, she fired off a round of questions. With wide-eyed disbelief, they listened to Estelle's rant. "Just someone tell me. I need to know. This man! Is he real or not? Perhaps I could speak to his relative in this ward."

"Like we've already explained to you, Miss Goldstein, privacy laws don't allow us."

"I don't need to hear about another death for today. Please tell me he is real."

The nurses looked at each other in bewilderment, then at Estelle, dazed and speechless as she started to pinch her own skin. "See! I mean does he have a human body that feels just like this?" Estelle looked at the nurses, begging with her eyes. "We're human, aren't we, or have I missed something vital today, apart from the fact that people, that are supposed to be alive and stop me from dying, are actually dead? Or at least can you give me an explanation about any other dimension that he may exist on?"

Turning to her colleague, one of the nurses uttered under her breath, "When was she due for release?"

"You guys don't seem to get it. I met my soul mate while I was in hospital and I have fallen really hard."

"On what?" challenged one of the exasperated nurses.

Estelle spun on the spot, up in arms.

"Looks like she's certainly checked out," muttered the ward clerk.

"Oh God, what if he has taken my heart to another dimension. It's quite OK. I don't care. I can live the rest of my life in his dimension." Estelle slowly moved a couple of steps away from the desk as another patient pulled in, wheeling a drip stand behind him. Taking a deep breath, Estelle quietly composed herself. "I am a rational person. I am a journalist and I help sway public opinion."

"God help the public," murmured the nurse.

"I will investigate all of this and prove to you good nurses that my soul mate visited regularly. I feel totally connected to him. He even asked me for breakfast."

Hesitantly, the male patient leaned over the desk. "What side effects do my medications have?"

They all watched in dismay as Estelle headed for the elevator. One of the nurses asked her colleague, "Can we start to write our own prescriptions any day soon, because I sure as hell feel woozy."

With the elevator door shutting behind her, an adjoining elevator door opened and a small group of people made their way out, including a tall, dark-skinned young man.

Chapter Six

Stepping out of her bathrobe, Estelle took a long, hard look at the pitiful body reflected back in the privacy of her own room. The small mirror in her hospital bathroom had mercifully spared her the shameful image in her full-length mirror, harshly magnified by a skylight. She looked like a skeleton clothed in skin, a clean-shaven pig ready for slaughter. She traced the thick, purple, two-inch scar running mid-line from her ribcage down. Timidly turning side on, she felt the hollowing between her ribs.

"Oh God!" She grimaced. Having a big butt was a problem, but having no butt at all was embarrassing. She pulled back her lacklustre hair and stared despairingly at her droopy boobs. Balancing on her weakened legs, she looked down at her wrinkled, aching feet. Even they had lost their youthful fullness. Sliding on a pair of previously tightly hugging jeans, Estelle was grateful they hid her scrawny frame.

Having been suspended for weeks between the forces of life and death, Estelle faced the same polarities emotionally and physically. Time and again she would find herself sobbing as she lay at the mercy of her wasted body. Often she felt as though she was waging a spiritual tug-of-war against a merciless God with whom she could not reconcile. Morally defeated and temporarily deflated, the next wave of energy and enthusiasm would build, only to break on the hard shore of reality. With each upswing, Estelle resolved to regain her freedom and independence. She'd grown used to the secure confinement of her single-bed hospital room with the constant flow of loved ones and staff attending to her every whim. Now she was alone for days on end, overwhelmed by the large open spaces as she shuffled about from one room to the next.

Today she was determined to lengthen her walking distance. Edging her way to the end of the block, Estelle inhaled the cool winter air. It was good to be finally breaking out. Winter solstice was looming and her legs needed a good stretch. She breathed deeply. Her initial increased exertions were tempered by an ominous awareness of a constriction as each deep breath felt restrained by fine elastic tentacles in her chest. It was as if fibrous cobwebs were covetous of her expanding heart.

LEANING OVER NAN'S BALCONY, Estelle slowly sipped on her warm lemon water. Below, Nan was fast surrounded by local cats of all shapes, colours and sizes. Competitively they inhaled the food as she dished it out. She gently picked up the scrawniest and gave it a special feed, helping it to gain a competitive edge. Rising to her feet, Esther turned to show affection to a dog barking for attention from his backyard.

"There, there, mate," she soothed, gently patting the lonely animal through a gap in the pickets. "Each species needs its own companion," she lamented as she made her way back into her home.

"You won't heal without a healthy breakfast," Esther's voice echoed as she juggled her way from the kitchen and her own pack, muffins in one hand and Marvin's feed in the other.

"Blueberry muffins. Yum!" Estelle's appetite was stimulated by the scrumptious aroma wafting up in front of her. Esther's nutritious vegetarian meals were fast doing the trick, allowing Estelle to slowly gain weight, gram by gram.

"I've made an appointment for you with Doctor Collette," called out Nan, simultaneously feeding the orphan galah in the room adjacent. "Soon ready for the wild, old boy?"

"But I've—"

"No buts. Collette is one of a kind," cut in Nan, closing the door behind her.

"I'm quite alright to—"

"She's seen me through the darkest of days," continued Nan as she made her way back into her cluttered, but otherwise tidy lounge room.

ESTELLE FOUND DOCTOR COLLETTE unusually open for a conventional doctor. It quickly became apparent that Collette's style was holistic patient care with a tendency to steer away from a symptom suppression-only method.

"You've probably had an episode of delirium. Nothing to be alarmed about," reassured the fit, attractive forty-three-year-old blonde as she listened attentively, curious and without judgement.

Estelle sighed, releasing the tightness from her shoulders.

"I once had a la-la land experience up in Papua New Guinea as a student. Dose of malaria, as it turned out. Any high fever can do it, and it looks like the Rifampicin has knocked your liver around," continued Collette as she checked Estelle's results on her computer. "She'll be right."

Focusing her attention on Collette's well-ordered desk, Estelle took an even deeper breath. "Sounds promising." She exhaled.

Collette reached across to Estelle's hand. "In the meantime, there's nothing like a good dose of woman."

"What?" Estelle frowned.

Collette obliged Estelle's curiosity, jotting down the acronym: Water, Oxygen, Meditation, Alkalinity, Nutrition.

"Looks like your zinc/copper ratio is a bit down. Ratio of 0.47: ideally 1.0. Some zinc and vitamin C combo, once a day, won't do you any harm and will enhance your immune system. And with your mother's history, you really should come off the Pill: drops your zinc/copper ratio. Carcinogenic effects can hang around for ten to fifteen years. Perhaps we can deal with that next visit." Collette pulled back, noting Estelle's frown.

"And the cobwebs in my chest every time I take a breath?"

"Your heart sounds were OK. I imagine you have some threads of scar tissue between your heart and lungs. This scar tissue will contract and stretch over a period of time, just like the one under your breastbone. It'll resolve in a few months: don't worry. Here's your referral to the cardiologist at St Vincent's."

Meeting Collette's eyes, Estelle smiled in gratitude. "Thanks."

"No worries. Give me a call if you need me. Here's my mobile." Collette handed Estelle her card. "Till you're out of the woods, that is." Collette paused long enough to ensure that her patient had absorbed the advice. "And one last thing: don't overdo it." Collette smiled. "Remember if you're too busy to laugh, you're too busy. Take a walk in the sunshine. Smell the roses."

ESTELLE DILIGENTLY PUT COLLETTE'S good advice into practice and within weeks was able to see noticeable improvements, especially in the restoration of her somewhat sallow hospital complexion back to a youthful glow.

Finally the day came when she triumphantly made the distance to Rose Bay Pier, less than a kilometre from home. Breaking out into the world, Estelle felt the sun beaming down on her face as she breathed in the invigorating harbour air. She could smell the faint scent of fresh seaweed offsetting the rich aroma of coffee at the pier cafe.

Estelle was in love with life again and overjoyed as she sheepishly renewed her God membership and begrudgingly called a truce with the Greater Intelligence. After all, she thought, who knows when she might next need to call upon her services? That's where Nan came in with her own inimitable style. She tactfully left a CD by Maryanne Williamson amongst Estelle's belongings. '*A Return to Love*' from A Course in Miracles was just the reassuring tonic Estelle needed to soothe her insomnia.

Estelle's ever-increasing loneliness drove her to beg Alex to restart her work schedule, against Collette's advice. Alex finally gave way with some misgivings. Concerned the company distance itself from any liability relating to Estelle's illness, she agreed to flick her protégé a little work, mainly from home, with a negligible number of office hours.

ESTELLE SETTLED INTO HER workstation, opening up the news. House of Commons in the UK had legislated to ban fox hunting.

Whoopee! Estelle silently cheered. Nan would be pleased.

World Meteorological Organisation publication: recent extreme weather may mark the beginning of changes in global climate caused by global warming.

"Someone's wiped my bookmarks. Damn!" she grumbled, rummaging around her desk for her files.

Estelle re-read an extensively modified article that had been completed and published by Alex, on her behalf, following her admission to hospital. Though grateful her article had been well received, giving strong acknowledgement and recognition to both herself and Alex, of course, for Estelle this was only the beginning. She could feel the tension in her chest.

"I've been away for less than three months and bookmarks on my computer have been deleted, print-offs have gone missing, USBs seem to vanish, only to turn up again. How can I research, for God's sake, when I can't leave anything unattended?" snapped Estelle as she stood before Alex, her hands on her hips.

"OK. Agree, Estelle." Alex motioned Estelle to take a seat. "It's been less than three months, but that's a long time in journalism." Her boss curtly peered over the rim of her glasses.

Estelle shut the door and sat herself down opposite Alex. "I'm sorry. I do appreciate you publishing my article."

"Our article, with you as first author—OK?" Alex reminded her, arching back in her chair, locking her hands behind her head. "Are you sure you're not getting ahead of yourself. When are you due for your next check-up?"

"Not for a month, but I think I can manage half a day a week." Estelle took care to recalibrate her tone, slowing the pace of her words.

"OK. Take your time. Your first AIDS article was a spectacular success—with my input, of course. How's about a follow up? You can research from home. You've got some contacts, have you not?"

CHEWING IT OVER, ESTELLE knew only too well, from her own personal experience, the wonders of modern day medicine and its life-saving drugs on which her life had depended, a stark contrast to the fate of the countless families in South Africa devastated by the cruel hand that had dealt them the death penalty of AIDS. The bittersweet truth: it was purely her position of privilege that had spared her a life cut short. What of little Innocence with her soulful eyes? Perhaps she had been long buried.

Underpinning all life force is an instinctive drive for survival, surely the birth right of every individual inhabiting the planet. She knew the unpalatable truth is that birth right is little more than a roll of the dice, a consequence of birthplace. All men are born equal? Not! The bottom line is survival of the fittest. Or is it biggest? That equates to little more than word power and voting power where it counts—in the cash till. I am a voice that votes, she proposed. Surely the people of Africa are as deserving of quality health care as my privileges have afforded me.

Estelle gritted her teeth. Her diligence in getting the word out had become an obsession. She was determined to try to help foster a ground swell of political action to push the pharmaceutical industries to provide cheaper access to antiretrovirals.

"And bugger the patents," she muttered.

Her almost manic focus on facts and stats had an unacknowledged secondary gain, helping shield her from the obsessive, unwelcomed and unwanted questions percolating beneath her consciousness. Who was he? Did he even exist? Why were the tormenting ghostly visions of this stranger so insistent on living rent-free in her head? Whatever the case, it, he, had served as a means to awaken her heart that had been walled off both physically and metaphysically.

"Damn it, Estelle! Stop being so goddamn delusional," she chided. "The man of your dreams is fast driving you insane. What a nightmare." From a fight for life to a fight for sanity, she thought wryly.

Then there was Angelica. Was she indeed some kind of guardian angel who had visited her in her hour of need, or just a figment of her imagination? Estelle paused for a moment, long enough to take a breath and regain her bearings in the room. She felt the spider's web around her heart and the pressure building again in her chest. She'd overstretched herself and needed to head home for peace, solitude and healing. She could handle an increasingly lengthy walk, but just couldn't handle the work stress she'd previously thrived on.

Her full recovery period seemed interminable. Nature, for the most part, was asleep within the coldest of winters and its howling nights. The days grew shorter and Estelle more restless. She had become increasingly fond of walking, braving the elements and the chilly sea breeze blowing off Rose Bay.

Walking home along Rose Bay esplanade, Estelle spotted something stirring on New South Head Road, thirty metres ahead. As she neared the spot, she identified the graceful movements as those of a tiny tortoiseshell kitten rolling on the road. From a distance the dark fur of the vulnerable critter blended into the bitumen, lit only by yellow fog lights.

"Come on, sweetheart, get off the road before you're hit," murmured Estelle gently as she bent over to pick up the feline. Stroking it, she tenderly placed the purring critter on the footpath.

Estelle continued to walk, the kitten following, right across the bay side esplanade. Her first impulse was to ignore it, then shoo it, then ignore it some more, then hasten her pace, and then shoo it again. Estelle's ever-increasing concern that the kitten would not recall its way home was to no avail, as it followed her to her door. Sensing she was in the clear, Estelle smuggled the little creature into her quarters.

NEXT EVENING FOUND SAM relaxing with a copy of The Economist, enjoying a glass of chardonnay, when he suddenly became aware of the covert addition to the house preening up against his leg.

"What? What's this fleabag doing in our lounge room?" he demanded, flicking the playful kitten away with his foot.

Estelle scurried away from the dishes and into the living space. "Oh, Dad! Be gentle," she insisted as she stooped to pick up the kitten.

"Gentle?" Narrowing his eyes, Sam grunted.

"She, Mellow, followed me home," replied Estelle, stroking Mellow under the chin.

"Mellow?" asked Sam, cringing at the kitten's loud purr. "Who does it belong to?" Removing his glasses, Sam hastily began polishing them.

"Me. I'm the new owner!" Estelle announced defiantly. "The vet traced her address through her microchip: a deceased estate." Estelle continued to stroke Mellow, allowing her to snuggle into her cardigan.

"New owner?" Sam ceased polishing his glasses. "This is your grandmother coming out in you! We'll have her moving in next," he moaned as he recommenced polishing his glasses, intermittently checking for grit. "Better still; let your grandmother have it. She doesn't seem to mind the smell, and animals slobbering around at dinner, or her lounge being used as a scratching post!"

"Oh, Dad, chill out. Besides, it's all a bit of overkill, refusing to share meals at Nan's place."

"Overkill? You need a tetanus shot just to fight your way inside the front door!"

Mellow's sleepy purr increased by several decibels, causing Sam's cringing to intensify.

"My new best friend!" Estelle defiantly held the kitten closer.

"Fine: just not in the house. We don't need cat fluff and cat piss all over the carpets," Sam grumbled. Putting his glasses back on, he dived back into his journal.

THE POURING RAIN WHITEWASHED Alex's car as she braved the elements on her way to a meeting with Estelle. Waiting patiently in a cosy downtown café, Estelle jotted relevant details in her small notebook while reformatting her article.

With a slow, pondering glance, she lifted her head just in time to catch a glimpse of a dark-skinned young stranger sheltering under a black umbrella as he walked briskly on the opposite side of the road. Springing to her feet without warning, Estelle sent the scalding tea flying across the room. She leapt out the door, through a sea of umbrellas, and into oncoming traffic. Swept by the angry tempest, she came within a whisker of collision as she was blown towards the bonnet of a car.

"Hey, lady! Got a death wish?" shouted the angry driver in his sixties, waving his hands about in the air.

Unconscious of the man's rage, her focus remained on reaching the anonymous stranger. As if in slow motion, Estelle watched as a beautiful, dark-haired young woman sporting a red umbrella approached from the opposite direction. With an instant kiss, the umbrellas united as one, and with that, he put his arm around her and they vanished behind a rolling billboard that read: I'd rather go naked than wear fur. Dazed, Estelle stood on the curve, wet, and feeling just as emotionally naked, watching as the two faded from view, never quite revealing their faces.

Estelle and Alex sat at a window table sipping their hot beverages, looking on as cars did a Strauss waltz, sloshing through the wet.

"He's the last thing I think about before I go to sleep and the first thought I wake up with," volunteered Estelle sheepishly.

"Sounds special: do tell," requested Alex, narrowing her focus.

"I don't know. I'm so goddamn confused. I can't get him out of my head." The tormented look in her eyes was a testimonial to her emotional disquiet.

"I'm always up for a hot romance. Who is he? What's he like?" urged Alex attentively, leaning further forward.

"He's gentle and strong at the same time: has the warmest, beaming smile, the most perfectly sculptured six-foot-plus body." Estelle beamed.

"All in proportion?" solicited Alex.

"His eyes exude confidence, yet there's a vulnerability about him—the man of my dreams," sighed Estelle.

"He sounds too good to be true."

"Mmm. Like I could almost reach out and touch him," continued Estelle with a dreamy, faraway look.

"How come you haven't come out with it earlier, girl? How long has this been going on? The suspense is killing me."

Slipping further into a trance, Estelle reached for the sugar, knocking her tea into a swirl, spilling some. "I'm so in love. Damn it!"

"Just give me his name and vital stats," cajoled the experienced older woman.

"I don't know his name."

Alex leaned back into her chair. "Hmmm: anonymous sexuality? Intriguing; I could be up for that. Now, the vital stats—please continue." Alex rubbed her hands together in anticipation.

Playing with her spoon, Estelle looked wistfully out the window onto the glistening street with its sea of umbrellas and slowly replied, "I can't fill you in on much. All I know is that he is my soul mate."

"Aah! I get it. He's married." Alex sat attentively waiting.

"Not sure. He may be married, or he may not be."

"Minor detail." Alex shrugged with a half-smile. "Although kids can get in the way," cautioned the older veteran.

"I don't recall seeing a wedding band: don't know if he has any children."

"Hmm, I'm starting to see the attraction."

"You do?"

"Sure: the strong, elusive, secretive type."

The women sat in silence for a moment. Estelle, lost in thought, stared out of the water-blurred window. Alex sat studying Estelle's face.

Suddenly Estelle snapped her attention back to Alex. "Oh, one other thing; I'm not sure if he's dead or alive, or if he even exists."

"Hetero or gay?"

FEELING MORE RELAXED, ESTELLE researched online with her computer notebook balanced on her legs. Mellow had become competitive with the notebook, persistently attacking it, pouncing on the keyboard. The unnecessary document changes frequently ended with the screen question about saving the changes, to which Estelle sharply replied, "Of course I don't want to save the bloody changes. They were made by my cat, you fool!"

The gentle purring of little Mellow soothed the night gremlins and enhanced Estelle's deep, restful sleep. She often awoke to little Mellow perched up on her chest, her purring dissolving away the spider's web around her heart. Regaining more of her core strength, she had become increasingly productive and independent, and was finally beginning to flow more and struggle less.

Nan is right, she thought. Animals are healing!

DRESSED IN CANARY YELLOW with champagne in hand, triumphantly trotting into the Goldstein living room, Esther's elation had been dampened neither by tempest nor gale. The ink had fast-dried on her property settlement. "I have successfully averted every devious plan Frankenstein has viciously plotted for my demise!"

"I see." Sam grimaced, wide-eyed at the high-pitched clanging resonating from the garishly oversized gypsy symbols hanging from Esther's ear lobes.

"Good for you, Nan!" Estelle scurried about setting the table for the evening meal.

"Not bankrupt! I still have my business and my home," ranted the old lady, helping with one hand, glass of champagne in the other.

"Whole new chapter of your life about to commence, eh, Nan," asserted Estelle, placing a platter of lasagne on the table.

"God help husband number three," muttered Sam from behind his newspaper.

"Finally put that bastard out of my misery. Optimum health! Love of family and friends. Still a loyal following. And in spite of his best campaign efforts to all and sundry, I still have my well-earned reputation." Esther took a long, hard slurp from her glass. "Poor bastard might have spared himself the effort. Least we can now add two more letters after his name. BF: Bloody Fool!"

"May God have mercy on his weary soul," Sam quietly mumbled, clearing his throat as he approached the table.

"Unseasonal weather, eh, Nan?" deflected Estelle as the three sat to eat.

"You're suggesting that we still have seasons? Haley's Comet, 1986; that November we had the most unseasonal weather. The heavens poured without mercy. No one could quite believe it. We had always had such regular weather patterns. Very important time for the planet."

"Here we go," muttered Sam, slathering his bread with a thick coat of butter.

"Psychics, astrologers, and all wise ones speculated that there would be great changes brought to bear upon our planet as a consequence of its visit."

"You lot are an advertisement as to why we need to add lithium to our water supplies," grunted Sam.

"Dismiss me if you will. The insurance companies will prove me right!"

"So where's the logic? This is a crazy assertion."

"Oh Dad, you know Nan's a lateral thinker."

"My point precisely, sweet pea! Lateral thinking always provides us with a fuller perspective on life. Just like auras; look at them straight on and you won't see them," quipped the old lady.

"That sort of intrigues me a little more these days, I must confess. I've even attempted to see auras recently," revealed Estelle reluctantly, sipping on her water.

"Now just watch who you disclose this to, young lady, or the shrinks will force lithium on to you too!" Sam frowned.

"Your father may be right there. Always keep your wits about you. Left brain for linear thinking: connects us to the practical world. That's what our five senses are for. Right brain for lateral thinking: connects us to the abstract world. Our sixth sense is the fine tuning of our other five senses," rambled the old crone. "God didn't give us two hemispheres by chance. Anyone who uses half a brain is a half-wit."

Sam shook his head and reached for another glass of red.

"One thing's for sure. Our left-brained education system marginalises right-brained kids and makes them feel inferior. I will never stop applauding those in right-brained professions like artists, psychics and storytellers: all those professions that require imagination and lateral thinking. Just look at Elton John. Now there's a gift to the world!"

"Well, let's agree on that," sighed Sam, hands held up in surrender.

The trio went quiet, each to their own as they savoured the lasagne. Estelle quietly mulled over the puzzle of life: almost as confusing as the Rubik's cube. She searched for some meaning as to what might have happened to her during the course of her illness. Was it all just some bio-chemically induced delirium or had she slowed down her critical, analytical left brain, allowing her right brain to kick in? Another possibility: it might have been explained by Nan's theory of time. But how can all time be now, she questioned. Einstein may have understood that linear time was an illusion—but a comforting illusion? She wasn't altogether sure what she apprehended most; the shattering possibility that her mystery man and Angelica did not exist, or even worse—that they did.

"Oh, sweet pea, before I forget. Do you mind filling in at the desk for me tomorrow morning; I have a client's funeral to attend?" asked Nan, glancing in Sam's direction.

WITHOUT WARNING, ALBERT LUNGED at the reception desk, infuriated. "Just look at her, will you? Sits around reception dressed like a tart in outfits that start late and end early. Totally unprofessional! It's so distressing for me to tune in, knowing what the male clientele are thinking when they walk in looking for service," raved the fifty-four year old palmist, eyeing off Lena as she sat cross-legged on the reception lounge in a skirt short enough that it might have doubled as a belt.

"Drama queen", muttered Estelle under her breath. One didn't need Nan's gift to instantly recognise the true source of Albert's distress. At that moment a client walked in, requesting to consult with Lena. Estelle inhaled deeply, before letting out a sigh.

Albert rolled his eyes. "OK, Estelle, give me your palm and I'll read your destiny!"

Humouring him, Estelle offered her palm.

"Oh I see you have a Stevenson's birthmark," Albert dramatically announced as if performing to a gallery. "You, my dear child have been burnt before." He gently stroked a jagged, rope-like mark that ran across her left wrist. "Easy to understand why you shy away from your spirituality this time round."

With curiosity Estelle looked down at her birthmark. "Perhaps I prefer to rely on scientific validation," she dismissed.

"Self-preservation, more likely," informed Albert boldly. "The good news is that he's coming back for you."

"Who's coming back?" Estelle frowned.

"This time he won't let you down." he added, flouncing his arms about as he moved off to greet a client.

"Would you like me to look into your eyes?" suggested Roberta, magnifying glass in hand.

Estelle had a lot of time for Roberta's iridology skills. She was a grounded, well-read, sweet thirty-two-year old single mother who, unlike the rest, spoke the Queen's English. Estelle looked through the magnifying lens at the distorted eye studying her.

"Keep still and look into the distance. Just relax," requested Roberta soothingly. "Hmm. Hmm." Roberta periodically jotted notes against an iridology chart. "Your constitution is strong. Seems you may have a little defect in the upper chamber of your heart. My advice is you check this out with your cardiologist."

"Funny; my cardiologist didn't mention it," replied Estelle.

"I suspect he'll only see this from behind the heart." Roberta put her lens down. "You know you're lucky to get this done right now. I've just been made aware the system is trying to force us out of the market. There is a proposal for a scheme to bring herbalists, naturopaths, acupuncturists, and the rest of us under the so-called rubric of evidence-based medicine. Control or eliminate!"

"I thought traditional medicine distanced itself from alternate therapies?" questioned Estelle dispassionately.

"Not if they can monopolise them through the pharmaceutical body, or eliminate via the Health Care Complaints Commission. Just a witch hunt!"

"Surely consumers have a right to complain. Too many shysters around. Bring it on, I say!"

"The Commission doesn't need a consumer complaint to launch an investigation. The Commission can be directed to investigate so-called shonky practices by those in power."

"What's so wrong with that?"

"Well, take my profession, for instance. Iridology would require the co-operation of a score of medical specialities to validate our value. Optometrists have to tread carefully around the territory claimed by the ophthalmologists. I can't see that level of collaboration being forthcoming any time soon. We'll be forced out of practice by the medical profession."

"Still, I do think some kind of regulation and control is called for," replied Estelle.

"What the drug companies are really about is to regulate and control the lining of their own pockets."

"How about people who die through misuse of these therapies?" Estelle protested. "And what about people who are persuaded to avoid evidence-based chemotherapy in favour of so-called natural approaches? What about that woman who recently refused chemotherapy and died of bowel cancer?"

"Well, in truth, only a small percentage of adult cancer sufferers benefit from chemo. It may contribute three percent to five year survival, if that," grumbled Roberta defensively.

"Still, I do think we need tighter regulations. Health is way too important a matter."

"Though, often, doctors bury their mistakes. The statistics of thousands of people dying annually during the course of medical treatment is astounding, but if just one person dies during the course of alternate treatment, it makes front page headlines," insisted Roberta. "Besides, there are other ways of doctoring. The Ian Gawler miracle is just one of the many medically documented cases of cure from terminal cancer using intensive meditation and nutrition. But hey, you can't put Zen in a bottle and retail it through the supermarkets!"

"What about Doctor 'Jekyll and Hyde' who's on trial for sexual misconduct?"

"OK, there are a few misfits, but a sexual misconduct charge is always a sure way for the system to eliminate dissent: took Clinton down!"

The two women looked up abruptly.

"I'd like to make a booking to see Roberta," requested a client.

Estelle was left reflecting on the story reported in the media about the disgraced doctor. Behind the polite, gentle facade were the depictions of a sociopath with no conscience. All accounts of him read much like some B-grade horror movie. The detailed depiction was of an immature, promiscuous gay who had seduced one of his dying patients. The doctor neglected to administer the correct life-saving treatments available to his terminal patient and many of the other vulnerable, sick and dying in his care. It was beyond Estelle's comprehension that this sort of negligence could go on, in spite of all the modern-day medical advancements available.

WITH ALL LIGHTS OUT, Estelle lay awake contemplating her life. She felt solid, grounded, present, and eager to re-integrate more fully with normality. It seemed as if all her perceptions, choices and actions thus far had been the artistry of her inner self expressed on a blank canvas. Her internal expressions reflected back to her as external manifestations. She felt both powerful and fragile in her newfound awareness of how she could never escape herself. The realisation hit her like a thunderbolt. She, alone, was fully responsible for herself. Estelle was able to finally make sense of karma.

Paradoxically she also conceded that she was being governed by some greater destiny over which she had little control. Feeling her vulnerability, she resolved to be more fully responsible for those elements she could control: and what she could control were both attitudes and choices; her attitudes being the springboard of the sum total of her choices.

Mellow leapt up onto her pillow, a reprieve from the intensity of her thoughts. Wrapping herself around Estelle's neck, doubling as a warm winter scarf, the two drifted off to sleep.

DRESSED AND READY TO face the day ahead, Estelle joined her Dad for breakfast. Sam pushed Mellow off the stool with his well-mastered technique that didn't involve lifting his eyes from the morning paper. Mellow sauntered off indignantly, giving Sam the tail.

"Out!" he sternly ordered.

"Oh, Dad, she only wants a little affection."

"Eh?" He barely lifted his eyes from the paper.

"Dad, I'd like your take on my AIDS article. Alex said she sent you a copy while I was an inmate." She dutifully opened the back door to allow Mellow out.

"Excellent debut, sweetheart. Very insightful."

"I'm working on a follow-up," coaxed Estelle.

"That's good, Stella," applauded Sam.

"What can you tell me about the new antiretroviral for AIDS? There's a heap on the net, but very confusing."

"We have a number of promising products ready for trial. All going to plan, Stella, one of these drugs could be the miracle breakthrough we've been working for," replied Sam, looking at Estelle reflectively. "Perhaps I could arrange a little chat with Doctor Schaffell. After all, it is an area of his expertise."

ESTELLE BRAVED THE HARROWING early morning traffic. She'd forgotten just how brutal it felt to forge her way through the dense frontline charge to work.

At her desk she downloaded and read a number of documents on AIDS prevention and management, focusing primarily on the antiretroviral therapy. It wasn't that straight forward, with vehement opinion for and against. She saw little Innocence in her mind's eye. The newborn of a HIV-positive mother had a twenty-five percent chance of being infected around the time of birth. The best outcome for the newborn seemed to be antiretroviral cover during labour and a caesarean section for a transmission rate reduction to one percent. Then breast-fed infants had a four percent risk of infection for every year of breast-feeding, and another little Innocence may face a death sentence if not breast-fed in rural Africa. There were the naysayers. President Mbeki had his supporters fighting against the introduction of antiretrovirals into South Africa. CD-4 counts and CD-8 counts? Data overload! Estelle figured she'd need Doctor Schaffell's help to cut through the avalanche of data.

Turning her attentions to AIDS vaccines, she came across a multimillion-dollar class action lodged against her father's pharmaceutical company. Far from preventing the deadly spread of AIDS and being the panacea for those sexually liberated souls who wanted to continue the quest for flesh-to-flesh communion, the vaccine, according to the class action, had not lived up to its hype. Not only did the case-controlled trials not prevent AIDS, but they showed a perversely increased rate in those who knowingly received the vaccine. Despite ethical approval of the trial and vigorously

109

documented counselling on behavioural risk management, it appeared those who received the vaccine may have been lulled into a false sense of security. An area of research fraught with hazard for all involved.

AT THE END OF the day Estelle and Alex headed out to their familiar haunt. Strutting back from the bar, bottle of red and another of mineral water in hand, Alex began a predatory survey of the room.

"I'm thinking I'd like to organise an interview with the doctor responsible for lodging a class action on behalf of those affected by the failed AIDS vaccine," announced Estelle.

"What's this guy's agenda, hmm?" Alex raised her eyebrows.

"That's what I'd like to explore."

"After a quick buck, no doubt."

"There were quite a number of individuals affected by this vaccine that was said to give protection from infected partners. I believe he is crusading for them and their loved ones."

"So he's a misfit crusader after a quick buck? Controversy sells, but let's not bite the hand that feeds us." Feasting on the male menu on offer, Alex began to narrow in on the night's potential prey, her olfactory senses sent wild by the scent of male pheromones. "Just keep our end in mind, hmm." Alex raised her eyebrows.

"I'm not out to derail any process." Estelle mirrored Alex, raising her eyebrows.

"Anyway, kiddo, here's to your recovery. What's the latest with lover boy?" prodded Alex, further tracking her potential prey's moves while stroking the long stem of her glass between her fingers.

"Don't know. I'm having a hard time battling my feelings," admitted Estelle, lowering her gaze onto her glass.

"What do they say? Love is a battlefield." Alex smirked as her unwary prey headed towards a nearby table and settled in to drink with his pack.

"Strange as this may sound, it's as if I can sometimes feel him so, so close to me, then as soon as I turn around, he mysteriously disappears."

"Get over it! You're his conquest and it's all just a game. By what you've told me thus far, his behaviour is typical of a guy who has already visited the Promised Land, marked his territory, had a drink, and now you're kidding yourself that his disappearance is some grand mystery."

"No. It's not like that. This is different."

"Don't give me that soppy love shit."

"I believe in love!"

"It's OK, kiddo, I don't expect you to break down with a lustful, tell-all confession."

"Love is real: just got to open your heart to it."

"Love: don't buy it, and I'm not about to be converted either! We humans are little more than walking hormones hanging for a hot night, after which we may barely be able to stand, let alone walk. It's called procreation and survival of the species." Alex laughed wickedly as she reached for another glass, continuing to track her victim over the rim of her full-bodied red.

"It's not a battle. I'm not a conquest." Estelle's eyes shone with conviction.

Alex licked her lips as if devouring her victim. Having savoured the final morsel, she then turned back to Estelle in response. "Get a grip, child."

Estelle shifted her gaze uncomfortably.

"Estelle, the merry war widow: cheers to you, girl." Swaying as she stood at mock attention, Alex raised her glass in salute. "He's either missing in action or went missing after he got some action. It's OK, kiddo. You don't need to come clean with me. Here's my best advice. Don't give over your heart. If you put all your faith in love, you'll be screwed. For all it's worth, just enjoy the latter."

SITTING IN HIS FAVOURITE armchair, Sam sat sipping on his favourite red as he listened to his favourite jazz.

"Dad, what do you know about the class action against your company's AIDS vaccine?"

"Why do you ask, Stella?"

"I read about it online while researching my follow-up AIDS article."

"Yes, a tragedy for all concerned. The recipients were all willing adults who were made fully aware of the potential risks involved in the trials. The cases will be settled. Just part of the landscape, I'm afraid, but litigation does frustrate the research process," replied Sam, carefully polishing his glasses.

"Surely, Dad, these are just desperate people clinging to any hope that they can find."

"Stella, the participants were mature adults who made lifestyle choices, and as fully informed adults, agreed to participate in an experimental trial. There was no hidden agenda here. The principal research scientists were anticipating a favourable outcome, and it wasn't. There's a race all over the world to find a cure for AIDS. Unfortunately it may take a number of trials before anyone gets it right." His voice was restrained.

"I'd like to interview individuals involved in pursuing the class action," declared Estelle, gauging her father's response.

"I'm sure you'll get their version of the truth. As your grandmother often says, we all have our own truth. Take care you're not accused of having a conflict of interest though."

IT WAS FRIDAY, EARLY evening, and the end of an intense working week. Grandmother and granddaughter met in one of Esther's favourite eateries, Vegetarian Butcher, a trendy vegan cafe in Newtown. At Esther's suggestion, the two women grabbed a bite before attending a lecture by Greg Fitzgerald on nutrition and disease reversal. Greg was an osteopath and naturopath much revered by Nan. As a groupie, Esther would get her fix by stalking him from one lecture to the next, year in, year out, then after each session, parroting him, word-perfect, as if his information were all her own.

"Now you're sure you're up to taking care of my brood this weekend, sweet pea?" asked Esther as the two women enthusiastically tucked into eggplant parrmiagiana.

"Up to it? Hey, I'm not the one placing myself between shooters and ducks for a weekend's recreation," teased Estelle between bites.

"Small, gutless wonders targeting harmless creatures." Esther groaned.

"Well, let's just hope that those small, gutless wonders don't target old ladies this year."

"Little men with little hearts—and little else—compensating with big guns. Bring it on!" Esther clenched her fist around her serviette.

"Maybe you can at least manage not to tumble into the freezing water as often this time," cautioned Estelle.

"I'll be fine. Wish I could say as much for the suffering of all those poor, defenceless birds."

"Just be careful, Nan. Don't want you sick."

"The least of my concerns; this year's season coincides with both mercury retrograde and moon-void course."

Estelle recalled Nan's lectures concerning Mercury retrograde; periods of three weeks that occur three times a year. When Mercury, the planet of communication, is retrograde, it is said to appear to be travelling backwards, taking as captive both communication and travel, so that things often don't run smoothly in either department. Nan had always kept a keen eye on the media during those times, frequently noting communication failures, especially in politics. As for the moon-void course, it occurred as the moon travelled from one sun sign to the next for a varied amount of hours, up to two days. These were often times of much effort, little result. In order to counteract any potential trouble spots at these times, Nan diligently checked and re-checked all details.

"Hi there," interrupted a gushy young brunette.

"Lorna! This is my grandmother, Esther. Lorna and I work together, Nan."

"Pleased to meet you, Esther; Estelle tells me that you are a gifted psychic," enthused the young journalist.

"Why, thank you, my dear." Esther smiled in gracious acknowledgement.

"How do you do all that?"

"I read tarot, tea leaves and astrology," informed the proud older woman.

"Oh, what an interesting way to make a living," responded Lorna vivaciously.

"I think so. I dare say it would make a great story for your readers," encouraged Esther enthusiastically.

"And tell me, do you believe in all that stuff?"

Esther's eyes narrowed fiercely, burning through Lorna's psyche.

"Well, nice to meet you. Must run. See you at work tomorrow, Estelle." Lorna awkwardly excused herself, scurrying off into the distance.

"Least we're not all still being burnt at the stake these days," grumbled Esther as she hurriedly settled the bill.

PULLING UP OUTSIDE THE public reception venue, Esther and Estelle alighted from the old jalopy and headed for the auditorium. Arriving on the first floor, Greg Fitzgerald, the sixty-something, balding hygienist lecturer was bouncing about the stage, spreading the gospel of natural health.

"I'm not here to impress you." He paused. "I'm here to impress upon you. The greatest weapons of mass destruction are the knife and fork."

The crowded auditorium laughed with approval as their guru warmed up.

"I don't know it all. I'm not young enough for that." Laughter. "But I do know we are killing ourselves with an acid lifestyle! That's right, ladies and gentlemen, not the GI index, but HI—that's right— Human Interference index."

He strode energetically across the stage, appearing to eyeball every one of the several hundred members of the public who had come mid-week from kilometres away to hear his health gospel.

"We are the inflammation nation, ladies and gentlemen. That's right: the inflammation nation. Did you know that of over four thousand, seven hundred mammals, we are the only species to suckle off another species after we've been weaned: still breast-feeding by proxy into our old age? Good God! And the medical profession continue to push the propaganda that dairy is good for you."

The crowd was silent, awaiting his next utterance.

"Researchers at Yale University in the US have found that the countries with the highest rates of osteoporosis, including the United States, Sweden and Australasia, were those whose people consumed the most meat, milk, and other animal products."

Estelle could almost feel the disbelief ripple through his predominantly female audience.

"Hard to believe? *The China Study*, the largest epidemiological study of its kind, found a strong correlation between animal consumption and cancer. Don't believe me, ladies and gentlemen? Look it up for yourselves." He waved a copy of the book, *The China Study*, high above his head.

There were further restless murmurs as the guru steamed on.

"As for us men, 'The Physicians' Health Study' confirmed that men, who over their lifetime consumed the most dairy products, had double the rate of prostate cancer and four times the rate of metastatic prostate cancer. That's right, guys. Four times the rate."

The auditorium hushed.

"Nothing has changed since Genesis, ladies and gentleman. It's what our grandmothers drummed into us. That's right. Eat your greens. A higher intake of fresh seasonal fruit and vegetables is associated with lower rates of cancer and heart disease."

His audience nodded in agreement.

"And finally the queen of fermentation: sucrose. That's right, ladies and gentleman, just a teaspoon of sugar to make the medicine go down, added to everything from antibiotics to salsa. Sucrose is broken down to glucose, that the body can metabolise, and fructose that is converted to fat and pumps up uric acid: toxic to our vascular system."

Estelle frowned as the energetic guru showed off his washboard abs and rippling muscles barely contained by a close-fitting shirt.

"And ladies, it's not just the pharmaceutical jabs that can cause cancer? Women who consume more than one glass of alcohol a day have higher rates of breast cancer. Cancer loves an acidic environment."

Estelle went pale.

"That's right. Check it out. For myself, coming into summer, I go eighty per cent raw, eighty per cent of the time. That's raw food, ladies and gentlemen." He grinned from ear to ear.

The audience chuckled.

"And," he paused, "we're all human. So go gently with yourselves," he added softly.

After an action-packed three hours and several glasses of the pure water provided, the show was over for another few months.

"What did you think?" quizzed Nan as they journeyed back home.

"He's either an over-energised ringing endorsement for a super healthy lifestyle, or he's forgotten to take his lithium today." Estelle laughed.

"I owe much of my vitality to him."

"Thought you always claimed it as a result of all your spiritual healing?"

"Healing, to be effective, must be psycho-spiritual as well as physical. You see, sweet pea, the trouble with modern medicine is its failure to recognise that we are not bodies without heads, nor heads without bodies, for we are embodied spirit."

"Plausible." Estelle shrugged matter-of-factly.

"And then there are planetary movements; they have as much an impact on us, if not more."

"Meaning?" Estelle frowned.

"Well, take the Pluto transition through Scorpio during the AIDS explosion, for instance. Pluto's lesson—change or break."

"Change or break what?"

"Our set patterns of behaviour. Pluto's generational transits always force us to dig roots deep."

"So what are you trying to say?" Estelle furrowed her brow.

"The threat of death aside, sex as an addiction can certainly kill the spirit."

"Not always," countered Estelle.

"Well, it may temporarily stop the dull ache from within. Love making, its heavenly polarity, is other-focused," suggested the old lady softly.

"Sounds like fundamentalist religion re-packaged to me," protested Estelle.

"Fundamentalist religion, like the so-called sexual liberation movement, can be equally shaming."

"Not sure I follow your gist."

"Well, one shames the flesh, the other the heart. Both systems equally encourage heart-pelvic disconnect as socially acceptable norms. Of course, when individuals act out, we punish them as perpetrators, instead of eyeballing the system."

"And the transits that follow?"

"Sagittarius and its lesson will, in part, shake up religious institutions, followed by 'Capricorn's transit', which will prick the ego of testosterone-driven capitalism—which may just implode."

COMMOTION GAVE WAY TO shock, shock to silence, silence to deafening sounds. Shooters held back, nursing their deflated egos amidst the confusion as to what to do next. Their firearms pointed to the ground as they watched on in disbelief. Floating along the beautiful Victorian waters was Esther, along with other ardent animal libbers. Dancing about energetically, banging tambourines and rice-shakers high in mid-air, they had volunteered themselves as a support act to the band they had hired for the day. Unlike the startled ducks that had fled for their lives, it seemed that someone had hit the pause button on the shooters. Immobilised, they stood mouths open wide and eyes even wider. The vision of the protesters in their psychedelic wigs and bright yellow attire, and the blaring sounds of the band as they went floating past on a barge, might have ruined their day's recreation, but a boat load of tree-hugging hippies jumping about to the sound of the Village People all singing 'Macho Macho Man'? Now that was adding insult to injury.

Then, as if someone had suddenly re-hit the pause button, the shooters all regained consciousness. Scrambling for their small boats, they sped towards the activists, hurling more and more abuse the closer they got.

As the day wore on, the confrontation became louder and louder. Hunters in chequered flannelette shirts shouting for their right to kill ducks on one side, activists in iridescent colours doing all they could to protect the defenceless birds on the other.

"Don't mess with our sports, you bastards," shouted one of the shooters.

"Violence isn't sport," Esther shouted back, her rage matching his.

"Shut your fuckin' mouth, bitch, or I'll shut it for you," he yelled with bravado, waving his rifle above his head.

"Big gun there, mate. What are you compensating for?" mocked Esther.

And so it went on. The day grew longer, reaching a crescendo before finally dissipating to an uneasy quiet.

Satisfied with their day's success, the activists disembarked and headed home. Zero death count of beautiful animals, zero maimed ducks left gasping for life in the water, often for several days on end, with open and bleeding wounds before an agonising death, accounting for one in four ducks shot. No orphaned duck left disorientated without maternal protection, unable to feed, fend or defend itself from predators. Instead these majestic birds would all live to see another day.

"As for Mercury retrograde and moon-void course, the shooters should have done their homework," mocked Esther.

ESTELLE ARRIVED PUNCTUALLY FOR her meeting with Doctor Schaffell. Standing at reception, she announced herself with poise. Aware of her newly redefined feminine curves, she adjusted her dusk pink suit and with head held high, marched down the corridor towards the office.

Extending her hand, she greeted Doctor Schaffell with eye contact and a firm handshake.

"Miss Goldstein, a pleasure to see you. Tell me, how have you been since your recovery?" asked the doctor, motioning Estelle to take a seat opposite his large mahogany desk.

Centring herself in a plush, black leather chair, Estelle rested her open notebook on her knee. "Estelle, please. I've been doing quite all right, thank you. Certainly nice to be back at work."

"Yes, your father tells me just how impatient you've been to return to your position: chafing at the bit, as they say. So how can I be of assistance to you today?"

Pausing for a moment, Estelle calibrated her approach. "I believe we have a common interest in seeing the expansion of your antiretroviral products into South Africa and other regions affected by HIV."

"Do go on, Miss Goldstein." Schaffell smiled.

"Well, for starters I am most interested in hearing about any plans that your company has to get your new antiretrovirals into South Africa."

"I am pleased to tell you that we are currently awaiting approval from the Medicine Control Council, the South African national regulatory agency. I am confident that we will soon be given the green light to go ahead."

"I'm aware of the difficulties your company has come up against. There seems to be an influential group of naysayers who have held sway so far. Are their concerns bio-ethical or budgetary? I note that some eminent scientists, Omar Bagasra, for instance, have raised concerns about rogue recombinants emerging in the process of developing an AIDS vaccine, giving rise to even deadlier strains of HIV." Estelle noted how her name-dropping got a rise out of Doctor Schaffell.

"Well, I see you've been diligent in your preparation, Estelle. Of course we take Doctor Bagasra's cautions very seriously. However our main focus has been on antiretrovirals, and as you know, our main blocks have been petty politics."

"How so?"

"Well, if I were a South African politician with a background in economics, I'd be primarily concerned about the budgetary implications, more especially in a post–Apartheid Rainbow nation."

"Would you mind expanding on that?"

"Like a lot of third world nations, South Africa has a dual economy. The first world White economy, predominantly urban, and the third world Black economy, nominally rural. The demand for these products are coming from the literate middle class and big business—the mines primarily—and they want the state to pay for these drugs, arguing that the HIV/AIDS epidemic is hitting their bottom line and the nation's GDP. Of course, the major impact of AIDS is on poorer blacks and those in the informal cash, or barter economy, and they, by and large, are an impoverished tax base and may consume more than they produce. Keeping these people alive with antiretrovirals will inevitably have downstream costs. Their opportunistic infections will then have to be treated, et cetera."

"I see."

"Our argument is that there are strategic opportunities, for instance for the provision of antiretroviral therapy to HIV-infected mothers at the time of labour, and our company has offered to donate the initial three years' antiretrovirals for such an enterprise. I believe such a program would reduce the HIV rate in this cohort of neonates from twenty-five to less than five per cent. A small cost for a big outcome. The potential years of life saved would be substantial."

119

"Quite so."

"Of course the mines are already covering their miners. It's cheaper to provide the antiretrovirals than train new recruits."

"It all sounds very dollar driven."

"We provide a good product and try to ensure optimal outcome for our clients. How these drugs are distributed and financed are matters of public policy. Each country has to live within its means."

"What is the anticipated time frame for this next stage?"

"Our forecast time is within the next nine months, and I am happy to say that we are well on track." Doctor Schaffell sat back smugly in the comfort of his high-backed, black leather chair, hands clasped at the base of his neck.

"Sounds promising." Estelle smiled.

"Promising indeed." Schaffell smiled triumphantly. "The New York conference will provide a strategic forum to facilitate political action and get our products into the South African market."

"I see." She nodded.

"All the major pharmaceutical players will be in one place at one time," continued Schaffell with obvious satisfaction.

Goose bumps rose over the entire contour of Estelle's arms. Swallowing hard, she surveyed the room: Schaffell's large mahogany desk, his high-backed, black leather chair, the feel of her dust pink outfit, and the open notebook on her knee.

"That sounds promising too!" Blushing, Estelle riveted her attention on the large ruby ring adorning Schaffell's meaty hand. "Another matter that has come to my attention is the legal action lodged against your AIDS vaccine?"

Schaffell shifted uncomfortably, then rose from behind his desk and moved across the room, pouring himself a glass of water. "I appreciate your question, Estelle." He paused. "Keeping in mind the enormity of all our efforts to get it right, there are great complexities within the field of medicine. Can I interest you in a glass of water?"

Estelle shook her head. "No thanks. What do you believe will come of this matter, Doctor Schaffell?" she pressed.

"We take an optimistic view that this matter will soon be successfully resolved." Schaffell moved towards the window.

"But perhaps, with what I have read of the case—"

"This matter is sub judice. Perhaps we ought to leave this one for the lawyers to sort out," Wolfgang cut in decisively.

"There seem quite a number of deaths alleged as a result of this vaccine. What is the company's mood about these deaths and the individual who has lodged the class action?"

An uncomfortably long silence fell between them. Facing the window, his back to Estelle, Schaffell abruptly replied, "I'm very sad for all those affected." Rubbing his ruby ring, Schaffell turned and retraced his steps back to his seat.

"How do you anticipate these deaths will impact on your company?" persisted Estelle.

"Estelle, I don't have a crystal ball. I cannot give you any answers on that one." Wolfgang's face was flushed as he took another sip of water.

Looking at his watch, he extended his hand. "Thank you so much for coming and I look forward to reading your next instalment. I trust our mutual interests will find common ground."

TOILING HER WAY THROUGH a swamp of information, Estelle rubbed her forehead as she sat at her desk. Diagonally across, Alex's door was slightly ajar. Seizing the opportunity, Estelle hesitantly knocked. "May I?" she requested.

"Sure, be my guest." Alex motioned Estelle to take a seat. "How's the article coming along?"

"That's what I need to talk to you about." Estelle turned to shut the door behind her.

"I'm all ears."

"Doctor Schaffell spoke of an international pharmaceutical conference to be held in New York where all the main pharmaceutical players are to be present. Vizard is aiming for market saturation of their antiretrovirals. The sub-Saharan market is a fertile void, so to speak, and the Asian market soon to follow."

"And?" Alex stroked her jaw, her eyes piercing straight through Estelle.

"And we currently have a very successful market with the suppliers of condoms. Why not expand our horizons to include Vizard as a major sponsor?"

"I like. And how do you propose facilitating this strategic partnership?"

"I propose you send me to New York to cover this process and promote Vizard's endeavours. It's a win-win."

"Send me a one-page proposal this afternoon. I'll sleep on it."

A WEEK LATER SAW Estelle at the Sydney International Terminal. Her mobile switched off, she missed a series of messages from her Nan's mobile, each one requesting that she urgently return her calls. Nan's final text to her: 'Keep safe, sweet pea.'

Chapter Seven

Stepping out from the Roosevelt, Estelle was immediately entranced by the smell of the place, the excitement of the place, the colour of the place, the loudness of the place, the movement of the place. It was a city of numbers: street numbers, Wall Street numbers, numbers and numbers of people; hundreds of thousands of loud, proud New Yorkers bustling, buzzing, pounding the pavement, rushing about their everyday lives. It was a constant city: constant movement, constant talking, constant eating, constant noise. It was a city of congestion: congested pathways, walkways, traffic, cars, yellow taxis. It was a city in competition: for tallness, loudness and time: tall buildings, tall people; tall, loud advertising; loud emergency vehicles competing against time itself. It was a city that inspired, demanded, and brought out the best one had to offer. A city of quality: quality musicians in tube stations, quality food in quality eateries, quality fine goods in quality shopping boutiques. This loud, proud city of colour, movement and excitement was as equally uncompromising and unforgiving of all things mediocre, for in its condemnation of such things, it would unrepentantly and viciously devour them. Estelle imagined that behind its vigorous demand for quality and competition lay dormant an equally unforgiving enemy, a sleeping giant with its looming threat concealed by its exuberance. Nan would have called this enemy the shadow, or perhaps the underdog, the denied part of oneself, a dormant shadow that in time could rise to threaten the heart of its own existence, perhaps by way of oppression, recession and depression.

Estelle scurried towards a yellow taxi. The driver was loud, direct and aggressive as he charged around town, claiming the road, darting unpredictably from one lane to the next, his technique a cross between a rally driver and a precision driver on an obstacle course. Sydney's drivers were no match for this lot. The ride was a shock to Estelle. Her driver impatiently honked his horn, fighting his way through the congestion. Language code amongst road users, as they snarled at the bumper-to-bumper gridlock, was mainly reduced to provocative hand and fist gestures backed by the obligatory shouting of obscenities.

"How are you guys coping after 9/11?" asked Estelle of her loquacious driver.

"Well, lady, yeah; a kick in the teeth, but we're not going to be intimidated by the bastards. They knocked down a couple of buildings, but not our spirit."

Her taxi driver continued his running commentary, swinging eastward towards the United Nations building. Estelle held her breath the entire journey, taking in as many sights as possible along the madcap route.

Entering the UN building, Estelle was overwhelmed by its grandeur. The eighteen acres of international territory, stretching from 42nd to 48th Street, showcased a thirty-nine-story complex overlooking the East River. Donated by John D. Rockefeller Jnr, it stood as a working monument to world peace, serving as a neutral space for arbitration and development for 180 nations.

Inside the main entrance, Estelle, like the other tourists, marvelled at the temple she'd entered. Grandeur has a way of evoking respect from people the world over. Her mind cast back to the Sandton Sun in South Africa, a world away, yet in the investigative trail of her story, opulence seemed to follow, as too the great divide between the visibly wealthy and those invisibly left wanting.

At the door of the main conference room, an obliging waiter greeted Estelle with an offer of refreshments. She had just entered a galaxy of world-renowned experts, VIPs, and a veritable who's who of international greats, amongst them Nobel laureates, eminent scientists and representatives of the pharmaceutical empire.

The conference banner boldly announced: Antiretrovirals for the 21st Century: Excellence in Research—Equity in Access.

Estelle scanned the program. The usual welcome speeches, an overview of the history of infectious diseases by a Professor Pascal, break down into various workshops. Four major themes:

HIV the evolving epidemic: Sexuality, host behaviour and sexually transmitted diseases; Evolutionary forces at the molecular level.

Bio-technical research: Approaches to prevention and control of HIV.

Public – private partnerships: Funding of research initiatives.

Community Participation: Presentations and discussion by advocacy groups, consumers and third-world concerns relating to patents on antiretroviral and new anti-tuberculosis drugs.

A list of participants and registered presenters was provided and the usual plenary sessions at the end of each day. A lot was being packed into three days.

Estelle's major aim would be to network with other press representatives covering this most prestigious of scientific meetings and get a nose for the politics behind the scenes. One name jumped out at her from the program. A rural perspective from South Africa: Mr S. H. Enoch Mabunda. Estelle was incredulous: surely not the same man? She scanned the hundreds of delegates, pharmaceutical reps and academics: a plethora of international attendees. He could be anywhere. Noting his workshop presentation scheduled for day three in theatre C, Estelle determined to track him down, if indeed this was the same Mabunda.

THE KEYNOTE ADDRESS BY Professor Pascal was an overview of the history of sexually transmitted infections and their impact on human biology and culture. Before HIV, Syphilis held centre stage one side of the border as the French disease, and the Italian Disease on the other. In the same way, AIDS was initially referred to as GRID, the Gay Related Immune Disease, European heterosexual communities reluctant to embrace their own vulnerability to this grim reaper.

The distinction between HIV, the Human Immune Deficiency Virus, and AIDS, the Acquired Immune Deficiency Syndrome, Estelle had a little difficulty getting her head around. Why should one identical twin of a HIV-infected mother die swiftly from fulminate AIDS-related disease, while the genetically identical twin remained apparently unaffected?

Then there was the issue of CD4 counts and the definition of AIDS. Perplexing! HIV rapidly infects and destroys CD4 cells and T lymphocytes, white blood cells essential for our protection from predatory pathogens. If two identical individuals have the same strain of HIV infection and the same health status, then why is one with a CD4 count less than 200, classified as AIDS, whilst the other with a CD4 count of greater than 200 is said to be living with HIV?

Professor Pascal addressed the hitherto frustrating efforts to find a vaccine for the ever-elusive HIV that mercurially changes its face to the world, eluding recognition by the many failed antibody-based vaccines. Baffling! The scientist seemed more excited in exploring the notion that promiscuity in primates could be an important determinant in the molecular evolution of our immune system.

Wow, thought Estelle, so mating behaviour and our immune system could be inter-related.

Estelle was grateful for a morning coffee break. She fortuitously bumped into an odd couple of sparring partners, Doctor Jan Kellerman, wearing the obligatory South African rainbow tie and a tell-tale Springbok badge next to his name tag, and his erudite Russian comrade, Doctor Boris Matyuk, peaceably discussing the pros and cons of antiretrovirals. HIV rates had spiralled in both South Africa and the former Soviet Republics, and the two scientists found common ground in the war on AIDS.

"Good morning, gentlemen. Do you mind if I join you?" Estelle boldly pushed in.

"But of course, you are very velcome." The goatee-bearded Boris courteously stepped back, allowing Estelle to join the triangle. "And you are?"

"Estelle Goldstein, New Woman magazine from Sydney, but not long back from assignment in South Africa."

"Ya, ya, do join us," greeted the gently spoken Afrikaner.

"Please don't let me interrupt your discussion," Estelle pleaded coquettishly, having done just that.

"Vell, is a qvestion of perspectives," explained Doctor Matyuk. "My comrade is looking for a—how do you say?—magical bullet."

"We need access to cheap antiretrovirals," argued Doctor Kellerman earnestly, "and patent-free anti-tuberculosis drugs."

The Russian shrugged, sceptically raising his bushy eyebrows. "Perhaps."

"What's your take, Doctor Matyuk?" probed Estelle.

"Vell, it's a qvestion of philosophy, is it not?" replied the shrewd Russian.

My God, these Russians and their philosophy, thought Estelle, nodding to the expectant Russian.

126

"Vell, if I may say, ve had the right approach at Alma Ata... Kazakhstan, 1978," emphasised the Russian. "Twenty-five years ago: a comprehensive approach." Pausing as Estelle diligently scribbled into her notebook, Boris went on. "It's a qvestion of social justice and eqvity. People have a right to health, do they not? This is not communist propaganda. It was the British who demonstrated the relationship betveen social class, income and health. Do ve not all have a right to a fair share of the cake?"

"Yes, of course, but hopelessly inefficient," retorted Doctor Kellerman, becoming more animated. "A selective approach to primary health care has had better outcomes targeting immunisation, clean water and essential drugs," argued the South African, targeting Estelle with the counterpoint.

The atmosphere suddenly became tense, the three stepping back a little from each other.

The Russian nodded in pensive agreement. "Of course, ve have to thank Mr Rockefeller for this efficient approach—and this beautiful venue."

"How so?" questioned Estelle.

"The Rockefeller Foundation funded the Bellagio Conference in Italy in 1979, the year after the Alma Ata declaration," explained Doctor Kellerman, regaining his composure.

"And who attended this Bellagio Conference?" interjected Estelle, sensing the undercurrents.

"James Grant, director of UNICEF, and Robert McNamara, president of the Vorld Bank. I don't recall ve got an invitation," replied the somewhat disgruntled Russian.

"Is that the same Robert McNamara, the former defence secretary for the Kennedy administration in Vietnam?" queried Estelle, eyebrow raised.

"Ve have our ideological differences." The Russian shrugged. "But I agree. Fresh vater, immunisation and essential drugs make a difference. Rather vage var on AIDS than each other," he agreed magnanimously.

"Yes, indeed," interjected an elderly African with pink, de-pigmented lower lip, "but who owns the water? And who owns the vaccines? And who owns the essential drugs?" The older black South African glared at Doctor Kellerman.

"Of course, Solomon," replied Doctor Kellerman deferentially. "Have you met Boris Matyuk?"

The Russian reached out to greet the older African, shaking his hand.

"Molo, Miss Goldstein," greeted the African, regaining his composure.

"Molweni, Doctor Mabunda," replied Estelle, to the surprise of the two other doctors.

An awkward silence was pre-empted by the warning bell recalling conference delegates to their respective workshop rooms.

"Ve're very democratic in Russia," boasted Boris. "The vater in Moscow is not so good, but everyone has access to vodka." The four chuckled as they started to go separate ways.

"Doctor Mabunda?"

"Miss Goldstein. We must talk," the elderly doctor emphasised before leaving. "Tomorrow afternoon—after the conference: Main Entrance, south."

"You know this place?" replied Estelle.

"I am a former Wa-Benzi," whispered Doctor Mabunda conspiratorially.

"Pardon?" Estelle frowned, and half-smiled, caught midway between puzzlement and curiosity.

"W.H.O. employees drive Mercedes Benz," jested the aged doctor.

"Oh? The World Health Organisation?" Estelle became less surprised by his cryptic banter.

"This temple was to be a house for all nations. It has become a robbers' den," replied Doctor Mabunda enigmatically. "Tomorrow then."

"Look forward to it. See you there," replied Estelle, mustering all her charm.

With no further ado, Doctor Mabunda showed her his back and hurried off.

Shrugging off Mabunda's eccentricity, Estelle began to network with the pharmaceutical reps as the other scientists disappeared into their respective workshops. This conference was a veritable bazaar of the latest antiretroviral agents, anti-bacterials and anti-fungals, all pertinent to living a full and dignified life with HIV. Various products, from diapers for the incontinent to remedies for halitosis for those with HIV-related gingivitis, were on display, with California leading the way through special state-funded programs for those fortunate enough to fit the criteria. The drug representatives, both male and female, were all beautiful people.

Estelle zeroed in on a display desk highlighting the benefits of AZT, the drug that it was believed would prevent the transmission of HIV from infected mothers to their newborn, at birth or during breastfeeding. The pharmaceutical representative was a young, passionate blonde from Yale, not so much older than Estelle. Estelle felt immediate rapport and was impressed with the erudite presentation by the young New Yorker. The two women exchanged email addresses and declared their intention to keep in touch.

THE MORNING'S TWO ANTAGONISTS were conversing with a much darker African, Doctor Mabunda nowhere to be seen. Estelle joined their table for lunch. Controversy was raging over the merits of antiretrovirals for HIV positive mothers, during delivery and breastfeeding.

"President Bush's initiative on funding for the war on AIDS in Africa will make a big difference," insisted Doctor Kellerman.

"Perhaps," replied Boris Matyuk sceptically, "but who vill look after the surviving orphan when the mother dies?"

Estelle's thoughts went back to little Innocence at Holy Cross.

"What are your thoughts, Doctor Rewzori?" asked Doctor Kellerman of the Ugandan silently stirring his tea.

"We are grateful for any assistance—of course," his accent was clipped, almost British upper-class, "though some aspects of the program are a yoke around our necks. A third of the budget is spent on promoting abstinence before marriage, and that's quite a large proportion. But we have a condom crisis in Kampala and that has been pivotal in our campaign to prevent AIDS."

"And the antiretrovirals? How has that initiative fared in Uganda?" asked Estelle, inserting herself into the discussion.

"The impact has been ambiguous, Miss?" replied the Ugandan.

"Goldstein. Estelle Goldstein."

"Undoubtedly some infants are protected from getting HIV infection, during birth or from their mother's breast milk, but the side effects of AZT and some of the newer antiretrovirals are not insubstantial. Of course if our children are not breastfed, a lot die from diarrhoea, malnutrition and infection, but on the other hand, some twenty per cent of our children given these drugs have serious side effects, some lethal."

"But surely, overall, there is mainly benefit," defended Estelle.

"Qvite so," agreed Doctor Matyuk.

"Yet some normal children are sacrificed," replied the Ugandan coolly.

"What do you mean by that?" asked Estelle.

"Well, the HIV test is imperfect, especially in pregnancy. Biological false positive results are not uncommon for Syphilis, or HIV, for that matter. So some healthy mothers are being treated with antiretrovirals and their offspring are dying from drug-induced liver failure or infection, whereas less than a third of our so-called HIV-positive infants go on to develop AIDS," replied the Ugandan, his expression deadpan. "But we Africans understand the need for sacrifice."

Estelle felt suddenly uncomfortable under his gaze.

"You see, Miss Goldstein," interceded Doctor Matyuk, "the qvest for a golden bullet is a poison chalice," quipped the Russian, mixing his metaphors. "The Vest has been seduced by Pasteur and ignored the noble truth of Claude Bernard."

"And Pasteur is to vaccination as Bernard is to?" responded Estelle, regaining her feistiness.

"Vell, it's the milieu interieur, is it not? If ve have a healthy interior environment, ve have a better chance of fighting off disease. Our bodies have natural intelligence. Ve can adapt. Adaptation is built into our DNA, if ve can resist tampering with it."

The Ugandan nodded his black head in assent.

"But surely you cannot ignore the positive impact of the pharmaceutical industry," Estelle argued, irritated by the Russian's scepticism.

"Of course everyone remembers the brilliance of Pasteur, but who recalls Metchnikoff?" asked the Russian defiantly.

"And who was Metchnikoff?" obliged Estelle.

Doctor Boris Matyuk nodded at Estelle, a headmaster awaiting silence from the class, before delivering his lesson.

"Doctor Elie Metchnikoff, my compatriot, vas the pathologist who discovered the phagocyte, our first-line defence against disease. He vas avarded the Nobel Prize for Medicine in 1908—and he didn't experiment on guinea pigs." He nodded to the Ugandan opposite. "Metchnikoff and his co-vorkers demonstrated the power of our immune system by standing before an assembly of physicians and drinking a decanter of fluid contaminated with cholera bacilli, highly infectious cholera bacilli from human faeces. Not a single participant in this informed and voluntary experiment fell ill with cholera!"

The Russian was defiant.

"Magic bullets cost," agreed the Ugandan. "Of course we welcome the American aid to pay for their magic bullets," sighed Doctor Rewzori, getting up to leave. "We are grateful for the crumbs off the rich man's table."

As the luncheon meeting dispersed, Estelle felt less enthusiastic about the spiel fed her by the young Yale graduate. Nothing was straightforward in the war on AIDS. Estelle spent the remainder of the afternoon wandering from stall to stall, mindful of her jetlag.

CONFERENCE DAY ONE HAD come to a close. Heading the long way back to her hotel, Estelle decided on the scenic route via Manhattan and a stopover at one of those world famous New York delicatessens renowned for their richness and range. Standing at the counter, Estelle eyed off just about every conceivable type of meat and animal produce available alongside an array of delicate pastries and sickly syrup-soaked sweets in just about every colour imaginable.

She found herself a seat and awaited table service. Gazing out across Wall Street's congested sidewalk, the young Aussie's eyes fixed on the oversized charging bull, an iconic image symbolising aggressive financial optimism and the re-emergent power of the American financial system following the stock market crash of 1987. Many from around the globe had come to worship the majestic bronze bull.

Her waiter appeared, prompt and polite, and recited an inexhaustible list of menu options so vast and varied that Estelle's palate went into overdrive. Before she knew it, she found herself hoeing into her supersized portion of pizza oozing and overflowing with thickly running mozzarella cheese. As she sat savouring her death-by-chocolate dessert alongside a pot of hot pouring chocolate, Estelle observed America's largesse. There was nothing small or diminutive about America, its people, its food portions, or its welcoming, gregarious attitude.

Finally, with the heavily mounted calories stacked against her, Estelle decided to walk part of the distance back to the Roosevelt, vowing to restart a diet and responsible girth control the very minute she'd land back on home soil.

COMING OUT OF HER food-induced coma, Estelle found it hard to feel motivated the next morning. She sluggishly got out of bed and headed down to breakfast, minus a healthy appetite. Thumping her nervous system with an extra-strength coffee, she managed to drift out the door and roll into a taxi.

Day two of the conference found her more grounded in the ambiguities and competing interests made more explicit by the war on AIDS. Employee assistance programs being touted for the miners highlighted the potential benefits for public-private partnerships in delivering services for people with HIV and AIDS. Cash-strapped third world countries were eager to push for corporate partnerships in collaboration with central governments in the targeted provision of antiretroviral agents to financially sensitive segments of the community.

Some governments were eager for the non-government mining sector to pick up on the philosophy of corporate provision of private health insurance to cover its skilled work force. The benefits for the company would be in maintaining a skilled work force, and for government these workers would continue to provide taxation revenue and minimise the impact of HIV on the country's GDP. Differential policies would target vulnerable segments of the community without sucking government funds into a black hole of need.

These corporate initiatives, together with the very short duration, government-funded antiretroviral coverage around delivery, promised to salvage some infants without exorbitant costs. Third world governments were desperate to maximise the benefits and limit the costs for their already overstretched health budgets. As always, the health budget would benefit the middle class preferably, as their benefit would provide a positive ripple through the whole economy. It may have been a cynical approach, but the best option in an imperfect system. Estelle was looking forward to the community participation models the next day that would provide a counter-balance to this economic-driven philosophy.

Next was the presentation by the International Mining Council and its proposal for lifelong health care plans for the miners that generated a lot of interest. The big mines were looking to present themselves as a positive generator of socio-economic growth, and thus good corporate citizens. Now well into a post-Apartheid era in South Africa, a newly energised National Union of Miners was restive and hungry for compensation for mining-related lung disease incurred during the Apartheid years, and big mining was now eager to rebrand themselves as philanthropic enterprises.

Estelle's thoughts went back to the men languishing in the wards of Holy Cross. The only compensation they would get would be a few thousand rand to cover funeral costs. Under the old Apartheid government, blacks would get a lump sum following confirmation of their silicosis at autopsy. Whites, on the other hand, were provided with an annuity till the miner reached sixty-five years, and then a death benefit. It seemed everyone had their own agenda in participation in the war on AIDS.

Estelle felt exhausted by day's end as she wandered through the swarming, complex maze. At the top of the stairs she faced an assorted crowd of rebellious protestors: People Living with HIV and AIDS; People for Third World Justice; People for the Ethical Treatment of Animals. The mixed crowd of several hundred protestors juxtaposed an expanding thin blue line of the Police Force facing the restless crowd.

Suddenly her attention riveted on a lone male. Unmistakably it was Doctor Solomon Mabunda standing out from the crowd of leaving delegates. Respectably dressed in a dark navy suit, his tie striped with bright South African colours, he stood above the rebellious fray, senatorial in his aloofness. Estelle made her way across to where he was standing. At that very moment, a beanie-clad figure in battle fatigues and high-collared wind jacket approached the elderly doctor. Doctor Mabunda stepped towards him as if in recognition.

"Molo, Dada," greeted the shorter, robust black man. The two men embraced. Estelle noted the surprised look on the elderly doctor's face as he looked at her over the right shoulder of the younger man embracing him. The two disengaged. The thickset young man turned to face Estelle, his dark eyes wooden. Turning again, he disappeared into the engulfing crowd.

Doctor Mabunda slumped to a sitting position as if he'd had one too many. He slid down onto the footpath. A shiny, narrow object projected from the left side of his chest. The kerbside crowd erupted into chaos. Estelle rushed to his side. Numb with confusion, she held up his head. The old doctor looked dumbly at the shiny metallic spoke protruding from his chest. His proud South African tie partially hid an expanding island of blood staining his pristine white shirt.

"Doctor Mabunda!" cried Estelle helplessly, cradling his head.

The dying man tried to talk, bloodstained froth foaming to his de-pigmented lips. "Conggaahhh..." He gasped as the pendulum ceased to swing. The darks of his eyes dilated as they glazed over.

Estelle screamed. The crowd encroached around her. Suddenly she felt a strong brown hand pulling her to a standing position. "It's you!" gasped Estelle, looking up at the young man in bewilderment.

"What happened?" enquired the familiar stranger, his attention riveted on her ashen face.

"This man's been stabbed."

"Back in a moment!" The young man rushed off.

"Doctor Mabunda!" uttered Estelle in disbelief, seconds seeming like hours as the strong masculine presence returned with police.

Estelle stepped back from the body. A ring of blue converged around them. Paramedics arrived and finally disengaged from their attempts at resuscitation, all transfixed by the silvery spoke protruding from the corpse's chest.

"Mabunda," she uttered again, numbly, staring at the lifeless corpse.

"Mabunda?" The dark-skinned stranger echoed back. "You know this man?" His large, firm hand supported her elbow as he listened intently.

"Yeah. We met in South Africa earlier this year," responded Estelle with a thousand-mile stare.

Two police officers stepped towards Estelle. Pulling herself together, she managed to assist them with some on-the-spot information while the young man stood vigilantly by her side.

"You'll have to come down to the station and make a statement, Miss."

"Of course. Anything to assist."

"How you faring, Miss?" The young New Yorker's voice was warm and consoling, genuine concern clearly written on his face. "Can I get you something? Some water perhaps?"

"I've got to go down town with the police to make a statement," murmured Estelle.

"Please allow me to escort you. I take it you're not all that familiar with this part of town. Correct?"

"Sure," answered Estelle blankly.

"The Aussie accent. Sorry, Miss. Ryan. Ryan Knight," volunteered the young man courteously, monitoring her trembling body and shallow breathing.

"We've met before?" Estelle looked at Ryan.

"Yes, I do believe we have. Miss?" Silence fell between them. His deeply penetrating eyes searched hers.

"Goldstein. Estelle Goldstein. Thanks. I could do with some support." Estelle nodded, her eyes glazed. She studied the man's golden-brown complexion, large, dark brown eyes and chiselled features, taking succour from his strength. "Sorry. Yes, we've met. In Sydney; I was in St Vincent's Hospital at the time," she responded sharply, breaking the intensity of the moment.

"Yes. Seems we meet in unconventional circumstances."

"Seems so," conceded Estelle, releasing a gentle, but apprehensive smile.

Ryan returned a reassuring smile. "Your squad car is awaiting you." He looked over his shoulder at the approaching officers.

"I'm accompanying Miss Goldstein," he announced to the officer.

They both hopped into the back of the police car as a gentle rain began to fall. It was chilly inside and they rode without speaking, the silence broken by the sound of the windscreen wipers, the crackle of the police radio and intermittent sirens.

Estelle's breath frosted the car window. Her mind wandered back to Mabunda's dying moments, the pink froth bubbling from his lips, and his lifeless eyes. Stopping abruptly outside the police department, they were ushered in.

"Good evening, Miss Goldstein? Detective Saul Winterbottom," greeted a greying, paunchy detective with a New York accent. "This must be a terrible shock for you. Would you like a coffee—or water?"

"Water. Thank you," replied Estelle numbly.

"Mr Knight, we'd like to interview Miss Goldstein in private. I gather you were not a witness to the murder. However we'll take a separate statement from you," directed the detective.

Estelle was escorted into an interview room where she was greeted by a scrawnier fellow, Detective Arnie Herschowitz, sporting a five o'clock shadow.

"Thank you for coming in, Miss Goldstein," Winterbottom opened gently. "You're a journalist. You say you'd met Doctor, Mr Mabunda previously in South Africa and you witnessed his killing here."

"Yes. That's correct." Estelle nodded.

"Unusual coincidence," he remarked.

"Yes, I suppose so."

"Go on," he further invited.

Estelle relayed her initial meeting with Doctor Mabunda at Holy Cross Hospital, and his apparently crazy behaviour.

"So you say Doctor Mabunda was a discredited virologist, an alcoholic, and that he'd studied in Belgium and worked here in the United States," summarised the paunchy detective.

"Yes." Estelle frowned.

"OK—and his apparent ravings at Holy Cross?"

"He was drunk. I didn't pay a lot of attention at the time. He was raving on about chimpanzees, anthrax, depo-contraception, AIDS and cancer," replied Estelle, rubbing her temples.

"And then you meet him here at a UN-sponsored AIDS conference?" interrogated Herschowitz.

"Yes. He claimed he used to work for the World Health Organisation. He was a bit cynical." Estelle faltered in her reply. "He was adamant we should meet this afternoon. He was due to make a presentation tomorrow."

"And he never made that meeting with you," stated the gaunt detective with piercing eyes.

"No," replied Estelle blankly. She trembled. The expressionless eyes of Doctor Mabunda's killer, whose features had been mainly concealed by his beanie and jacket, sent shivers up her spine.

"Did he say anything before he died?" asked Winterbottom.

"He just moaned."

"We'll need you to sign a typed statement, Miss Goldstein, and we'd like you to assist us in building an Identikit image of Doctor Mabunda's assassin."

"Of course, detective. Anything I can do to be of assistance."

"We'd like you to stay around for a few days till we've completed our preliminary investigations. There's no need to hand in your passport, but we will require a contact phone and address till our investigations are concluded."

"Of course."

"One other thing, Miss Goldstein." Winterbottom scrutinised her intently. "Do take care of yourself. Caution is always advisable in this city of ours."

Estelle nodded and was shown to the door.

The two detectives looked at each other. "What's your take, Arnie?"

"What have we got? Doctor Solomon Herbert Enoch Mabunda comes to this conference as Mr Enoch Mabunda. Murdered, literally yards away from our finest, their backs turned, pre-occupied with a ratbag crowd. The assassin vanishes without a trace. Then there's the Goldstein coincidence."

Saul stroked his jaw.

"I smell a bit of monkey business here," quipped Arnie.

"Let's drill down, shall we?" replied his paunchy colleague. "What about her risk, Arnie?"

"Nah. She'll be out of here in a few days. Zip risk."

ESTELLE WAS GRATEFUL TO meet with Ryan at police reception. He quickly whisked her out onto the kerb and hailed down a cab.

"Where are you staying, Estelle? I'll take you back to your hotel," volunteered Ryan.

"Thanks." Estelle smiled in gratitude. "The Roosevelt, please."

"Any further questioning—or are you free to go?" probed Ryan.

"Go?"

"Home? Your conference badge. I'm guessing you're here on a visitor's visa: some kind of assignment?"

"Not yet. Seems I'm on standby for further questioning?" Estelle frowned. "His killer knew him. They embraced. Why did he insist on seeing me this afternoon? He was just a harmless old man. Why would anyone want to kill him?" Estelle babbled while Ryan listened attentively.

Arriving at the Roosevelt, Ryan inquired, "May I escort you to your door?"

"Thanks, but I think I'll be right. Just need a good night's sleep."

"I'd like to stay in touch if you don't mind, Estelle: just to know that you're alright. Please feel free to call me if you need anything—anything at all," invited Ryan, placing his business card in her hand.

"Thanks. I appreciate it," replied Estelle, smiling back nervously as she stepped away.

Estelle ascended to her room and immediately dialled her dad.

"Dad? Dad!"

"Stella. How are you, sweetheart? Is everything OK?" asked Sam, noting Estelle's agitation.

"Not really. I'm not sure if you recall Doctor Mabunda? The crazy old doctor I met at Holy Cross. He was killed this evening. Stabbed!"

"Good God! Stella!" cried Sam in dismay.

"Why would anyone want to kill a harmless old man? Dad...it's just terrible."

"You've got to get out of there. Come home. Get an early flight." Sam's voice was stern and emphatic.

"I can't leave till preliminary investigations are completed. I witnessed his assassination."

"You what? Have the police offered you any protection?"

"Dad, I'll be fine. The police aren't concerned. Murders happen here every day. I'll be careful."

"You need to ask for police protection if you're a witness," demanded Sam.

"Don't worry, Dad. I'm street-wise."

"Stella!" spluttered Sam.

"Dad; the security here at the Roosevelt is five-star. Mabunda's assassin has no idea who I am. No need to get excited."

"Excited!"

"OK. OK, Dad; I'll be very careful. Got to sleep. Ring you tomorrow. Got to go."

"Estelle!"

AMIDST THE RECLUSIVE CONFINES of her pristine room, Estelle ran her fingers along the crisp, sharp white edges of Ryan's business card. The bold, black, elevated lettering defined him as Ryan Knight, Veterinary scientist, PETA—People for the Ethical Treatment of Animals. His mobile phone number helped buffer her against an enveloping cloud of sensory overload. As Estelle closed her eyes, Ryan's card dropped from her hand, fluttering softly by her cheek and onto her pillow.

Estelle spiralled into a twilit descent, a foreboding corridor of rambling, jagged images of the day's events. Thrust into a string of troubled stirrings, she awoke repeatedly throughout the night.

The sound of galloping encroaching upon her consciousness, gathering apace as Estelle heard her name called out. She woke abruptly, relieved by the break of dawn streaming through her bedroom curtains.

Estelle wandered down for breakfast, settling for a glass of fruit juice.

SHE ARRIVED LATE FOR the start of day three, but in time for a minute's silence for the fallen Doctor Mabunda. No details were given of his death. Estelle found it hard to bring any enthusiasm to Community Participation. It seemed to her that participation meant the community just needed to show up for their jabs and be rewarded by not having their government benefits withdrawn.

Finding herself a bit split off in the morning, Estelle was surprised when lunchtime arrived so soon. Following the one-minute's silence, it was as if the tragedy that befell Doctor Mabunda never happened. The young Yale rep was as exuberant and erudite as ever, and the show just went on.

Estelle was grateful to engage with the trio she'd lunched with the day before. Doctor Mabunda's absence was at least noted at their table, their sombreness a sharp contrast to the general exuberance and idle chatter of the dining hall. The conversation revolved around speculation as to how Mabunda died—and why.

"Did he have a cardiac arrest? There were rumours he was stabbed!"

"It's as if he never existed," declared Estelle.

"Life just goes on," replied Doctor Kellerman. "When a lion takes out a zebra on the veldt, the surviving herd quickly settle down, just yards from the feeding pride, as if nothing happened."

"You see, Miss Goldstein, ve have more in common with the animal kingdom than ve'd like to admit," added Boris Matyuk, his eyebrow raised. "Once the herd's sacrifice has been offered, and accepted, ve all feel a little safer. Lightning doesn't strike tvice, even in New York. Ya?"

"But why must anyone be sacrificed in the first place?" demanded Estelle.

"God only knows. Sometimes there is no rhyme, nor reason," shrugged Doctor Kellerman.

Estelle could feel her anger rising at Kellerman's dismissive comments. "But who was Doctor Solomon Mabunda? And why was he presenting himself as Mr Enoch Mabunda, a community representative at this forum?" asked Estelle.

"A lot of Africans have an alias: different name for different situations. Solomon the wise: Enoch the lost sheep, perhaps." Kellerman shrugged his shoulders again.

"Lost sheep or not, he still had enough pull to be put forward to present at this forum. He was, after all, a brilliant virologist who formerly worked for the WHO." Estelle's blue eyes were ablaze.

"But of course. Prior to his fall from grace, he was one of South Africa's most brilliant virologists," added Kellerman, blushing above his collar and lowering his eyes, averting Estelle's fierce gaze.

"Quite a feat for a black South African of his vintage, one would think." Estelle also flushed, then regained her composure.

"In the old South Africa, the Africans had to do their further studies abroad. Solomon did post-graduate studies in Antwerp, London, here in New York, and worked for a time back at the

South African Institute of Medical Research," explained Doctor Kellerman.

"Yes. I gather the University of Witwatersrand was quite progressive," Estelle agreed begrudgingly.

"Will you be joining us this evening for the conference dinner, Miss Goldstein?" asked the South African.

"No, thanks; I think I'll pass. May I take this opportunity to thank you gentlemen for tolerating my inquisitiveness."

"The pleasure is ours, my dear," volunteered the Ugandan.

Estelle left the conference early, Doctor Mabunda's presentation replaced by a backup extolling the virtues of the Bush administration's pledge of support for the war on AIDS in Africa.

RETURNING TO THE ROOSEVELT, Estelle crashed out for a few hours, exhausted, following a succession of calls to and from her dad.

Opening her eyes, Estelle felt momentarily hazy taking in her oversized room. Galvanising herself, she flicked open her laptop, checked her email and proceeded downstairs.

Cutting a solitary figure, she quickly found refuge in a quiet corner of the hotel eatery where she looked out onto the sidewalk. Sipping on water, Estelle flicked through a Wall Street Journal. 'Coca Cola accused of stealing water from Varanasi.' Who would want to steal water from the Ganges? Is nothing sacred, mused Estelle. The struggle to control water had already started, as Nan would say.

Confident footsteps made their approach. Estelle looked up instinctively.

"Hello, Estelle, thought it was you. Mind if I join you?" requested Ryan, pulling up a chair.

"Feel free," invited Estelle, flushing slightly.

"Actually I was hoping you could do with some company," ventured Ryan hesitantly. "Are you alright? Any further contact from the police?" Ryan sat down, his broad frame leaning in towards her.

"Not yet: just waiting to hear. I'm doing a little better though. Just slept some of it off," replied Estelle pensively, running her fingers through her hair.

"Nevertheless, all still a little nerve-racking, I imagine. You might even be a little homesick by now?"

"I'm trying not to dwell on things too much—if I can." Estelle shrugged, looking down into her glass.

"That's fair enough," agreed Ryan, "though you do need to take care, young lady. Having someone keep an eye on you might not be such a bad idea." He smiled warmly, his almond-brown eyes deeply focused on the pretty, blue-eyed Aussie blonde.

"And who might you be suggesting?" She cautiously released a guarded smile. "You seem to notice an awful lot of things and ask an awful lot of question," challenged Estelle coyly. She studied his pleasantly symmetrical, well defined facial features and tightly curled dark hair.

"Hey, sorry if I'm making you feel uncomfortable," apologised Ryan, pulling back.

"Maybe just a tad," responded Estelle, lifting her eyes to meet his gaze.

"I am a true gentleman, I assure you," quipped the cheeky Afro-American.

"I'm sure you are," replied Estelle in mock agreement. Estelle's features softened and with a widening smile, she reluctantly let down her guard.

"Now, can I get you something to eat?" offered Ryan.

"Sorry, not hungry."

"A tea? Coffee? Chai, per—?"

"Off caffeine: heart palpitations," broke in Estelle.

"Oh? Not my presence?" teased Ryan.

"Chai might be nice—non-caffeinated." Estelle chuckled, finally breaking the sombre trance that had shrouded her.

"So what's brought you to my town, Miss Goldstein? Researcher? Drug Rep?"

"None of the above; I'm a journalist, actually, covering AIDS in Australia and South Africa, hence the HIV conference at the UN."

"You look too young to be a journalist."

"You look too young to be a vet."

"Touché!"

Reclining a little, Estelle laughed at the cheeky New Yorker, then frowned. "I still can't get over Mabunda's death."

"It's barely twenty-four hours—and you said you knew him from South Africa?"

"Yes. It's just weird. At first I thought he knew me. He was pissed as a parrot, barely able to stand, and raving on about Project Coast and anthrax in Rhodesia, amongst other things."

"What's Project Coast?" Ryan raised his eyebrows.

"Top secret chemical and biological weapons program developed by the South African government during the Apartheid era and headed by the personal physician to the then Prime Minister, P.W. Botha: a certain Doctor Basson—cardiologist apparently."

"Ahh, the loyal physician."

"Yes," agreed Estelle, "just doing his duty for the state. A year or so back, some character by the name of Daan Goosen, the former head of the program, tried to do a deal with the FBI, wanting to offload their bacterial stock in exchange for green cards in the US. Declined apparently."

"Anthrax?" Ryan furrowed his eyebrows.

"Don't know, but the reports on the anthrax story in Rhodesia during Smith's rule appear to have legs: over 10,000 human cases and 182 deaths. Quite extraordinary! Only in African Tribal Trust land apparently, and mainly in Matebele Land, south of Victoria Falls."

"Must say I have a veterinarian interest in anthrax, but have not heard of this."

"Obscure reference: East African Medical Journal. A certain Doctor Davies noted that during the war of independence, anthrax, a rare disease, became one of Rhodesia's major causes of admissions to hospital."

"In blacks?"

"Yes: in blacks." Estelle paused, swallowing her chai. "I didn't follow up on it as it was outside my brief to focus on AIDS, but I can understand why Mugabe is such a bitter old bastard, looking more Hitleresque the older he gets."

"Sure," agreed Ryan. "Mugabe's dictatorship has led to Zimbabwe's ruin, but ironically, it sounds like the pukka English gentlemen in colonial Rhodesia were dabbling in germ warfare—and that's been swept under the carpet!"

"Yes. I guess you're right."

"And I guess, perhaps, not too big a stretch of the imagination to suggest possible research links between colonial Rhodesia and Apartheid South Africa," added Ryan, stroking his forehead.

"Geographical neighbours, tribal cousins," agreed Estelle.

"White tribal cousins at that!" added Ryan with emphasis.

"Perhaps. Yep, very possible." Estelle shrugged, slumping into her chair. "I guess I wrote off Mabunda as just a drunken has-been. I still don't get it. Then he turns up here? He must still have connections, and now he's been killed: just too much of a coincidence," conceded Estelle, shaking her head.

Ryan scratched his head.

"My mind's still spinning. I'm grateful to chew this stuff over with someone." Estelle massaged her temples.

"And home?"

"Home is Sydney. With Dad, Nan, and my cat, Mellow." Estelle smiled.

"Tell me about Mellow," encouraged Ryan, returning her smile.

With developing rapport, the two sat talking, Ryan mainly listening while Estelle reminisced about home. Ryan just sat, like her oldest friend, catching up on lost years, absorbing the vulnerability and vitality in her voice.

Estelle pulled herself up abruptly. "Look at the time." she gasped, realising she had prattled on to an almost-stranger for over an hour. "I think I might call it a day. I'm sorry; you know all about me and I've monopolised the conversation."

"That's quite alright, young lady. That will cost you a dinner date, and next time I'll bring my couch," teased Ryan. He escorted Estelle to her door.

"Thanks for listening." She smiled.

"Do we have a date?"

"That'd be nice."

HAVING SLEPT HEAVILY, ESTELLE awoke in the middle of the night. Ryan was right. Estelle did feel homesick. Reaching for her mobile, she again dialled her dad.

"Dad, no. Trust me, Dad, I'll be fine. I'll be home just as soon as I can. Don't worry, Dad. Give Nan a big kiss for me, and of course," Estelle smiled, "perhaps a tickle under Mellow's chin from me. Love you, Dad."

SLUMPING INTO HIS LEATHER chair, Sam rubbed his forehead. Yet another call, and yet another futile attempt to get his daughter home. With frequent calls, father to daughter, daughter to father, father to authorities, and so on up and down the line, Sam was exhausted, the reward for his efforts now resting solely in the hands of the police, as did her safety.

Sam's concentration was broken by a loud knock at his door. Examining sales data, Wolfgang made his entry into Sam's office. His mood elevated and exuberant, he laid the spreadsheets across the desk.

Unable to match Wolf's elation, Sam stared back at him coolly, allowing his boss to go on boasting.

"Don't worry, son, I'm sure that the problem will be soon blown away and you'll get your little girl back safely on Aussie soil," volunteered Wolf, rubbing his ruby ring, belatedly aware of Sam's less-than-elated mood. "Let me know if there is anything I can do to help."

"Sure," replied Sam, his voice stilted.

AT THE END OF a day that seemed to have no end, Sam made his way home, took off his tie and headed out for some fresh air.

Traversing a local footbridge, he leaned over to observe the reflection of a lone figure in the water. As the light began to fade, so too did the figure. Sam rubbed the back of his neck and felt for his pendant ring, softly caressing it between his fingers.

With the disappearance of the last of the remaining light, Sam headed home. There he found Mellow patiently waiting at the front door. He picked her up with both hands and tickled her under the chin. The two sat side by side for their evening meal.

With all lights out, Sam could hear the growing feline bouncing down the hallway and up the stairs, pouncing onto his bed. Snuggling into his chest, she purred herself to sleep.

THE NEXT DAY ESTELLE found herself back at the police station. Her help in building the killer's identikit was a little sketchy, given that his features were largely concealed, though his dark, wooden eyes still haunted her. Drained by an intensive couple of hours, she was escorted out of the interview room and again thanked for her assistance.

"Call me any time if you remember anything else. Anything at all," entreated Winterbottom, leading her to the door.

"Look, Detective, I need to get home," protested Estelle meekly.

"Another forty-eight to seventy-two hours, thanks, Miss Goldstein, and you should be free to go," replied Herschowitz.

"OK. I guess I've got a good reason to do some sightseeing."

"Yes, Miss. Enjoy our city," enthused Winterbottom.

After Estelle's departure, the two detectives looked at each other pensively.

"What have we got now, Arnie?" questioned Saul.

"Mabunda's hotel room was broken into: computer missing. USB file found in the lining of the deceased's coat: hole in his pocket. Fortuitous! USB held two PowerPoint files, due for presentation the next day, same time, at this UN-sponsored AIDS conference," replied his bespectacled colleague.

"Did he plan to switch presentations, or what?" Saul scratched his head.

"A contentious presentation at the UN avoids the hazards of getting an article published." The detective rubbed his chin. "I'm no scientist, but this looks like it would have gone off like a bomb shell!"

"Contentious PowerPoint presentation dedicated to one Professor William Hamilton, who died in London following a trip to the Democratic Republic of the Congo in January 2000. According to his passport, Mabunda also flew into and out of the capital, Kinshasa, in January 2000."

"And Hamilton?"

"According to Who's Who, the most significant evolutionary biologists of the twentieth century!" concluded Arnie.

"What's the connection here? What are these two contemporary researchers doing in Kinshasa in January 2000? And now they're both dead," muttered Saul. "And then we have the Goldstein factor."

"Yep. Monkey business alright," concluded his lean colleague.

OUT ON THE FOOTPATH, Estelle was unexpectedly swept into a torrential downpour as she struggled to hail a taxi.

"Estelle!" called a familiar voice. She looked up to spot Ryan dashing across the road towards her through the rain.

"Where's your umbrella, young lady?" He grinned.

"Thanks heaps," she replied, delighted and surprised to see him. "You seem to pop up when I need you the most. But you're always late!" She flicked large drops of rain off her shoulders.

"I do apologise, Miss!" replied Ryan with mock earnestness. "Come on!" Taking her hand in his, Ryan carefully navigated Estelle across the road, all the while sheltering her under his umbrella.

Estelle allowed herself to be guided by his chivalrous presence and it just felt right. Her hand surrendered to his. This just felt like home somehow.

As he opened the door of his car, Ryan put his arm around Estelle to keep her from shivering. "I'll try to be on time next time," he apologised. "You did mention you were due in at the station this morning. Thought I'd pick you up."

Estelle smiled in gratitude, rain dripping from her forehead. They drove through the heavy downpour.

"How did this morning's session go?" quizzed Ryan.

"I almost feel dizzy from having gone round and round in circles: many of the same questions, only phrased differently. Thankfully I'm done for the day." Estelle rubbed her forehead. "Not so very different from my own craft."

"Anything I can do to make it any easier?"

"You've been great. Thank you." Estelle paused, looking Ryan in the eye. "I really mean it. Thank you, Ryan."

"What say you dry off, get on a warm change of clothes, and we grab a quick bite?" he suggested.

"Sounds good." Estelle nodded.

Dried off, and with a warm change of clothes, Estelle and Ryan opted to share their meal at the Roosevelt.

As Ryan ordered, Estelle brought him up to speed with the latest details of the investigation. "I'm beginning to second-guess myself so far as to what else I might remember. Is there anything else? Perhaps some small overlooked detail, some seemingly insignificant clue."

"Go easy on yourself. You've been through quite an ordeal," soothed Ryan.

"I just want the bastard brought to justice," Estelle seethed, her jaw tightening. Gazing out of the entrance, she became distracted, the colour draining from her face.

"Are you OK?" asked Ryan, following her gaze.

"I guess I've just got the spooks," replied Estelle, her sudden disquiet palpable. "I keep imagining that I see his eyes. Sometimes I imagine that I've seen him at a distance, or that I hear his footsteps following me."

"I don't like the idea of you being alone. I'd rather you don't continue to stay here."

"Here?" Estelle frowned.

"At this hotel: by yourself." Ryan's voice elevated a decibel.

"Five-star security: I'll be right. Besides I'll probably spend the rest of the afternoon in my room: a lot of work to catch up on," she reassured with cocky bravado.

"I'm sorry to have to leave right now. Work: afternoon shift at the clinic."

"Hey, I don't need constant babysitting," protested Estelle indignantly.

"Who says I'm babysitting?" Ryan got up, ready to escort her to her door.

"Thank you, Ryan." Estelle smiled. She hesitated for a brief second and then tiptoed up to kiss him on his left cheek.

EXHAUSTED AFTER AN INTENSIVE afternoon of researching, formatting and reformatting, Estelle pulled the drapes for an early evening in front of television. More relaxed, she drifted off to sleep.

"Conggahh!" exclaimed Estelle. It was the middle of the night. She sat bolt upright. A sharp revivification of the dying man's final murmur riveted her attention. She diligently scrawled it into her notepad and slept till morning.

"GOOD MORNING, MISS GOLDSTEIN," greeted Winterbottom offhandedly. "Would you care to come through?" He directed Estelle into an interview room.

Estelle noted his aloofness.

"You say that you have further information for us?" asked the paunchy detective impatiently.

"That's correct! I clearly recall Doctor Mabunda's dying word."

"Word. Is that so?"

"It was conggahh—or something." Estelle shrugged helplessly.

"Conggahh or something, that's hardly a dying declaration, Miss Goldstein." The paunchy detective grimaced. "Thank you for all your help. It has been much appreciated, but we were about to phone you anyway. Doctor Mabunda's murder investigation has reached closure."

"Closed? What? You've found his killer?" Estelle frowned, perplexed by the abrupt change and tone of Winterbottom's voice.

"Doctor Mabunda's assassin was taken out in a shootout with our guys last night."

"Who? When?" asked Estelle, incredulous. "What do you mean by a shootout?" She struggled to take in the revelation.

"His assassin was identified on CCTV. We raided his residence. He was shot violently resisting arrest. Doctor Mabunda's computer was retrieved from amongst his possessions."

"His computer? Why?"

"I guess some crack-heads will kill you for a cup of coffee. Anyway, he's off the streets. You can relax now, Miss."

"Will I be needed for anything?" Estelle's eyes glazed.

"That won't be necessary. Looks like Doctor Mabunda's death has all the hallmarks of a ritual killing. Bicycle spoke through the heart: a Soweto specialty, apparently."

"Soweto specialty?"

"One of our crew's an ex-South African. Tsotsies, I think they're called. Any which way: case closed for you, Miss Goldstein. You're free to go home."

"Home?"

"Have a nice trip and do take care of yourself." Winterbottom was hasty but civil.

"I see!" Estelle frowned. She was briskly led out of the interview room by the impatient detective, who nonetheless hailed her a taxi.

"Out of our hands now." Winterbottom slapped the Pole's back.

"Yeah. Fucking FBI bullshit," muttered Arnie. "Shit! I need a coffee."

Chapter Eight

$\mathcal{B}$athed by autumn sunlight, Estelle strolled through the late morning perusing bric-a-brac, cheap clothing and souvenirs. A beautiful handmade carving caught her attention, her spontaneous smile crowded out by a pensive look as she reached out. A large brown hand engulfed hers.

"Hear no evil. See no evil."

"Shit!" Her eyes widening, she jumped aside. "What the hell? You!" Goose bumps rose over her arms.

"Speak no evil," jested Ryan. "I'm sorry. Didn't mean to—"

"Don't creep up on me like that." She laughed. "Bloody well frightened the bejesus out of me."

"I'm sorry." The New Yorker chuckled. "Allow me." He reached across to retrieve the carving of the Three Wise Monkeys, his warm hand enfolding hers. Their eyes meeting, he carefully laid the carving in Estelle's hand.

"Wow. It's beautiful. Thank you."

"Got here just as fast as I could," apologised Ryan.

"Where's your late note, Mister?"

"Must have left it at work, Miss."

"Well, thank God you're here. I guess I really am still a bit jumpy," she confessed begrudgingly, looking down at her gift.

"Just a little," agreed Ryan, placing his arm protectively around her shoulders.

"Do you make a habit of stalking women?" teased Estelle as they proceeded to weave their way amongst a sea of local and international tourists.

"Habit? Uh-uh. I see what you're getting at. Only good-looking Aussie blondes." Ryan smirked boyishly, taking in Estelle with her tight, cream turtleneck sweater, hip-hugging jeans and knee-high boots.

"Is that so." Estelle laughed.

"My modus operandi," Ryan agreed cheekily. "How did this morning's interview go?"

"Case closed," replied Estelle sharply, throwing up her free hand in frustration. She smiled forcibly.

"What do you mean, case closed?" Ryan's dark eyebrows furrowed.

"I was informed the assassin was taken out by a police shoot-out last night. They were about to notify me: no longer required for their investigations."

"Well, that must be a relief."

"It is! Tell the truth, I'm glad he's off the streets. Though—"

"Almost unbelievable?" cut in Ryan.

"Yes, almost unbelievable." Estelle fell silent, looking down at the Three Wise Monkeys.

Ryan furtively scanned the crowd. "Your plans now?" He refocused his attention back to Estelle.

"Well, I'm booked home Friday. I guess I could—"

"Great! You've got a few days for me to show you around." Ryan grinned enthusiastically.

The two continued to stroll as the big hands on their watches rotated again and again. Together they marvelled at individual pieces of sculptured craftsmanship as they yielded to, and were blessed by the sun's radiance. The fluffy clouds overhead refused to coalesce and a brilliant blue allowed the day to gently warm. The outreaching branches of the trees quietly quivered in tender response to the occasional cool breeze as they drifted through the park. Hosted by a shady glade, they laid back to enjoy the smooth richness of a local jazz band. As the band played, clouds gathered, billowing into myriad creative formations. With the conclusion of the band's final number, Estelle declared it time she made her way back to her hotel.

"And that one right over there?" pointed out Ryan, slowing their pace.

"I see a newborn, a little chubby newborn drifting towards a set of hands," suggested Estelle.

"A scientist with a test tube." He gestured with a theatrical flourish. "That's his hand decanting a test tube right there. See?"

"Oh yeah, I see it now," replied Estelle, playing into his fantasy.

"Did I tell you the one about the scientist writing up his lab findings?"

"No, but I'm sure you're about to." Estelle grinned.

"There was a scientist recording his lab results," shared Ryan. "In front of him stood an insect. The scientist cut off one of the

151

insect's legs, clapped loudly and ordered the insect to jump. At his order, the insect jumped high. He then cut off the insect's second leg, clapped loudly and again ordered the insect to jump. Again the insect jumped high, and again and again, and again as third, fourth and fifth legs were removed. Finally the scientist cut off the insect's last remaining leg and ordered the insect to jump. Much to the scientist's surprise, the insect did not jump. Nor did it respond in any other way. The scientist's conclusion, as he wrote up his findings for publication: When you cut all the legs off an insect, the insect becomes deaf."

Estelle crinkled her nose. "Three out of ten, Mister!" She laughed.

"Dinner tonight?" probed Ryan as they neared the entrance to the hotel.

"Tonight?" teased Estelle with a feigned frown.

"You still owe me." Ryan mirrored her frown, feigning exacerbation.

"I do?" Flirtatiously raising her eyebrow, Estelle bit her lower lip.

"All that patient listening. Come on, you do remember?"

"But of course." Estelle blushed.

"What say I pick you up from reception at six?"

"Looking forward to it!" called out Estelle, glancing seductively over her shoulder as she headed toward the hotel lift.

Awake with fifteen minutes to spare, Estelle sprang out of bed and landed under a hot shower, followed by a shivering rinse. Racing to her closet, indecisiveness followed decisiveness, back to indecisiveness, and again back to decisiveness. What to wear? Too formal: not formal enough. Too long: too short. Too revealing: not revealing enough.

"Ah! The piece de resistance!" she exclaimed, slipping on a mid-calf length midnight blue dress that contoured her body. The front of the dress crisscrossed over her breasts and nipped in tightly at her waist. Her knee-high boots elongated her legs and her handwoven shawl added elegance, pulling together her outfit. Her final touch: a dab of alluring perfume.

Flushed with anticipation, Estelle entered the dimly lit, cosy, log-cabin restaurant. The ambience was intimate and inviting. A large mirror backdrop reflected a crackling open fire in the corner, along with a dozen or so delicate candles strategically placed in the centre of each table. Placing his hand on the small of Estelle's back, Ryan guided her into the room. Shown to their table by their waiter, Ryan pulled out Estelle's chair.

"Thank you." Estelle smiled, turning to face her tall, handsome, well-dressed date.

Ryan returned her smile, taking obvious pleasure in her appreciation.

The service was prompt and the meal scrumptious. The two communicated like intimate friends. Their easy rapport allowed for multifaceted conversation. They talked of politics, philosophy and love. They discussed life and the afterlife, perception and reality, crime and social justice, eco and the economy. They spoke of history, both recent and ancient, themselves and their observations of each other. They hit upon topics on which they agreed and those upon which they agreed to disagree. They debated, they reflected, they laughed. They spoke of times past and times yet to come. But most of all, they were just entranced in this moment of time.

"What led you into being a vet for PETA?" quizzed Estelle.

"I just figured there had to be another way." Ryan shrugged.

"Do tell," invited Estelle.

"As veterinary students we practiced our surgery on many healthy, live animals, some operated on repeatedly, up to seventeen times with little time, if any, for recovery," reflected Ryan. "I'd often go to them in the middle of the night just to sit by their side, to talk to them, to stroke them, to comfort them. But mostly I was comforting myself—for doing what I thought I had to do!"

"Sounds like that was traumatic for you," reflected Estelle.

Ryan shrugged. "Not as traumatic as it was for them." Lapsing into a moment's silence, he sipped on his wine. "I just wasn't being true to myself," he continued.

"All this was done in veterinary school?"

"Yeah. I became a vet to help animals, not destroy them." Ryan grimaced, shaking his head.

Both Ryan and Estelle sat silently.

"And all your protest rallies, do you think they make a difference?"

"Organising rallies, like the one in front of the UN, makes some difference—but there's so much more to be done."

"What's your ultimate goal?"

"An end to vivisection, for starters." Fiddling with his spoon, Ryan's voice was low and precise.

"An anti-vivisectionist and a vegan. My Nan's an animal liberationist and borders on being a vegan. The two of you would get on like a house on fire," Estelle added enthusiastically.

Ryan looked up to see Estelle crinkling her nose at him. "I'd love to meet her some day; I'm sure we would get on. Like a house on fire." His eyes lighted.

"She runs a business, psychics and new age practitioners, called the Psychic Sanctuary."

"So what do they do? Do they all get together and read each other's minds?"

"Something like that."

"Sounds insane." Ryan laughed.

"You got that right: a bit like walking into the Mad Hatter's Tea Party." Estelle chuckled. "A lot of people running around the place, and not all of them sane."

The two laughed out loud, drawing attention from other restaurant patrons.

"So she's a little off the beam then?" Ryan whispered.

"Just a tad; her psychic powers takes a bit of getting used to," Estelle whispered back conspiratorially.

"You sound almost sceptical?" quizzed Ryan. "I'd imagine you'd be used to all that by now?"

"I found it magical as a child, and invasive as an adolescent."

"Aha! Sprung!" roared Ryan, swaying his neck and twinkling his fingers in Estelle's direction.

"You got it," snickered Estelle. "Far too, too many times for my liking."

The two of them roared even louder, Estelle throwing her head back, Ryan shaking his.

"Later, of course, the time came when I decided that I was far too sophisticated in my thinking to believe in all that mumbo-jumbo, so I chose to keep it all at an intellectual distance," stated Estelle in mock sophistication.

"I can just imagine you being that way, Miss Estelle Goldstein," bantered Ryan, reflecting back her tone.

"I still loved my Nan, and I believed that she really did believe that she was a psychic," admitted Estelle.

"And now?" questioned Ryan.

"Now I just accept it, and maybe at times I even respect her for it. Beneath all her eccentricities, she may be the wisest person I know, and way too right, way too often for comfort. But I won't be telling her that any time soon." Estelle lowered her voice.

"Why? Got something to hide, young lady?" smirked Ryan "Mind you, I'm not all that sure what to make of people who claim to have psychic abilities."

"Ever had a psychic reading?"

"Been tempted." Ryan nodded. "I'm open-minded: found Arthur Koestler's writings on the psychic fascinating."

"Arthur who?"

"Koestler. Set up a parapsychology unit in Edinburgh University. But no: never. Do you think you inherited some of your Nan's psychic ability?"

"Doubt it, though Nan calls me a left/right brainer."

"A left/right brainer?" Ryan scratched his head.

"Yeah: someone with left-brained logic, though often right-brained intuitive."

"So let me test out your intuitive abilities: purely in the name of science, of course."

"But of course," acquiesced Estelle.

"Hmm. Can you guess what I'm thinking right now?" Ryan seductively taunted his gorgeous date with his exploring eyes.

"No idea," replied Estelle, tilting her head to one side. "Let me in on it?"

"Oh, I'll let you in on it alright: maybe a bit later." Ryan's tone was suggestively smooth, his eyes smouldering.

"Oh, you!" responded Estelle, smacking the back of his hand. "Behave."

"Sorry." He grinned unapologetically.

"Cheeky bugger." Estelle smiled reflectively. "All Nan's psychic stuff aside, I often think of death and dying and reincarnation. Sometimes I call on my mum when I'm in trouble and don't know what to do, and not ready to open up to anyone else." Estelle went quiet. "I'm sure she hears me."

"Must have been hard growing up without your mum," sympathised Ryan.

"Made me more independent. Dad tried, but he was often at work. Nan became my mum, but she never replaced her. Funny." Estelle paused. "I often wonder how my life might be different if I knew the due date and time of my own death: bit like an annual pre-death anniversary."

"Interesting thought." Ryan watched Estelle carefully. "Bit of a morbid gestation though," he lightly jested.

"Not really. Death's as important as birth. Perhaps mortality forces us to focus on our real priorities. Perhaps I'd put those ones first." Again she paused. "I've never told anyone this my whole life, but when times get really, really tough, I swear after all these years, Mum always advises me to play it backwards."

"Backwards?" invited Ryan.

"Yeah, like she might have done had she somehow known that her own time would be cut so short." Estelle shrugged. "I try to imagine those situations as if I'm looking back in my final moments."

"Never looked at it that way." Ryan scratched the back of his neck.

"I see how death frames my life."

"Some insight." Now it was Ryan's turn for a pause. Gazing deeply at Estelle, he narrowed his eyes in search of hers.

"What are you thinking?" asked Estelle, interrupting his silence.

"I'm just thinking how beautiful you are." Ryan noticed Estelle blush. "So what else about your Nan? Did she predict that you would meet a tall, dark, handsome stranger?"

"Maybe." Estelle flirted, playfully easing the intensity of the moment.

"Maybe, huh?" responded Ryan, taking hold of Estelle's hand, then without warning diverting a spoonful of vegan chocolate mud cake into his own mouth.

"Hey! Eat your own," protested Estelle, smacking his hand again. "She strongly suggested I pack a couple of nice things to wear, especially for one evening." Estelle relinquished some privately guarded space.

"I like," responded Ryan, eyeing Estelle's clinging outfit.

"Oh, you do, do you?" Estelle smiled cheekily, stroking the long stem of her glass.

"Only one flaw with that suggestion, Miss Goldstein."

"Oh?" puzzled Estelle.

"She should have suggested you pack an entire wardrobe of those dresses, as I fully intend to see each and every one of them."

A fuzzy, warm glow radiated throughout each of Estelle's senses. She had him, and she knew it, but now too, she was a goner. Nan's good advice echoed softly in her mind. 'Always allow a man to chase you until you catch him, sweet pea.'

"Oh. And what if this is the only evening dress that I possess?" teased Estelle, secretly catching her breath.

"Then I will make it my business to see to it that you will, in time, have an entire wardrobe of them."

"Like that, uh? I see." Estelle blushed.

"Does Nan see that you have a soul mate," he pushed.

Goosebumps rose over the entire contour of Estelle's skin. "She talks about sacred contracts that we have entered into with those who play a major part in our lives."

"Sacred contracts." Ryan tilted his head. "Sounds interesting." He reached across the table, the soft, naked candle flame highlighting Estelle's gold bracelet as it flickered in the shadowy light. Tenderly he ran his fingers over the back of her hand. She blushed again as she looked down at his large, square brown hand.

"Yeah, like we reincarnate to fulfill these sacred contracts."

Gently Ryan turned Estelle's hand, resting her hand in his. Estelle sighed deeply, yielding to Ryan's hand.

"What's this? Burnt yourself ironing?" Ryan caressed the rope-shaped mark across the inner part of her left wrist.

"Nan says it's my Stevenson birthmark."

"And who is Stevenson?"

"Ian Stevenson, the Galileo of twentieth century psychiatry: claims to have scientific proof of reincarnation by tracing tell-tale birthmarks!"

"Sounds intriguing?" With his other hand, Ryan reached across the linen tablecloth and lifted Estelle's chin.

"And you, Estelle, what do you believe? Do you believe we've been here before," asked Ryan, looking into her sparkling blue eyes.

"I guess I do believe in reincarnation and the stars," she responded. She could feel the tenderness of her heart as it fluttered within her chest.

"With a name like Estelle, I guess you'd have to."

"I was sort of named after Nan: Esther," elaborated Estelle.

"Stella. Star: a star that shines." Ryan paused. "I'm sure we've been here before and that we'll be here again." His voice was so quiet that he could just about hear Estelle's heart begin to pound as her breathing intensified.

"So why do you keep following me? Sorry. I mean, how is it that you just keep showing up in my life?"

"Sorry, Estelle, I didn't mean to make you uncomfortable." He apologetically pulled back.

"No, please just pretend I didn't say that. What I meant to say is my life has been so crazy this last six months; you couldn't even begin to imagine. It's like my whole world has been turned upside-down and inside out, and I've woken up in some other kind of reality."

"Any of this got to do with your illness?" pressed Ryan, confused by the sudden change.

"Illness?"

"You know; your stay in hospital?"

"Yes. Yes. That." Estelle frowned. "What were you doing there?"

"I was visiting my mother."

"I didn't see any African woman in any of the other beds on my floor."

"My mother's Lebanese background but an Aussie through and through. Why were you looking at all the other beds?" He laughed, pulling back and looking at her with mock indignation.

"Oh, you know how it is. A long time in hospital, nothing better to do, obviously, than go wandering around all over the place meeting people: in fact, some extraordinary people."

"Well, appearances can be deceptive. My paternal grandfather was a Knight—from Ireland. Grandma was a Bakare from West Africa. So Dad's a black knight, so to speak. Mum's people, West African Lebs. The Khourys settled in Sydney."

"I thought you said your mum's Lebanese."

"Yes. That's Khoury, not Koori," explained Ryan. "Not that it bothers me being perceived as Aboriginal. I'm Afro-Arab-Aussie-Black American, whatever." Ryan chuckled, amused at Estelle's faux pas. "Next?"

"So where were you born?" inquired Estelle.

"Born and raised in the Eastern Suburbs, Sydney, in fact."

"You!" She frowned. "That's crazy. I was born and raised there too!"

"Mum and Dad split up when I was sixteen and I first came across to live with Dad in the States. I remember the day we moved here really clearly. It was the ninth of November, two days before my birthday, and I know it must have upset Mum a real lot."

"Wait! Your birthday falls on the same day as mine." Estelle leaned forward, eyes wide open.

"Yours is on the eleventh of November? Hey, are you for real? Nah."

"I've been asking myself the same question," murmured Estelle.

"What year?" asked Ryan.

"What year? Ah. Oh, ah, every year."

"You're really funny. What year were you born?" Ryan jutted his jaw toward Estelle.

"1976: the year of the dragon. I'm a Scorpio dragon!"

"Hey, man, that's really so, so cool. You're not about to believe this but—"

"No! You mean? Oh no, now you really are spooking me. Please, I've got an uncanny feeling with everything that has been happening in my world lately. I thought I was finally in the real world. Now I'm not so sure. Please don't tell me same year at the Royal Private," pleaded Estelle.

"Are you sure you don't have some kind of sixth sense like your Nan?"

"Please don't tell me, please. No! Do tell me." begged Estelle.

"Tell you what?" Ryan hesitated, vacillating between raising his eyebrows, frowning, nodding, and shaking his head almost simultaneously.

"You're not going to believe this, but all this stalking each other may have started a long time before you and I had any say in it. It was our mums and dads that started it all," rambled Estelle.

"Now I'm not sure if you're starting to intrigue me more, or scare me."

"I think I have a photo of you taken soon after your birth."

"You're pulling my leg. Right?"

"I wish I was. Oh, how I wish I was," sighed Estelle.

"You mean you have a picture of a baby that looked like I might have looked at a few days old?"

"No! You don't get it!"

"No. You've got that one right!" Ryan contorted his face.

"You were born at about six am. Correct?"

Rising to his feet, Ryan took off his coat. "Getting a bit warm in here. Correct! Your ESP thing you have going. I think you're really good." Ryan nodded, scratching the side of his head as he sat back down.

"No, I'm serious. My Nan took the photo. I saw it shortly before I collapsed and got rushed into hospital." Estelle took a deep breath. "I've got to go." She stood up abruptly, turning to leave. "I don't feel so good."

Grabbing his coat, Ryan pursued. "Wait! Wait! Where are you going? What's going on?"

"No. I think I need to be on my own. Stop following me," demanded Estelle, turning on him.

"I'm not sure I follow. How it is you think that I am following you? You might be the one following me. After all, you're the one who's in New York right now! Right?" protested Ryan, struggling to put on his coat.

"Please! You don't get it."

"I'm all ears. Please, Estelle, don't run out on me. Do you need some help?"

"It's like I know too much about you."

"Does that mean you think I'm going to need to kill you." Ryan hurriedly settled the bill, the bewildered cashier scratching his ear.

"Hey, that's not funny."

"Sorry." He followed her out into the street.

Estelle turned to look at him. "It means I've been feeling this strange connection for months: maybe even longer," babbled Estelle. "It's like I've known you my whole life, or maybe longer: some kind of karmic bond. Oh God, I'm starting to sound like Nan. Please say something before I dig myself an even bigger hole. Oh, wait. And then there was Angelica. Please don't tell me you know Angelica."

"Who's Angelica?"

"She's an angel, I guess. I don't know."

"You don't know, but you think I might know her?"

"She existed—until she didn't. She forgot to tell me just one minor detail—like that she was dead."

"Dead? This Angelica is dead? And I might know her? OK, now I'm being spooked. Next you're going to tell me that I might be dead, only I don't know it. Have I got the gist?"

"Please, Ryan, I've got to go," begged Estelle.

"You're not the only one," called out Ryan.

Estelle immediately recoiled as Ryan's tone became sombre. She instantly ceased to speak. A puzzled look came over her face: instant recognition of a voice other than her own inside her head.

"The only one what?" Estelle took a couple of steps backwards.

"Hear me out, Estelle. Please."

"I don't need to hear or see anything else as or more confused than I already have."

"You're not the only one who has fallen in love here."

A surge of cold air hit Estelle's face. She inhaled in shock and turned to wave down a taxi. With tender force, Ryan pulled her towards him, his warm breath on her cheek.

"Somehow it feels like I have known you my entire life. You've just pulled through some crazy times and maybe you're not yourself right now; maybe neither of us is behaving like we normally would. And yes, you do come out with some strange things, but that's what I love about you. My world is straight: I'm a scientist. Sometimes fighting for what is right, I have to deal with some pretty horrific stuff. Each day I just keep fighting. I'm confronted with stuff too horrendous to see, too unbearable to deal with, too heartbreaking to comprehend. It's just how it is for me. Estelle, listen to me. I know it's only been days, and if you're crazy, then so am I, but how often do we get to feel a connection that makes us feel so intoxicated and alive. You want to talk about the dead and the dying. Estelle, right now, here with you, I feel more alive than I can ever remember feeling my whole life. Estelle, please don't leave me or I will follow you, and that's a promise."

Estelle looked at Ryan as if it was the first time she had laid eyes on a man: his warm breath, getting warmer against her cheek; his strong, masculine arms pulling her to his chest; his eyes swimming in hers. Slowly he ran his fingertips across her quivering chin, the back of his hand across her trembling cheeks, then over her hair, gazing at her. Brushing back several strands of her hair, he breathed deeply, raising Estelle's chin with his fingers. Slowly their mouths met. Pressing his lips against hers, he kissed her deeply and passionately. As he held her to his chest, time stood still. She could hear and feel his heart. They had just tasted life as if for the first time.

"Goose bumps?" Ryan took off his coat and draped it around Estelle's shoulders, his left arm buffering her from the chill. Together they began strolling through the streets of Manhattan. He was eager to show her the best his city had to offer. With its electrifying sounds and dazzling neon lights, New York nightlife was intoxicating. Estelle was thrilled by the city that never sleeps. They had now become a part of the greatest show on earth. The expression on her face, the look in her eyes, the radiance of her smile as she looked up at Ryan: Estelle was charged with excitement. Taking her in, her excitement became his. It seemed as if the party had been turned on just for the two of them.

Leading her across the Brooklyn Bridge was a fairytale come true. She had never felt this before. He had never felt this before, and as they traversed, it was as if they were traversing into another world. Moulding her body into his, his protective arm around her waist, Estelle held her breath at each entrancing vision. She marvelled at the bridge with its network of cables, amazing arches, and the plaques that told of its incredible history. Looking back, she delighted at the spectacular sight of lower Manhattan in all of its psychedelic brilliance. She relished the joy and exuberant chatter of locals and tourists alike: a melting pot of every race and ethnicity. In the main she could identify the tourists by their unlimited variety of poses and clicking cameras, all set to capture the stunning backdrop of tall buildings and monumental structures: the Empire State building with its magnificent architectural excellence, especially a crowd favourite; and then there was The Statue of Liberty, New York's greatest showpiece, and the proudest display of them all. As the night buzz of city traffic moved beneath them, Estelle struggled to take in the breadth of the never-ending skyline.

Their stroll across the world famous suspension bridge neared its end. Crossing the bridge planks, Ryan whisked Estelle onto a waiting ferry. As they rode across the waves, he held her closely and stroked her back and shoulders. Looking deeply into her eyes, he pulled her to his chest. Enveloped in his arms, he again kissed her tenderly, the enchantment of the unforgettable night captured in the reflection on the shimmering water below.

Slowly Estelle and Ryan strolled back to the Roosevelt, their idle chatter and carefree laughter captured and carried through the night by a gentle breeze.

SWIPING HER SECURITY CARD, Estelle stood motionless, surveying her room. "Ryan!"

"What is it?"

"Someone's been in my room."

"Room service?"

"No! I swear this is not how I left it, and this is not how they would have left it either!" She grimaced, shrugging off Ryan's amorous advances.

"Well, thank God for that," Ryan joked, noting Estelle's bras and panties spilling from her suitcase onto the carpeted floor.

"I had most of my stuff packed ready for check-out!" she insisted, collecting up her scattered items.

Ryan swept into action, checking wardrobes and windows. "Anything missing?"

"I left cupboards all neatly shut," replied Estelle, rummaging through drawers left ajar." My computer! It's missing! I've been robbed!"

"Are you sure?"

"I thought I saw him in the street." Estelle was wide-eyed.

"Saw who?" Ryan moved towards her.

"Mabunda's assassin. I'll never forget his eyes."

"He was taken out by the police," reassured Ryan, his hands firmly planted on Estelle's shoulders.

"It doesn't make sense." Estelle held her breath. "I might have seen him before then. Nothing makes sense. I've got the creeps."

Ryan searched Estelle's eyes. "Right! I'm calling hotel management." Pulling Estelle in close, Ryan called for security. "I don't want you staying here by yourself. You're coming with me," he commanded as he hung up the phone. "I've got a convertible lounge. You'll be safe. Trust me." He rubbed her upper arms.

Estelle paused. "OK. Thanks. Just not comfortable here, um, OK."

Management arrived within minutes, giving Estelle time to collect herself. She was irritated, but quiescent as the security staff re-checked drawers and closets, and under the bed, for her missing computer.

"This type of event is not known at the Roosevelt," apologised the assistant manager as he processed Estelle's official investigation request. "Another room perhaps?"

"Miss Goldstein will be checking out tonight," instructed Ryan.

"We'll get a porter to assist," complied the assistant manager.

"It's OK. I'll take care of it. I was a porter in my early uni years," quipped Ryan.

Out on the kerb, Ryan hailed down a cab and they bundled into the back.

"Nan did mention the death of an innocent man, and not to hesitate in changing hotels. Her psychic messages are always so cryptic."

Ryan listened in silence. Within twenty minutes their taxi pulled up outside a vintage brownstone building. Ryan quickly unloaded Estelle's luggage and whisked her out of the cold.

Entering his ground floor apartment, Estelle and Ryan were greeted by an excitable white, black and tan beagle.

"Back home soon, Buddy. Will miss you." Ryan squatted to give the canine a big hug. "Go on then: just like reading the paper, eh." He smiled as the affectionate beagle went berserk, wagging his tail and sniffing his human companions for information.

"Where's home?"

"Buddy lives at my dad's country property. He's been keeping me company while Dad's been out of town. You OK?" Ryan rose to his feet to meet Estelle face to face.

Throwing her head back, Estelle inhaled deeply with her eyes closed. "So, so sorry: massive overreaction."

"No need to apologise. You've been through quite an ordeal. To be expected. Besides I get to play the knight, eh." Ryan smiled.

"Thanks, Ryan." Estelle sighed. "God!"

"Now can I tempt you?" He raised his left eyebrow. "A hot cacao? Chef's specialty!" he offered with a cheeky grin.

"Sounds good."

"Make yourself right at home," he invited as he slipped into the kitchen.

Estelle cruised across the room, scanning a floor-to-ceiling bookshelf: *You Can Conquer Cancer; The Wealth Within; Eat to live; The China Study; Green for Life.*

"Hey! You have some of my Nan's favourite books. Do you read much?" called out Estelle.

"I'm the original bookworm," replied Ryan enthusiastically as he re-entered the room, warm drinks in hand.

"Cosy old fireplace!" Estelle rubbed her hands together.

"Even cosier lit." Ryan obliged, lighting the gas. "Lovely fake coals."

Having warmed the room, he placed his mug on a carved wooden box beneath a window facing the street and moved to the next room to collect fresh sheets and towels.

He answered his mobile in a lowered voice: "All set to go. Got metal cutters? Right. Spoke to the others. Problems with security all seen to." He paused to listen. "We enter from back lane. Park vans closest to the left side entrance. Will send a signal on approach," instructed Ryan. "Two a.m. sharp. Staff all left."

After settling Estelle, Ryan turned in, setting his wrist alarm for one a.m.

Creeping out of his darkened room, Ryan quietly entered the lounge room. Sitting by Estelle, he watched her stir in her sleep.

"Called out for a sick animal, back shortly," he whispered apologetically, kissing her on the forehead. "Buddy will keep an eye on you."

Estelle groaned and rolled over.

Her hooded beau scudded out the door.

MORNING LIGHT STREAMED IN courtesy of an old leadlight window. Estelle stretched and lay awake, quietly entranced by the many hues. She inhaled deeply in anticipation, smelling the rich aroma emanating from the kitchen, Ryan clattering away. Her attention narrowed to a number of degrees hung on a nearby wall not far from the window and the carved box beneath the window, then the bookcase not far from the foyer entrance.

"Eerie," she murmured.

"What? You're not keen on breakfast? You haven't even tasted it yet?" Ryan entered the room with breakfast tray in hand.

"It's like I've been here before."

"Was breakfast any better that time?" asked Ryan, placing the tray on the wooden box by her side.

"I'm having a déjà vu moment."

"Damn! I missed a hottie in my apartment. When was that?"

"No. I'm seriously having a déjà vu experience."

"I have them all the time," replied Ryan coolly.

"When?" Estelle frowned.

"Every Thursday night."

"What do you mean?"

"I'm part of the déjà vu society. Didn't I mention it?"

"There's a déjà vu society?"

"Yeah, we meet every Tuesday night at eight p.m. and then again on Thursday night, same time, same place."

"Not funny," replied Estelle, swiping him across the shoulder. "This is so freaky! It's like I've been here before: in this very room." She continued eyeing her surrounds.

"You don't believe me?" Ryan hung his head with a pout. "Now stop talking and eat up before it goes cold. After breakfast we're off shopping."

"Shopping where and what for?"

"To answer your first question, hopefully somewhere you haven't been before. To answer your second question, to find some outfits for a fancy dress. We have a masquerade ball tonight: thought you might enjoy it." He grinned.

"You are one strange kind of guy."

"As you may appreciate, Mademoiselle, this fabulous French gown from the fifteen hundreds is made of our finest white linen. The inner kirtle is lined with our softest velveteen and is pulled together with this wide black belt, which will enhance your womanly curves. As you move, Mademoiselle, you will feel the drop of the gown as it sweeps the floor with its length," jested Ryan. "Perhaps, Mademoiselle, you shall attend the ball as a damsel in distress."

"The weight in this thing." Estelle chuckled, struggling to hold the garment up against her body.

"Though I have heard from reliable sources that women do fancy men in uniform. So what do you think?" Wearing an army jacket of the 13th Light Dragoons, Ryan leapt out from behind an overpacked clothing rack.

"You are seriously insane."

"Or we can take a walk on the wild side: me Tarzan, you Jane." He stood with his legs astride, thumping his chest with one hand, African jungle attire in the other.

"Anything skimpier?"

"Wait! Wait, Miss Goldstein, a nurse's uniform. Men love a gal in uniform. Haven't you heard?"

"Your State's mental health programme must be seriously underfunded." Estelle giggled.

"Yes, Nursie."

Stepping out onto the pavement, Estelle lapsed into an uneasy quiet.

"What's up?" nudged Ryan.

Goosebumps quickly spread, claiming her upper arms. "Weird. Like someone's just walked over my grave," replied Estelle with a shudder. "Like some weird kind of familiarity. Where to next?" she deflected.

"Allow me." Squeezing her hand, he escorted her across the road and pulled her in under his arm as they headed for Central Park.

There Estelle observed humans and animals in their recreation: humans on vacation, wildlife in migration. Birds took to the wind in flight with their flocks while humans took to the pavements, jogging in droves. The sounds of birdsong filled the cool air while the cacophony of children's laughter was buffered by lush greens. The elderly strolled by sedately, the young skated by independently. Animals enacted their mating rituals, humans their courtship rituals.

Strolling across a lawn, they made their way to Strawberry Fields, a memorial in remembrance of John Lennon. The monument was dedicated by his widow, Yoko Ono, and stood as a lasting tribute to her beloved husband and soul mate.

Amidst the black and white mosaic monument was just one single word: Imagine. It was that one single word the whole world recognised, that one single word the whole world could never forget. That one single word had touched the world, soul deep; that one single word had challenged the whole world to its very core.

"Imagine?" reflected Estelle, taking in the endless floral display that adorned the temple.

"Simple enough message," acknowledged Ryan.

"You guys really copped it with 9/11."

"Yeah. Bad: real bad, but we refuse to let it get on top of us. If anything, the legacy of 9/11 has made me remember not to take life for granted."

"Sounds like it's still very raw."

"Yeah. I had a mate in the South Tower. Chris. He texted all his loved ones before it collapsed. He just told us all he loved us, and his parting words?" Ryan smiled. "Life's short: eat dessert first!"

Arriving back at Ryan's apartment, Estelle pleaded exhaustion, showered, and acquiesced to crashing out on Ryan's bed, sans Ryan.

Estelle fell into a dead slumber, punctuated by an occasional whimper. Ryan refrained from waking her, until some two hours into her sleep, she called out his name. "Ryan. Ryan!"

Responding to her fretful cries, Ryan gently interrupted a presumed nightmare.

"Ryan!?" exclaimed Estelle, confused. "I thought you'd be too late."

"Too late? We will be too late if you don't get dressed. Andiamo!"

"My God, where am I?"

"You're in my bed, Mademoiselle, and we are late for our engagement!"

Estelle ordered Ryan out of his bedroom and scrambled to dress for the occasion.

"OK. You can open your eyes now," announced Ryan as their taxi pulled up.

Estelle opened her eyes to the bedazzling brilliance of Broadway. Stepping out onto the kerb of New York's Theatre District, Estelle was instantly and magically transported into another world. This was a world of glamour, rich in talent extraordinaire, with its rows and rows of plays and productions, theatre and musicals, song and voice, dance and movement: at every corner the spectacular showcasing of yet another theatrical event; at every step another larger-than-life famous name, set in lights; at every turn, the delights of yet another gourmet eatery. An intoxicating atmosphere of excitement filled the sidewalks and waffled through the air from theatregoers of every age and stage from all around the world. Estelle was enthralled by a world of make-believe, a magical place that somehow held extraordinary power with its bewitching sensations of liveliness as it captivated and catapulted the imagination from the real to the surreal.

Ryan led Estelle into a splendid old theatre. It was as if, upon their entry, they had stepped back in time and into the pages of a bygone era. Observing their visitation were the ghostly figures from the photographs that lined each wall, each a celebrated name of those who once graced cinema and stage with their performances, their autographed images a reminder of a career that had blazed so brightly and now acted as a beacon for those brave souls daring enough to follow in their footsteps.

Standing in the foyer, Estelle could almost hear the chatter of nobility, all to be seen in their finery. There were refined ladies of poise and etiquette and distinguished gentlemen of wit and charm. Ladies wore elegant white gloves to the elbow and beautiful ball gowns that swept the patterned carpet. Gentlemen wore bow ties and tuxedos. Courteously they stood alongside the ladies they escorted. Sipping on fine wine from long-stemmed glasses, pleasantries were exchanged as too, commentary on the finer details of the etchings proudly showcased above the hand-carved railings.

From deep within the chambers, Estelle could still hear the operatic arias reverberate from the stage, rebounding against each crimson wall, with even the most critical of audiences rising from the gallery, tears in their eyes, the resounding applause so deafening it would have shaken the crystal chandeliers hung from the ornate ceilings. The sounds of yesteryear still echoed from beyond the final fall of the heavy velvet curtains and Estelle could still hear the murmuring of those who had attended. Each giving verdict, be it lavish praise or scathing criticism.

Entering one of the smaller theatre rooms, they were acknowledged by the nods of other masked partygoers.

"You know these people?" she whispered to Ryan.

"They all know me. Work colleagues fund-raising for PETA. I guess I'm always the knight." Ryan adjusted his plastic helmet.

"Feels like everyone is staring at us."

"That's because you, Miss Joan of Arc, are one hot woman. Come, I'll introduce you." Ryan forged ahead into the crowd, Estelle beside him.

"Why? It's not like I'm going to recognise any of these people by morning," protested Estelle. Swept inside, she felt instantly devoured by an endless parade of colourful masks that observed her every movement.

"Are you OK?" asked Ryan, noting Estelle's reserve.

"Yeah, I'm fine." Estelle took in the colour, noise and movement of the room, all set against the backdrop of a phantasmagorical yesteryear with both its finery and eeriness.

Several dances and a couple of drinks later, Estelle began to relax. The pressure of idle small talk with masked bandits abated as the increased volume of noise entranced a mass of dancing couples. She felt less claustrophobic and more comfortable swanning about, smiling and making eye contact from one mystery guest to the next.

It was definitely smoke, not cigarette or weed. An icy chill ran down her spine. Turning, Estelle became aware of a cold, sinister stare stretching out to her from across the room. Her menacing adversary was dressed in full cardinal's regalia, a large ruby ring adorning his meaty left ring-finger. She looked away, and went off to find Ryan, who'd excused himself to get drinks.

Ryan sidled up to Estelle in her Joan of Arc garb. "Here, gorgeous." He smacked her inviting butt.

The blonde spun around. "Why, thank ya, honey. Don't mind if I do."

Ryan handed over the champagne mechanically. This was not Estelle's mouth and not Estelle's voice. "My pleasure, Mademoiselle." He bowed gallantly.

"I'm Carol. Carol Hughes," announced the blousy blond, presenting her hand.

"I'm a knight on an errand, m'lady." Ryan obliged the unfamiliar blonde by pecking her hand, then about-faced and melted back into the crowd, leaving a confused Carol to sip her champagne.

Estelle continued to scuttle, wide-eyed behind her mask, from one end of the room to the other. She dared not look back, sensing intimidation from the stranger's eyes, his chilling focus following her every move. Estelle made her way through the crowd and slipped out onto the terrace. She was immediately aware of the genuine chill of the evening and the warmth of the flaming gas lantern towers surrounding her. She scurried to a secluded corner of a small balcony and stood motionless as she struggled to regain her breath. A full moon had risen.

"Estelle!"

Startled, she jumped. "Ryan, where have you been? I thought you'd forgotten me."

"Been looking for you, sweetheart; you just slipped away from me."

"Don't warm to the cardinal dude!" Estelle swallowed and coughed fitfully.

"Are you OK? Can I get you some water?"

"I'd like to get out of this place."

"Perhaps getting out of the cold night air might be a start." Ryan gently guided Estelle back towards the main room.

"I don't want to go back in there. I just want to get the hell out of this place."

"What? Don't care for the mask? Must confess I don't care for them much either," soothed Ryan, holding her clammy hand in his.

Rapid pulsations were visible in Estelle's neck. "If this is your idea of a joke, it's a bad one."

"OK. OK. We can go."

"Thank you." Estelle looked furtively back into the crowded room. "I'll just say goodbye to—."

"I'm leaving now, with you or without you."

"Estelle, take it easy."

"Damn you, Ryan, I'm serious." Estelle's voice raised several octaves against the competing backdrop of entertainment.

"Oh. I get it. You want me to take you home now. All you had to do is ask." Ryan calmly led her out of the venue.

The taxi ride home was frosty, Estelle aloof to Ryan's efforts at physical closeness.

Inside his apartment, Ryan's continued conciliatory efforts bounced back off Estelle's deafening cold wall of silence as she hurriedly went about gathering her belongings, crashing, banging and slamming every step of the way.

Standing by the door, Ryan grabbed her wrists. "Talk to me, Estelle," he pleaded. "Remember, I will follow you forever."

"I just needed to get the hell out of there."

"Come on, cool your jets. Take you to a masquerade ball and you put on a big enough performance to carry the entire theatre district. I just want to know what's going on for you. OK?"

"When is everything going to stop being one big joke to you, Ryan?" she shouted, struggling to get away. "So insensitive."

"OK. OK. I take the insensitive bit. I really did believe the advertising claim—the mask—you know, one size fits all. Umm—not funny?"

Estelle went to hit him, struggling even harder to get away. Ryan locked her into a tight bear hug. Estelle's eyes began to well.

"It's OK," he soothed.

"Sorry," she whispered.

"I get it. I totally get it."

"No, Ryan, you don't get it. I thought I saw his eyes." Estelle's face was deadpan.

Ryan lifted her chin, holding her gaze. "Saw who?"

"The killer: whoever. I swear I've come across him before. It's like his eyes kept following me from behind his mask. They just kept following me, Ryan." She stopped and looked at him. A cold shiver ran up her spine. "I just keep imagining that I see him. I can't get his eyes out of my mind."

"I know. I'm sorry you had to go through all that. I should have thought. You do remember the assassin was killed in a police shoot-out?" Assured Ryan, gently rubbing Estelle's left wrist.

"Yes, but, all the flashbacks, and not just…just when I think it's all over."

"I'd never put you in harm's way. You've got to know that." Ryan's voice softened further. Lifting Estelle's wrist to his lips he planted a soft kiss on her birthmark.

ESTELLE FELL SOUNDLY ASLEEP. Having offered her his bed, Ryan withdrew to the couch and collapsed into slumber, his long legs dangling over the end of the foldout. Buddy was agitated. Vigilant, he paced from one room to the next, checking in on both of them as they slept.

A sharp, ear-piercing siren woke both Ryan and Estelle. Buddy began frantically barking and circling the apartment, claws scraping along the polished wooden floorboards as he dashed from one room to the next. Snarling, he began to lunge at the windows, Ryan's in particular, his aggression uncharacteristically out of control. He charged to the front door, snarling and biting in a lather of relentless determination to be let out.

"Quiet, Buddy!" commanded Ryan, throwing on shirt and pants and heading for the door. He went outside to survey the street for any mischief. Noting nothing out of the ordinary, he calmly walked back inside, only to hear the deafening sounds of emergency vehicles. "Buddy! Sit! Quiet! What's wrong with you?"

"Ryan?"

"Are you alright?" he enquired as he sat by Estelle on his bed.

She remained silent for several moments. "The sirens?" she asked, huddling in his quilt.

"This is New York—regular as sunrise." Taking Estelle in his arms, they both fell asleep.

UP AT THE CRACK of dawn, Ryan rustled around in the kitchen, preparing coffee while Estelle slept in. He switched on the news quietly in time to catch "...fundraiser was marred by suspected arson attack, and strangulation of twenty-five-year old Carol Hughes. Police investigations are continuing. Stephanie Wright reporting. N.B—" Ryan hurriedly flicked off the TV.

"What's that, Ryan?" Estelle yawned.

"How'd ya sleep?"

"Good. Sorry for taking over your bed." She laughed.

"Coffee and muffins?"

"Yum!"

"Get this into you and your stuff together and we're out of here."

"I'm tired. Sleeeep," she pleaded.

"Nah. Day trip. Surprise. We're leaving. Beautiful day. And the mountains beckon."

Chapter Nine

"Come on, Buddy!" invited Ryan, waiting for the mutt to enter via the rear door as Estelle clambered into the passenger seat.

"Don't expect I'll do the same." Estelle grinned and rolled her eyes as Ryan turned the ignition.

"Do the same what?"

"That whole slobbering over your hand bit."

"Aha! As they say, dogs are a man's best friend. Right, Buddy?" Ryan laughed, raising his eyebrows, checking rear-vision mirrors and easing into traffic.

"No hard feelings, Buddy, but I prefer my little Mellow."

"Dogs are loyal and will serve their masters," responded Ryan enigmatically as Buddy barked for attention.

"Cats are independent and can fend for themselves."

"Buddy fetches the paper the minute we let him out. Isn't that right, Buddy?" again checking his rear-view mirror.

"Mellow lets herself out through her cleverly self-crafted, ripped screen hatch. And no, she will not be lowered to such menial tasks."

"Like any true aristo-cat, she has you all jumping through hoops. Right?"

"Something like that." Estelle laughed.

"As they say, 'Cats have servants: dogs have masters.'" Ryan chuckled.

"You still haven't told me where we're going," quizzed Estelle as Ryan manoeuvred his old Chevy around traffic.

"Catskills! Cat country!"

"Bring it on!" hooted Estelle.

Buddy gave a whimper and plonked himself on the back seat.

Heading nor'-west, Ryan kept monitoring the surrounding traffic, periodically checking his rear-view mirror. The bustle of the city soon gave way to a monotony of stop-lights and overhead electric wires. Eventually they rendezvoused with Route 23 and headed for the distant mountains.

Ryan's light hearted banter evaporated as they gained altitude, twisting and turning fast up the steep mountain highway. "Shall we take the scenic route?" He swung sharp right onto a gravel off-road, skidding to an abrupt halt as the short offshoot came to an unexpected dead-end. "Sorry."

"Scenic route, ha?" Estelle looked at Ryan, perplexed. "You really don't expect me to go parking here, do you?"

"Sorry, Estelle: wrong turn." He hastily turned back to the main route. A blue sedan flashed past just before they joined the highway. Ryan paused.

"And?" Bemused, Estelle looked at Ryan.

They re-entered the highway, turning back to where they'd come from.

"This is a better way. The scenic route." Ryan frowned, checking his mirrors.

"Sure you're OK?"

"I'm OK. This car doesn't feel right though." Ryan abruptly turned off onto another gravel road. "We'll drop in to see an old friend who can look at it."

"This is not the Belanglo State Forest, is it?"

"What?"

"You're behaving erratically, Ryan." The Chevy rattled, following the gravel road. "What sort of facial coverage might I expect from this one?" Estelle clutched the dashboard to steady herself.

"He's more of a hoodie," teased Ryan.

"They say you know people by the company they keep," mocked Estelle.

The tree-lined road formed a tranquil archway as they drove further into a green silence.

"Here we are," announced Ryan, cruising to a halt.

Estelle sat surveying a vast open green with several horse and cow enclosures framed by distant mountains. On it stood a humble wooden dwelling adorned by a brightly coloured plaque: 'St Francis of Assisi.'

An old man waved.

"St Francis? He looks a bit derelict," muttered Estelle, unbuckling her seat belt.

"Not quite. Mel's his caretaker, mechanic, jack-of-all-trades, whatever," Ryan replied under his breath.

"Well, hello there, stranger," greeted the old man, ambling towards them.

"Mel, this is Estelle: from Sydney, Australia."

"Lovely to meet you, my dear," charmed the old fellow with a subtle lilt in his voice. On closer inspection the slightly rotund man almost looked like Santa Claus, sans beard. Fresh blisters bubbled his face. He had a full head of white, curly hair, slightly thinning on top, and evidently had spent more time in the sun than his skin could handle.

"Got a bit of a rattle; mind if I put the car over the pit? Might do an overnight swap with the van, if that's OK?"

"Be my guest, son. Just drive around," obliged the old guy as he opened the gates.

"So, Estelle, welcome; your first trip to our lovely land?" He guided Estelle around the corner of the building as Ryan swung his car into the garage, out of view from the roadside.

"Yes. You live in quite an impressive part of the world."

"Mel, can you check this out?" called Ryan.

Excusing himself, Mel obligingly strolled over.

With bonnet up, the two engaged in secret men's business while Estelle kept amused with the over-enthusiastic beagle busily sniffing the grounds.

"No problem," Mel soothed, patting Ryan affectionately on the back. Motioning to Estelle and Buddy, the merry old man waved them towards his humble abode. "Come on through for a little tipple," he invited, opening the back screen into his kitchen.

"Think we might just keep going: still got a way to go. I take it Pete's already been in for the day?" questioned Ryan.

"Come and gone. All's well. Now you enjoy yourselves," nodded Mel cheerfully. The Christmas cake will keep till the morrow."

"I'll be by tomorrow," responded Ryan.

"Your car will be ready. See you then, son."

"Thanks, Mel. I owe you." Ryan hugged the older man.

"Be good," the older man added sagely.

"As always, Mel."

Mel watched as the visitors threw their luggage through the slide door before clambering into a spacious van with tinted windows.

Ryan and Estelle drove off, Mel waving before closing the gates behind them.

"I get the impression that you and Mel go back a while."

"Yeah. He's been around for quite a number of years now. I do rounds on his brood; the original environmentalist back in the day. Enjoys a party." Ryan laughed.

"Father Mel?"

"Mel. St Francis. Whoever. Quite the party boy. The more things change, the more they stay the same." Ryan smiled at Estelle. "These guys don't take themselves too seriously. If the sun was higher, I'd join Mel for a tipple."

"Who's Pete?"

"Another vet who keeps a check on the animals," replied Ryan watchfully. A blue sedan cruised past them back down Route 23. Ryan remained alert, donning cap and sunglasses. "Whoopee!"

"You're a funny bugger. Is it that glary?" Estelle shook her head in amusement.

"It's the altitude," replied Ryan, fishing around in the central console for a beanie and sunnies for Estelle.

The light-hearted banter resumed as they relaxed into the afternoon, cruising through town and out to the Catskills countryside. Ryan took Estelle's hand and the trio ventured out onto an open-level green park leading inward and down a trail to a densely wooded area.

Climbing through a diversity of natural landscape, they were invigorated by the twitter and fluttering of bird life rejoicing high within tree hollows above them. Beneath them a rustling diversity of critters scurried about industriously in the undergrowth. In the foreground, the trickling sounds of multiple streams.

More so than New York City, this place of wonder was cold, the air clean and crisp, and the ground more fertile. Crossing a bridge, Estelle stood gazing at the cascading beauty of the Kaaterskill Falls.

"These mountain flowers are so vibrant," she gushed.

"Autumn is big in our part of the world. God's own country," bragged Ryan proudly. "People come from all over just to check out our wonderful nature."

"My favourite is spring in Australia. I especially love the sweet smell of jasmine at night. I always loved the long walks with Nan during my childhood and troubled teens."

Ryan grinned back nostalgically. "My favourite: the Aussie summer. Nothing compares."

"Favourite flower?" Estelle tilted her head, gazing deeply into Ryan's big brown eyes.

"Rose; no other flower holds a candle to its simple elegance."

"A rose," echoed Estelle, softly returning Ryan's smile.

Hopping back inside the van, they made their way further into the countryside. The green scenery was bursting with life: rolling hills, rows and rows of fenced paddocks, and majestic horses. The dwellings along the way varied from the humble to the rambling and everything in-between. Folk they greeted in little hamlets were courteous and polite.

Ryan turned off onto a narrower, unsealed road that forked into an uphill path to Eagle's Ridge. The van pulled up over a crest and down to a hidden plateau looking out onto the valley below. Nestled on the highland was a sizable rustic log cabin.

Estelle held her breath in silence as she surveyed the magnificent vista before her.

"Welcome home. This has been my home with Dad on and off since my teens. Not exactly social; Dad's a bit of a recluse." Ryan beamed, taking Estelle's bag. "Don't always lock up, but with Dad being away..." he explained almost apologetically.

Buddy charged around the house, sniffing his territory. Pushing open the back screen door, he careered down wooden steps to the backyard.

"What do you think?" invited Ryan.

"It's amazing." She sighed, struck by its old-world perfection.

"Yeah, Dad has good taste. He'll be away until tomorrow night."

Inside, the cabin was clean, private and cosy. A large plush rug held centre stage on polished honeycomb wooden floors. The one stone wall encased a welcoming open fireplace. In front of the rug was a comfortable deep green lounge and positioned to one side, a matching old-fashioned lazy-boy reclining rocker. Across the opposite wall was a floor-to-ceiling built-in bookcase teeming with a diverse range of topics. Overhead were large timber beams and extending an invitation to the outside world were rustically decorated herb-filled planter boxes held securely in place beneath big wooden window frames on either side of the entry door. To the right was a generous open-plan kitchen with a solid old fuel stove, large pantry, and a large bowl of fruit holding centrepiece on a carved wooden kitchen table.

"Grand tour?" offered Ryan.

"Sure!"

"Visitors' bathroom: just in case." Ryan smiled awkwardly as they headed down the hallway. Inside, on a black slate floor, stood an old free-standing bath alongside a towel rail holding fluffy green and white towels. Off to the side, with door slightly ajar, was the master bedroom that hosted a massive four-poster timber bed, nightstands either side, two antique wardrobes, and in a corner, a large, round antique swivel mirror. In each of three bedrooms along the hallway, there was a variety of books and literature.

Ryan quickly put on some music and lit a fire. Opening the French doors, Estelle wandered out onto the west-facing sun deck. Dusk was fast setting upon the unspoilt panoramic views. The sapphire skies retired yet another day and a soft blanket laid claim to what was left of the light softly falling upon the russet earth, its rolling emerald and grey mountains shaded with different hues of olive and jade.

With the surrender of daylight, the mysteries of the night would soon be revealed, bursting into uncensored pleasure beneath a blanket of stars. Estelle wondered about the microcosm of her life and how it might unfold from this microsecond onwards.

"Dance with me?" Ryan invited. His voice smouldered, his eyes on fire. His arms rippled as he pulled her into the heat of his chest. "I am the man who will fight for your honour. I'll be the hero you're dreaming of. We'll live forever, knowing together—"

"Chicago," delighted Estelle.

Inhaling her sweet perfume, their lips met. Passionately they kissed. Scooping her into his arms, Ryan stepped back inside the fire-lit cabin. Delicately he lowered her onto the soft plush rug in front of the flames. With a rush of excitement she began to tear off his shirt. For a second he knelt before her, drinking her in with his eyes. He undressed her, kissing her naked skin as it appeared, before lowering himself towards her femininity. They kissed sweetly, tenderly, deeply. Delirious, they caressed, stroked, touched each other's flesh, mind and soul. He ran his fingers through her hair, his tips on her lips, and contoured her face with his hands. He gazed deeply into her eyes, losing himself in her soul. He stroked the softness of her back, the smoothness of her thighs, and kissed her silky breasts. She ran her mouth over his naked flesh, his neck, throat, shoulders, and arms. She tasted the salty sweat of his firm chest and rippling stomach. They inhaled each other's essence, moaning and breathing heavily, hot blood rushing through their veins, occupying their extremities. She quivered as she rose and lowered, repeatedly meeting his hardened body, his naked flesh pressing against hers.

Lost in the sea of their love, she surrendered, opening herself to him, merging with the hardness of his torso. He penetrated her soul, infusing her with his love. Melting beneath his pulsating body, she breathed and panted, losing control as the gates of heaven opened before them. Lying in their ecstasy, they each came home to themselves in the glow of a timeless oneness.

Throughout the night he reached out to her through an intimacy of touch far beyond the flesh. Had he loved her more, he might never have left and come home to himself. Only now, holding tightly his true joy, he was able to repeatedly come back to himself, giving her more of who he was. Hearing the pounding of his heart, she connected to the heartbeat of life. She surrendered all that she knew, only to know more: know more of who she truly was. Together in their loving embrace, they danced the gentle sway of the universe, and in the silent moment of their soul's breath they were again united as one. It was as if they had always been one, only to rediscover it in their moments of love. Finally they'd come to understand how their soul's true ecstasy was in constant renewal of their own self-discovery in each other's eyes.

During the early hours of the morning, she stirred as Ryan rose to stoke the fire. Wrapping themselves in a doona, the young lovers ventured out onto the wooden deck to marvel at the mystery of the night. Estelle looked skyward, eyes cast on the perfect illumination of the clear sky with its millions of twinkling, shining stars.

"Wow!" she cried, surprised by the dashing brilliance of a falling star. "I've never...My God!" gasped Estelle as she turned to face Ryan with her feminine smile and eyes of wonder. "Beautiful."

"You're beautiful," whispered Ryan in her ear, pulling her in even closer under the doona. "I love you, Estelle. I've always loved you. I'll always love you," he whispered in a moment heard by God, captured by eternity, a moment where the heavens rejoiced and the angels danced. Tomorrow she would be gone, but for now they were at one with all of life's creation. The spirit of creation had blessed them. It was a moment that would fuse them together forever.

Again they kissed. A smile travelled from the depth of her being, giving way to a moment of reminiscence.

"Star light, star bright," she whispered, "the first star I see tonight. I wish I may, I wish I might, have the wish I wish tonight." She smiled: a tender remembrance of her mother's voice swept up towards the heavens as they made their way inside.

MORNING ROSE TO GREET their eyes, their spirits awakening to a brand new day. Their hearts radiating with joy, the two lovers greeted the morning with a sun-blessed kiss.

Buddy came thundering through the hallway, nuzzling the lovers with his cold, wet nose. Fetching his ball, he was up for a game. Any game would do: fetch, piggy in the middle, wrestle for the ball, hide and go seek—all as long as he could play with his pack.

Ryan rose and sprinted to the kitchen, preparing to satisfy all of the hungry tummies. The aromatic smell of breakfast permeated the cottage. As Buddy tucked into his food with a ferocious appetite, Estelle immersed herself in some of Ryan's father's books.

"Pronto!" announced Ryan, placing breakfast on the table.

With a relaxed smile, Estelle wandered across to the kitchen and poured Ryan a juice.

"Yum!" responded Estelle, having taken in the first mouthful of banana and oat pancake. The fresh, organic, home-grown foods were a melt-in-your-mouth treat.

"You never did get round to telling me why you took off at the speed of light when I asked you for breakfast that time," questioned Ryan.

"Took off?"

"You know what I mean."

"I do?" she replied with taunting innocence.

"Hospital cafeteria not good enough for you, young lady?"

"No. Not really."

"So?" He paused.

"Pay back."

"Pay back?"

"Pay back," she again repeated, as if he were meant to instantly know his crime.

"Let me in on it. What did I do? Or didn't do? Or should have known to do or not to do?" He grinned, bemused.

"You borrowed something very, very special from me, and you never returned it, never apologised, never even acknowledged it," she teased, as if drawing out a long piece of string.

"No way; I didn't, did I?"

"Remember the smile I gave you as I stood by the water-cooler?"

"Temporary amnesia: tell me more."

"There I was, barely able to get about—at death's door, you know." She raised her eyebrows and tilted her head in a tease. "I made my way to the water-cooler down the hospital corridor. Quite nasty really: could have caught anything—a chill, an infection. I stood waiting for you to walk past and as you did, I gave you one of my smiles. You, you just walked directly past me as if you'd stared right through me."

"Are you kidding me? I would never do that to such a pretty girl. Sure it was me?"

"Of course I'm sure! I'd sustained heart damage, not brain damage." She giggled.

There he sat holding her hand, with the biggest grin, just looking into her eyes.

"What?"

"Paid back with interest." And with that, breakfast was quickly forgotten for more pressing matters.

AN HOUR LATER, BUDDY had finally managed to drag them both out of the wooden cabin and onto the lawns for a game of piggy-in-the-middle. Running around chasing ball, attempting to out-bounce Buddy, Ryan was exhausted. Waving the flag of surrender, Ryan grabbed Estelle's hand and they made their way back inside.

"Score: Ryan four, Estelle six, Buddy ten. Clearly the winner!" teased Estelle.

Growling and playing, Buddy coaxed Estelle off the couch and onto the floor for a wrestle.

"No wrestling in the house," protested Ryan, shamefully unable to regain his strength. And there it was: calamity. Estelle was no match for the energetic pup. Slamming into the bookcase, several books toppled onto the floor.

"Whoops!" She giggled, pausing to look at an inquisitive white mouse on the front cover of the book in hand. "The Costs and Benefits of Animal Experiments. Andrew Knight. Any relation?"

"Nah. Some Aussie vet in Oxford. He's done all the serious scientific grunt work: lands a body blow on the orthodoxy that animal experiments are useful for combating major illness in humans. Good science."

"I guess animal experimentation is big business over here."

"You're right there, and expanding exponentially with genetically modified food. But hey, Australia comes in at number four internationally, and possibly number one in terms of animals sacrificed per capita."

"You're bullshitting me." Estelle frowned.

"I'm afraid not: rabbits and rodents mainly. Well, eighty per cent."

"Well, news to me. But surely some animal research is necessary," defended Estelle.

"Doesn't stand up to scrutiny, Estelle. Take penicillin, lethal to many lab animals and a veritable lifesaver for millions of humans over the decades. Or Vioxx, the arthritis drug considered heart-safe, or even beneficial, during animal studies, then withdrawn from the global market after causing 140,000 heart attacks or strokes globally, and 60,000 deaths in the US alone."

"Wow! I didn't realise the extent."

A moment's silence as each withdrew into their thoughts.

"Something I'd like to share with you."

"Sound serious." Estelle frowned.

"On the way back, perhaps." Ryan extended his hand towards Estelle. Obligingly she sat beside him on the sofa. Snuggling in, he closed his eyes and inhaled the scent of her skin. "But for now…"

LATER THAT MORNING ESTELLE gathered her belongings, then stood by her luggage watching Ryan as he went about seeing to it that Buddy had enough food and water for the day, and that the cottage had been secured. She surveyed the cabin for a final time, each room, each space, each corner permeated with a ghostly imprint of the night before. Estelle drew a breath and closed her eyes to the movie reel still playing in her mind. She was both her own private audience and participant as she returned to the moments she'd never leave, the tangible images so real, her heart pierced with the pleasure and pain of knowing too much tenderness and the sweet agony of longing for more. She was held captive by two sovereign masters—the master of loving and the master of longing—so very deeply they each infused her every sense as they swam through her veins. In an instant she could still inhale Ryan's essence. She recalled him as he searched her soul with his eyes, and her surrender in response to the soulful sound of him calling her name. She could still taste the sweet sweat of his manhood. She was overcome with a fuzzy, warm glow of knowing that she had found what she had come to find, returning to a place she'd searched for her whole life: a return to love. As the door shut behind them, a part of her would remain, standing guard for all those precious memories.

"Are you OK?" Ryan put his arm around her shoulders. His touch was able to retrieve her back to the bittersweet present.

"I'm fine," she replied, breaking her silence with a wistful smile.

Ryan smiled at her, as he had so often done before, only now it was with subtle unease. Buddy moved between them, bringing relief to the awkwardness. "Dad will be home shortly," assured Ryan, crouching to say goodbye to him, then stood to take Estelle's luggage.

"Goodbye, Buddy." Estelle smiled, crouching to pat the canine.

"She'll see you again very, very soon, Buddy. I promise." He looked to Estelle for confirmation.

Buckling in, Estelle followed Ryan with her eyes as he jumped into the driver's side. He looked across and took her hand, placing it on his thigh as they took off. In stark contrast to their anticipatory drive up, and their animated discussions, the drive back to New York felt stilted. They were leaving a rustic paradise and heading back to cold, hard reality.

Arriving back at St Francis, Estelle alighted to open the gate.

"Thank God you're here, Ryan. Hello, my dear. I'm going to borrow your man for a moment." Turning back to Ryan, he said, "Lucy needs your attention."

"Right: come and meet Lucy, Estelle," invited Ryan, following the old man.

Estelle followed the two, walking briskly to the back of the animal enclosures. Mel unlocked the cage. Noting the oozing wound on her abdomen, Ryan cautiously leaned in and removed the little old female chimp from the confines of her almost barren cage. Whimpering, the critter offered no resistance, aside from a feeble attempt to cover her eyes with both of her hands.

Ryan gently soothed her with his deep, sympathetic voice. "Let's fix you up, darling." He followed Mel into the animal clinic inconspicuously tucked away behind the main enclosures, washed his hands and put on surgical gloves while Mel opened a dressing pack. Once laid out on the table, the severe scarring all along her abdomen was revealed. Ryan kept soothing Lucy with his soft voice as he went about examining and cleaning her inflamed stitches. "Hatchet job." He grimaced.

"Why's she so compliant?" uttered Estelle as she looked on.

"Institutionalised. Depressed." Ryan deftly cut through and removed a blue suture, the chimp barely moving. All the while Mel gently stroked the little animal's head, his lips moving silently, a tear in the corner of his eye.

"The tattoo on her chest?"

"Her ID. Lucy's spent over twenty years enduring invasive procedures in an animal research institution. Isolated, caged: known only by a number." Ryan gently swabbed down her inflamed suture line with saline. "Discourages any familiarity with laboratory staff," he continued.

"We'll look after you here, Lucy." Mel held her firmly, but gently.

"Where to from here?" Estelle's gaze didn't move from the forlorn chimp.

"When she's fit to travel, the network will take her to a more social setting. You need your own kind. Too long on your own, eh, Lucy," Mel added softly.

"Oh, God." Estelle moved closer to hold Lucy's soft hand, the chimp's eyes vacant. "But how...Her human handlers?"

"Lucy has endured multiple operations." Ryan gestured to the chimp's battle-scarred body. "Her only contact the indifference and brutality of humans."

"Why?" Estelle placed her hand over her mouth.

"Removal of ovaries: cancer research," replied Ryan as he applied a firm compress.

"I guess this has been going on for decades." Estelle mused aloud.

"Yep." Ryan grimaced. "As far back as the 1920s, chimpanzee testes were grafted into wealthy Europeans with limps dicks."

"What?" Estelle gasped.

"Yep. Surgical Viagra: ended in disaster. Over 500 recipients died from infection or graft rejection. It must have been quite distressing for them to see their scrotums turn black, given their paranoid rejection of African testicular tissue!"

Estelle went silent, observing the inert primate with a faraway look in her eye.

"No pain?" Estelle frowned.

The chimp's eyes were glazed over.

"Dissociated; she's learnt to cut off from her bodily sensations. Haven't you, sweetheart?" murmured Ryan gently.

"Like she's not here," reflected Estelle, falling silent. She recalled Mabunda's drunken words: 'Our blood debt to the chimpanzeeees.'

"Lucky or unlucky, she's a survivor: rescued finally, at least. Ritually, they're killed and discarded after serving their purpose. It's massive. Lucy is only one of over a hundred million non-human vertebrates sacrificed each year worldwide—and growing," Ryan spat out.

"No rehabilitation?"

"Voiceless creatures mercilessly experimented on, often without pain killers, held in place by restraining devices," raged Ryan quietly.

"What's with her cage?" queried Estelle as Ryan moved to gently place Lucy back on her soft bedding.

"Let's get you comfortable, old girl." He gently stroked Lucy's hand. "The only home she may have ever known."

"Unbelievable!" uttered Estelle as she and Ryan exited the room.

"Chimpanzee are the species most closely related to us, so you might think the most likely to be predictive of human outcomes when used for biomedical research. Yet for all the thousands of chimps wasted annually, the contribution to human research is minimal. Less than fifteen per cent of invasive chimpanzee research is ever cited in the human research literature, mostly distorted, in any case. Just a waste."

Estelle was mute.

"They feel, relate, communicate just like us, but non-human persons—not seen. No justification." Anger simmered below his controlled voice.

"Man has perverted God's word to have dominion over the creatures." The old man sadly shook his head.

"Buddy was an inpatient not so long ago: a rescue pup," explained Ryan as he continued his ward rounds.

Lost for words, Estelle followed Ryan as he soothed and attended to one needy critter after another.

"And this poor baby?" She turned to Ryan as he settled his last patient, a sleepy beagle pup attached to intravenous.

"His mother forced to deliver her litter on bare, cold concrete in the middle of winter. Most died of hypothermia, others perished from starvation."

"She couldn't feed them?"

"Not when her milk had dried from radiation. She just gave up and watched helplessly as her whimpering babies died, one after the other."

Estelle knelt before the small puppy. Quietly she stroked him with her middle and index finger. "So trusting," she murmured.

"The beagle's non-aggressive nature makes them easy subjects. We managed to save this one." Ryan smiled wistfully.

Estelle swallowed hard.

"Thanks, Ryan. Now you won't run away before having some of my Christmas cake." Mel lightened the atmosphere as they exited the clinic. "Too much for me." He patted his ample girth.

"Sounds good." Ryan nodded. "Might unload our luggage from the van first."

"You do that, son. I'll boil the kettle," obliged Mel.

Scrambling to unload, Estelle and Ryan went about transferring baggage from van to Chevy.

"A balaclava and torch?" queried Estelle, holding up the two items from a bag she'd just rummaged through.

"Party hire." Ryan winked cheekily. "Come on: tea's ready." He smacked Estelle on the butt.

Entering Mel's kitchen cum living space, Estelle was struck by the somewhat cluttered appearance of the room. Some shelves sat astride an old television, above which was framed a poem. A video, 'Hidden Crimes', was partially slotted into an archaic video cassette player.

Estelle stood silently reading the poem on somewhat faded, yellowing paper:

WILL IT BE YOUR CHILD OR A DOG?

I live behind locked gates in a basement so cold
Knowing only a cruel life of pain, fear and isolation
I've been starved, electrically shocked and set ablaze,
I've been poisoned by chemicals, disinfectants
and detergents.

My brothers and sisters live horrors untold
As one by one they are restrained for mutilation.
Everyday I wonder how man can do this, I'm in such a daze.
I plead to you, release us, our anguish is urgent.

Without anaesthetic or pain killers we face
many an operation,
Restrained and unable to speak the horrors of our pain.
Our skulls scalpel open, we are put to sleep,
Our heads violently bashed, we are unable to defend.

All done in secrecy with grants and government
co-operation.
Man, in his greed, heartlessly pursuing profit and gain,
While the public are enchanted by the wonder of
scientific leaps.
To keep this horror going, on deception they depend.

My brothers and sisters in terror must die,
Many millions a year in many cruel hands in many nations.
Forced to chain smoke, drink petrol and become alcoholic,
Given tumours, heart disease and drugged to blindness.

My family in secret underground basements will cry.
While immaculate heroes conduct research operations.
Humanitarian demi-gods with no time to frolic,
Revered as pillars of society for their love and kindness.

They convince man to believe in them for health and beauty,
As man in the wonders of an optimum life still seeks.
With millions of us a year condemned to a life of abuse,
Yet with the way man chooses to live, we must die.

With cigarettes, alcohol, coffee, animal flesh and fizzy
drinks so fruity,
To line his shopping trolley he feels delighted with his treats.
Air too thick to breathe and soil unworthy of use,
Undrinkable water, as man is operated upon, he then
asks, why?

My brothers and sisters, they wish you no harm.
They are rabbits, pigeons, monkeys and mice.
They are the guinea pigs and others that serve you well.
They are the sheep and the goat and even the hog.

Your beloved cat put in a pound should raise your alarm.
Before you believe it's only rats, as shown on TV,
just think twice.
By now you are thinking of what they do tell—
In order for your unquestioned support—'Will it be
your child or a dog?'

The persistent whistle of the kettle interrupted Estelle's silent
reflection. Ryan stepped forward to rescue it as Mel bustled about
preparing a tea set and Christmas cake.

"Who wrote the poem?"

"My memory fails me, my dear." The old man scratched his
head. "We'll be putting in another enclosure to the back of the
paddock. Demand not getting less." The old man was enthused,
though walking with some discomfort, balancing cake and tea on an
old wooden tray.

"Always room at the inn." Ryan opened the door to the porch.
"So what are we going to do about your health, old boy?" he asked,
observing the old man as he struggled to get comfortable in his seat.

"Ah. The bone doctors want me to have new knees. The skin
doctor wants to hit me with a blow torch every time I see him, and

my cardiologist suggests I drink too much red wine." He directed his complaint to Estelle: "Outrageous!"

They all laughed at Mel's expense. The collective laughter came to an abrupt halt as the phone rang and Mel excused himself from the table to take the call. Ryan and Estelle remained out on the porch overlooking the valley, each sipping their beverage: Estelle her tea, Ryan his percolated coffee.

"So here we are, Antipodeans on the other side of the world. What's kept you in The States, Ryan?"

"Long story: a little rat."

"A little rat." Laughing, Estelle wrinkled her nose.

Ryan didn't respond. "Remember that cute little fellow on the front cover of Andrew Knight's treatise?"

Estelle cast her mind back to the book cover and the little mouse's pink eyes, attentive ears and button nose surrounded by ever-so-long whiskers. "Yes, cute." She smiled.

"I didn't tell you I started veterinary studies in Australia." Ryan looked at Estelle intently.

Estelle looked back at Ryan in surprise. "Why, no; you have a flawless New York accent, though you don't quite talk ninety to the dozen."

"As part of our initiation into veterinarian lab work, students were expected to kill lab rats by slamming them over a lab bench."

The smile on Estelle's face froze.

"I participated in that ritual killing, along with my macho mates." Ryan paused. "Andrew Knight, on the other hand, had the guts to initiate legal action and a mass media exposure of curricular animal killing before Murdoch University would allow him to use humane teaching methods in sections of his training." Ryan paused again.

Estelle felt her heart contract. "Why are you telling me this, Ryan?"

"I guess sometimes we—I compromised myself for the sake of belonging." Ryan looked down at his hands. "My hands aren't clean. I owe that rat."

"Isn't that all of us, Ryan?" Estelle massaged the back of her neck.

"I guess. I felt so ashamed of my brutish behaviour; I eventually dropped out of Vet School. With Dad's help I was able to restart studies here in Tufts. So here I am."

"So my knight has a dent in his shiny armour. Any more bombshells?"

"No. That's probably enough over-disclosure for one day," Ryan jested grimly.

Silence befell Ryan and Estelle. The distant skies filled with the cries of soaring birds.

"It's estimated some four animals a second, around the globe, are tortured to their death, all in the name of science. That's hundreds of millions of innocent animals globally each year. Sadly a large percentage are channelled through charity funding, the donations produced by good-hearted charitable individuals deceived into digging deep into their wallets."

"You're a bit of a tortured soul, Ryan." Estelle looked across at him, his eyes grimly riveted towards the distant cries.

"The scientists involved are paid to show an agreed outcome."

Estelle sat silently taking it all in.

"For over a decade monkeys forced to chain smoke were used to prove that smoking doesn't cause lung cancer." Ryan grimaced.

Estelle raised her eyebrows.

"It all comes down to who's funding what outcome," explained Ryan sombrely. "In spite of all of the animals sacrificed, pharmaceutical drugs are still the third leading cause of human death in the US."

Estelle cast her eyes to the floor.

"In truth, everyone is protecting themselves from the lawyers. These animals are sacrificed to protect the vested interests they represent from costly public litigation."

Estelle sighed. "I don't think I mentioned my Dad's occupation, did I, Ryan?" She blew on her tea to cool it down.

"No. I don't recall you did." He cocked his head to the side.

"He's a senior executive with Vizard."

"Big Pharma?" Ryan took another sip of his coffee.

"Yep."

"So here we are. Strange bedfellows." Ryan looked squarely at Estelle.

For what seemed like an eternity, the two gazed out over the distant vista.

"And those horses?" Estelle interrupted the stilted silence.

"Discarded race horses. The one to the far right we rescued from the knackery while in foal. Her daughter, Mia, is the little chestnut beside her," replied Ryan. "Not so different to the dairy industry: nothing more than waste products."

"Now I insist you both have some of my Christmas cake," exclaimed Mel, returning to the relief of both Ryan and Estelle, who obliged by taking a piece of cake each.

Ryan checked his watch. "Estelle has a plane to catch, Mel."

As the trio wandered back inside, Ryan carrying the tea tray, Estelle was struck by a large, old black-and-white photo of an elephant hunter with his trophy. It hung in solitude, incongruously facing off the poignant framed poem she'd only just read. A proud hunter stood in a safari suit cradling what was presumably an elephant gun. A pre-pubescent African boy stood off to the side, his right hand missing. With his overdeveloped left arm, he helped balance a massive elephant tusk, a trophy hewed from an elephant's skull. In the bottom right-hand corner of the photo: 'Leopoldville, 1895.'

"Father Mel, what is this photo?"

"My grandfather on safari. This photo was taken in the Belgian Congo." Mel sighed.

"Sins of the father, eh, Mel?" quipped Ryan cheekily.

"Always the jester!" Mel grimaced. "Father, forgive them, they know not what they do."

"What happened to the boy's hand?" Estelle's question hung heavy in the air, waiting for Mel's reply.

"Punishment: perhaps his parents didn't make their quota of rubber or ivory."

Estelle stood speechless.

"Ten million Congolese died during King Leopold's reign of terror; the Association Internationale Africaine. So much for European philanthropy in Africa." Mel shrugged before escorting the young couple out the door. "Do come again, dear, and don't leave it too long." Mel looked at Estelle and Ryan kindly.

ESTELLE GAZED OUT THE window, observing the world as they passed. Ryan focused on the road ahead as they journeyed back down toward sea-bound New York.

Estelle broke the silence. "I didn't ask about your mum. Is she OK now?"

"Yes. She's doing OK. Had a pig heart valve transplant at St Vincent's, and it's given her a new lease on life."

"That's good."

"Dad wasn't overly happy."

"That she's doing OK?"

"No. I think Dad still loves Mum, but he's vehemently against transplantation across species."

"Even if it's life-saving?"

"Dad's argument—well, pigs carry many retroviruses that currently do no harm to humans. By accepting a pig valve, if infected, well, it's like inoculating the human species with a pig virus. A fusion of a human and pig virus could give birth to a killer recombinant and these retroviruses could remain dormant in the recipient for years, an incubating culture medium just waiting to mutate."

"Gee: hadn't considered that."

"We've learned nothing in the last hundred years," grunted Ryan.

"Your dad works for W.H.O?"

"Used to: resigned some years back." Ryan glanced at Estelle briefly.

"Would he have known Mabunda?"

Ryan shrugged. "Dad's an epidemiologist, a number cruncher. Mabunda may have been on the technical research side. Big organisation. Can ask him. Unlikely."

"Mabunda was deeply disillusioned with the W.H.O.," mused Estelle aloud.

"Yes. A lot of Wabenzi left the W.H.O. disillusioned. Dad found the organisation's ties to the pharmaceutical industry disquieting."

Estelle shifted uncomfortably, the intimate space between them all but evaporated. "Am I missing something?" asked Estelle, looking to Ryan. "Apart from cancer research, what else are chimpanzees used for?"

"HIV, Hepatitis, Polio vaccine development—they're our closest relative—lots."

"Mabunda was silenced for a reason."

"He wasn't perchance involved in the oral polio vaccine development?" pressed Ryan.

"Not that I'm aware of. He was South African, remember, and a black South African at that. Why?"

"You mentioned he did some postgraduate training in Antwerp."

"Where are you going with this, Ryan?"

"The most hated hypothesis in contemporary medical circles. The Oral Polio vaccine–HIV narrative," Ryan stated matter-of-factly.

"Refresh my memory." Estelle had a far-away look in her eye.

"Controversial hypothesis, all but dismissed. That the AIDS epidemic was spawned by a monkey immunodeficiency virus called S.I.V. that may have contaminated batches of early live oral polio vaccines."

"Mmm," murmured Estelle.

A pregnant silence filled the space between them.

"I thought it was taken for granted that AIDS came from monkeys," broke in Estelle.

"Sure! In the early eighties, AIDS had the epidemiologists stumped. Then it was finally discovered that H.I.V. had a cousin in S.I.V., a similar virus found in chimpanzee," explained Ryan.

"Is that cousin or ancestor?" interjected Estelle. "S.I.V.?"

"Sorry. Simian Immunodeficiency Virus: cousin, ancestor, whatever." Ryan continued. "There's only two ways this cross-species contamination could occur: body fluids through broken skin, or mucosa."

"Mucosa?"

"Oral, vaginal, rectal, whatever," replied Ryan.

"And what about the chimpanzee?"

"Ground up chimp kidneys were used in the production of a cell culture for the oral polio vaccine used in the Belgian Congo trials in the late fifties: denied by the principal researchers."

"Got it!" Estelle clenched her fist.

"Got what?" Ryan frowned.

"Mabunda spoke Afrikaans. He had postgraduate training in tropical medicine in Antwerp. He was a virologist. The blood debt to the chimpanzees…"

"Dad reckons the whole polio-HIV debacle's been swept under the carpet and that the pursuit of prestige and profit has blinded some scientists to the dangers of messing with genetic heritage. For instance, the odd one or two pig valve transplants is neither here nor there, perhaps, but with an ageing baby-boomer population and their voracious appetite for longevity, well, transplanting hundreds of thousands of pig valves into a population with waning molecular immunity is a potential recipe for disaster."

"So your dad supports this polio vaccine-AIDS hypothesis?"

"He's not alone. Many eminent scientists privately agree this epidemic is man-made, either by accident or design. It's not a new theory. It was said to have come to the attention of the scientific community early in the piece. The threat of cross-species contamination, I mean. Harvesting chimpanzee organs in a compliant third world country would have been irresistibly economical. It would have been a far more costly exercise to go the synthetic route, so I guess they took the short cut."

"My understanding of the cross-over from monkeys to human was that it was open wounds on the bush-meat hunters that came into contact with monkey body fluids. I mean, isn't AIDS blood-borne?" asked Estelle, deferring to Ryan's biological background.

"Yeah, that's right, Estelle. For centuries humans have hunted and eaten monkeys, but the question is why now? Why the Congo? And the vaccine was delivered orally, not by injection."

"Yes, and I guess newborns and young children can get HIV from breast milk," recalled Estelle.

"Right on. An immature or damaged gut could render a host vulnerable to infection. We forget the gut is one of our most important immune organs."

"So an oral vaccine could have delivered the king-hit."

"That's the suggestion," acknowledged Ryan. "AIDS has only been around for a few decades. It all seems to trace back to a sentinel hit on Central Africans sometime between the late fifties and mid-seventies. Over a million were conscripted into the oral polio vaccine trial."

"My God, how did they get that many people to participate: and why a remote African country?"

"The vaccine needed to be trialled in populations naive to previous vaccinations. Hey, they were given no choice."

"And those who did not conform?"

"The Africans had no rights in colonial Belgian Congo. Well, maybe a little more than the chimpanzee sacrificed for their benefit," sneered Ryan sarcastically. "Dad lived through all that crap."

"This is personal for you, isn't it, Ryan?"

"Sure, Estelle, isn't that all of us? If it doesn't touch us personally, it really doesn't touch us."

"There's truth in that," reflected Estelle.

"You know, Estelle, historically the Europeans considered blacks just one up from the great apes. My dad's ancestors were brought to America in chains."

"The human species!" uttered Estelle.

"In the race for a Nobel prize-winning magic bullet, there's been a lot of collateral damage. And a costly exercise now, with the cost of AIDS globally," added Ryan.

"Whatever happened to the Hippocratic oath: first do no harm?"

"We're all humans first and scientists second. Even the eminent Louis Pasteur lied about his research, stole ideas from competitors, and was downright deceitful in his methods. But I guess history rewards the victors," he reflected. "In the long run, there are no short cuts."

"So you think the AIDS debacle could be repeated?" added Estelle, her concern impossible to disguise.

"Oh yeah, Dad's adamant it will happen again."

"My God!" Estelle fell into quiet reflection. "Congo!"

"Pardon?"

"It's in the river. They tried to hide it. His dying word was Congo," Estelle replied, almost in a whisper. "I was circling this the night my computer was stolen. This is no coincidence. Ryan, I need to go back to the police."

Ryan became suddenly pensive. Slowing down, he pulled off to the side of the road.

"Why've we stopped?" Estelle frowned.

Undoing his seat belt, Ryan leaned forward, placing his hands either side of Estelle's face, looking her square in the eyes. "Listen to me, Estelle. You may well be putting yourself in harm's way."

"An innocent man has been murdered. I'm heading straight to the police."

"I'm putting you straight on that plane, Estelle." Ryan's voice was calmly assertive.

"Why are you blocking me, Ryan?" protested Estelle.

Ryan paused, taking a deep breath. "Sweetheart, this is bigger than you and I."

"Don't patronise," fumed Estelle.

"Listen to me, Estelle. The night of the fancy dress ball, another Joan of Arc look-alike was found strangled."

"What?" Estelle visibly whitened.

"These people mean business. I'm getting you on that plane." His voice was dead calm.

Estelle sat frozen, the colour completely drained from her face. "And you're telling me this now?"

"I'm sorry. I wasn't sure. I thought it best to get you out of New York. I imagined we were being tailed. I'm not sure, hence the vehicle swap."

"I don't understand. Why?"

"I don't know, Estelle, but somehow you're linked to Mabunda."

Estelle fell silent, her head in her hands.

Looming up in front was the distant horizon of New York City. The remainder of the trip passed mainly in silence as Ryan focused on the emerging busy traffic.

Zipping about the airport, Ryan quickly found a spot to park. Unloading Estelle's luggage onto a trolley, they walked into the departure lounge, hand in hand, and headed for check-in.

The two kept physically close, exchanging small talk.

An escapee tear snuck from Estelle's eye and vanished down her cheek as she looked back at Ryan a final time before disappearing behind the customs and departure screen.

Ryan watched as Estelle's plane took off down the tarmac before disappearing into the distant skies.

Chapter Ten

The Qantas 747 touched down on a Botany Bay runway. Estelle reached for her overhead hand luggage. A flashing incoming text brought a smile to her face: Missing you xox.

Cleared through customs, Estelle looked up to see a relieved and beaming Sam.

"Hi, sweetheart, good to have you home safe and sound!" He gave his daughter a big hug before helping with her luggage.

"Thanks, Dad." Estelle kissed him on the cheek. "Where's Nan?"

"Oh, you know your nan, her ceaseless monologues: barely made it out with my life."

"I see nothing's changed." Estelle grinned at her exasperated father.

"Well, I see you know your nan," agreed Sam.

Her luggage loaded into the boot of the Merc, Estelle slid into the passenger seat.

"How was your trip?" asked Sam, unable to disguise the concern in his voice.

"Dramatic. Especially with Mabunda's murder."

"And the rest of the conference? I guess this tragedy must have shaken you up quite a bit. I can't imagine the horror of it all."

"Mabunda's death was shocking, but I feel I gave the conference my full attention."

"You prolonged your stay a few extra days?"

"Yeah, the police wanted me to stay on till preliminary investigations were completed. There's more to his death than meets the eye."

"Yes. Sounds like it," agreed Sam pensively as he navigated the solid Mercedes through the traffic.

Stepping inside their Point Piper hideaway, Estelle was delighted to see Mellow racing around, playing in a nylon tunnel. "Must have weaved her magic on you while I was away." Estelle grinned.

"I guess stranger things have happened." Esther nudged Estelle cheekily.

Sam stood back as grandmother and grand-daughter embraced. Esther had a wicked look in her eye. "I see you've brought me home a little surprise." She chuckled, her sparkling blue eyes dancing with delight.

"No use trying to hide anything from you, Nan." Estelle smiled, shaking her head in resignation. "Now or after dinner?" She reached for a muffin.

"Now for my present," demanded Esther, smacking Estelle on her outstretched hand. "Muffins after dinner."

Estelle produced a carefully wrapped gift. The accompanying card was of a Texan-looking dude holding the bronze testicle of the Wall Street Bull, a popular tourist pose in New York.

Esther roared with laughter, tears streaming down her face. "Well! Indeed! Who's got who by the balls?" she snorted. "I'm sure Wall Street has Main Street by the balls. After all, someone has to pay for this war."

Even Sam had to laugh at Nan's antics. "What can you do with this crazy old woman?"

Esther proceeded to impatiently tear off gift wrapping, revealing a beautiful porcelain cat from the Catskills.

"This one doesn't need kitty litter," explained Estelle, kissing Nan on the cheek.

"And did you get yourself something special?" asked Sam.

Estelle produced the sculpture of Three Wise Monkeys to the admiration of all.

"Hear no evil, see no evil, speak no evil. How appropriate." Nan laughed.

Tears of laughter were interrupted by the oven timer.

"Dinner's ready. You sit," Nan imperiously directed Sam. "Sweet pea, help me serve."

Sam complied, serving himself a glass of Taylor's Cab Sav as daughter and mother-in-law served.

The three broke bread and savoured the pie. Sam hoed into bread slathered with butter, pouring himself a second glass of red. Esther held her tongue, also pouring herself a glass.

"Well, out with it, Missy," cajoled Nan.

"What?" Estelle frowned. "Doctor Mabunda's assassination?"

"Oh, that dear man; we'll catch up with him later. Now who's the new man around you?" With raised eyebrows and a knowing smile, Nan held her breath. "Well?"

With a gulp of wine, Sam raised his eyebrows. "Have you no boundaries, Nan? The poor girl has just witnessed a homicide, for God's sake."

"Perhaps she hasn't." Estelle smirked.

"Now don't play coy with me, sweet pea? Remember you can't hide anything from your nan. Hmm?"

"If Stella has met a man, I'm sure she'll tell us in due time. Isn't that right, Stella?" coaxed Sam, leaning towards his daughter, an eyebrow cocked inquisitively.

"If you must know, I've known him since birth. Well, we did cross paths while I was in hospital," announced Estelle boldly.

"Known who since birth?" Sam pulled back.

"Well, there's certainly a lot to be said for not rushing into things." Nan threw her head back dramatically and chortled loudly.

"Nan, do you recall the photo taken immediately after my birth?"

"What photo?" Nan leaned forward.

"Mr Triple Scorpio. Remember? He also turned out to be the same guy that stood in my hospital doorway that night."

"Truly? Mr Triple Intensity; where on earth did you manage to find him?" Nan's excitement and curiosity danced as one.

Putting down his wine glass, Sam looked painfully bemused. "Are either of you going to let me in on this joke?"

"No joke, Dad. Seriously. His name is Ryan Knight. I told him how Nan had a photo taken within a day or so of my birth. He and his family were in the background. Isn't that right, Nan?" She looked towards Nan for support.

"Quite a couple of coincidences?" muttered Sam.

"He just materialised as Doctor Mabunda lay dying and has supported me every step of the way since," Estelle shared emphatically.

Sam looked over the rim of his glasses, his eyes narrowed with a confrontational glare. "Have the two of you both totally lost it?"

"No! Looks like she's found it—him! A karmic reunion, if you ask me," bubbled Esther.

"Spare me that crap," spluttered Sam.

"Didn't I suggest romance coming your way?" cackled Esther smugly.

"Stella, it's wonderful to have you home safely. Don't jump into anything impulsively: just be sensible."

"Oh, Da-ad!" Estelle sighed while Esther continued to cackle away.

"Don't worry about your father, dear: just listen to my suggestions."

Sam glared hard at Esther. "There's a great many things I'd like to suggest for your grandmother, most of them, unfortunately, not legal. As for you, Stella, I suggest you stay on the better side of caution."

"I can take care of myself. Relax, Dad."

"Take care of yourself? Some random stranger turns up, firstly while you were in hospital and then again in time to witness some random murder half a world away. You tell him about some random photo taken after your birth, and some random child in it, and this Casanova suggests that it might be him. Please, Stella. Give me a break."

"I suggest you follow your heart." Esther smiled warmly, a gleam in her eye. "Look at her; she's positively glowing." Esther raised her glass in silent toast.

"I'm twenty-seven, almost twenty-eight, for crying out loud. I'm old enough to know my own mind."

"Well, your grandmother has positively lost hers. Safety first, Stella. I mean it." Sam's eyebrows furrowed sternly.

"You're right on track for your karmic schedule. How exciting." The old lady rubbed her hands together.

"You're right on track to be scheduled," groaned Sam, glaring at Esther with his bloodshot eyes. "So what's he do for a living, this miraculous stranger who has turned up out of nowhere after almost three decades?"

"He's a scientist for PETA."

"OK. OK. Sound like he at least has a rational background. Does he at least wear shoes and pay his taxes?" interrogated Sam.

"That's a bit unfair. You haven't even met him and already you're passing judgement," retorted Estelle sharply.

Rubbing his eyes behind his glasses, Sam looked across at his daughter. "Believe me, Stella, I know the type: dreamers. Imagine they can change the world."

"So do I: the type who fight with passion for animal rights and social justice. A noble calling," rallied Esther.

"I'd just prefer you meet someone with a real job. The last thing this world needs is another welfare dependant do-gooder," blurted Sam, his face visibly reddening as he poured another glass of Cab Sav. His distress was rescued by the arrival of Mellow, alias Velcro cat. She landed on his lap and began to purr.

"One of the best things PETA ever did was take on Doctor Taub over the appalling treatment meted out to the Silver Spring monkeys for over a decade," provoked Esther.

"Taub has been vilified! He should have won a Nobel Prize. His ground-breaking research shed crucial insight into neuroplasticity," spat Sam, folding his arms across his chest.

"Pity those Nazis had neither insight nor neural plasticity of their own to boast about," retorted Esther defiantly.

"These scientists have worked, and still work tirelessly for the welfare of humanity." Sam's jaw tightened.

"Is that why, for centuries now, they have centred much of their experimentation on Jews, blacks, Gypsies, orphans, prostitutes and animals. Ah, I guess, to the pharma-culture, some life is of lesser value than others. All scaled to fit the profit margin, of course," hissed Esther.

"Bullshit!" muttered Sam with contempt.

"I'm with Nan on this one, Dad," interjected Estelle. "Experiments involving severing the nerves of harmless monkeys, then brutalising them with electric shocks and depriving them of food for days on end, just to observe their neurological survival functions, can hardly be condoned and upheld as good science." Estelle's jaw tightened.

"You're misinformed, both of you. Please calm down," patronised Sam. "This entire argument was long settled in court back in the eighties."

"Couldn't be too hard to settle court disputes around experimental animals with no legal rights," fumed Esther.

"We've come a long way since those days. We now have ethics committees overseeing the welfare of experimental animals," retorted Sam.

"And who elects these so called ethics committees? Is it not an inside job? Besides there's a vast difference between legal rights and ethical rights," stormed Esther.

"Surely, Dad, you can't possibly suggest that the end justifies the means. Would you have Mellow subjected to that level of cruelty?"

Sam stopped to pat Mellow, who had continued to unconditionally purr loudly on his lap.

"Careful, you may begin to mellow, Sam," suggested Esther, crinkling her nose at her son-in-law.

With dinner over, Esther trotted out the door and headed down the pathway. Banging her way into the old clanger, she sped off into the night.

"She must do something about that muffler before the police catch up with her. I keep warning her," muttered Sam.

"Some presents for you, Dad: three, in fact," soothed Estelle.

"Ah. Thank you, Stella. That's wonderful." Sam carefully unwrapped his gifts. "*Dream Work?*" read Sam, holding the soft cover at a distance.

"Mary Oliver, America's favourite poet. I often see your light on about one am—and Doctor Brasch's *A Book of Forgiveness*. And," presenting a third gift, "a little Bach: soothes the nerves."

"Stella." He softly smiled.

Estelle turned to go off to bed. "Oh, Dad?" She turned back. "What do you know about the link between the polio vaccine and AIDS?"

Sam stood silent for a moment, lost in his solitary thoughts. "A plausible theory: refuted by the evidence."

"Quite a lot of evidence, don't you think, Dad?"

"Two plus two doesn't equal twenty two." Sam yawned.

BACK AT WORK NEXT morning, Estelle downloaded articles and other research material on AIDS: the science, the money, the politics, and perhaps a major cover-up of one of the greatest medical disasters our planet has ever known, reaching back into the dark mists of the Congo in the late 1950s. And Mabunda? An obituary in The Sowetan: 'A stellar career: Fort Hare, University of Cape Town, Institute of Tropical Medicine, Antwerp, and an M.Sc. at the London School of Economics, then W.H.O.'

Gifted alright, mused Estelle. Reference to his political and community activism: tragically dead at 72 years, his alcoholism discreetly omitted.

Estelle stepped towards the water cooler, then strolled around to view Sydney Harbour: water sparkling blue; a Manly Ferry ploughing through choppy water, a catamaran dashing cheekily across its bow; the No War graffiti faded from the Opera House shell.

So many competing issues in an oversaturated media: North Korea boasting its nuclear weapons program; the Genome completed, big business waiting to make a killing; David Kay's report—zip evidence of weapons of mass destruction in Iraq, but the clandestine network of biological laboratories—interesting. Would they ever get to the truth? Project Coast buried in Apartheid South Africa—a lot of shredding there, I'll bet—and Rhodesia's dirty little anthrax secret buried in obscurity, the Rhodesians let off the hook. Zimbabwe's President Mugabe, archetypal black despot, Hitleresque moustache a wonderful touch, and Southern Africa: thirty per cent of pregnant women HIV positive. No access to antiretrovirals and the whole issue fraught with hazard anyway. AZT was not exactly a magic bullet.

"God! What a catastrophe."

Back at her desk, Estelle took a deep breath. Ten o'clock meeting with Alex. Hell: a bit of explaining to do. How to angle this, she mused. The AIDS crisis is now: can't get derailed, but the cover-up by the scientific establishment...Mabunda's death? Estelle felt an increasing deep unease.

"Estelle, you're back?" Alex checked her wristwatch, shaking her finger, but smiling. "Let's have a chinwag. You have a deadline, my girl."

"Hi, Alex. I can explain."

"Got your email: calamity or controversy? You're looking more and more like a femme fatale, my girl," jested Alex to Estelle's chagrin.

Estelle followed Alex into her office, Alex enthroning herself in typical fashion, waving her underling to a utilitarian chair across the desk.

"A week in New York: got to be worth a three-part series. Pitch it to me." Alex lounged back, hands clasped behind her head.

"OK—in three parts. The new South Africa: the rainbow nation still overwhelmingly male chauvinistic; thirty per cent of pregnant women HIV positive. The female Minister for Health, Zuma, a puppet to President Mbeki: a remote cold fish, HIV sceptic. No access to antiretrovirals, legacy of an oppressive regime. Denial of access to potentially lifesaving medication; AZT reduces transmission rates to newborn babies and from breastfeeding mothers: access to lifesaving AZT for women and children."

"The relevance here?" cut in Alex, frowning.

"Well, it's a question of context." Estelle faltered.

"Context? Rural Africa: urban Australia. Our readers are thoughtful women: twenties, thirties, predominantly unattached." Alex gave Estelle that piercing look.

"Maybe we need to be looking at the ecology of the AIDS epidemic and the peculiarities of how it may be emerging in Australia."

"Ecology: it's not a four-letter word." Alex looked over her gold-rimmed glasses at Estelle.

"OK. Here's the thesis. The HIV epidemic is heterogeneous: not one epidemic, but multiple epidemics dependant as much on the subspecies of HIV as the peculiarities of class, race, ethnicity, and the success of the parasite in carving out a niche position in the market of sexual behaviours."

"So if I'm HIV–C subspecies—C being for cock-sucking—and cock-sucking is in vogue in gay men in San Francisco, then I'll thrive there?"

"Right on! You have a way with words, Alex!"

"It's a question of taste, don't you think?" Alex winked. "Fortunately I don't have a degree in science journalism." She smirked. "And the conceptual links between the South African AIDS epidemic and a would-be epidemic here?"

"Apartheid: profit-driven; disregard for impact on families, communities, and the black population. Apathy: scepticism of the subservient classes. Rural women: poor, malnourished, coerced into depo-contraception, impacting on their ability to resist infection, thinning of vaginal mucosa, et cetera. The whole issue of the potential for oral infection by HIV dismissed: inadequate attention to effective barrier methods like condoms and the devastating consequences for the spread of HIV."

"You're losing me, Estelle." She tapped her right index finger on the desk.

"OK. Australia: impact on marginalised people likely to be more significant. Similar to South African blacks: poor, marginalised, malnourished, cut out of the metropolitan global economy."

"Sure. Blah-blah: convenient scapegoats. Estelle, what does your generation think of HIV and how it may impact them personally?"

"Well, it's known about. It's joked about, at least. It's never going to happen to me."

"Precisely. Now how can we provide infotainment that will boost our sagging sales?" Alex glared. "Our special edition on the glories of fellatio was sensational, our advert for flavoured condoms and dental dams not so successful. Sex sells. There's just so many ways you can serve it up."

"So the local context: apathy. She'll be right, mate. Pass me a tinny: booze, parties, let the good times roll; the market saturation of recreational drugs, alcohol, and the liberalisation of sexual mores. And thanks to our initial success with the gay lobby, mainstream still sees AIDS as a gay disease. We have a low-level epidemic of chlamydia that peaks every so often."

"Yeah: boring middle-class disease."

"Yes, but it does provide a portal for the entry for HIV," countered Estelle.

"Your generation?"

"Well, sex has become an adult recreation for my generation, but the ecological hazards include fly in-fly out labour, family breakdown, travel, alcohol, depression and stress. Moreover, my generation is much more sexually assertive than my mother's generation."

"OK, your generation's more sexually assertive when drunk. Play with it. Do what you can with it: the more controversial, the better."

"And there's a bigger story here, Alex," suggested Estelle cautiously.

"I'm listening."

Estelle felt Alex's icy gaze transfixed on her. "I reckon Doctor Mabunda's death was not random. He was taken out because he knew too much. He was due to meet me the evening before his presentation to the conference. I just have a gut feel that—"

"You need more than a gut feel, Estelle."

"But—"

"Estelle." The older lady softened. "This has not been an easy year for you. Your deadline for your assigned piece is Friday. I expect it in my in-tray. You can give me a one-page brief on the Mabunda assassination and," she cut Estelle's interjection, "I want you to make an appointment to see Doctor Dinah Roberts, or whoever, downstairs."

"I'm OK. Really, Alex."

"If I'd witnessed an assassination, I reckon I, Alex, hardened veteran, might just need a little professional debriefing. Go and have some counselling. It's covered by E.A.P. Go and get the counselling—and I expect your article by Friday."

"But there's been a cover-up—"

"Go!"

Estelle nodded in assent, turned and left Her Majesty's office.

Mulling over details, Estelle read her father's reply to her interrogation list. Sam was a fund of information on vaccine research and a redoubtable sceptic on the oral polio vaccine–AIDS connection.

At his desk, munching on a cheese and ham sandwich, Sam sent Estelle his final reply. 'I'll bring home any further information I come across.'

A familiar double knock was punctuated by the intrusive entry of the looming figure of Wolfgang.

"Come in," welcomed Sam redundantly. Sam shifted his focus from his computer to Wolfgang, motioning to a lounge chair in the corner of his office.

"Well, how are things going: happy with the figures?"

"Steady as she goes. May need to trim our strategy a little, but we're on track to exceed quarterly profits," replied Sam.

"And how are things on the domestic front? Your little girl home safe and sound now."

"Yes. Home safe and sound, thank God." Sam stroked his jaw, pensively.

"Terrible shock, I suppose: Mabunda's homicide. Remote South Africa and metropolitan New York: quite a coincidence."

"Yes. Quite a coincidence. Too much of a coincidence," agreed Sam, carefully scrutinising Wolfgang's reaction. "Must say I was shocked by his death."

"Yes, terrible business. Controversial in life: controversial in death. Poor Solomon," Wolfgang intoned sympathetically.

"Yes, controversial character alright. Who could forget his farewell speech?" spluttered Sam, thumping his chest and reaching for the dregs of his cold coffee.

"Of course the door that shut on his soured career coincided with an opening for you with Vizard," reminded Wolfgang.

"Yeah, amazing. Half a lifetime ago. Judith was also gobsmacked by his departing speech. Such a charmer to meet. Outrageous bugger: remarkably prescient though, old Solomon." Sam continued to stroke his jaw, a distant look in his eye.

"Yes, brilliant man. Pity about his people skills: personality disorder—his own worst enemy. He obviously made a few along the way," spat out Wolfgang. "Generous redundancy package; he would have been better to keep a low profile and just enjoy it, ungrateful bastard. Yeah, he trod on the wrong toes alright." A callous satisfaction coloured his voice.

Wolfgang's tone jolted Sam. "Mabunda's killing was just a coincidence?" Sam looked Wolfgang in the eye.

Wolfgang was unmoved. "Grapevine says it was a ritual Sowetan-style killing. His assassin taken out by the police, I believe. I guess it's up to the cops to make the call. I understand the investigation is closed." Wolfgang rubbed his ruby ring.

"Yes, closed." Sam's face was blank. He continued to cough, hand over his mouth.

"Does Estelle know of your association with Solomon?"

"No. It hasn't really come up."

"Perhaps it's best to let sleeping dogs lie." Wolfgang rose to leave.

"Yeah, perhaps you're right." Sam glared coldly at his boss.

"You know, Sam, loyalty can't be bought." He slapped Sam on the back.

Sam did not reply.

AT POINT PIPER, SAM drove through the gates to the seclusion of his safe haven. He smiled at the vision of Estelle's Mazda parked, albeit a little carelessly, declaring herself home. Just like her grandmother, he thought. Sam took a deep breath, contemplating his castle with satisfaction. His thirty-odd years with the company had been deeply rewarding. The options he'd sold off, on Wolfgang's advice, just prior to the '87 crash had paid off handsomely.

As Sam put his key in the front door, Estelle pre-empted the turn of the lock, greeting her Father with a kiss on the cheek.

"Hi, Dad, home early today? It's only seven o'clock."

"Yes. I thought I deserved an early mark." Sam looked down to see the tortoise-shell swanning seductively around his legs, stroking him with her tail.

"Your number one admirer." Estelle chuckled.

"She's a tart." Sam smiled. "Mmm. What's cooking?"

"Thai green curry. Basmati."

"Smells great." He inhaled deeply.

Father and daughter sat and broke bread, the silent intimacy between them punctuated by small talk. Estelle had laid out a linen tablecloth and a couple of little candles between them.

"What do you think of Ed Hooper's hypothesis that the early oral polio vaccine trials in the Congo may have caused the AIDS epidemic?"

"Well, you're like a dog with a bone, aren't you?" grumbled Sam.

"It does seem a reasonable hypothesis."

"Sure, not unreasonable, and journos need to make a living. Let's not let the truth get in the way of a good story."

"What are you inferring, Dad?"

Sam put his hands up, surrendering in anticipation. "I didn't mean you, Stella. But that Rolling Stones character…"

"Tom Curtis?"

"Yes, Curtis, and Hooper: just a bunch of no-hopers trying to make a quick buck out of a catastrophe."

"Ed Hooper spent seventeen years researching the whole thing and Tom Curtis is a very ethical journalist. They both are."

"Look, I've got you some solid information. Just read it and draw your own conclusions."

"But Dad, can't you discuss this dispassionately?"

Sam put his hands up in surrender again. "Estelle, I don't want to argue with you over this. I just want peace."

Sam walked across to open his briefcase, left inside the front foyer. Digging deep, he handed Estelle several scientific publications downloaded from the net, as well as a weighty manuscript.

"Here. Read through this." Sam handed over an inch-thick tome. "Philosophical Transactions of the Royal Society Sept 2000: Polio vaccine and the Origin of AIDS. It's all there. Sensational journalism is no substitute for good science—as you should know."

"OK. Thanks, Dad. You don't have to be so prickly though."

"The only place I have peace is here—when your grandmother is not around."

"Sorry, Dad, I just wish you wouldn't dismiss me. I do have a solid science background. Stop treating me like a little girl."

"OK. Let's hit the reset button. Sorry, Stella." Sam kissed Estelle on the cheek. "I'm sure this will satisfy any further questions." Sam watched as his daughter greedily perused the documents he'd provided.

"Thanks, Dad: bedtime reading."

Estelle pensively flicked through the manuscript. Hearing the sounds of Bach, she smiled as she made her way towards her pool house.

Lights all low, Estelle sat in her study speed-reading through the mass of articles, underlining here and there with a purple biro and making occasional notes on her research cards: quote on one side, careful referencing on the back. In three hours, she'd managed to speed-read a dozen odd articles, including the Transactions of the Royal Society.

Finally she put some more meat into her article. Trusting Alex would be happy with the title, 'AIDS, Sex and Rock and Roll', Estelle rechecked her schedule for meetings with representatives from PLWAHIV (People Living with AIDS and HIV) starting at ten am at Circular Quay.

"Hey, stranger."

Answering her phone, she smiled softly at the pleasant interruption.

"How are you?" His voice was warm and inviting.

"Panic stations: deadline for the follow-up AIDS article this Friday. Still trying to piece together any information I can get my hands on about the polio-AIDS link. Dad's been helpful. He's printed out some articles and publications."

"Well, here's one for you. William Hamilton is worth looking up: a world-renowned evolutionary biologist from Oxford University and formerly from the London School of Economics. A fellow of the Royal Society and a mentor to Ed Hooper, he was apparently ninety-five per cent sure of the validity of Hooper's hypothesis. Died following a trip to the Congo in 2000: got malaria doing field research collecting chimp faeces at the age of sixty-nine."

"Hamilton, the name rings a bell. Wait. Wait. Backtrack a little." Estelle's voice raised a couple of octaves. "Mabunda also had a degree from the London School of Economics; I wonder if there's a connection?"

"Wouldn't be surprised; keep yourself safe though," cautioned Ryan. "It won't be of any value for you to colour outside of the lines at this point, though it does seem way too many coincidences."

Ryan and Estelle prattled on, barely noticing the time.

"My God, sweetheart, we've been on the phone over two hours. It's almost two am here. I've got a ten am appointment. Better get some shut-eye," announced Estelle.

Turning over, Estelle noted her dad's light still on and the melody of Bach softly audible in the cool night air.

APPROACHING THE EASTERN SIDE of Circular Quay the next day, Estelle strolled past several Quayside restaurants. The Opera House was some fifty-odd metres ahead. It being a beautiful October day, she sat in the sun, ordered a coffee, and waited for her contact. At ten her mobile went off. It was the girl sitting just opposite.

"Hello, Jodie?" welcomed Estelle, surprised they'd been sitting so near.

"Estelle?" The younger woman checked her out.

Jodie appeared ten years older than her years. Apart from a few greys that streaked through her chestnut hair, and a little acne, she looked surprisingly well. Estelle was struck by her expressive eyes.

"Thank you for agreeing to this interview," acknowledged Estelle with an easy smile, pulling her chair across to the girl's table. "Can I interest you in a tea or coffee?"

"Perhaps an orange juice."

"You're twenty-four? How long?" opened Estelle, mindful to not appear too intrusive.

"I've been HIV-positive for a little over three years. Night of my twenty-first birthday: still a virgin at the time. I'm told I look older." Jodie shifted self-consciously.

"I guess we all feel a bit older with illness."

Jodie shrugged. "Yeah: just a funny pneumonia that didn't go away."

"Must have come as quite a shock to learn of your HIV status."

"I thought it could never happen to me," reflected the younger girl. "Then again, perhaps I never thought at all. Easy to feel invincible 'n'let ya guard down." Jodie shrugged.

"None of us are invincible." Estelle jotted in her notebook.

"I thought I was in love. Imagined I'd met the guy that I would spend the rest of my life with," explained the young girl candidly.

"Love has a way of making us feel invincible," agreed Estelle.

"Invincible?" The young girl frowned, a pained look in her eyes. "Perhaps love is blind, or just blind drunk on the night." Jodie bit her lower lip before recovering. "Guess it was the ecstasy: if anything, that made me feel invincible."

"I'm sorry. This must be hard for you."

"Please don't apologise. I'm doing this interview with you because I want my life to mean something to maybe even someone." The younger girl regained a little more composure.

"Sure. I understand," Estelle added gently.

"By the way, thank you for understanding that I don't want my photo taken. Anyway, getting back to what I was saying, I was never going to spend the rest of my life with him. Just the legacy of loving him, believing in him and taking his bait…" Jodie continued candidly.

Estelle flicked back in her mind to her Nan's wisdom: the difference between hooking a mate versus attracting a mate. For Jodie, that difference was lethal.

"I guess it could happen to anyone," replied Estelle softly. A cold shiver travelled up her spine.

"The funny part of all this was that I didn't listen to my gut feelings at the time: desperation for love and a cocktail of drugs and alcohol, a deadly concoction. Well, maybe not deadly. I try not to think of myself as dying from AIDS as much as living with it."

"God! We've all been caught out ignoring our gut feelings," agreed Estelle as she set about trying to soothe the young girl's brokenness that had treacherously entwined itself around her self-worth and self-condemnation. "So Jodie, you're convinced you got HIV on the night of your twenty-first birthday."

"Yes. That's what my doctors say."

"Do you mind if I ask about your dating history prior to that night?"

"Sure." She shrugged. "Only ever gone out with two other guys."

"And have you ever had any other forms of sexual contact, aside from intercourse?"

Jodie frowned, then answered, "Well, you know, just kissing and touching; that sort of stuff."

"And oral sex?"

"Oh yeah, on a few occasions, but that's not really sex."

"Did your partners wear a condom?"

"No. These things are kinda spontaneous. Came in my mouth on a few occasions. I didn't really mind." The younger girl frowned. "My doctors told me how dangerous butt sex was; I didn't have any cut on my lips or anything."

"Sure," agreed Estelle. "No doubt anal sex is the more dangerous, regardless of your orientation. "

"They seemed to focus on the vaginal sex." She blushed. "Do you think oral sex is dangerous?"

Estelle paused. "Maybe: body fluids are body fluids."

"Yeah, I guess. Whatever, I've learnt to accept that there's no crying over spilt milk," shrugged the younger woman.

"So if there was just one message you could give to anyone out there willing to listen to you, Jodie?"

Jodie looked away a moment before her reply. "To all of my friends; drugs, sex and alcohol can be a deadly mix."

"Yes, who is it?" A silvery-headed woman in her seventies with a melodious voice unlatched a guard chain and peeped around the partially open door.

"Good morning, I'm Estelle Goldstein from New Woman. Is Jim in?"

"Oh yes. He's expecting you," the old woman said, nodding, a slight Russian accent detectable. "I'm Natalie, his landlady."

She smiled vivaciously, welcoming Estelle into the small Edwardian anteroom, continuing through a slate-floored terrace corridor doubling as a laundry. Striding through the back door to a courtyard overrun with opulent greenery, she reached a solitary backroom off to the left, the entrance draped by a roll-down bamboo screen.

"James. You have a visitor. A young lady," announced the old lady with barely subdued excitement.

"Coming," answered a disgruntled voice. After a long pause the bamboo screen was rolled up. "Keeps the mozzies out," explained the tall, unshaven man in his early fifties. "Estelle?"

"Yes, from New Woman." She reached out for a handshake with his slightly trembling, yet firm hand.

"Jim Dwyer: pleased to meet you." His blue eyes studied her intently.

Natalie withdrew as Jim invited Estelle into his cramped bedsitter. A single bed was partially hidden around to the left in an alcove. A round kitchen table occupied most of the room, three chairs to boot, one laden with an ironing basket. The tiny room was surrounded by bookcases, an old black-and-white TV sitting on a cupboard. A single kitchen sink was half-full with dirty plates and a few utensils. A lone hot plate, a microwave and a bar fridge were the other items in the cluttered bedsitter.

"Tea?" Jim pulled Estelle a chair, then put on the kettle. He was at pains to find a space on a table piled high with legal and research documents. His gaunt hands were thinner than could be accounted for by his lean build.

"Well, it's very courageous of you to agree to see me, Jim. People living with HIV and AIDS were effusive in praise. Have I seen you somewhere before?"

"Others have said the same: must have one of those faces."

"How long have you lived here?"

"Going on two months now; I'm very grateful Natalie has taken me in. She was my tutor in first year Med: my chemistry demonstrator."

"You've known each other a while?"

"Yes, pure serendipity. Julian, my partner, died. Contested will: ran into Natalie at Julian's funeral."

"So how are you coping?"

"Well, good on the whole. Losing my registration was gut-wrenching. I was hoping to do some counselling for men's health, but the Medical Board assessed me a potential risk to society, quite apart from my HIV status."

"How did that come about?"

"After Julian's death, had been seeing a shrink, dealing with my divorce, coming out and all that. My relationship with Julian: mentioned he'd been a former patient of mine. Copped a mandatory notification to the Board for that: OK, but all the family stuff—psychosexual stuff from my teens—my failed marriage." Jim grimaced. "Grossly distorted."

Estelle gasped. "Gee! I thought medical records were confidential."

"Yeah, so did I. I'd been seeing this guy, on and off, for eighteen years: good reputation, apparently very ethical. I told him he needed to look at his own shit. Anyway, he dumped on me: most common political trick in the book if they want to get rid of you. Either concoct or embellish some sexual misconduct allegation, or schedule you." Jim grimaced. "Bullies in pin-striped suits." He sat observing the shock as it swept across Estelle's eyes. "Often they just bide their time, then they strike when they think that no one is watching."

"Did you lodge a complaint to the Health Care Complaints Commission?"

"On legal advice from my medical defence union, yes: dismissed. Old boys club; they just closed ranks."

"The end justifies their means."

"Julian's dead, for God's sake. I'll never meet anyone like him again." Jim looked across to a small, framed photo of himself and Julian. "Medical defence slapped a twenty thousand deductible on my policy for defamation or whistle blowing." Jim's laughter turned to a hacking cough.

"Both of you are familiar." Estelle scrutinised the photograph.

"He was my father, my brother, my lover. Just once in a lifetime. I'd do it all over again—in a heartbeat."

"You really loved him," acknowledged Estelle.

"Yes. His death has given me the strength to take up the cudgel on behalf of so many duped into taking part in this AIDS vaccine trial. Based in Thailand at the time: fewer legal implications and less red tape for them: promises, promises. Distorted the HIV test. His suspension from teaching just floored him: lost his will to live. Such crap." Jim stopped to catch his breath. "Suspended for allegedly groping a prepubescent girl in a public swimming pool—one of his pupils. Trial by media."

"Were there any witnesses?" Estelle shifted her focus uncomfortably to her notepad.

"Hundreds, possibly, but he was gay: my lover, for God's sake."

"So he was accused?"

"Accused: trial aborted. Outed by radio shock jocks but never exonerated. No vindication. Disturbed kid, no witnesses to testify, just..."Jim's frustration and helplessness were palpable.

"It must have been devastating for him."

"Indeed. He was born to teach. His suspension almost destroyed him. At least we had each other."

"Your love was very deep." Estelle's chest tightened.

"Have you known love, Estelle?" Jim looked at her smack in the eye.

"Yes. Yes, I have." Estelle nodded quietly, the wistful look in her eye overshadowing her smile.

"I went to this psychiatrist in confidence—damn mandatory reporting to HCCC—used as a weapon against me."

Estelle shook her head, pursing her lips.

"If you want confidentiality, go to a lawyer."

"Or a clairvoyant?" jested Estelle awkwardly.

"Yes." Jim laughed. "Funny you should say that."

"You've still got your sense of humour." Estelle smiled.

"Laugh and the world laughs with you: Julian's favourite saying. You know, Estelle, at the end of the day we're all just human beings with tender hearts and clay feet."

"And AZT?"

"And the rest." Jim opened the bar fridge, choc-a-block with pill bottles. "I take AZT, blah, blah, blah, vitamin C, B6, Selenium, Nilstat for my thrush."

"Wow! That is a mouthful."

"If only Julian was still alive. He was my lifeline. You know, Estelle, if you just feel loved—that can keep you going."

"And now?" Estelle reached for Jim's icy hands.

Jim shrugged. "Before I'm cremated, I just want to get my story out."

"For whom do you write?"

"Well, for a start, all those lost youth attending the federally funded Mental Health Clinics. No confidentiality, down the track, for them either."

"Still, I thought...?"

"It all depends. Relationship doesn't count any more. It's all just throughput and medication," Jim spluttered, wiping the phlegm from his lips. "You know, Estelle, in the late seventies, eighty per cent of psychiatric consultations were talking therapy. Thirty years later, eighty per cent of psychiatric consultations are for ongoing medications. The Medical Board is very censorious of any boundary violation by individual practitioners—and sure, there's a place for that—but the profession seems to have a blind spot when it comes to its own enmeshment with the pharmaceutical industry."

"A pill for every ill?"

"So it seems: till death do us part."

"You're saying the medical establishment are in bed with the drug companies?"

"Of course; about half of all research completed is never published and the raw data upon which their evidence is based is not open to third-party scrutiny. Researchers are totally dependent on the giant pharmaceutical companies for funding: afraid to speak out."

"I guess your stance with the class action hasn't endeared you."

"Ah! What the hell. Life's short: got to do what you can." Jim broke into a paroxysm of coughing, reaching for a tissue to spit out another gob of phlegm. "Thanks," he spluttered.

"No. Thank you," replied Estelle with an apologetic smile.

"You know, Estelle," he added, as she got up to leave, "often the final curtain falls and our exit is made through the door of regret."

Estelle paused in order to take in his statement. "I guess." She smiled.

"Love is what makes the difference." His eyes softened.

Estelle closed both her eyes, nodding in agreement. She took both of Jim's hands, bowing in gratitude—and he towards her.

Estelle left to catch the ferry to Lavender Bay. As her ferry cruised to its destination, she weaved together in her mind the four phases of AIDS, with a face for each: Jodie, Jim, and little Innocence—and she hadn't yet faced death. As always, the leering face of Moloch greeted her from Luna Park.

BACK AT HER DESK, Estelle sat, fire in her belly, bullet-pointing her article. Jodie and Jim, just like every other person in the world, wanted to be heard and validated. They wanted to know their existence somehow had meaning. Estelle wondered how long before Jodie would drop the excruciating pain of her shame and allow herself to be seen by the world in the way that Estelle perceived her.

She cast her mind back to Jim: the look in his eye at the mention of his beloved. Closing her eyes, Estelle pondered on how we exist in the way we do. We really need to be seen by another; it's what makes us feel fully human, fully alive, she concluded. A smile rose on her lips, enlivened by the remembrance of the way in which Ryan had glimpsed her soul, as she did his.

For Estelle, this article had to count: count for the Jodie's of the world who didn't feel loved; for the Julians and Jims condemned for their love; for the number of South African wives that lined up, but never felt counted; for the underground miners that never felt seen, for the prostitutes that never felt wanted; for the children that lay dying, who the world would never come to know.

'AIDS, SEX AND ROCK AND ROLL.
THE MANY FACES OF AIDS: PART ONE

'ON A HOT SATURDAY night in a lust-filled bar, blinded by drugs and alcohol, a young woman by the name of Jodie exposes herself to a deadly mistake. On her twenty-first birthday, Jodie trades her sexual innocence for intimate contact with a man she barely knows. Jodie is a marketable commodity in Sydney's lucrative nightlife and party culture.

'Half a world away, in South Africa, in smoke-filled bars, migrant miners ply themselves with alcohol. As 'foreign' miners, they are a lucrative commodity for the mining industry. Away from their wives for most the year, they trade their loneliness for sexual contact with the prostitutes in the brothel next door.

'Having long lost their innocence, the women and girls in the brothel next door trade themselves as sexual commodities to the lonely migrant miners. In their desperation for survival, both miner and prostitute make deadly sexual contact.

'Lined up, standing in the dust in the heat of the day, the miners' wives expose their buttocks to an innocent little white needle. They are a lucrative target for the contraceptive market. With pregnancy-free sex, they are now available for a deadly trade-off as their men return to greet them with a deadly gift for Christmas.

'Lying in a South African hospital bed, a little girl clings to life. In a world that has built its trade upon humans as commodities, she is little more than collateral damage. As she lies dying, she dies to a world that has lost its innocence.'

Estelle rubbed her eyes. It was time for her morning break. She checked her inbox. Ryan had photoshopped himself as an angel in several of their many photos taken together. "Now that's some self-delusion," she muttered, chuckling. Cheeky, light-hearted banter, along with a few romantic exchanges, and it was soon time to get back to meeting that deadline.

HANDS SCROLLED THROUGH THE reams of microfiche files, pausing, and scrolling again. "Fucking archaic." Scrolling again. Finally pausing, vision riveted on the contents imprinted on the clear plastic film: 'Monolayer culture development utilising kidney cells of Pan troglodytes- troglodytes.' Central African Mirage Journal. Vol 160, 1960. Coetzee, J.; Mabunda, S.H.E.; De Lange, J.M.'

"Gotcha!"

ALEX LOUNGED BACK, TAKING in her protégé's pitch as she sipped on a small Scotch on the rocks. "Goodo. Don't get too preachy. And part two?"

"Yeah, thought I'd run a line from Pasteur, Louis Pasteur."

"Do tell." That expectant silence again.

"Well, like his often quoted recantation: 'The microbe is nothing. The terrain is everything.' I was thinking of linking Jodie's personal journey of being HIV-positive with a consideration of the challenges facing a consumer—the victim: looking through the lens of different individuals as they pass through the different phases of this evolving epidemic—more an environmental look at the AIDS epidemic.

"Blah, blah, blah," replied Alex, deadpan, cutting through Estelle's waffle.

"Well, it fascinates me how South Africa, probably the leading nation on the African continent, was the last to be affected. The epicentre was in the Congo, and yet now South Africa has by far the highest case-load of AIDS. What do we have in common here?"

Alex yawned.

"Well, our sexual culture can be pretty toxic, and all things being equal, why is it that some succumb with a seemingly trivial encounter whereas others can sleep with an HIV-positive partner for a decade and somehow avoid getting infected?"

"So a sub-heading for part two might be The Many Phases of AIDS?" Alex frowned.

"Four phases:– Phase One: toxic culture, dangerous behaviour, silent infection, proliferation. Phase Two is the sickness phase, some three to ten years later, lasting years, and characterised by chronic ill health punctuated by increasingly frequent admission to hospitals. Phase Three: death and all that entails when the victim is in the prime of their life, a breadwinner or mother. We could interview others further down the illness spiral from where Jim is now. Finally, Phase Four: prolonged aftermath; in Africa the epidemic has been like a slow-moving tsunami, it's impact rippling across the generations, impacting GDP and creating socio-economic ghettos. Widows, having lost their breadwinner, are more likely to trade sex for survival, increasing risk; orphans more likely to be malnourished and more prone to casual sex—comfort sex, I guess—and more likely become HIV-positive."

"And relevance here?"

"Look, we may have got a head start here in the eighties, but apathy has caught up with the Lucky Country—again. I'm sure there are parallels here: mobility and social isolation, issues for our workforce—not just for miners. Our technology is driving a wedge in our social interactions. Internet sex was unheard of a decade ago. People are sacked via a text message. Sexting a new phenomenon—"

"OK, OK. Good. Sex it up."

"The party culture is dripping with alcohol, ecstasy, and casual sex. We need to educate. Jodie, for instance, didn't consider oral sex as sex. These kids don't stand a chance."

"OK, but don't be a killjoy. Don't mind a bit of safe butt sex for novelty. Remember size matters," smirked Alex.

Estelle looked at Alex, perplexed.

"The size of our sponsors." She half-smiled. "Yeah, I like it." Alex was momentarily reflective. "OK, you're looking at the environmental context. See if you can get some idea of policy direction—but no matter, keep it sexy! Controversy sells."

"Well, that brings us to Part Three: The Origin of AIDS." Estelle grabbed the opening.

"OK," agreed Alex. "Just get these first two rolling. Give me another one pager."

PARTS ONE AND TWO of 'AIDS, Sex and Rock and Roll' were completed—'The Many Faces of AIDS' and 'The Many Phases of AIDS'—the two ready for publication consecutively over two weeks. Estelle dropped both in Alex's in-tray and set off for home.

Father and daughter sat sipping wine over dinner. "Interviewed a doctor by the name of Jim—gay guy, early fifties—sure we've crossed paths somewhere. Photo of him and his lover: eerie looking at the photo of his deceased lover." Estelle paused. "Felt I'd met them both at some stage."

"Perhaps you may have." Sam shrugged.

"He's got AIDS. His lover died after a failed HIV-vaccine trial."

"It's always tragic to lose a loved one," replied Sam, sipping on his full-blooded red.

"They loved deeply and were equally punished for it. Still a lot of hatred projected towards the gay community."

"I'm sure there is," replied Sam. "Does he have friends or family for support?"

"Fair weather friends, and as for family: bystanders when the chips are down."

"I see." Sam blinked.

"How many people claiming to be accepting of gays would stand proud if their son or daughter came out?"

"You're right, Stella. I suspect not many."

"I reckon he's dying from a broken heart—can kill you. Perhaps in more ways than one," reflected Estelle. "What do you reckon, Dad?" Estelle gazed steadily in Sam's direction.

Sam silently raised his eyebrows without immediately commenting. "I'm sure you're right, Stella."

"I really felt for him," continued Estelle. "Too easy to pass judgement. What do you think? Where are you, Dad?" challenged Estelle, frustrated by Sam's lack of connection.

"I guess you're right, Stella. It's a shame," replied Sam, rubbing his eyes and refocusing his attention.

"Shaming seems to be a bloody powerful weapon: favourite tool of society to keep us all in line."

"Stella, you are starting to sound more and more like your grandmother," grumbled Sam, irritated by Estelle's bolshie attitude.

"No wonder the world's in such a mess. The whole bloody system's out of balance. We're all treated like mushrooms—fed bullshit and kept in the dark—taking as gospel whatever the authority figures feed us."

"The world needs more cooperation," grunted Sam.

"It needs someone prepared to ask the difficult questions, then stand up and fight for what is right. 'The only thing for evil to triumph, is that good men do nothing'."

"Sometimes you've got no control over the big picture, Stella. All you can do is try and look out for your family," deflected Sam.

The night continued in animated discussion and challenging repartee; major controversy was sidestepped, father and daughter concluding on a pleasant note. Team Goldstein washed up before making their separate ways to bed. Sam embraced his daughter at the bottom of the staircase and Estelle headed to her outhouse.

"HELLO, BEAUTIFUL." IT WAS a late night call from Ryan, his voice smooth, smouldering, sexy.

"Hello, stranger," she responded, her instantaneous smile lighting the dark.

"I've been missing you badly. I can't stop thinking of you. God, I just want to hold you and kiss you all over," opened Ryan.

"I think of you every spare minute." Estelle sighed. A tingling sensation danced beneath her skin.

"How's your day been?"

"Finished off and submitted parts one and two. Quite good pieces, even if I say so myself."

"Your interview with the young girl; how did that go?"

"Heart-wrenching; something Nan said to me not so long ago is hitting home."

"And what's that?"

"Just how much our course through life can change based on the people we choose to sleep with. Kind of eerie when I stand back and look at it from Jodie's perspective, as well as Jim's, the other guy I interviewed."

"Sounds like they both made an impact on you."

"Jim lost his lover to AIDS after a failed AIDS vaccine trial—continues to haunt me. I remember reading something about an accusation brought against his lover for molesting a teenage girl that he was teaching at the time." Estelle drew a deep breath." I was so bloody fast to pass judgement back then."

"We've all fallen into that trap at different times."

"He has taken up a crusade and launched a class action against the pharmaceutical company that let them down so badly. If anything, it put Jim at greater risk of AIDS."

"That's fair enough. I imagine he'd be seeking compensation for loved ones left behind?"

"Perhaps?"

"Do you know which pharma company this guy has launched the class action against? Not your dad's, I hope."

"Class action's just par for the course for all pharma companies."

"STRAIGHT INTO MY OFFICE. I'd like a word with you, Estelle," commanded Alex sternly.

"Sure." Estelle followed nervously.

Alex eyeballed Estelle for several long seconds. "Well done! You've excelled. The response to your article has been a resounding success."

"Are you kidding me?" exclaimed Estelle, her eyes widening.

"No, kiddo. The readers' response has been unprecedented. Letters just keep flooding in, all thanking the magazine for its open and sensitive approach to the dangers out on the streets: mothers everywhere writing to thank us, saying how it has opened dialogue between themselves and their teenage sons and daughters; young girls writing in, thanking us for our timely warnings; boys and men thanking us equally as much for reminding them to stay safe; and a few more, who have already contracted AIDS and other STDs, for our compassion. Well done, Estelle."

"That's great."

"Our October sales spiked. Keep it up," added Alex, softening to a smile.

"Guarantee you'll love part three. Bring on November." Estelle beamed.

"I've no doubt." Alex smirked. "Now get out of here. I've got some work to do and I'm sure you do too."

Head held high, Estelle marched straight to her desk. 'Two thumbs up. Article a success,' boasted Estelle in her email to Ryan.

'You're a star.' His instant reply.

'Those poor people in central Africa will never get access to antiretrovirals, unless as part of some experimental drug or vaccine trials. At least in South Africa the country may afford some universal access to drugs as a right. And Mabunda's death?' she wrote back.

'PART THREE – THE ORIGINS OF AIDS'

The issue had already received a lot of publicity since Curtis's Rolling Stone article. Louis Pascall and Julian Cribb had succeeded in giving the theory oxygen, and Hooper had put in a sterling effort, but still the injustice to the Africans has not been acknowledged or the issue of compensation addressed. Blacks and gays are still the object of crass stereotyping and scapegoating.

225

Notwithstanding the chaotic nature of post-colonial Africa—political instability, social breakdown, war, and a lack of human rights, the ensuing food shortages and malnutrition—something big hit the continent some half a century ago and the scientific establishment is running for cover.

Back to where it all started. It is now widely accepted that AIDS had its origins from monkeys, specifically the chimpanzee: the first cases ever diagnosed stemming from the Belgian Congo, Rwanda and Burundi. Having established who were initially affected, when it began, and where the AIDS pandemic started, the still unresolved question plaguing many minds is what actually happened? How did SIV evolve to HIV, and why? Why has this catastrophe happened? Could something similar, if not worse, happen again?

The geographical fit of the initial AIDS cases in the Congo with the targeted region for the 1950s polio campaign is pretty compelling. The overwhelming initial victims were from the Congo.

The Royal Society's conclusion of the September 2000 conference on the Origin of Aids had been all but dismissive of Ed Hooper's meticulously researched tome. There are jarring inconsistencies: senior researchers from the Laboratoire Medical de Stanleyville have denied using chimpanzee in their research, yet archival contemporaneous footage from the Congo would appear to contradict their assertions.

African assistants from that time volunteered that four to six hundred chimpanzee from Camp Lindi had been sacrificed to provide kidneys for the purpose of virological culture. Why the denial? The gentlemen doth protest too much, methinks.'

Estelle whipped off a one-pager to Alex and continued to fine tune her document before heading home.

Kicking off her shoes, Estelle headed to her kitchen. Startled by the whirring sound of the garage door opening, Estelle just missed seeing a hooded man in dark clothes as he leapt out of the glass doors of her pool house. He'd rummaged through her belongings, taking a handful of disks and USB sticks, and stuffed them into the oversized pocket of his jacket. He lightfooted it between the swirls of steam coming from the spa before disappearing into the night like an apparition. Inquisitively peering through her window, Estelle noted nothing more than shafts of light from the main house piercing the eerie mist.

FRIDAY CAME AROUND ALL too quickly. Estelle felt a little anxious about how Alex might receive the final article in her trilogy. The precedents were not favourable. Bill Hamilton was incensed that lawsuits were being used to terrorise individuals and journals that tried to promote discussion of plausible, but inconvenient hypotheses that might be a threat to the prestige of the discipline of medical science. His unpublished letter to the Editor-in-Chief of Science Magazine of 23rd Feb 1994, had concluded:

'Surely you must realise that the development of this sort of situation in science is terrible—literally terrible for all mankind. Thinking only of the narrow escape in the SV40 case, leave alone the possibly worse and determinedly under-investigated case of AIDS, anyone should see that the situation ought to terrify us.'

"COME IN, ESTELLE," INVITED Alex politely. The older lady took her usual place on her throne and motioned Estelle to sit. Estelle noticed an empty glass of Scotch on her desk and detected the faint scent of nicotine.

"Well, what do you think?" Estelle pursed her lips.

"Meticulously researched. Well argued." Alex stroked her upper lip. "What's your agenda here?"

"What do you mean?"

"My understanding is that the general thrust of this three part series was to rally public interest in the AIDS epidemic locally and foster support for access to antiretrovirals for sub-Saharan Africa—part of our ongoing philanthropic endeavours—not to dig into fanciful conjecture of what may have happened in the Congo over fifty years ago." Alex's jaw hardened.

"But the question logically follows."

"Yes. Hooper, Pascal, Curtis have all aired this Polio–AIDS hypothesis more than adequately."

"But there's more evidence," cut in Estelle. "Mabunda's death—"

"Did you go and see Doctor Parsons?" Alex cut her off.

"I'm fine."

"This article is off track. It lacks balance. Redraft it: include this data—and this conclusion." She handed Estelle a two-page document.

Estelle skimmed quickly over issues with which she was well familiar. The cut hunter or bush meat hypothesis was to be given premier focus, as was the issue of phylogenetic dating analysis proving the other viable theory, that random accidental contact of monkey hunters with simian body fluids allowed entry of chimp SIV into man, becoming HIV-1.

"The timing and locations of the first clinical cases don't fit," argued Estelle.

"A recent look-back analysis of molecular sequence data suggests a date of origin for HIV as early as nineteen-thirty," responded Alex.

"Yes, assuming a gradual Darwinian-type evolution, chance mutation, and a slowly evolving epidemic mutating randomly over years, but this pandemic doesn't look like that."

The older lady scratched her head, hearing her protégé out.

"I'm familiar with the research you're referring to," Estelle continued. "Korber and Co. The phylogenetic tree analysis of the group M-HIV viruses look like a sunburst: looks like the Congo was cluster-bombed with up to ten different sub-types of HIV over a very short period of time, a Lamarckian-type event, not like the feline AIDS virus that shows a more classic, Darwinian-type evolution."

"Please explain," encouraged Alex.

"The African AIDS epidemic involved ten or more synchronous epidemics. The sunburst pattern of the group M viruses signifies a synchronous entry of ten or more viruses into a human population: a punctuated origin, not a slow-branching evolution." Estelle halted, noting the glazed look in Alex's eyes.

"Look, kid. Keep it simple and upbeat. This is what's to be presented and there's your conclusion," dictated Alex.

"But the truth about the polio campaign—"

"We all have our truth, Estelle, and I will not let any truth get in the way of a good outcome. The world is on the brink of eradicating polio. I won't get in the way of that noble outcome. Will you?" provoked Alex, peering over her glasses.

"But—"

"I had a message from God this morning. He doesn't often contact me, but when he does, I listen and obey—and so will you."

"You're shutting me down, aren't you?" protested Estelle. "Who is he?" she asked, anger rising in her voice.

The editor of New Woman stood up and poured herself a glass of Johnny Walker. She offered her young protégé a glass. Estelle declined. Alex walked across to look out over Sydney Harbour, shining and tranquil. "I'm not at liberty to say who he is, but I suspect he's closer to you than to me."

"What are you talking about?" Estelle visibly stiffened.

"Prior to your South African assignment we received a generous donation with a request tailor-made for you," Alex span around and looked Estelle straight in the eye, "to investigate the AIDS situation in South Africa."

"What?" Estelle blushed. "I've got the necessary credentials," she protested.

"Really, Estelle? Why would we send a twenty-seven-year-old rookie to cover such an important assignment?" baited Alex. "I should have known then, but put it down to serendipity." The older lady turned away, sipping her Scotch, musing. "When we had an action replay before New York, I twigged."

"What are you saying? What's going on?" Gob-smacked, Estelle inhaled hard.

"You have a powerful benefactor, but something went very wrong in New York—and I do not want to know anything about it." Alex downed the rest of her Scotch and turned around to face her confused and embarrassed protégé.

"I don't understand."

"I want the revised and upbeat version on my desk by two pm. 'The Origin of Aids' will go out in your name or mine, but it will go out. Southern Africa could do with the antiretrovirals. Do I make myself clear?"

"Yes. Sure." Estelle got up and left.

"Ryan, I've got to talk to you," pleaded Estelle impatiently.

"Hey, beautiful, what's going on?" soothed Ryan.

"My third article on the origin of AIDS has been canned."

"No surprises there, sweetheart. It wouldn't be the first time this issue's been suppressed. Sorry, Estelle, just take it from the top."

"I don't know where to start. I feel terrible."

"I'm here for you," he calmly assured.

"I think my dad's company may be involved. I don't know what to think."

"Involved in what?"

"Mabunda's murder."

"Not surprised."

"What do you mean?"

"Too many coincidences, sweetheart. Did a literature search on old fiche disc files. Solomon Mabunda declared a conflict of interest on one of his research papers: seems he was a recipient of a funding grant for Hepatitis B vaccine research from Vizard back in the early seventies."

"Oh, God."

"Damn! Sorry, Estelle."

"Oh, God. Oh, God. Ryan, how long have you known?" Estelle asked, humiliated.

"About Mabunda's financial connections? Only since yesterday, but I was concerned for you since our weekend in the Catskills."

"Why didn't you say something?"

"Look, Estelle: please, sweetheart. I know you had nothing to do with Mabunda's death."

"Oh, God, I feel sick."

"It's the system, Estelle. Litigate if you can, character assassinate if you can't, eliminate if you must."

"For God's sake, stop it. Stop it. I can barely breathe. I feel like I'm going to throw up."

"It's not your fault, Estelle," pleaded Ryan.

"Please just stop. Ryan, I've got to go."

"Estelle—".

The line went dead.

SAM GOLDSTEIN STRETCHED OUT in his chair. He looked across to a father-daughter photo sitting on top of a bookshelf: Estelle's twenty-first birthday.

The familiar double knock preceded by a millisecond the entry of Doctor Wolfgang Schaffell, ebullient as ever. "How's it, Sam?"

"Good, Wolf." Sam waited.

"Happy with the figures?"

"We're doing well."

"And how's the little girl going? Settling after her traumatic trip?"

"She's doing OK, thank you: birthday this weekend. Getting good reviews for her AIDS articles; she's really got her teeth into it and seems to be settling, thank God. Thanks for those Royal Society Conference Transactions on the Origin of AIDS. I'm sure that's pointed her in the right direction."

"I'm sure her efforts will help foster much needed public support for antiretrovirals to be embraced in South Africa," added Wolf.

"New Woman is just a local rag. I'm just grateful she's finding her feet here at home."

"Local maybe, but good pieces of journalism are syndicated to our stable partners offshore. We have a certain degree of synergy with the UK and US. I see us working on strategic partnerships with the South Africans in the twenty-first century."

"I'm sure there are many possibilities for her."

"We'd welcome a constructive relationship with rising young stars in the media. Has Estelle considered a move sideways into television? She's got the brains and good looks. I could put in a good word."

"I'm sure you could." Sam looked at Wolf, poker-faced.

"I'd be only too delighted: just the left hand washing the right." Wolf beamed, turning to leave. "I take it Estelle has dropped the Mabunda conspiracy?"

"She hasn't mentioned anything. New boyfriend is keeping her occupied, I suspect."

"Goodo. Mabunda always has been the fly in the ointment. Best let sleeping dogs lie."

"SOMETHING YOU'RE NOT TELLING me?" prodded Sam, his daughter having remained withdrawn throughout dinner, picking at her food. Sam had arrived home to an unusually withdrawn daughter. The table had been set for two, with linen tablecloth and silverware, the candle unlit.

"Few little upsets at work," replied Estelle nonchalantly.

"Oh? I thought your boss was wildly enthusiastic about your efforts."

"Yes. Very impressed with the first two: less impressed with the third instalment."

"I guess two out of three's not bad," soothed Sam, pouring himself another glass of red.

"Yes. She would have been very happy had I followed the script," snapped Estelle.

"The script?" probed Sam, viewing her over the rims of his glasses.

"Yes. You know the script. The script you gave me right out of the transactions of the Royal Society. You know!" Estelle eyeballed her father, the anger in her tone unmistakable.

"What's this? One moment as demure and as delightful as your mother at your age, the next as volatile and as crazy as your grandmother," Sam jested.

"Don't play dumb, Dad. It's about time you levelled with me."

"What on earth are you talking about, Stella?" Sam put his glass down.

"Don't bullshit me!" Estelle hit out, her rage barely contained.

"What?"

"You knew Mabunda. Don't lie to me."

"OK. OK. Yes, I knew Solomon Mabunda." Sam crossed his arms.

"Did he work for your company?" Estelle demanded.

"Yes, but—"

"Why was Mabunda persona non-grata with the company?"

"Solomon was perturbed by the ongoing use of primate organs as a base for viral culture for vaccines. The SV-40 debacle, that had contaminated one of Doctor Sabin's vaccines, had been ignored. Solomon was adamant the use of primate organs should be stopped. His intransigence on this led to his resignation. He used his farewell as a platform to slag off at the company for ignoring demonstrable risks of cross-species infection," explained Sam. "In hindsight, his prescience of the AIDS pandemic was remarkable."

"So is Vizard still using primate organs for vaccine culture?"

"Yes, but it's being phased out. These things just can't happen overnight. Huge costs involved, and a polio pandemic to wipe out.

"What are you saying?"

"Estelle, it's easy to be wise in hindsight. We did the best we could with the technology we had at the time," placated Sam.

"When was the mishap with SV-40?" challenged Estelle.

"Late fifties."

"So fifty years after Sabin's mishap with SV-40 and twenty-three years since the AIDS pandemic was recognised, you're still using primate organs for vaccine production. What's all that about?" snarled Estelle.

"But, Estelle—"

"You know—you're pathetic!" Estelle spat the words out. "And Mabunda, why was he sacrificed?"

"What nonsense," Sam blustered.

"You couldn't manipulate him. Character assassination failed, so he was eliminated."

"That's crazy," gasped Sam

"A forgotten has-been on his last legs, was he, Dad? Don't need another fucking class action, eh, Dad? In whose best interest that nothing else is investigated or leaked? Is that right, Dad?"

Sam looked at his adult daughter as if for the first time, speechless.

"And then—Oh, Dad!—currying favour for me with financial inducements behind my back. How could you betray me like that? Humiliate me?"

"You've got the wrong end of the stick."

"I didn't tell you my double was taken out in New York, did I?"

"My God! What? What do you mean?"

"I've been groomed. May I expect any further inducements?" snapped Estelle.

"Estelle. Please—"

"Oh, Dad, just stop. Just stop!" Estelle turned away from her father, slamming a door behind her.

SAM PULLED HIS MERCEDES over to the side of the road, away from the early morning gridlock. Exiting his vehicle, he headed for a park bench, where he sat in silence.

Cold sweat poured down his pristine white shirt as he caressed his pendant. A sudden excruciating gasp for breath and he clutched his chest. He fell hard to the ground. A group of startled birds took to flight over a cliff edge.

Chapter Eleven

*N*an clutched Estelle's hand, giving a gentle squeeze. Together they looked on, nodding to the passing mourners as they dribbled out of the Eastern Suburbs Crematorium. One by one, they lined up to offer their condolences, Estelle and Nan acknowledging each with appreciation.

"How you holding up, sweet pea?" whispered Nan.

"Don't recognise half these faces," she replied, just in time to glimpse Wolfgang shifting his calculating gaze in their direction. From the core of her gut, nausea welled up in Estelle's throat.

"Condolences," Wolfgang muttered. "Your father was a good man."

Struggling to contain her contempt, she acknowledged him with a frosty look. A moment of chilled silence fell between them before Wolfgang excused himself for being unable to attend the wake.

After a few consoling words for both Estelle and her Nan, their solemn duties concluded, the funeral attendants departed. Minutes later, so too did the lingering mourners, leaving Estelle and Nan to walk away in privacy.

A pathetic, teary drizzle spewed its way towards them, droplets of water taunting the parched earth beneath their feet. Withholding any succour, the water rolled across the dry cracks, fast disappearing into drains by the side of the road. Without warning, its final tears exhausted, the rain suddenly stopped.

Estelle turned in time to see Wolfgang heading off into the distance. She lifted her reddened eyes skywards, observing the predatory grey clouds as they hovered above the crematorium. Hungrily they sucked up the grey smoke billowing from the chimney, as if feeding on the grief.

"No. Enough!" Motioning Nan to stay behind, Estelle ran after Wolfgang's receding presence.

"Doctor Schaffell."

Wolfgang paused and swung around to confront the breathless young blonde flushed with anticipation. "Yes, Estelle. Sorry I cannot attend your father's wake."

Estelle took a deep breath. A sudden, unforgiving southerly buster arrived, bracing her determination. "I know all about Solomon Mabunda."

"Really?" Wolfgang looked puzzled.

"I know of Mabunda's involvement with the Polio and Hepatitis B vaccine development. I know why he was assassinated."

"My dear girl, you really do need to get some help." Wolfgang looked down with feigned sympathy.

"Mabunda was on to your screw-up with the Polio vaccine trials, wasn't he?"

"My dear girl."

"Don't dear girl me. Dad told me everything. It was you who provided the inducements for my overseas assignments, wasn't it?"

Wolfgang's face hardened. "No. Not I. Your father was just trying to assist you in your career."

"It was you who pulled the plug on my 'Origin of AIDS' article, wasn't it?"

"We needed to protect you from yourself. Publish that nonsense and you'll wake up in the garbage pail."

"And the millions of innocent orphans left in the wake of the unethical Congo trials? Who protects them?"

Wolfgang's upper lip curled. "You have no idea, Miss Goldstein. Vaccines have saved millions of lives. We will eliminate Polio, and in time, we will eliminate AIDS."

Glancing at the hallowed ground surrounded by plaques of the deceased, Estelle's mind flicked back to Nancefield Cemetery in Soweto. "And the twenty million wiped out by your stuff-up? Just collateral damage, are they?"

"These are wild and reckless allegations, Estelle. Allegations to which no respectable scientist would put his name, and no respectable journal will publish—and more than adequately refuted by experts in the field."

"And Hamilton?"

"Proved nothing," he snarled.

Estelle paused, watching Wolfgang carefully. "But Mabunda's evidence is pretty damning, isn't it? No longer buried in dusty archives," she bluffed.

Wolfgang's eyes widened. "You have nothing."

"Sooner or later I will expose you." Estelle lifted her chin in defiance.

"You're playing with fire, Miss Joan of Arc," he warned, rubbing his ruby ring.

Guests wandered into the Goldstein home, Estelle and Nan greeted each with an offer of refreshments. Estelle made polite conversation, stoically acknowledging their expressions of shared grief.

"Sorry I'm late," apologised a sombre voice from behind her. "Got here just as fast as I could."

Estelle turned to face his deeply sympathetic eyes. "Hi," she quietly acknowledged.

"Are you OK?" asked Ryan, reaching out to touch her upper arm.

"I have to be." She frowned, nodding, before gently releasing a subdued smile.

Reaching to take Estelle's hand, Ryan observed a subtle tear-trace faintly etched into her dried make-up.

"How did you…?" Estelle awkwardly pulled back.

"Your Nan rang: tracked me down through PETA."

"I see." She moved to greet other guests.

"Thank you for coming," interrupted Esther, alleviating the awkwardness of the moment. Recognising the welcoming tone of her voice, Ryan turned to face the old woman, returning the warmth of her eye contact.

"I'm grateful for the call. Quite a shock," replied Ryan, following Estelle's every movement across the room.

"I'm sure it did come as quite a shock for a number of people," replied Esther. "You'll be sticking around then?" The old lady followed Ryan's steady focus.

"Yes, till Thursday. I was able to cobble together a few days leave." Ryan shifted his attention back to meet the old lady's eyes.

Esther dropped her voice, eyeballing Ryan over her glasses. "She's going to need you around."

"I intend to be here for her."

"Pleased to hear." Esther nodded approvingly.

The onset of early evening carried with it a humid stillness, drowned out by the serenade of cicadas competitively vying for a mate. With the last of the mourners departed, Estelle sat quietly by the edge of the pool, her feet dangling in the water, her attention centred on a single ripple from a fallen seed. She watched as ever expanding, concentric circles took perfect formation.

"Mind?" signalled Ryan as he slowly approached.

"Sure." She shrugged.

A stilted silence fell between them.

"I'm here for you," broke in Ryan. "Till Thursday, at least."

"Thanks for coming."

"You haven't been taking my calls or responding to my emails or texts."

"I needed, still need to clear my head." Estelle grimaced, head down, stirring the water with her toe.

"It's OK, sweetheart, however long it takes."

"What's that supposed to mean?" snapped Estelle, her face reddening with anger. "You think this will all go away?"

"I didn't mean that," soothed Ryan.

"Then what?" She looked through and beyond him.

"I mean however long you need me. I just want to be here for you," emphasised Ryan, gently coaxing Estelle out of her resistance to him.

"There is no however long; however long will not bring him back. I killed my father. I killed him!"

"No! Stop that. None of this is your fault, Stell." Ryan summoned all his strength to quash Estelle's demons.

"It is my fault. None of this should have happened. In digging for the truth, I dug his grave, and Mabunda's, and—"

"Shhh!" whispered Ryan, his index finger pressing gently over Estelle's lips.

Estelle pushed his hand away. "Can't you see?"

"You are not responsible for your dad's death! And neither of us really know why Mabunda was killed."

"Mabunda's death was not some random event. Dad knew, Wolfgang knew," she looked straight at Ryan, "and you knew."

Ryan nodded in assent.

"I confronted Wolfgang this morning. He admitted shutting down my article; threatened an end to my career."

Ryan went to speak, but refrained.

"He was aware of the relationship between Hamilton and Mabunda." Estelle looked at Ryan sharply. "I bluffed about Mabunda. Led him to believe I have possession of Mabunda's evidence.

"What have you done, Stell?" Ryan frowned.

"No longer buried in dusty archives; I threatened to expose him." Estelle looked across to Ryan.

"What?"

"His parting words to me were, 'You're playing with fire, Miss Joan Of Arc.'"

"Shit!" Ryan whispered.

"Dad was somehow involved. Why? Why?" Her ferocity quickly gave way to helplessness.

"Hey," he whispered, again raising his finger to her lips, "although you can't see it now, in time you will come to see things differently. You did not kill your father, or anyone else, for that matter. You are not to blame. You must believe me, Stell," persisted Ryan tenderly.

"As if his death means nothing?" Slowly raising her glance from the palms of her hands, Estelle looked tearfully at Ryan. "I just need to be alone. Please, Ryan, I need some space." The torment of guilt clearly written in her eyes, Estelle broke her gaze with Ryan. "Blood on my hands…Dad's death…Mabunda's blood…and Carol. No more, Ryan. No more." She stared at her hands.

"Please don't shut me out. Please don't throw us away," pleaded Ryan, observing Estelle's presence fade with the last of the light.

"Sorry, Ryan," whispered Estelle, turning to cast her gaze shamefully down into the pool.

"I want to see you again before I head back. Maybe we can do coffee somewhere quiet." The young man paused. "Maybe tomorrow, after you get yourself a good night's sleep." Ryan's voice echoed through the chill of early evening. "How's I pick you up tomorrow morning, say ten for breakfast?" he suggested gently.

Several long seconds passed, each stuck inside their own merciless cell. She broke the silence, her reluctance to reach out palpable. "OK, I guess coffee'd be good."

The two parted company, each vanishing into the night, taking with them their own private grief.

NEXT DAY SAW ESTELLE and Ryan wandering on to the pier at Rose Bay. 'Sydney Harbour Escapes', read the promo.

Yes, mused Estelle.

At that moment she felt like escaping on her own out onto the wide ocean. The little cafe on the edge of the pier offered breakfast and coffee. The sun was generous, but not overbearing, allowing both to sit in its warmth in quiet contemplation. Together they watched the tranquil rows of sailing boats and a few deckhands here and there preparing to sail.

"I know this coming year will be a better year for you, Stell. Trust me," coaxed Ryan.

"Maybe," replied Estelle, slowly shifting herself out of her self-induced trance. "Seems I've become enmeshed in our family's twenty-seven year curse."

"Twenty-seven year curse?" Ryan rested his chin between his index finger and thumb, his eyes intensely focused.

"Twenty-seven, according to Nan, comes to a nine, an end of a numerological cycle."

"I don't understand."

"Twenty-seven precedes Saturn return, a twenty-seven year cycle of growth, according to Nan. We've all been affected. Mum was diagnosed with breast cancer at twenty-seven: took her own life. Me: critically ill, Mabunda, and now I've had to bury my dad. The twenty-seven year family curse, it seems, has welcomed me with open arms."

"Your dad wasn't twenty-seven," challenged Ryan gently.

"No: sixty-three. Six and three: a nine." Her bitterness was palpable.

"God, this is so heavy," muttered Ryan.

"Apparently numerological nines belong to the world and can't be used for self-gain."

"It's been really challenging for you, Stell," acknowledged Ryan, continuing to try to peer through her jagged wall of defence.

"Right now, I feel so weather-beaten," admitted Estelle, an uncertain, far-away look in her eye.

"You're courageous, Stell. You may be weathered, but you're not beaten," comforted Ryan.

"Can't say I feel all that courageous right now." Estelle lowered her gaze to an orange juice that had just arrived.

"Breakfast? I'm hungry," announced Ryan, enthused by the aromas wafting from the cafe.

"Juice is fine for me. You go for it." Estelle smiled, amused at Ryan's irrepressible male appetite.

Ryan lightened up as Estelle's mood lifted somewhat. "I'm hoping this will help." Ryan handed Estelle an envelope. "Happy birthday, Stell."

"What's this?" Estelle frowned, puzzled.

"A birthday present," replied Ryan, carefully monitoring her reaction as she peered inside the envelope.

"Oh, God, just come and gone: too busy with funeral arrangements. I didn't get you anything," replied Estelle awkwardly, reaching inside mechanically. "An airline ticket?" She frowned.

"It's a twelve month open ticket to the States. I'd already bought it before your Nan rang," Ryan rushed to explain.

Estelle shook her head, having sat speechless for several moments. "I can't accept this."

"Sure you can," encouraged Ryan. "I thought a break, with a little time in the Catskills. Just what the doctor ordered: when you're ready."

"Ryan, this is so sweet of you, but I just need time. Time alone: time to get my head together."

"I'm OK with that, however long."

"However long what?" interjected Estelle, irritated. "I think it's best we cool it. No contact for a while. Please respect my wishes, Ryan. I mean it." She cut off his attempt at salvaging his faux-pas.

"This has also been a nine for me. I'll be damned if I'll lose you. Not after all this."

"I'm so, so sorry," apologised Estelle, suddenly aware of the soul-deep grief in Ryan's eyes.

"Sweetheart, I'll wait. I love you, Stell," pleaded Ryan gently. "However long, I'll wait."

Ryan left his breakfast half-eaten, their dismal reunion leaving both reluctant to connect prior to Ryan's return to the States.

With Christmas fast approaching, the stress of innumerable deadlines was all taking a toll on Estelle's physical and mental wellbeing. She dragged her body around lethargically, with poor concentration and a loss of appetite. Finally she conceded that Nan might well be right and that a trip to the doctor was in order.

Startled by Doctor Collette's diagnosis, Estelle sat in motionless silence staring blankly at a paper clip on Collette's desk. "Pregnant?" Stunned, a flicker of joy smothered out by cold reality, Estelle rubbed her temples, leaning forward into the open palms of her hands.

"Pregnant," confirmed Collette with a warm, open smile. The doctor scrutinised Estelle's face, studying her eyes, quietly waiting for Estelle's shock to pass. "Are you alright? Seems this has come as quite a surprise?"

A long pause allowed Estelle to catch her breath. "I'd just put it all down to stress, with Dad's passing and all," she replied, struggling to take in the revelation. "Still, I'm not altogether surprised. Just wasn't ready to hear it."

"Can I get you a glass of water?"

"I'm quite alright," replied Estelle with a distant look.

"Are you OK with this pregnancy, Estelle?"

"It's just a shock: need some time." Rising to leave, Estelle looked back over her shoulder, releasing a subdued smile as she left the room.

"I ALREADY KNOW." THE old lady gleamed with a knowing smile. Her look of heartfelt anticipation had been hard to disguise as the two women sat together over dinner. "You're going to be a wonderful mother." Tears of joy trickled down Nan's cheeks as she rose from the table with open arms to kiss and congratulate her granddaughter.

"How did you?"

She clicked her tongue against the roof of her mouth. "I'm your Nan, remember," admonished Esther. "I've waited patiently——"

"Waited for?"

"Waited for you to be ready to find out."

"Since when?" demanded Estelle.

"Since you arrived home with the little surprise for me." Esther chuckled. "And the dad? When are we going to tell him, hmm?" cajoled Esther, a glint in her eye.

The air stirred with agitation, briefly blanketing the entire room. "He doesn't need to know," snapped Estelle sharply.

"Oh, sweet pea, it'll all be OK. You and Ryan have a karmic destiny," soothed the old lady.

The sudden arrival of two of Nan's cats in a crash'n'tackle helped discharge the tension between grandmother and grand-daughter. "You must do what you think best then," conceded the old lady with a gentle smile as she reached for her grand-daughter's hand.

After supper, the two women ventured out for a leisurely walk. It was a perfect summer evening. A southerly breeze carried with it the sweet smell of jasmine, gardenias, and the delicate scent of rose. The clear night sky was sprinkled with millions of flickering stars. The full moon seemed to magnify Estelle's feelings of fecundity and vulnerability. Its vigilance lit the way for the two women as they strolled, arm in arm. Memories of earlier times lapped at Estelle's consciousness. She was drawn back to the echoes of a childhood filled with laughter, her long blond hair dancing in the breeze as she hopscotched across the neighbourhood paths in the back streets of Paddington. Nan had many stories to tell to the young Estelle, a mesmerised true believer in life's magic and enchantment.

Now here she was. Whatever happened to all the magic? Where had all the enchantment gone? Estelle's mind was drawn back to a vivid image. It was that of a colourful self-portrait she had illustrated in her diary that she'd held under lock and key. With a wistful smile, she revisited the words in the rhyme she had carefully penned beneath the illustration on the first night of her periods. She had begun to shed a part of herself earlier that day. Now she was finally ready to present herself to the world as a young woman.

> She sits and waits for life to come, so delicate and young.
> She regrets the past, and worries for the future.
> What will it be? What will I become?
>
> Then she takes it by surprise.
> She's all grown up.
> And then she realises, her outlook has changed.
> And it was hope that was on her side.

"The magic of a dark night is always its illumination," suggested Nan, as if she had just read Estelle's thoughts. "Some call it the dark night of the soul."

"Are you suggesting I'm depressed?"

"Perhaps: you've been through a lot. You're grieving." The older lady was pensive. "There's sacredness in grief—and depression."

Estelle slowed her pace. "I'd considered taking antidepressants before finding out."

"The little life growing inside?"

"Collette cautioned against them. It's bloody unfair."

Esther took Estelle tightly under her wing. "Sweet pea, you'll feel better the minute you let go of the illusion that life owes you happiness: but you can choose to be happy."

"Sometimes I just feel like giving up."

"Ah, there's a difference between giving up and surrendering. Surrendering is all about giving up control, but not your responsibilities."

"Then what is life all about?" demanded Estelle.

"Our evolution, my dear, just our evolution," replied the old crone. "We're here to love and be loved—and belong. And that starts with forgiveness—and all forgiveness starts with self-forgiveness, sweet pea." The old lady paused. "All the self-punishment in the world will not bring back your father."

"But—"

"Listen to me." Esther faced her granddaughter as the two women stopped strolling. "Your father's death does not require atonement by you or by anyone. You don't need to forego your heart's desire." Esther waited for signs that Estelle had taken her message in. "And this little life deserves a daddy." Looking deep into Estelle's eyes, Esther gently patted her grand-daughter's tummy.

Hooking her grand-daughter's arm through hers, the two women resumed their stroll. "We do not walk this earth alone: angelic forces walk beside us. All we ever need to do is ask for their guidance."

"When I was in hospital—"

"Yes. She was real," cut in Nan. "I called her in for you."

"You never said."

"You never asked." Nan chuckled.

"Guess I wasn't ready to know."

"She was alive: just missing a body. Our spirit doesn't need a body: life just goes on because life is what we are. We can be just as active without a body: in fact, more so."

"I had a series of dreams and déjà vu-like premonitions."

"You astral travelled through time and space, sweet pea, lots of sign posts along the way."

RYAN AND PETE SLOWED cautiously, pulling up behind the flashing lights of a police vehicle signalling them to stop. Watchful for speeding highway traffic, Ryan leaped out of the cabin and walked over to the patrol officers as Pete lowered the hydraulic loading platform.

"He's taken quite a nasty fall." The female officer's concern was obvious, her male partner directing the late morning traffic.

Spurred on by fear, and in spite of his broken leg, the young calf managed to move several feet further away from the approaching humans, fortuitously further away from traffic hazards.

"Yeah. Looks like his hind legs have taken quite an impact." Ryan observed the stricken calf.

"The transport owners are on their way back with a gun." Officer Tobias was almost apologetic.

"That won't be necessary," replied Pete as he and Ryan moved into action.

Ryan crouched to examine the baby's injuries, his snout and hind quarter a bloodied mess, the deep grazes and lacerations further evidence of the force of impact of the calf hitting the road at high speed. The terrified calf looked up helplessly into Ryan's eyes as if pleading for mercy. His traumatic truck ride had torn him apart from his grieving mother, the only protection he would have known.

Ryan jabbed the calf with a syringe of pain relief. With Pete's assistance, they gently lifted the shocked animal into the back of the van. Having tended to the bleeding, Ryan connected an IV line to the bag of intravenous fluid.

"Damn!" he muttered as his fumbled mobile clunked to the floor and broke in pieces, pinned beneath the animal.

Covering the calf with a blanket, Ryan crouched to comfort him. "Not quite your mum's milk, hey, mate," apologised Ryan, stroking the quivering animal's head. The infant began sucking Ryan's hand as the van drove cautiously off.

Though Ryan had done this many times before, his soul somehow still stirred. The calf's distress had compounded his own personal grief, blurred by the collective guilt that the young vet felt for the callousness of his own species. The young calf's only crime was to be born, and more so a male. Without an udder he was little more than waste product to the dairy industry. On his way to slaughter, tightly packed in amongst countless, nameless others, all crying for their mothers, he had fallen from the livestock truck. As any baby, this non-human person needed his mother, just his mother, and the nurturing and nutrition she alone could provide. Now he was hooked to this IV, a far cry from his mother's milk. Meanwhile the milk nature had provided for him would be stolen by humans.

As for his mother, like millions of other mourning dairy cows enslaved to the dairy industry, she would spend her days and nights crying forlornly for her stolen babies, one stolen newborn after another. Trapped in a perpetual cycle of trauma and abuse, she would forcibly undergo repeated artificial impregnation on a rape rack, give birth, then with just enough time to clean and bond with her calf, mother and infant would be torn apart, her milk extracted by machines with ruthless efficiency. In her final, crippling exhaustion, she would be slaughtered for another consumer market. If pregnant at the time, her live unborn baby would be cut from her womb, its blood drained without anaesthesia and skin stripped and turned into soft leather. As for the supermarket consumer, for the most part they would remain blissfully unaware of the dark secret of this lucrative industry and the trauma their morning cuppa would have delivered. And if they did know, would they truly care?

Finally at Saint Francis, it was again time to recruit human strength to lower the weary calf from the van and carry him into the barn. Greeted at the paddock, Mel swung into action, helping the two young lads with their latest delivery.

"What's happened to your phone, son?" asked Mel as he examined the pieces.

"Ah! Butter-fingers."

The old man eyeballed Ryan. "Too bad." Putting his index finger over his lips, he signalled Ryan not to speak further.

ONLY WEEKS AND THE festive season rolled in. Nan had insisted Estelle accompany her to Carols in the Domain. "You and your father were both too busy with office parties last year. It's my turn this year!"

A Sydney tradition the weekend before Christmas, Carols in the Domain was abuzz with the joyous sounds of 'Hark the Herald Angels Sing' and 'Away in a Manger' mixed irreverently with 'Jingle Bells Rock'. The Domain is an area bracketed by the New South Wales Art Gallery and the old Sydney Hospital. Here, family and friends, backpackers and the homeless, a cauldron of cultures and denominations of young and old from every walk of life, united in the season's good will.

Mums and dads with their littlies pushed prams and wheeled strollers as they weaved their way amongst the festive crowd. Grandmas and grandpas shuffled up the rear. They were constantly vigilant with the slightly older siblings who darted here and there, hopscotching around picnic blankets that marked out a family's territorial rights. As for the teens, they charged on ahead of the pack, targeting their way towards the front of the stage. They carried glow-sticks and other souvenirs, and identified themselves by the latest fads and fashion trends. Claiming the night as their own, they showed little concern for the rest with their skylarking.

Then there were the lovers to whom the night truly belonged. Hand in hand, laughing and smiling, they strolled in the open, delighting in their togetherness. They had little concern for where they might ultimately end up sitting, nor for how the night might unfold.

The night was brilliant with a twinkling heaven reflected in the starry eyes of thousands of little shiny-faced souls. They were mesmerised by the stage and the nativity set. There lay baby Jesus wrapped in the manger in the loving presence of Mary and Joseph. In unison, children sat miming and swaying to the melodies and the words of their favourite carols.

As the evening progressed, Santa was evicted from a noisy helicopter to the squealing delight of excited children. Lowered from the sky, showering the little ones with cheap trinkets and lollies, the white-bearded visitor sweated under his polar attire. Parents were cheered by the innocent delight of children, even as the teens guffawed from the sidelines.

The festive night of food and fun drew to a close. Singing along with the final carol, 'Silent Night', many littlies slumbered, their tiny faces shining in the moonlight.

Estelle looked across a sea of flickering candles, the collective luminosity lighting the faces of the enormous crowd. She turned her gaze upon a young family on a nearby blanket and watched as a young dad, fast to the rescue, relit the tiny wick of his dismayed toddler whose candle had just blown out. Having relit the flame, he gazed lovingly upon his beautiful young wife who had been nurturing their newborn, snuggled into the warmth of her breast. Protectively, he put one arm around his wife, and with the other, shepherded in the restive toddler.

"A joyful Christmas is how the church redeems itself in my eyes." Esther was leading Estelle towards the exit gates.

"Depends. Last Christmas service was almost a requiem: church oppressive and condemning."

"That's because of its misinterpretation of sin, sweet pea."

"And your interpretation?"

"The splintered self, my dear: the parts of ourselves that we are taught to shamefully deny, then project onto one another." Taking Estelle's hand, Esther sharply cut a way across the crowds as she continued. "Then we reincarnate time and again until we finally heal. Hurt people hurting people."

"Make love, not war. Nan has spoken." teased Estelle.

"If we could accept all parts of ourselves with compassion, and others with equal compassion, there would be peace on earth," replied Nan with restrained passion.

RYAN SAT WITH MEL for a pre-Christmas tipple, the fading light rapidly slipping away as they looked out over the porch.

"Thanks Ryan, you've worked wonders with Snoopy."

"Thanks to you and Saint Francis; we couldn't do it without your benevolence," replied Ryan reflectively. "You were right, Mel. How did you know?"

"I'm no expert on cell phones, but I know that phone. That small black device did not belong inside it. Besides, after you and your young lady left, I had an odd couple snooping around."

"Sorry, Mel."

"No apology necessary, son," reassured the old man. "I played dumb. You were in desperate need of the van for a good reason."

"The only time my phone was out of my sight was when it was taken going through Customs on the way out to see Estelle." Ryan paused to sip on his whiskey.

The old man observed the younger man, who'd withdrawn into his silence. "You're staying away as much for her protection?" Mel reached across to pat his young mate on the shoulder.

Ryan swallowed his whiskey and looked down into his empty glass.

CHRISTMAS MORNING HAD FINALLY arrived. A gentle light filtered through the blinds. Estelle had relinquished the outhouse in favour of the downstairs bedroom, opting for the security of the main house. Yawning, she tumbled out of bed and sluggishly headed for the bathroom.

"Mellow!" she grumbled, having almost trod on a red bauble.

The Christmas tree, courtesy of Nan, had been sabotaged by the feline. The multi-coloured tree decorations had provided the mischievous minx with hours of entertainment. Scaling the furniture with dainty dexterity, she manoeuvred to knock each bauble to the wooden floor. As they bounced, she would sit in a hypnotic trance, watching as they rolled noisily along the shiny surface. As the baubles ceased to roll, she would crouch on the ground for closer inspection. Skilfully stalking each one, she'd gently bat them back into motion while remaining vigilant for further signs of life. Without warning, Mellow would then catapult herself into a mid-air somersault, landing with a calamitous thump, taking her hunt by surprise and causing some to roll away out of reach. Game on. Charging about in a frenzied rampage, Mellow would vigorously scurry in pursuit of her victims, room to room, corner to corner, up and down the hallway, under furniture, in and out of dark and narrow places. They had nowhere to hide. She had each within her sights as she continued, without mercy, pursuing, striking, pouncing and tackling. Many hours later, as her lifeless prey lay inert with exhaustion, Mellow watched with immense satisfaction, her mission completed. She'd grace Estelle with her prized gift, leaving it by her bedside, then elegantly saunter back down the hallway and up the stairwell to Sam's pillow, where she would curl up to await his return, as she'd done since his passing.

TREE-FILTERED SUNLIGHT BATHED THE upper deck of Nan's semi, providing a private glade where the old lady loved to read surrounded by her shrubs, vines and flowers. On this, the first Christmas without Sam, it seemed the perfect peaceful setting for lunch. As carols harmonised pleasantly in the background, Esther and Estelle scuttled about preparing lunch as they awaited Nan's special guest.

Called to the door for a Christmas delivery, Nan excused herself to answer. Peering inquisitively into a darkened box, she whispered reassuringly to a shocked month-old bat orphaned by a recent heat wave. After attending to the infant's immediate needs, she quietly placed the critter in the spare bedroom.

Estelle stopped to smile at the neighbourhood children as they played next door. "Seems bikes were high up on Santa's list again this year."

"Hey, kids," called Esther in delight, tossing a handful of lollies in their direction. Estelle watched as the excited children tore towards the flying candy, amongst them a couple of Afro-Aussies, a girl of about ten and a younger boy of about six with clipped English accents.

"Thank you, cat lady." They enthusiastically waved with open arms and wide, smiley faces.

"Cat lady?" Estelle raised her eyebrows.

"Well, if somebody needs to be the cat lady of Spicer Lane, it may as well be me." Esther beamed.

"Good neighbours?"

"Terrific. Just moved in. Dad's some sort of tech expert at IBM and Mum's a teacher. Kenyan, I think."

"Mabunda's family has been left fatherless this Christmas," muttered Estelle. "I often wonder..."

Esther gazed compassionately at her granddaughter. "Mabunda would have recognised your mother in you, the minute he laid eyes on you." A silent pause fell between the women. "Your mother would have seen an integrity in him that your father was slow to recognise."

"How so?"

"His determination to raise the alarm—"

"And taken out for it."

"Yep. One mother of a stuff-up." Esther shook her head. "I have a strong feeling he was never meant to leave his own country, and that somehow things just went terribly wrong."

Estelle furrowed her brow, scrutinising Nan's face. "So much loss for all of us."

"Your dad's at rest now. His heart no longer aches for your mother: together at last this Christmas." Esther's assurance was interrupted by the doorbell.

Estelle turned to the sound of a familiar raspy voice.

"Merry Christmas all."

"Jim?" Estelle swallowed, her shock at his deterioration hard to disguise.

"Great article," he wheezed. "For the table." He offered Esther a colourful arrangement of flowers with one hand while leaning the rest of his skeletal frame on his walking stick.

Nan quickly moved to assist him to get comfortable in his seat.

"I've thought of you, wondered how you've been," Estelle opened.

"My bum's still above ground, if that's what you mean." He laughed with a wheeze. "Mainly thanks to your wonderful Nan."

"Oh, Jim," Esther glowed, "you and Julian will never know how much you've both given me."

"Family; you've been our only family," replied Jim, his blue eyes still very much alive with warmth.

"Nan really is amazing," agreed Estelle, beaming with pride.

Estelle couldn't help but note Jim's loose-fitting clothing that slid around his frame as he moved to keep comfortable, picking throughout the meal.

"Julian always loved your Nan."

"A man of immense compassion and sincerity in a world that had done him such wrong," added Esther.

"Loyalty like your Nan's is as rare as hen's teeth." Gasping for breath, Jim began to cough. Estelle quickly moved to pour him a glass of water. "To loved ones absent." Jim raised his trembling hand to toast.

"Have I taught you nothing?" rebuffed Esther. "Never absent, always in our midst. Right, JC?" She leaned to take Jim's hand, his cold, spindly fingers disturbingly translucent.

Estelle flashed back to the cream-coloured farewell card with gold lettering retrieved from Nan's tatty shoe box. She shifted uncomfortably, her face whitened. "Of course."

Nan looked at her grand-daughter. "You look like you've just seen a ghost, sweet pea?"

"To Mum and Dad," she toasted, her goblet raised.

"To Judith, Sam and Julian." Esther drew a quiet breath. "Incoming message from Sam: love never dies. From Mum: a love eternal. Message from JC: laugh and the world laughs with you." She softly cackled.

A moment lapsed and the three chinked glasses.

ALONE WITH NAN, ESTELLE finished drying the last of the dishes. Esther sneaked into the spare room to retrieve the orphan. "Come on, little one: time for your dinner."

Reclining, with lounge cushions to support her back, Estelle watched as Nan firmly, but gently, angled the juvenile upside-down, ready to feed.

"So tiny." Estelle observed the helplessness of the critter as it endeavoured to attach to its bottle.

"She really needs her mum." Esther stroked the baby's jaw with firm tenderness as it latched on to its bottle. "Still, in life we must make the most of the hand we're dealt."

"I guess survival is more about adapting than anything else." Estelle wriggled to get comfortable.

"This little girl will soon adapt and will come to recognise me as Mum, won't you, darling?" Esther paused to remove the bottle from the juvenile's mouth, allowing more air into the teat. "She'll grow strong, ready for release back into the wild, where she'll come to recognise a friendship group of about hundred or so other bats. Amazing facial recognition."

Smiling softly, Estelle gazed upon the little bat's delicate face, milk dribbling from the side of her mouth as she guzzled away greedily.

"She'll always remember me, won't you, sweetheart? Gave me so much joy when, by chance encounter, Eli and Sunray flew from their trees to me for cuddles. What shall we call you, missy?"

"Bella," piped up Estelle.

"Bella." Nan's eyes shone with tenderness. "In the wild, mum and bub spend much of their time gazing into each other's eyes. Mother bats constantly stroke their baby as they feed." Esther continued stroking the tiny bat with her spare thumb as it continued to suck.

"The maternal instinct is about the strongest instinct on the planet." Estelle unconsciously rubbed her belly.

"A couple of years ago a little mother dropped off her infant at my home before flying off to find food."

"She obviously knew she was leaving her baby in safe hands."

"Sadly, mother bats often get shot while foraging food for their infants." Esther's flicker of sadness filled the air. "Man destroys their habitat, so they are forced to venture for food onto farmers' properties. All too often they meet their fate at the wrong end of a shotgun. I wonder what would happen if wildlife had guns?" snarled Esther. "About the most abused wild animal in Australia…" Esther's voice trailed off.

"Somehow I'm sure your babies are protected after release," reassured Estelle.

"Babies often throw tantrums when Mum leaves to find food," added Esther. "Left orphaned, their fate is slow starvation high up in the trees. Gut-wrenching to hear their cries, waiting for mums who never return."

"A lot of people are scared of being infected by them," deflected Estelle.

"Environmental vandalism fuelled by misinformation, hysteria and Hollywood horror movies. That's all the ridiculous provocation man seems to need to turn a gun on them. More people die from road accidents in one day than by bats in a century—only three suspected deaths ever recorded—yet we don't gun down motorists. We've no right to destroy a keystone species, do we, sweetheart." Esther cast her gaze back to the juvenile. Exhausted from guzzling, the sleepy juvenile ceased suckling. "Three thousand perished from one colony alone during last week's high temperatures."

"I've seen people turn on deafening gardening equipment during heat waves so as to exhaust them out of their trees, then watch with satisfaction as they fly around in terror, disorientated," added Estelle.

"May the good Lord help the ignorant and the arrogant," scolded Nan as she positioned the critter to be burped.

Farmers aside, bushfire season was always the worst, Estelle thought, with so many arsonists deliberately setting hectares of bushland alight so that they could sit in admiration of their handiwork, callously indifferent to the tens of thousands of creatures screaming as they burnt to death. There were never enough skilled volunteers to help, so Nan gave of herself tirelessly. Estelle reflected upon a young female possum that had been dropped off by a fire fighter one year. Her feet badly burnt, the young mother had carried her terrified baby to safety as it clung tightly to her back. Her own injuries were so horrific she later died an agonising death in Nan's living room. Still, she had managed to save her tiny offspring.

Nan never moaned or complained. If she'd ever shed a tear, she would have done so privately. Estelle had never really seen Nan cry. She just got on with the task at hand, year in, year out. Now here she is, Christmas Day, another year and another tiny critter needing Nan's maternal care.

Having burped the infant, Esther made her way to the next room where she hung her sleepy baby by her feet, upside-down on the clothes hanger.

ARRIVING HOME, ESTELLE ENTERED the downstairs foyer. The house stood empty: silence.

"Dad?" she was tempted to cry out.

Several long seconds passed. Estelle clutched her chest, pressing both hands tightly to her heart. An unbearable pain pierced her soul till she could no longer breathe, a merciless wave of grief, then another and another, each pounding at the last of her protective wall of numbness that had served to hold her upright.

Slowly she summoned the strength to climb the staircase. Several agonising seconds passed as she looked around her father's room. It had been untouched from the time he'd last left the house on that fateful day. By his bed, a shrine to his beloved; amongst the shrine, several photos, one especially, had always held centre stage. It was her mum and dad's favourite wedding photo, her mother in delicate white lace, an assorted spray of colour in her posy, beside her an adoring groom in tails and bow tie, both beaming into the camera. The young couple were undeniably in love.

Adorning the shrine were several seashells Judith had sneaked back from their honeymoon in the Whitsunday Isles. Newly picked, prior to his death, was a small vase of wilted gardenias, her mother's favourite.

Estelle stepped forward, her focus riveted on a happy snap of the three of them building sandcastles at Bondi Beach. It had been taken the year prior to her mother's death. Clasping the photo in her hands, she lightly caressed the picture with her fingertips, yearning to remember, reclaim and relive what might have been amongst the happiest times of her life.

Estelle slipped into bed. A deluge burst its banks, soaking her pillow. A little angel sprinted lightly onto the bed, claiming her space on Estelle's chest, where she licked away the salty tears.

RYAN'S SWEAT-SOAKED SHIRT STUCK to his back as they voyaged deeper into the river's archaic origin. A rare puff of breeze provided precious little respite from entombing humidity, the expansive waterway wide, thick and brown. Twenty minutes further on, the little ferry pulled into a small brown tributary. Inching their way forward, ducking overhanging branches and detouring around partially submerged logs, they finally arrived at their humid destination.

Disembarking, Ryan followed his guides as they carefully probed into the soft green womb of an earlier time, preserved now only in photographic images. Joseph's long, brown, sinewy legs brushed through the swirling undergrowth, Francine bringing up the rear. Ryan swept aside the soft green fronds as he followed rheumy-eyed Joseph deeper into the dense green forest. Sweat trickled down his face, stinging the corners of his eyes. He squinted, ploughing further and further inward. Their idle chatter had ceased for a while, the forest buzzing with the constant static of insects.

Suddenly Joseph stopped, crouching to finger old debris. "Nous sommes arrives."

"What? This is it?" Ryan viewed the dense undergrowth with dismay. A few rusted metal frames were all that remained of the camp. Overgrown and devoured so long ago, the smell of decay hung thick in the claustrophobic jungle. "So this is where the chimps arrived for processing sixty years ago?"

"Oui...leur destination finale."

"This was the end of the journey for the chimps," translated Francine, her petite prettiness marred by a faded, but disfiguring scar over her right eyebrow.

"Their last resting place?"

Francine and Joseph dialogued briefly.

"Yes. The kidneys were harvested here and transported back to Stanleyville."

"How were they transported?"

"In the cold boxes, the boxes for organ transport," explained Francine.

"And the chimpanzee were alive when their organs were removed?"

"Yes, but given some sedation. They needed live, fresh organs," Francine explained carefully.

"Why weren't the organs harvested back at the lab in Stanleyville?" asked Ryan.

"C'etait leur secret....peut etre.....on sait pas......on était jeunes," muttered the old man. "C'etaitcomme ca." He shrugged despondently.

"It was their secret. Maybe: don't know. They were just young lab assistants. That's how it was then," explained Francine.

"Merci, Joseph." Ryan surveyed the archaeological traces of what was Camp Lindi. His body slumped almost imperceptibly. "Oui. C'est la vie."

"On y va?" asked the old man timidly.

"Shall we go?" translated Francine.

"Oui. Thank you, Joseph." Ryan shrugged.

The three retraced their steps back through the dense rainforest to the river. They boarded the little rocking ferry. Their captain ignited the putt-putt engine that immediately spurted back into life.

Gently the little ferry negotiated the tributary as it merged out of nowhere back into the mighty river. Ryan gazed out over the swollen river's brown majesty. "Slaves, ivory, chimps and vaccines," muttered Ryan. "The river has its secrets alright."

"Pardon?" asked Francine, wanting to translate.

"This is a great and ancient river," replied Ryan. "Many secrets."

"Oui. Un grand fleuve," agreed Francine.

"Votre premiere rencontre avec le Congo?" Joseph took Ryan's hand affectionately in his.

"Déjà vu: must be in my blood," Ryan answered pensively, and smiling, gently let go of the old man's grasp.

"Le cœur reste en Afrique, mon fils." The greying, but otherwise boyish old African smiled.

"Our hearts remain in Africa," explained Francine.

Ryan nodded in agreement.

In no time at all the ferry landed about ten kilometres out of what is now known as Kisangani. In the distance, up a sodden clay path, stood the dilapidated ghost of the laboratory.

Strolling along at a leisurely pace, Ryan took in the vacant white elephant slap-bang in the middle of Africa. Its former colonial grandeur stood in sharp contrast to the surrounding suburban shantytown huts.

Approaching the entrance, a derelict sign, 'Entree Interdite!' hung on its side. Front doors appeared bolted, but windows everywhere were smashed: a haven for squatters perhaps, but with no electricity.

"Suivez-moi, camarade." Joseph barged his way towards the locked doors, levering them open with a screwdriver, and made his way in.

"You've done this before," noted Ryan, frowning momentarily as he hesitated.

The smell of the place was mouldy—not a hint of disinfectant—disused decades before. The decrepit, whitewashed walls were now patchy grey, with a film of indigenous fungus.

Joseph pushed aside a door, slightly ajar, stretching and breaking cobwebs. Light brown dust clung to myriad laboratory vessels—flasks, test tubes and glass tubing—finger marks everywhere in the dust-coated lab. Fans froze overhead. Disused and disabled fridges lined the spacious lab.

"Visitors—recently?" Ryan asked, looking to Joseph.

"Ah, oui?" replied Joseph. "Wabenzi, la semaine derniere."

"Wabenzi?" queried Ryan, frowning.

"Researchers, like yourself—American, French, Belge. Melange de langues," explained Francine with a shrug. "Tourist, like yourself." She watched Ryan cautiously. "Oui. They wanted to see for the old times."

"Old time's sake. Hmm," mused Ryan aloud.

Joseph led Ryan down a dimly lit corridor to the archives. The musty smell of age filled the room. "Mon Dieu!" Joseph gasped. "Vandales!"

Files littered the room, scattered on the floor and benches. Ryan gently fingered through the decaying folders, checking the bindings on which were written the year and month of their records. He bent to pick up some folios strewn on the floor.

"Halte la!" shouted an authoritarian voice from behind.

Ryan held up his hands instinctively. "Pardon. Je suis American scientist."

The African soldier grunted in contempt. "Passport! Passport!" screamed the African, pointing an AK 47 at Ryan and Joseph, then Francine.

"Pardon, pardon. C'est ma faute—ah!" The old man's cry was cut short. The soldier savagely butted Joseph in the solar plexus and slammed the butt of his rifle over the old man's head. Ryan jumped to intervene, the black stepping back, smiling as he pointed the AK 47 at Francine's head. "Wallet!"

Ryan pulled back instinctively, sensing the callous indifference of his heavily armed opponent. "OK. OK." Holding his left arm high in surrender, Ryan slowly reached for a money belt hanging around his neck. He carefully removed a slender plastic wallet, placing it on the dusty archival bench.

"Bien. Bien." The black lips smiled, eyes dead. Stepping back into the light, the soldier, dressed in faded and decayed battle fatigues, flipped open the wallet, withdrew five US$100 bills and viewed the greenbacks with contempt.

"Non. Non. Euros, Euros!" screamed the soldier, pointing the AK again at Francine as she crumpled to the floor, all but paralysed by fear, holding her hands protectively in front of her face and head.

"OK. OK. OK." Ryan shrugged, loosening his belt, standing astride, his waistband slipping to sit just over his hip. Pulling up a hidden money belt, Ryan unzipped the sweaty wallet with fumbling fingers. "Shit!"

"Oui, Oui. Euros! Euros!" demanded the soldier aggressively.

Ryan handed across a wad of euros. The African grabbed the bundle and flicked through, smiling with satisfaction and pocketing the money.

"Reculez." The black motioned Ryan back further into the dusty archives.

Ryan hesitated.

Francine cowered in fear, whimpering, "Do what he says."

"Damn!" muttered Ryan, turning to observe a fleeting look of relief pass over Francine's face before the darkness.

AN EXPLOSION OF COLOUR lit Sydney Harbour, the bursting, luminous display falling towards the reflective waters below. As the clock struck midnight, Estelle's mind drifted across the shores. 'Auld Lang Syne' played as the party crowd sang along, mostly out of tune. Embracing lovers passionately kissed in the New Year and a cacophony of mobile sounds all set off at the same time, congesting networks and breaking the sound barrier of Estelle's fragile mind.

Melancholy swept through Estelle, flooding her mind with images of Ryan so real she could almost feel him breathe, so real she could almost touch him, so real she could almost talk to him. Passion, relentless as wildfire, swept through her heart, scorching her with memories that devoured her with bittersweet desire. Just one more night; the sovereign masters of loving and longing had again made their return. She could see before her the swagger of his walk, hear the timbre of his voice, imagine his dark, penetrating eyes as they pierced her soul; the way they laughed together, the way they danced together, the way they loved; the way they'd come together as one. The way they'd created life together.

Estelle dared to glance at her mobile, her right hand gently resting on her belly. All of Ryan's texts erased, yet she could not erase him from her heart. Amongst the crowd she felt more alone than ever. A quiet tear sneaked out with a silent prayer. As she turned to merge with the leaving crowd of rowdy partygoers, she left behind the most turbulent year of her adult life.

Hours later she awoke sobbing into her pillow. Her head pounded with discordant emotions, as if ghostly baritone sounds of a discarded old piano.

A CACOPHONY OF GUNFIRE erupted as scattered fireworks lit up the city, a shabby parody of its former colonial prominence. Alcohol and gunfire farewelled 2003, welcoming in a New Year still full of promise for a lasting ceasefire to a civil war.

Ryan tossed and turned on the narrow bed, the pillowcase soaked with blood and sweat. "Oh, non. S'ilvous plait, mon Dieu," he cried. "Je te le promets. Je te le jure devant Dieu. Je mettrai fin a ce carnage," he whispered with grim determination into the ear of his younger companion, her teary face, framed by golden ringlets, buried deep in his chest.

The old grey priest mopped the young man's brow. "C'est bon. Tu es en securite. Repose -toi."

"Estelle? Estelle?"

The old priest gently stroked his shoulder. "C'est bon. C'est bon. Ce n'est qu'un cauchemar."

"No. Not a nightmare. Like a memory," replied the young man emphatically.

"Quel est ton nom, mon fils?" the old man asked, almost in a whisper, watching the young man intently.

"Ryan." He opened his eyes, grimacing as he felt the back of his head, squinting at the priest in the candlelight. "Ryan Knight," he replied.

"Vousetes en securite. Vous avez fait un cauchemar. Voulez vous de l'eau?" The priest offered Ryan a glass of water.

Ryan drank greedily, the overflow escaping his parched mouth, dribbling onto his chest. The priest topped up the glass, waiting patiently as Ryan soothed himself, rolling the rim of the cool glass against his temple. "Thank you. Merci," replied the young man, resting back into the pillow as he looked into the sad, drawn face before him.

The kindly old African priest waited expectantly.

"Who are you? Where am I?" spluttered Ryan warily, holding his forehead.

"Je suis lepere Jean- Marie. C'est la Cathedrale Kisangani. Vous etes en securite ici."The old priest handed Ryan two scored white tablets. "Pour vosmaux de tete."

Ryan frowned, then nodded . "Merci beaucoup." What time?" Ryan felt for his wristwatch. Gone.

"Ah, c'est le nouvel an." The priest smiled, shrugging as if in resignation. "Qui est Estelle, mon fils? Estelle en danger?"

"A friend." Ryan gestured in confusion.

"Tu as parle d'une promesse sacree. Quelle est cette promesse?"

"Non comprendez." Ryan looked to the old priest, confused. "I don't speak French."

"Mais mon fils, vous parliez couramment francais dans votre reve."

"Pardon?" Ryan frowned in confusion.

The old priest looked at Ryan, perplexed, then shrugged. "Parlez vous français, mon fils?"

"A little. Un petit peu," Ryan stumbled, hesitantly.

"OK. Rest now."

RYAN AWOKE TO A rich aroma as the priest knocked, bringing an old tray with coffee and a somewhat stale croissant.

"Merci, padre." Ryan drank the coffee. He sat up, holding his head through a bandana of bandages that felt renewed.

The old priest nodded. "Ca va?"

"Oui. Thank you." Ryan studied the old priest's face, lean and lined: a lot of suffering in the Congo. "I'm looking to understand why a man was killed." Ryan studied the priest's face for signs of understanding.

"Pardon." The priest's face was blank.

Ryan reached into his top pocket, handing a slightly creased Sowetan photo of Solomon Mabunda across to the priest. "L'homme killed. Homicide. Morte."

Holding the photo with reverence, his old hands trembled. "Mon dieu." The priest shook his head. "Solomon!"

"Solomon! You know him?" Ryan almost screamed, leaning in with excitement.

"Attendez, s'ilvous plait." The priest excused himself, returning with an old album. He sat with Ryan, slowly flicking over the yellow pages of the flimsy album as if turning the pages of a bible. He removed a group photo. The old priest pointed to the photo. "Joseph, Jean-Marie, Solomon." Ryan froze, his attention riveted on the old photo. It was Solomon Herbert Enoch Mabunda, late twenties perhaps, the determined look in his eyes unmistakable.

"You knew him." He grasped the photo, trembling.

"Solomon? Oui. Un homme bon. Tres bon. How you say? Good man."

"Do you know, Father, of the AIDS sickness caused by the polio vaccine here over fifty year ago?" Ryan searched the old priest's long-suffering face.

"Oui, mon fils. I know." The old priest nodded, hand over his heart. "Ici, tout le monde sait. Here everyone knows. La verite doit sortir. The truth it must come out." He struggled to explain.

Ryan nodded in silent assent, holding the old photo. Turning it over, he scrutinised the almost calligraphic handwriting on the back. 'Camp Lindi, 1959. Regards, Solomon.'

Estelle awoke to a distant call.

"Estelle! Estelle!"

"Ryan? Dad? Ryan?"

Her morning sickness had abated. Estelle stretched, in wondrous awe of the rapidly growing new life as she felt her baby's first movements. Closing her eyes, her thoughts vacillated, debating her options like an incessant metro-meter ticking from side to side: to contact or not to contact? What was he up to? Was he happy? Did he still think of her, long for her? Love her? Perhaps she had become little more than a pleasant memory that might occasion some cold and lonely night—or an unguarded moment—or not. Perhaps he no longer felt that special connection to her. Perhaps he had banished her from his mind, or worse, from his heart. Perhaps he was angry at her: furious. Could Ryan have moved on? A mild wave of anxiety rippled through her being. Her breathing became shallow and intense. Perhaps he had met someone else. Sadness gripped her heart with ferocious intensity. Overwhelming thoughts, charged with anxiety, took over with increased speed, swinging wildly from side to side as if time was running out. Was it already too late?

Estelle lay quietly, deliberately slowing her breath, feeling her baby's life force moving inside. Massaging her tummy, she soothed her unborn child with a tender caress.

FOUR WEEKS INTO THE New Year saw in Australia Day, a day of national pride. Australia, the lucky country, built on the backs of convicts and defended by the heroic courage of those who fought to protect their great land. Australia grew strong, its strength an attraction to migrant folks from all around the globe who, over decades, had headed down-under in search of a better life.

For many Aussies it was a day to party, for others, a day of rest following the first four weeks of return to work. Whatever the case, on Australia Day the frantic pace of Christmas, with all of its round the clock shopping, gave way to frolicking amongst the waves of its most famous beaches. Hot family roasts gave way to relaxed backyard barbies. Church attendances gave way to pub attendances and holy carols to 'Advance Australia Fair', the oft-forgotten anthem her people mumbled through.

Patriotic Australia had expanded its melting pot of ethnicity for those migrants choosing citizenship by pledging before the Australian flag to uphold the Australian way of life and its democratic values. This day was also designated a time to publicly acknowledge the worthy few whose endeavours had made enormous contributions to the lucky country and the welfare of its inhabitants, from sportsmen and women to scientists, from artists to those in the armed forces, from the aspiring to the inspired, and from the ordinary man to the extraordinary women.

Nan had arrived pronto, baby bat hung upside down from a towel fashioned as a poncho, the infant sleeping soundly. The two worked their way through the last of Sam's paperwork and other office items that had earlier been delivered to Estelle's door: business, legal, sentimental, and toss-outs.

Their heads-down task of sifting, sorting and separating had been abruptly interrupted as, in unison, they stared at the television screen.

"Arsehole!" exclaimed Estelle.

"Serious or bloody well delirious?" Nan's jaw hung open. "Doctor Wolfgang Schaffell? The Order of Australia?"

"For his invaluable contribution to AIDS research?" cringed Estelle. "If I wasn't pregnant, I'd still want to vomit."

"Why don't we turn this thing off, sweet pea?"

"The show must go on, it seems." Estelle grimaced.

"The system, sweet pea, is set up to protect and preserve itself: its only loyalty—itself. We are all brought into the system and bought by the system. Everyone has their price. Those who dare defect pay the ultimate price."

"The system's fucked," snapped Estelle.

"Such is life. Don't know about you, but my knees are about to give way. I could do with a break. Besides, feed time for baby Bella. Let's put on the kettle, shall we?"

The two women sat with tea and scones, Estelle's quiet brooding drowned out by the bat as it suckled away noisily.

"I've been told this place shouldn't take long to sell," broke in Estelle, skimming through a real estate booklet left by a calling agent.

"All up to you: the sole beneficiary of your home," replied Nan softly as she stroked the delicate critter's tiny face. "As for me, the hide of your father: leaving me his pharmaceutical stocks." She hooted.

Estelle laughed, shaking her head. "Even from beyond the grave."

"I'll not be outdone by your father. I'll not be compromised."

"What will you do?"

"I'll, I'll cash out the shares and donate the lot to MAWA and the Humane Society.

"Ma-what?"

"Medical Advances Without Animals. Take that one, Sam." The old lady chuckled defiantly, looking to the heavens.

Wearily, they reached for the final box.

"Insurances, income protection plans, investment portfolios, charitable donations." Estelle divided the piles. Opening a small, white envelope, Estelle sat quietly scrutinising the words of a small newspaper clipping. "What do you make of this?" she asked, passing it across. "Julian Clarke's obituary."

"Must have really hit home with your dad."

"Dad knew him?"

"Knew of him; love and grief's a universal language, it seems. It would have been too hard for your father to acknowledge his own stuff."

"All a bit hard to believe," replied Estelle. "Guess there's a side of Dad I never knew."

"In becoming a rescuer, your dad became a little controlling." The old lady softened. "Still, we mustn't be too hard on him. He did what he knew to be best."

LATER THAT EVENING, ESTELLE propped herself up with a comfy cushion and a soothing, warm cacao as she sat in front of her television screen. The familiar title of the video, initially sighted in Mel's living room and rediscovered amongst Nan's selection, had ignited her curiosity.

She rolled in the old video cassette: Hidden Crimes. The quality was amateurish, sound echoing, but otherwise in clear focus. It showed six individuals in balaclavas breaking into a biomedical laboratory with metal cutters. Footage was taken of sickly, mistreated animals, most of which were close to death and left in filthy cages and on cold, barren concrete floors without food or water. Footage taken by scientists themselves was also seized. Contrary to the sanitised version, courtesy of modern media, these experimental animals were more than just a few small mice. The monkey specimen 1666 had an elongated head strapped into an immobilising block. Various monitoring devices were attached to his scalp and limbs. Suddenly a percussive device was triggered, slamming into the primate's skull. A sickening thud punctuated the footage; the strapped-down creature shuddered and went limp.

A monotone voice-over described the experiment in clinical detail. Another wisecracking voice was heard off-screen mocking the poor creature crucified on the lab table. Another section of footage documented third degree burning of a pig with a blowtorch, providing data for use with artificial skin. The strapped-down pig writhed in agony before all nerve endings were burnt down through the skin.

Estelle remained transfixed by the images on the screen. The footage catalogued a litany of cruelty: pigs burnt alive, monkeys electrocuted, dogs and cats rendered paraplegic. Then there were the lethal dose 50, or LD 50 tests, as they were more commonly known: poisonous substances, everything from dishwashing detergents to petrol, administered in varying doses to gauge how long it would take fifty per cent of the animals to die an agonising death after ingestion.

The grainy footage came to an end, leaving just a crackly, blank screen. Estelle sat in reflection of Lucy, her ovaries removed for cancer research, and the chimpanzee testis and ovaries transplants for wealthy Europeans back in the 1920s. A cold shiver ran up her spine.

Estelle rushed to get out of the office; her ultrasound was booked for ten. She walked briskly and jumped into a taxi, directing her Ethiopian driver to the Mater Hospital a kilometre up the road. During the fleeting drive, Estelle became aware of the number of men and women carrying roses. But of course, it was Valentine's Day.

Nan had suggested it would be a big vibration day for miracles through the collective consciousness of love. Perhaps, but that did not account for the sad and the lonely, those whose tender hearts lay shattered amongst the ruins of their broken dreams, those whose hopes and wishes had been shattered by the collective illusion of the fairy tale: 'And think not that you can direct the course of love, for love, if it finds you worthy, directs your course.' Oh yeah, not that Kahlil Gibran was ever pregnant, Estelle reflected.

She could feel the kicking inside pulling her attention back into herself. She could not deny her own yearning for the father of the restless life inside her womb, and yet the commercialisation of love seemed particularly ugly that day. She'd sent him packing back to New York. Was it appropriate to summon him back just because of her pregnancy, she wondered.

The taxi pulled up outside the Mater. Estelle glanced at a young suit carrying a dozen red roses. She wondered about the destination of the flowers. Were they anticipated? Would they come as a complete surprise? What might have been the illusion and the reality of their love? Would he still be buying flowers for the same recipient next Valentine's Day?

With the flashing walk signal, Estelle scurried across to the other side of the road and disappeared into the antenatal clinic building. Before too long she found herself laid out under an ultrasound probe, her lower abdomen wet with a slimy, cold gel, watching in anticipation of seeing her baby on the screen. With as much delight as relief, all was confirmed: spine, arms, legs, fingers, toes, and most important of all, a strongly beating, well developed heart. Then the second most important question.

"Sorry, Mum, not this time. Baby has decided to cross his or her legs," apologised the obstetrician.

THE GAUNT YOUNG AMERICAN sat cross-legged in a La-Z-Boy, fidgeting with a large white envelope headed 'St Mary's Infectious Diseases Hospital'. He looked up with jaundiced eyes as a dapper, bespectacled, middle-aged gentleman entered the room, white coat draped over his shoulders held magically in place by an impressive stethoscope.

"Good morning, Mister Knight. Or is it Doctor Knight?" inquired the consultant.

"Whatever." The younger Afro-American cleared his throat.

"You're lucky to be alive, Doctor Knight." The clean-shaven doctor spoke carefully, scrutinising his patient through titanium-rimmed glasses.

"So I believe. Thank you. I'm at Her Majesty's pleasure." The young man grinned cheekily.

"So you're a Royalist?" He raised his eyebrows in expectation. "But of course, you Americans secretly admire our Monarchy."

"I'm Australian born, but dual nationality actually," Ryan replied blandly.

"Oh. Well, a Republican then, as you say. Whatever, you'll be right to travel—with due care. Direct to New York, is it?"

"Yes." Ryan nodded gratefully, waiting as the older doctor scrutinised his papers.

"You will need careful follow-up though. No alcohol for three months. You'll have to watch your liver function."

"No problem." Ryan nodded.

"And," the consultant paused, "I'd strongly advise another HIV test in three months' time." He cleared his throat. "Can't be too careful with your travels in the Congo."

"I'm not at risk," replied Ryan.

"Of course; all you young people are bulletproof, but the Congo's a dangerous place. I still feel obliged to encourage you to have another HIV test in three months."

Ryan shrugged.

"The last admission arriving from the Congo with malaria, three years ago, if I'm not mistaken, bled to death. Previous infection with malaria doesn't necessarily confer immunity, and at this juncture, we have no vaccine for malaria. A rapid schedule for hepatitis A may have prevented this admission." He cleared his throat. "As you might know, hepatitis A is usually a benign illness in childhood, but can be pretty nasty in adults, Doctor Knight. I can't emphasise enough the need to attend a travel clinic before you go gallivanting back to Africa."

Ryan took a deep breath, nodded, and put his hand over his mouth.

"We've thoroughly worked you up: a touch of malaria and fulminate hepatitis A. I presume you were vaccinated for hepatitis B. So a HIV test in three months then."

"I hear you," replied the seated young man, shifting uncomfortably.

"And a travel vaccine clinic before your next adventure." The old Brit looked earnestly at the younger man, taking off his glasses to polish some imaginary smudge. "I hope I haven't offended you, Doctor Knight." He cleared his throat. "Even if we're professionals, sometimes we can have a blind spot." He cleared his throat again. "Just thank God you're alive. All the best then, and remember the travel clinic." The Brit stretched out his hand in farewell.

RYAN STOOD OUTSIDE ST Mary's Infectious Diseases Hospital, discharge papers stuffed inside his duffle bag. The sun broke through heavy cloud.

"Roses for St Valentine's, mista?" offered a young urchin, keen as mustard.

267

"Thank you. No. A little late for me." Ryan shrugged apologetically.

"It's never too late for love, mista," quipped the vagabond teen, holding a single rose out earnestly.

"I hope so. Why not then?" Ryan smiled, taking the last rose. "Here. Keep the change."

"Thanks, mista." The lad beamed, pocketing the twenty-pound note.

ESTELLE SAT AT HER desk composing herself, ready to add the finishing touches to her article, 'Blow his Mind.'

"How'd your ultrasound go the other day?" asked Alex as she marched past Estelle's cubicle. "Well?"

"All good." Estelle smiled. "Fingers, toes—"

"Good to hear," assured Alex, tilting her head as a summons to her office.

"The piece, 'Till Debt do us Part', is in your inbox."

"Kiddo," sighed Alex pensively, "you've got quite a bit of raw talent."

"Yeah, if you say so," replied Estelle flatly.

"Hey! Get rid of that crap," snapped back the older woman.

"What crap?"

"Listen, kid, you've got talent. OK. So what, your daddy arranged a few sweeteners as an intro: spared you screwing your way to the top."

Estelle blushed.

"Hey, nothing to be ashamed about; you had the benevolent papa and I the better looks." Alex smiled smugly.

"Alright, so you think I'm naive. I was naive, and I guess you might think I was born with a silver spoon in my mouth."

"Estelle, we all cut our teeth in this business in different ways. Talent's talent; get over your privilege."

Estelle took a deep breath and sighed silently.

"All I care about is you deliver the goods. And don't let your ideals get too much in the way of a good story."

Estelle shrugged in response.

"Sometimes we just need to recalibrate our ethics. That's politics." Alex laughed wickedly.

"I see," replied Estelle.

"See, kiddo, it may just be a game, but the name of the game is power: power in the bedroom, power in the boardroom. It's all about who's on top. I want you to stay on top. It's where you belong."

"Of course." Estelle shrugged.

"Really, kiddo, I want you to get back in the game. What do you say?"

Estelle gently placed her right hand over her lower abdomen.

"Oh! Of course," added Alex sympathetically. "Take a bit of time off when the kid arrives. At a few weeks you'll be able to get it a private nanny. You can afford it. They take babies in at day care from six weeks these days."

"I thought I might breast feed for a year or so," replied Estelle.

"What?" The older woman was wide-eyed. "You don't want saggy tits, do you?" She shook her head in disbelief.

RYAN KICKED BACK, TAKING in a coffee as he flicked through the Nature journal, enjoying the New York sunshine. 'Contaminated polio vaccine theory refuted.' Stroking his temple, Ryan carefully scrutinised the brief communication. 'The species of HIV's immediate monkey ancestor SIV cpz was identified as being endemic to pan troglodytes-troglodytes, or p.t. troglodytes.'

A colour-coded map depicted the p.t.t. chimps as residing in the green-coded West-Central Congo, near Kinshasa, the capital Ryan had not so recently flown out from. Kisangani, to the north-east and beyond a bend in the Congo River, was surrounded by a sea of red, territory of the so called p.t.s. clean chimps, carrying a divergent strain of SIV not in the same family tree as that which evolved to HIV.

"Well, there you go." Ryan shrugged. "That just about wraps it up, but why are the villains always found to reside on the west bank? Trust they carry a passbook." He laughed dismissively. "Disingenuous!"

THE HOUSE STOOD VACANT, stripped of its possessions, vulnerable in its emptiness. Estelle revisited her life there, room by room.

From beneath the upper level of her childhood bedroom, she could hear the far-away chanting of a ringlet golden girl, her mother by her side, the child's gaze cast towards the heavens, affirming to the vast, endless universe: "Star light, star bright, the first star I see tonight. I wish I may, I wish I might, have the wish I wish tonight."

From far beneath the covers, snuggled tightly in the night, the fairytale pages were read with great delight. Far-away fantasies filled the evening air, whereupon she ventured till the break of morning light.

Clicking and clacking down the hallway; her clumsy adolescent practice of walking in stiletto heels.

Giggly, girly gossip. Blessed by summer sun that filled her adolescent, lovestruck heart when a new boy settled only metres from her house, and as she and her friends stood spying from her wispy, white lace curtains, a new dawn had awakened something different within.

Silhouetted by the night, beneath the outside landing, her first romantic kiss, then sneaking to her room, tippy-toeing all the way, stilettos now in hand, having broken her first curfew. She soon discovered her father was no fool, his vigilance betrayed by the peering light beneath his bedroom door.

Bidding her final farewell to her childhood and adolescent memories, Estelle spiralled her way down the beautifully carved staircase as if seeing it for the very first time. Wafting up towards her, she recalled the aromatic smell of her Nan's hot apple pie and the echoing sounds of Bach that had filled the atmosphere only weeks prior to her father's death.

Hitting the final step, Estelle was startled by a sharp, shooting pain that surged through her, cramping her abdomen.

CONTROLLED, LONG, SLOW, DEEP breaths gave way to interspersed quick, shallow panting. Estelle and Nan paced the hospital corridors as one, pausing every few steps, allowing for each cramping contraction to pass, as with the next, the next again, and again the next.

Stoically Estelle refused all pain relief, opting instead for a natural, drug-free birth. It was simply a matter of timing. She paced and paused along the hospital corridors, supported by Nan's arms, the walls, the side of beds, and all other immovable objects along the way, as she stood regaining her breath from one contraction to the next.

Focusing on Nan's voice, Estelle remained calm, in control, and able to articulate her needs. There was the need for water. There was the need for refreshing face-cloths. There was the need for quick, steady, firm dabs, wiping away the perspiration that dribbled down her forehead. There was the need for back rubs, shoulder rubs, neck rubs, head rubs, leg rubs and foot rubs. There was the need for big, soothing, round, open palm rubs. There was the need for rubs with sweetly scented, cool, aromatic gel. There was the need for quick, firm, steady, up-and-down strokes. There was the need to stand, to walk, to bend, to move, to stop.

"That's right; just keep breathing, sweet pea. You're doing just fine," assured Nan as she continued to rub her grand-daughter's back with one hand while wiping the sweat from her forehead with the other.

"Thanks," panted Estelle in gratitude.

A few minutes, and again she was in the merciless grip of excruciating pain, akin to being sawn in half by a chain saw. Estelle pursed her lips, closed her eyes, and waited for the intensity of the pain to cease. Slowly breathing herself back, she reopened her eyes in time to witness a young couple down the corridor sharing their labour, the devoted father breathing in unison with his panting wife, pacing his breathing to match hers. Rubbing her back, he calmed her with words of encouragement and loving praise.

"That hurts!" yelped Estelle. "Where are the drugs—drugs!" She yelled out loudly enough to startle the expectant couple and to just about stop the entire ward in its tracks. A few moments passed and again she breathed herself back to a state of calm.

Within minutes her verbal skills had all but disintegrated to little more than incomprehensible primal moans and groans. The final stages of labour had finally set upon her. Legs wide apart, her obstetrician kept steady vigilance for crowning.

"Epi-eeuww-dural," she growled.

"Too late, blossom. Your baby's coming. Now. I need for you to push for me, sweetheart. Give me a hard push," ordered the midwife sternly.

"Oooohhhh!" moaned Estelle, pushing hard into a lather of perspiration.

"Come on, Stell, you can do it," came a deep, rich, recognisable male voice.

"Ryan?" A relieved smile rose from Estelle's mouth as her chest rose and fell in heavy panting. Sweat continued to pour out of every pore of her body, further saturating her already soaked bed linen.

"I got here just as fast as I could," replied Ryan.

"Not a moment too soon," muttered Nan under her breath.

"Late again," replied Estelle, tears of joy mixing with her sweat.

Nan moved aside, allowing Ryan to move in closer.

"OK. Nearly there: one more hard push," demanded the midwife sternly.

Looking into Ryan's eyes, Estelle gave another push.

"Come on, Stell, I've got you. Push," he echoed, squeezing her hand tightly.

"Ooohhhh!" groaned Estelle, pushing with all her might

A loud cry punctuated the air from between Estelle's legs.

"Congratulations. You have a healthy baby girl," announced the doctor, having quickly checked the infant.

The smiling midwife carefully lowered the warmly wrapped baby to Estelle's breast. "She's beautiful," she comforted, before stepping back, giving the family room to come together.

Shaking, smiling with tears of joy and relief, Estelle looked deeply into Ryan's eyes.

He smiled back at her. "I love you, Stell. You're amazing," he whispered. Leaning into her, he softly stroked her face. "I'm so proud of you."

"Congratulations, Mum," interrupted Esther, barely holding back her own tears.

"As for you, Nan, you and I need to talk." Estelle laughed.

"I thought I'd make an executive decision. The rest is up to you guys." Nan grinned audaciously.

"Thank you, Nan." Ryan smiled.

"I think I'd best call it a day then," announced Nan, leaning over to kiss both mum and bub, and playfully punching Ryan on the arm. "A watch for you for Christmas." She chortled. "I'm not sure about you guys, but I've had quite a busy day." She roared as she mischievously marched out the door.

"I'd like to name her Summer Rose." Estelle tenderly caressed her newborn.

"Let's see. We'll have to run it past missy first," jested Ryan. He picked up the tiny bundle and nursed her close to his chest. "Your mummy suggests we name you Summer Rose?" he asked in a mock-infantile voice. "Ohhhh! I almost forgot: busy day and all." Ryan took an envelope from his back pocket. "Direct from the Big Apple." Ryan placed the envelope securely into Estelle's hand. "An extra ticket for the Catskills."

Estelle looked puzzled.

"We can't exactly leave her behind. Right?" He grinned boyishly.

Chapter Twelve

Stepping out of a vehicle, the statuesque blonde crossed the road. A well-dressed young suit slowed his pace and turned to glance as their paths crossed.

"I see the more things change, the more they stay the same," sighed the elderly lady, spying from her upstairs window as the blonde briskly made her way towards the house. "I once turned many a head."

"I'm sure you did." The younger woman humoured her.

"Then one day I spun around just in time to notice a head turn, this time to the passenger's side as you stepped out of my car, my dear." The older woman looked lovingly across at the younger woman. "I knew from that moment it was your turn to steal the show."

"Those were the days," acknowledged the younger of the two.

"Mind you, heads do still turn as I hop out of my vehicle." The older woman chuckled, her hazy blue eyes dancing with amusement. "They just do a double-take on my jalopy." Both women glanced down at the vintage parked on the street below.

"By the way, look at what I found in the attic." The younger woman presented the older woman with a tatty old shoebox.

The older woman steadied the box on her dresser and carefully opened it. Inside was an old photo album. "Well! I haven't seen this in decades."

"What is it?"

"A letter from an old friend," reflected the older woman. "'Sadly, after his long battle with AIDS, Dave passed away last week, friends and family by his side. Take care, Stan,'" she read. "Unbeknownst to either of us, my dear friend Dave Barrow was sick the last time we met," muttered the older woman, a distant look in her eyes. Estelle slowly and carefully placed the letter back between the album sheets. "How the men we align ourselves with can alter the course of our lives."

Turning over the sleeve of the album, the old, wrinkled hands gently touched a photo of three young African men. "'Camp Lindi, 1959.' Hmm." Estelle carefully placed the fragile photo back into the album sleeve and turned the page. With reverence she picked up a card that had been tucked into another sleeve, some of the thick coating of glitter spilling out onto her dresser. "'To our beautiful Summer Rose beneath the night star.' I remember this card so very clearly." She softly smiled. "Your twenty-first birthday; a ticket to the States was your father's idea."

THE DOORBELL INTERRUPTED ESTELLE'S reminiscence.

"I'm Louisa," bubbled the statuesque blonde. "Thank you for granting me this interview."

"Not at all, dear. Do take a seat." Estelle led Louisa to a lounge chair adjacent her own.

"Firstly I'd like to say that I found your latest book quite a compelling read."

Smiling, Estelle nodded graciously.

"Though there are those who would like to see the back of you," Louisa challenged.

"I dare say that it is those in power who would like to see the back of me," agreed Estelle dryly.

"You and your late husband have been and continue to be controversial and disquieting figures, especially given your startling claims regarding cross-species contamination, and more specifically a major cover-up in the scientific community, the polio vaccine being a case in point?"

"Seems nothing is ever so controversial as the truth."

"What do you say to those who refute your claims arguing that vivisection and animal experimentation have helped save countless human lives?"

"Well, certainly not mine, at least," Estelle replied sharply. "You see, my dear, any time that I've fallen ill, I've never once booked myself into a vet. Have you or any of your friends?" Estelle delivered her line deadpan.

"Of course not." Louisa frowned. "Another group that would like to see the back of you are some environmentalists who claim that the culling of some species is necessary?"

"Some shooting is indeed necessary. I wholeheartedly agree." The elderly woman smiled mischievously.

"Oh?" Louisa frowned, sitting back.

"You see, dear, one of the greatest environmentalists of our era has been responsible for shooting millions upon millions of animals around the world. He is quite a legend." Estelle raised her eyebrows expectantly.

"I don't understand," replied the young journalist, shifting uncomfortably.

"Oh yes. You may have heard of him. David Attenborough. He shot each and every one of them through the lens of a camera, not through the barrel of a gun."

Louisa grinned.

Steadying her balance on the chair arms, Estelle slowly rose to her feet. Gingerly she shuffled across the room towards the window and looked out onto the world beneath.

"Man spends much of his life running in terror, aiming his weapons at each and every perceived enemy. For some it is the animals in the bush. His excuse; he's protecting one species from another. For some it is certain bird species. Again his excuse is the protection of one species from another. For some it is the smaller species from the larger species, or species of the ocean. His excuse; he's protecting his own species. He aims his weapons at the species that consume too much, breed too much, or inhabit too much." Estelle slowly swung around. Calmly she held Louisa's gaze. "A perfect depiction of man himself, I dare say. He is then handed a gun and told to go and kill his own species, often in a far-away land. Finally, in his exhaustion, and without triumph, he turns the weapon on himself. With a weapon he fights to eliminate every conceivable germ that lives beneath his own skin. Yet it is in his perceived defence that he creates his own enemy. To triumph, man must conquer himself, but he will not do so until he puts down his weapon."

"So true." Louisa smiled. Released from eye contact, she jotted in her notepad.

"The truth will set us free, but first we must be brave enough to seek it. The truth empowers us as people, for I believe that the power of the people is greater than the people in power."

Estelle steadily shuffled back and lowered herself into her chair. Leaning forward, she asked, "Tell me, how old are you? You're such a pretty and intelligent young lady. I'd guess about twenty-eight?" She raised her questioning eyebrows.

"Twenty-seven."

"Twenty-seven," echoed Estelle. "Seems like only yesterday." She sighed. "Still, every age has its compensations. Tell me, why did you take up journalism?"

"I guess I'd like to make our world a better place."

"And of course a name for yourself; am I correct?" prodded Estelle. "Sorry if I seem nosy: force of habit. Picked it up early in my career. Can't quite seem to shake it." Estelle frowned. "Has got me into quite a lot of trouble."

"I guess you may be right." The young woman adjusted her fitted business skirt.

"I thought as much." Estelle smiled knowingly. "Of course there will be much sacrificed if you choose not to give up your integrity for the sake of a good story, and so much more to be sacrificed if you choose to."

"Of course." Louisa looked down at her notepad.

"As we speak, our planet is in crisis and at a tipping point. We are all being called upon to make a difference."

"How so?"

"Through aspiration and inspiration. To be inspired is to be in spiritual commune with angelic forces appointed to guide us, but we must firstly aspire with an open heart."

"This is all very deep." Louisa frowned.

Estelle's eyes shone with her own knowing. "We do not walk this earth alone; angels take on many forms and when we inspire others, we too become earth angels." Estelle smiled softly. "With whatever we're called to do in life, we will either contribute to creating heaven or hell right here on earth. And what we create, we will, in time, come to inherit: in this life or the next!"

"Reincarnation? You have made mention of it in your latest book."

"Reincarnation: all part of our evolutionary journey," confirmed Estelle with a slow and deliberate smile.

"And your take on heaven and reincarnation?" quizzed Louisa.

"Heaven or hell is what we choose to see and how we choose to be." The old lady shone. "It's all very simple really; it is as if we each have two selves, the compassionate, loving self and the manipulative self. One helps create heaven, the other, well, you fill in the blank," she teased.

"Manipulative? How so?"

"Manipulative, fearful; whatever the reason, there's a part of ourselves that may at times live in frozen terror of love. If we don't recognise and conquer it, we only ever get to half-live, and what we fear, we seek to destroy." Estelle took a moment's silence, gazing gently at Louisa. "You see, dear, we must come to our hearts or perish." She smiled, releasing Louisa from her gaze.

"I have never really looked at it that way," conceded Louisa pensively. "And reincarnation?"

"Reincarnation makes perfect sense to me. Otherwise I'd have to believe in an unfair God, one that indiscriminately punishes an innocent child with horrific misfortune while rewarding another with blissful good fortune, seemingly for no good reason at all."

FINALLY ALONE, ESTELLE LOOKED around her room: her luxuriously fluffed-up pillows and comfortable bedding; her tallboy adorned by numerous photographs. Photos of herself and Ryan on their wedding day at St Francis; Mel their celebrant, and beside him, Nan, their witness, decked out in a fluorescent outfit and matching Aladdin shoes, proudly holding Summer Rose; photos of the young family splashing in the waves at Bondi; the poem handed to her by Angelica in a beautifully carved frame; a photo of Mellow proudly posing in front of a ripped screen; a photo of Buddy with a newspaper in his mouth. On a corner of an adjacent bookcase stood the carving of the Three Wise Monkeys, next to the carving, a series of books: Innocence Lost; Mabunda: Dark Knight of Truth; The Cathars' Return.

Peacefully, Estelle sat, book in hand, caressing Ryan's wedding band hanging from a gold chain around her neck. In elegant handwriting inside the front cover: 'I dedicate this book with all of its proceeds to my beloved late husband's foundation, Charity Without Cruelty.' And beneath:

'For all divine beings, the countless of them that have lived amongst us from the beginning of time, helping man carry his karma and gracing us with their feathers, furs and fins: may they become free of all suffering. My prayer for the human race is for the evolution of our consciousness, so that we begin to treat them with all the dignity and respect they deserve.'

Chapter One:

As we said goodbye to Mellow and drove away from the vet, I couldn't help but reflect on all the millions of other animals who also died that day, mostly nameless, with no one to say goodbye, or even thank you for being: most of them never knowing human kindness; most of them just numbers; many slaughtered brutally by humans. Many of them better off never being born. And as we said goodbye to our girl, to all of those nameless millions, I also wanted to say goodbye. There are many humans you would never have encountered who cared and loved you all. Rest in Peace.

ESTELLE'S EYES FLUTTERED, HER attention strangely drawn to her hands as they slowly released their grip on her book. As if in slow motion, the book landed on the floor, its pages flying open, moved by a mysterious breeze.

Her wrists exposed, she studied with quiet curiosity the pulsating artery tucked beneath her Stevenson's birthmark. Her eyes opened and shut in unison with the rise and fall of each pulsation. She softly smiled at the remembrance of Ryan and their date in the log cabin restaurant all those years ago, and his gentle caress as he traced her birthmark with his finger.

With defusing focus, Estelle continued to watch with detached curiosity as the jagged, rope-like mark began to increase in size, its coarseness constricting circulation to her veins. Her breathing diminished as she passed through the gauntlet of an excited crowd. The young healer winced as her wrists were further bound, left over right, behind the stake, binding her to the ground of her execution. She tried to relax as the crowd bayed for her life. To the left and right of her pyre, her sisters in crime protested their innocence, their collective confessions of fornication with Satan extracted under vile duress. How had her vocation of healing with hands and herbs, and tending to God's creatures, come to this?

She remembered their last parting moment, and how his gentle embrace had soothed her trembling body. Her mother had been burnt at the stake for healing her knight's lord from the Black Death. She was under the jurisdiction of the Inquisition. Pope Innocent III had declared her brethren intolerable, the Cathars a threat to the power of the one true Church.

The crowd cheered as the acolytes threw faggots around the three staked to the ground. The village cracked with excitement as the robed cleric proclaimed their guilt and solemnised the imperative to burn the witches. With grim satisfaction the cleric recited Exodus 22:18, "Thy shalt not suffer a witch to live." He nodded to the restive crowd. "We burn the flesh to redeem the soul."

"Burn the witches. Burn them all," screamed the crowd, men and women all eager to be seen on the side of righteousness in the presence of the Inquisitor.

His Grace held up his hand to quell the intemperate mob. A ruby ring, the insignia of his authority, adorned his ring finger as he blessed the hapless women. "In the name of the Father, His Son, Lord Jesus Christ, and the Holy Spirit, may God have mercy on your souls." His hands joined in prayer, an unspoken directive for the executioners to light the faggots.

"Our Father who art in heaven…" He solemnly prayed as the excited mob jeered and cheered with delight. "…and deliver us from Satan…" He looked on in satisfaction as flames began to take hold. With callous delight he rubbed his ruby ring as the young maiden struggled against the ropes burning into her exposed wrist. The stench of burnt flesh emanated from the burning pyres.

The young virgin coughed, struggling to breathe as she sensed the galloping of his approach. Charging in from the distance, the young man's heart sank as he saw the three pales of black smoke rising on the distant horizon. A Knight of the Templars, the power of his Lord was ebbing before the total onslaught against the Cathars. Arriving too late, he stood in helpless resignation, watching as the young girl's charred remains collapsed at the foot of the stake.

FOR A MOMENT THE pages ceased to ripple, allowing the book to quietly rest open. With another mysterious breeze, the pages flicked back to life, turning one after another, picking up momentum, a soft whistling sound, as if the sound of a distant locomotion entered via a corridor into the room.

As the train neared the platform, he stood before her halting carriage. In regimented uniform of the 13th Light Dragoons, he held himself upright, though pensive. On furlough from the Crimea, the young woman in a crisp nurse's uniform alighted from the carriage. Their gaze locked as if in soul recognition of a different time and place.

The whistle blew. Upon boarding, he turned in her direction, their transfixed gaze stolen by the vanishing train headed for Southampton. With the final echoes of the distant engine, the young nurse turned and walked away.

The atmosphere hung heavy with the stench of death and cries of the wounded. As terror rained from blackened skies, they thundered through a deafening barrage of artilleries, shells exploding around them. The young man and his horse as one, lead the front line charge at Balaklava. Felled by shell and bullet, they were flung through the air, their limbs shattered by splintered shards and shrapnel. Together they lay crumpled on the steaming ground surrounded by the ear-piercing screams of the wretched and the charred remains of the dismembered bodies of their compatriots.

The young dragoon's body slumped, sheltered by the breast of his dying horse. Hearing the pounding of his war horse's heart, the soldier let out his last breath as his companion let out a final whimper.

The roaring sounds of an approaching train and a whistle echoed through the young soldier's consciousness. Before him stood the young nurse, gaze transfixed, and though but a brief moment passed before them, she too carried his memory until her dying day.

THE STILLNESS OF THE breeze momentarily settled the pages once again. The doors all shut, the room became breathless as the prickly afternoon heat streamed in from the unopened windows.

The two children lay huddled in the long grass, their hidey-hole concealed by overhanging foliage. Taking care not to expose their presence, they kept very still, spying on the family gathering.

Mother, father and toddler were unaware of their presence, enjoying what was left of lunch. Father and daughter were engaged in a friendly wrestle as Mum basked in the sun.

"Can they see us?" whispered the younger of the two secretively, her delicate face framed by golden ringlets.

"I don't think so," whispered the African boy.

The tranquil scene was disturbed by cries of purple glossy starlings as they fled from overhanging branches. The male chimp jumped to his feet, alert to the disturbance.

A loud crack shattered the afternoon peace. A bullet penetrated below his left eye, exiting the back of his head. The female panicked, reaching for her toddler before being felled with a machete, a single blow decapitating her. The young chimp was petrified, pissing on the dusty ground. The kidnappers approached her, smiling, then grabbed her, bundling her into a bag. Before departing, the assassins cut off the hands of her deceased parents, bagging their trophies separately.

The young girl buried her tearful face into the black boy's chest. "You've got to stop it. Please, you've got to stop it. Promise me."

The older black boy looked with passion into the younger girl's teary eyes. "I promise you. I swear before God. I'll stop it. I'll stop it."

THROUGH THE BRIGHTEST OF lights, a large brown hand emerged as the pages rippled to closure. Together they had travelled through the chapters of their past life encounters. Having kept his sacred promise to her, he had come to take her home.

For the Curious

Chapter 1

Charles Darwin. *On the Origin of Species, by Means of Natural Selection. Or the Preservation of Favoured Races in the Struggle for Life.* John Murray. London 1859.

Enoch. *The Book of Enoch.* Trans. R.H. Charles. 1917.

Friedrich Nietzsche. *Beyond Good and Evil.* Trans. R.J. Hollingdale. Penguin Books 1973.

Lothrop Stoddard. *The Revolt Against Civilisation: the Menace of the Underman.* NY. Charles Schreiber and sons 1922.

Voronoff, Serge Abrahamovitch. *Rejuvenation by Grafting.* Adephi Publications 1925.

Chapter 2

J.D. Kark and J.H. Abramson. 'Sidney Kark's contribution to epidemiology and community medicine.' Letters to Editor. *International Journal of Epidemiology* 2003; 32: 878–885.

Chapter 3

Alliance for Earth, Life, Liberty & Advocacy: www.aella.org

Rene Girard. *Violence and the Sacred.* 1972 Paris Grasset.

Animals Australia: 'Dairy calf cruelty investigation' www.animalsaustralia.org.

Animal Liberation: Animal-lib.org.au.

Bellavite, P. Signorini, A. *The Emerging Science of Homeopathy*, 2e 2002 North Atlantic, Berkley.

Christopher I. Li et al. 'Effect of Depo-Medroxyprogesterone Acetate on Breast Cancer Risk among Women 20 to 44 Years of Age'. *Cancer Research* April 15, 2012.

Daniel W. Cramer, Allison F. Vitonis et al. 'Mumps and Ovarian Cancer: modern interpretation of an historic association'. *Cancer Causes and Control.* Aug 2010; 21(8): 1193–1201.

Deborah Cohen . 'Complications tracking down the data on Oseltamivir'. *British Medical Journal* 2009; 339.

Dimercheli, V. et al 'Vaccines to prevent influenza in healthy adults'. *Cochrane Summaries.* 13th March 2014.

Earthlings: www.earthlings.com.

Faith Javane and Dusty Bunker. *Numerology and The Divine Triangle.* Whitford Press. 1979.

Forks Over Knives: www.forksoverknives.com.

Florence Scovel Shinn. T*he Wisdom of Florence Scovel Shinn.* Simon & Schuster. New York 1989.

Kip Andersen & Keegan Kuhn. Cowspiracy.com: 'The sustainability secret'.

Linda Reid. *Astrology Step by Step.* Canopus Publication 2001

Howard Sasportis & Liz Green. The twelve Houses. LSA/Flare Publication. 2009.

Mark E.J. Woolhouse et al. 'Biological and biomedical implications of the co-evolution of pathogens and their hosts'. *Nature Genetics* Volume 32. December 2002.

Milk is Cruel: www.milkiscruel.com.

Mostad et al. 'Women using Depo-Progestin 2.9 times more likely to have HIV-1 cells in cervical and vaginal secretions'. *Lancet,* 1997. P350.

Occupy for Animals: www.occupyforanimals.org.

Montagnier, L. et al. 'Electromagnetic signals are produced by aqueous nanostructures derived from bacterial DNA sequences'. *Interdisiplinary Sciences: Computational Life Sciences,* 2009; 1:81-90.

Peter Singer & Jim Mason. T*he ethics of what we eat.* Text Publishing. Melbourne, Australia. 2006.

Preston Marx. 'Progesterone increases risk of getting AIDS in Monkeys. It causes thinning of vaginal mucosa, reducing the barrier to viruses and bacteria'. *Nature Medicine* 1996 p2.

Richard Tarnas. *Cosmos and Psyche: Intimations of a New World View.* Plume. Penguin. New York 2006.

Skegg & Noonan. 'Pooled Analysis of WHO and New Zealand Studies. Women taking Depo-progestins for two to three years before the age of twenty five had a 310 per cent increased risk of getting invasive breast cancer'. *Journal of American Medical Association* 1995.

Tom Jefferson et.al. 'Unintended events following immunisation with MMR: a systematic review'. *Vaccine* 21 (2003) 3954–3960. Available online at www.sciencedirect.com.

Thomas J. McFarlane. *Consciousness and Quantum Mechanics*. 1988.

Chapter 5

Ainslie Meares MD. *A Way of Doctoring*. Hill of Content. Melbourne. 1984.

Ainslie Meares. *Cancer Another Way?* Hill of Content. Melbourne. 1977.

Byron Kaye. 'HCCC power boosted after anti-vax feud'. *Medical Observer* 2nd May 2013.

Dr David Servan-Schreiber. *Anti-cancer, a New Way of Life*. Scribe. Melbourne 2007, 2010.

Meares A. 'Regression of Osteogenic Sarcoma metastases associated with intensive meditation'. *Medical Journal of Australia* 1978; 2: 433.

Gerson, M. *A Cancer Therapy: Results of Fifty Cases*. 1958. Totality Books, California, USA.

Ian Gawler. *You Can Conquer Cancer*. Michelle Anderson Publishing. Melbourne. 1984. Revised 2013.

Joel Fuhrman. *Super Immunity*. Harper Collins. New York 2011.

Joel Fuhrman. *Eat to Live*. Little, Brown & Company. 2011.

Money, Banking and the Federal Reserve. DVD Mises Institute.

Rory Freedman & Kim Barnouin. *Skinny Bitch*. Running Press Book Publishers. 2005.

Victoria Boutenko. *Green for Life*. North Atlantic Books. Berkeley, California. 2005. 2010.

Chapter 6

Al Gore. *An Inconvenient Truth*. DVD and YouTube.

Chan J.M. & Gionvannucci E.L. 'Dairy Products, calcium, and vitamin D and risk of prostate cancer'. *Epidemiological Reviews*. 23 (2001): 87–89.

Graeme Morgan, Robyn Ward, Michael Barton. 'The Contribution of Cytotoxic Chemotherapy to 5-Year Survival in Adult Malignancies'. *Clinical Oncology* (2004) 16: 549–560.

Greg and Dawn Fitzgerald. Health for Life: www.healthforlife.com.au.

Janet Raloff. 'Insurance payouts point to climate change'. Sciencenews.org. Jan 4th 2012.

Jui Tung Chen & Kazuhiko Kotani. 'Oral Contraception Therapy increases Oxidative Stress in Pre–menopausal women'. *International Journal of Preventative Medicine* Dec 2012; 3(12): 893–896.

Maryanne Williamson. *A Return to Love from A Course in Miracles*. Audio or book.

Martin Roosli et al. 'Sleepless night, the moon is bright: Longitudinal Study of Lunar Phase and Sleep'. *Journal of Sleep Research* Vol. 15, issue 2, p149–153. June 2006.

Omar Bagasra. *HIV and Molecular Immunity: prospects for the AIDS vaccine*. Biotechnique Books, 1999. ISBN 1-801299-10-4).

Richard Rohr. CD. *Spiral of Violence*. Centre for Action and Contemplation.

T. Colin Campbell & Thomas M. Campbell II. *The China Study*. Benbella Books. Dallas, Texas. 2006.

Chapter 7

Allan Combs & Stanley Krippner. 'Collective Consciousness and the Social Brain'. *Journal of Consciousness Studies*. Vol. 15, Numbers 10–11, 2008, pp264–276 (13).

Charles G. Gross. 'Claude Barnard and the Constancy of the Internal Environment'. *Neuroscientist* 4: 380–385. 1998.

Chandre Gould and Peter Kolb. *Project Coast: Apartheid's Chemical and Biological Weapons Program*. United Nations Institute for

Disarmament Research & Centre for Conflict Resolution. Cape Town 2012.

Davies, J.C.A. 'Transmission of Anthrax'. *Central African Journal of Medicine*, 1980; 26:126–129.

The Declaration of Alma-Ata. International Conference on Primary Health Care, Alma-Ata, USSR, 6–12 September 1978.

Gabriela Wlasiuk and Michael W. Nachman. 'Promiscuity and the Rate of Molecular Evolution at Primate Immunity Genes'. *Evolution*, 2010 August ; 64(8): 2204–2220.

John J. Hall and Richard Taylor. 'Health for all beyond 2000: the demise of the Alma-Ata Declaration and primary health care in developing countries'. *Medical Journal of Australia* 2003; 178:17–20.

Jonathan Hill. 'Coca Cola in India—a case study'. *CRS Asia Weekly.*

Kauffman, S.H. 'Immunology's foundation; the 100-year anniversary of the Nobel Prize to Paul Ehrlick and Eli Metchnikoff'. *Nature Immunology*. 2008 July 9 (7): 705–12.

Meryl Nass MD. 'Anthrax Epizootic in Zimbabwe, 1978–1980: Due to Deliberate Spread?' International Physicians for the Prevention of Nuclear War. www.ippnw.org/pdf/mgs/psr-2-4-nass.pdf.

Pol De Vos et al. 'Health through people's empowerment: A rights based approach to participation'. *Health and Human Rights Journal*. Vol. 11, no. 1(2009).

Richard Dawkins. 'W.D. Hamilton, an obituary'. 12th March 2000. Edge.org.

Wisner, B. GOBI versus PHC? 'Some dangers of selective primary health care'. *Social Science and Medicine*, 1988; 26(9): 963–9.

Chapter 8

Arthur Koestler. *The Roots of Co-incidence*. Hutchinson and Co Ltd 1972.

Caroline Myss. *Sacred Contracts*. Three Rivers Press, New York,. New York 2002.

Ian Stevenson MD. *Children Who Remember Previous Lives: A question of reincarnation*. McFarland and Co. 2001 North Carolina USA.

Jessica Utts. Replication and Meta-analysis in Parapsychology. Statistical Science 1991, Vol. 6, No. 4, 363–403.

Chapter 9

Adam Hochschild. *King Leopold's Ghost*. Pan Macmillan. London 1998.

Andrew Knight. *The Costs and Benefits of Animal Experiments. Animal Ethics Series*. Palgrave Macmillan 2012.

Hammer, C. Link, R. Wagner, F. Diefenbeck, M. 'Organs from Animals for Man'. *International Archives of Allergy and Immunology*, Vol. 116, No. 1, 1998.

Horse Racing Kills: www.horseracingkills.com.

Meredith Wadman. 'Chimpanzee Research on Trial'. *Nature*, Vol. 747, 16 June 2011.

Mark Twain. *King Leopold's Sililoque, a Defence of his Congo Rule*. New York. P.R.Warren 1905.

PETA. 'Animals Used for Experimentation'. www.peta.org/issues/animals-used-for-experimentation.

Supress. *Hidden Crimes*. YouTube.

Chapter 10

Bought: The truth behind Vaccines, Big Pharma & Your food. www.boughtmovie.net.

Brian Martin. 'Contested testimony in scientific disputes: the case of the origin of AIDS'. *The Skeptic*, Vol. 13, No. 3, 2007, pp52–58.

Dan Nosowitz. 'Largest Current Study of AIDS Vaccine Shut Down Because it Doesn't Work'. *Science*, 27th April 2013.

Gary Greenberg. 'The Psychiatric Drug Crisis'. *The New Yorker*, Sept 3 2013.

Hooper, E.J. *The River: A Journey Back to the Source of HIV and AIDS*. London: Penguin; Boston: Back Bay Books.

John de Wit. 'To curb rising HIV rates, we must target our human flaws'. *The Conversation*, 20 Feb 2014.

Korber, B. et al. 'Timing the ancestor of the HIV-1 pandemic strains'. *Science*, 288, 1789–1796.

Lawrence K. Altman. 'The Doctor's World; Revisionist History Sees Pasteur as Liar Who Stole Rivals' Ideas'. *New York Times*. May 16th 1995.

London, L. Kagee, A. Moodley, K. Swartz, L. 'Ethics, human rights and HIV vaccine trials in low-income settings'. *Journal of Medical Ethics*, 2012 May; 38(5): 286–93.

The Origin of AIDS. YouTube.

PETA. 'Animals Used for Experimentation'. www.peta.org/issues/animals-used-for-experimentation.

Philip Calder. Editorial. 'Study Raises Questions about Dietary Fats and Heart Disease Guidance'. *British Medical Journal*. 5th Feb 2013.

'Polio Vaccine and the Origin of AIDS'. *Philosophical Transactions of the Royal Society*, Sept 2000.

Robert Whitaker. *Anatomy of an Epidemic*. Broadway Books New York. 2010.

Tom Burr, J.M. Hyman and Gerald Myers. The origin of acquired immune deficiency syndrome: Darwinian or Lamarckian? *Philosophical Transactions of the Royal Society*. London. B (2001) 356, 877–88.

Professor W.D. Hamilton. 'Unpublished letter to Editor-in-Chief'. *Science Magazine*. 23rd February 1994.

Chapter 11

Andre Menache MRCVS. *An open letter to Dr Harpal Kumar: The Role of Cancer Research UK and Corporate Social Responsibility*, 20th January 2014.

Cowspiracy: www.cowspiracy.com.

Humane Society: www.hsi.org.

Medical Advances Without Animals: www.mawa-trust.org.au.

Michael Worobey et al. 'Contaminated polio vaccine theory refuted'. *Nature*, Vol. 428. 22 April 2004.

Stephanie Sorrell. *Depression as a Spiritual Journey*. O Books, Winchester, UK 2009.

Chapter 12

Bruce Grayson, M.D. 'Incidence and correlates of near-death experiences in a cardiac care unit'. *General Hospital Psychiatry* 25 (2003) 269–276.

Maria Tonnard et al. 'Characteristics of Near-Death Experiences Memories as Compared to Real and Imagined Events Memories'. *PLOS One*. 2013.

Parnia, S. 'Do reports of consciousness during cardiac arrest hold the key to discovering the nature of consciousness?' *Medical Hypotheses Journal* 2007; 69(4): 933–7.

For Lovers of Good Food

Suzy Spoon's Vegetarian Butcher: www.ssvb.com.au.